This
belongs
to
Angel

year 6
Age: 11

2013

CANDYFLOSS DREAMS

Angel. ♡

you can't
go back and
change the
past, so look
to the future and
don't make the
same mistake twice.

Jacqueline Wilson

CANDYFLOSS DREAMS

Candyfloss and
Cookie

ILLUSTRATED BY NICK SHARRATT

DOUBLEDAY

CANDYFLOSS DREAMS
A DOUBLEDAY BOOK 978 0 857 53302 9

CANDYFLOSS
First published in Great Britain by Doubleday,
an imprint of Random House Children's Publishers UK
A Random House Group Company
Text © Jacqueline Wilson, 2006
Illustrations © Nick Sharratt, 2006

COOKIE
First published in Great Britain by Doubleday,
an imprint of Random House Children's Publishers UK
A Random House Group Company
Text © Jacqueline Wilson, 2008
Illustrations © Nick Sharratt, 2008

This collection first published in Great Britain as CANDYFLOSS DREAMS
by Doubleday, an imprint of Random House Children's Publishers UK
A Random House Group Company

This edition published 2013

1 3 5 7 9 10 8 6 4 2

The Random House Group Limited supports the Forest Stewardship Council
(FSC®), the leading international forest certification organization. Our books
carrying the FSC label are printed on FSC®-certified paper. FSC is the only forest
certification scheme endorsed by the leading environmental organizations,
including Greenpeace. Our paper procurement policy can be found at
www.randomhouse.co.uk/environment.

Set in New Century Schoolbook

Random House Children's Publishers UK,
61–63 Uxbridge Road, London W5 5SA

www.randomhousechildrens.co.uk
www.totallyrandombooks.co.uk
www.randomhouse.co.uk

Addresses for companies within The Random House Group Limited
can be found at: www.randomhouse.co.uk/offices.htm

THE RANDOM HOUSE GROUP Limited Reg. No. 954009

A CIP catalogue record for this book is available from the British Library.

Printed and bound in Great Britain by Clays Ltd, St Ives plc

Jacqueline Wilson

CANDYFLOSS

ILLUSTRATED BY NICK SHARRATT

To Robbie and Callum

1

I had two birthdays in one week.

My first birthday was on Friday. Mum and Steve woke me up singing '*Happy Birthday to you*'. They'd stuck candles in a big fat croissant and put a little paper umbrella and a cocktail stick of cherries in my orange juice.

My little half-brother Tiger came crawling into my bedroom too. He's too tiny to sing but he made a loud *he-he-he* noise, sitting up on his padded bottom and clapping his hands. He's really called Tim, but Tiger suits him better.

I blew out all my candles. Tiger cried when the flames went out, so we had to light them all again for him to huff and puff at.

I had my birthday breakfast in bed. Mum and Steve perched at the end, drinking coffee. Tiger went exploring under my bed and came out all fluffy, clutching one of my long-forgotten socks. He held it over his nose like a cuddle blanket,

1

while Mum and Steve cooed at his cuteness.

Then I got to open my presents. They were wrapped up in shiny silver paper with big pink bows. I thought they looked so pretty I just wanted to hold them for a moment, smoothing the silver paper and fingering the bows, trying to guess what might be inside. But Tiger started ripping them himself, tearing all the paper and tangling the ribbon.

'Tiger, stop it! They're *my* presents, not yours,' I said, trying to snatch them out of the way.

'He's just trying to help you unwrap them, Flossie,' said Steve.

'You need to get a bit of a move on, darling, or you'll be late for school,' said Mum.

Tiger said *He-he-he*. Or it *could* have been *Ha-ha-ha*, meaning *Ya-boo-sucks-to-you*.

So I lost my chance of savouring my five shiny silver presents. I opened them there and then. I'll list them. (I *like* making lists!)

1.   A pair of blue jeans with lots of little pockets fastened with pink heart-shaped buttons. They matched a pink heart-patterned T-shirt with a cute koala motif across the chest.
2.   A pink shoebox containing a pair of trainers, blue with pink laces.

2

3.   A little wallet of gel pens with a
     stationery set and stickers.
4.   A pink pull-along trolley suitcase.

I left number 5 till last because it was big but soft and squashy, and I hoped it *might* be a cuddly animal (any kind, but not a tiger). He had torn off half the paper already, exposing two big brown ears and a long pointy nose. I delved inside and found two *tiny* brown ears and a weeny pointy nose. It was a mother kangaroo with a baby kangaroo in her pouch.

Tiger held out his hands, trying to snatch the baby out of the pouch.

'No, Tiger, he wants to stay tucked in his mummy's pocket,' I said, holding them out of his reach.

Tiger roared.

'Just let him play with the baby kanga a minute. He won't do him any harm,' said Steve, going off to the bathroom.

Steve talks a lot of rubbish sometimes. Tiger grabbed the baby kangaroo and shoved him straight in his mouth, ears, snout, his entire *head*.

'Mum, Tiger's *eating* him!' I protested.

'Don't be silly, Floss. Hang on!' Mum hooked her finger into Tiger's bulging mouth and rescued the poor little baby kangaroo.

'He's all covered in Tiger's slobber!' I said.

'Just wipe it on the duvet. Don't be such a baby, Birthday Girl,' said Mum, giving me a little poke. 'Do you like your presents, Floss?'

'Yes, I love them,' I said, gathering them all up in my arms away from Tiger.

I supposed I loved my little half-brother, but I wished we could keep him in a cage like a real tiger.

'There's actually another extra present,' said Mum. Her eyes were shining as brightly as my birthday candles. She raised her voice, shouting to Steve in the bathroom. 'Shall I tell Floss now, Steve?'

'OK, yeah, why not?' he said, coming back into my bedroom, shaving soap all over his face.

He put a little blob of shaving soap on the tip of Tiger's chin and pretended to shave him. Tiger screamed delightedly, rolling away from his dad. He wiped shaving soap all over my special cherry-patterned duvet. I rubbed at the slimy mark, sighing heavily.

'So, OK, what's my extra present?' I asked warily.

I very much hoped Mum wasn't going to announce she was going to have another baby. One Tiger was bad enough. Two would be truly terrible.

4

'It's a present for all of us. The best present ever, and it's all due to Steve,' said Mum. She was looking at him as if he was a Super Rock Star/Footballer for England/Total God, instead of a perfectly ordinary actually quite boring guy who picks his nose and scratches himself in rude places.

Steve smirked and flexed his muscles, striking a silly pose.

'Steve's got promotion at his work, Floss,' said Mum. 'He's being made a manager – isn't that incredible? There's a sister company newly starting in Sydney and Steve's been asked to set things up there. Isn't that *great*?'

'Yeah, I suppose. Well done, Steve,' I said politely, not really taking it in at all. The stain on my duvet wasn't budging.

'*Sydney!*' Mum said.

I blinked at her. I didn't quite get the significance. Sydney was just an old-fashioned guy's name.

'She doesn't have a clue where it is,' said Steve, laughing. 'Don't they teach kids geography nowadays?'

Then I got it. 'Sydney in Australia?'

Steve clapped me. He made Tiger clap his little pink fists too. Mum gave me a big big hug.

'Isn't it exciting, Floss! Think of all the

sunshine! You just step out of the city and there you are, on a fabulous beach. Imagine!'

I *was* imagining. I saw us on a huge white beach, with kangaroos hopping across the sand and koalas climbing palm trees and lots of beautiful skinny ladies like Kylie Minogue swimming in the turquoise sea. I saw Mum and me paddling, hand in hand. I sent Steve way way out to sea on a surfboard. I stuck Tiger in a kangaroo's pouch and sent them hopping far off into the bush.

'It's going to be so wonderful,' said Mum, lying back on the bed, arms and legs outstretched, as if she was already sunbathing.

'Yeah, wonderful,' I echoed. 'Wait till I tell Rhiannon and everyone at school!' Then I paused. 'What *about* school?'

'Well, Steve reckons we'll be in Sydney a good six months, though we're not permanently emigrating. You'll go to a lovely new Australian school while we're out there, darling,' said Mum. 'It'll be a fantastic experience for you.'

My heart started thumping. 'But I won't know anyone,' I said.

'You'll soon make heaps of new friends,' said Mum.

'I like my *old* friends,' I said.

Rhiannon and I had been best friends for almost

a whole year. It's the most wonderful thing in the world to be Rhiannon's best friend because:

1. She's the most popular girl in the class and always gets voted to be monitor and the lead part in any play and first in any team.

2. She's the prettiest girl in the class too. No, the prettiest girl in the whole *school*. She's got long dark black hair, utterly straight and very shiny. She's got delicate black arched eyebrows and long thick black eyelashes but her eyes are bright blue. She is quite tall and very slim and could absolutely definitely be a fashion model when she's older. Or a rock star. Or a television presenter. Or *all three.*

3. Everyone else wants to be Rhiannon's best friend, especially Margot, but she's my best friend, so there. Margot's never ever going to break us up. No one can ever come between Rhiannon and me.

I loved Rhiannon to bits even though she could be a bit bossy at times. She generally told me what to do. But I didn't really mind because mostly I just wanted to please her.

7

I tried to imagine this big new Australian school. I'd watched the soaps on television. I made the girls wear funny check dresses and smile a lot with their big white teeth. They all spoke together. 'G'day, Flossie, can we be your friends?' they chorused.

'Well, I'd normally say yes. But I'm Rhiannon's friend,' I explained.

'Hey, daydream Birthday Girl!' said Mum, giving me a kiss. 'I'm going to pop in the bathroom after Steve. Keep an eye on Tiger for me.'

You needed two eyes looking out for Tiger. Plus another pair at the back of your head.

I gathered up all my birthday presents and put them up on top of my bookshelf, out of his reach. I pictured myself wearing my new T-shirt and jeans and trainers, pulling my trolley-case, kangaroo under one arm, bouncing off to Australia. I saw how cleverly Mum had chosen my presents.

Then I looked at the stationery set. I fingered the writing paper and envelopes and the gel pens all the colours of the rainbow. Why would I be writing lots of letters?

Then my heart thumped harder. I dropped the stationery and the pens and ran to the bathroom. 'Mum! Mum!' I yelled.

'What?' Mum was larking around with Steve, splashing him like a little kid.

8

'Mum, what about Dad?' I said.

Mum peered at me. 'I expect your dad will phone you tonight, Floss. And you'll be seeing him on Saturday, same as always.'

'Yes, I know. But what's going to happen when we're in Australia? I can still see him, can't I?'

Mum's brow wrinkled. 'Oh, come on, Flossie, don't be stupid. You can't nip back from Australia every weekend, obviously.'

'But I can go sometimes? Every month?'

'I'm doing very nicely, thank you, but we're not made of money, kiddo,' said Steve. 'It costs hundreds and hundreds of pounds for a flight.'

'But what am I going to *do*?'

'You can write to your dad,' said Mum.

'I *knew* that's why you got me that stationery set. I don't want to write to him!'

'Well, if he'd only join the modern world and get a mobile and a computer you could text and email him too,' said Mum.

'I want to be able to *see* him like I do now,' I said.

'Well, we're not going to Australia for *ever*,' said Mum. 'Those six months will whizz past and then we'll be back. Unless of course it's so wonderful out there that we decide to stay on! Still, if we *did* decide to stay for good we'd come back on a visit.'

'Your dad could maybe come out to Sydney to see you,' said Steve.

He said it nicely enough but there was a little smirk on his face. He knew perfectly well my dad was having major money problems. He had barely enough for the bus fare into town. If flights to Australia cost hundreds of pounds there was no hope whatsoever.

'You're mean, Steve,' I said, glaring at him.

'Oh, Floss, how can you say that? Steve's the most generous guy in the whole world,' said Mum, deliberately misunderstanding. 'He's booked for us to go to TGI Friday's as a special birthday treat for you tonight.'

'I'd sooner have a birthday meal at home. A little party, just Rhiannon and me.'

'I haven't got the time, Floss. I've got one million and one things to get organized. Come on, you know you love TGI Friday's. Don't spoil your birthday making a fuss about nothing.'

I stomped back to my bedroom.

My dad wasn't *nothing*! I loved him so much. I missed him every week when I was at Mum and Steve's.

I'd forgotten I'd left Tiger in my bedroom. He'd got at my new gel pens. He'd decided to decorate my walls.

'You are a *menace*,' I hissed at him. 'I wish

you'd never been born. I wish my mum had never met your dad. I wish my mum was still with *my* dad.'

Tiger just laughed at me, baring his small sharp teeth.

2

I cheered up just a little bit when I got to school. I love Mrs Horsefield, my teacher. She gave me a great big smile when I came into the classroom and said, 'Happy birthday, Floss.' She gave me an iced bun to eat at break time. She gives each child in her class a bun when it's their birthday, but mine was a special big one with pink icing and a cherry on the top.

Rhiannon was looking at it enviously. She especially likes cherries.

'Want half my birthday bun?' I offered.

'No, it's yours,' she said, but she looked hopeful.

I gave her the biggest half of the bun with the cherry.

'Yum!' said Rhiannon, sucking it like a sweet. 'OK, open your present from me, Floss.'

She gave me a pink tissue parcel tied with pink ribbon, and a special card. I really wanted us to go off together so that I could open my present

13

privately, but Rhiannon seemed to want me to open it with everyone gathered around. She'd given me a proper shop-bought card of two girls hugging. It said at the top in pink lettering, YOU ARE MY BEST FRIEND. I started to be glad that Margot and Judy and all their gang were lurking. *See!* I wanted to say. *Rhiannon's* my *best friend*.

'Open your present, Floss. You're such a slowpoke,' said Margot.

She meant slow*coach*. She's got this irritating habit of talking in a fake American accent and using silly American expressions. She thinks it makes her sound sophisticated but *I* think she sounds plain stupid.

I could make a l-o-n-g list of reasons why I can't stick Margot. She used to be ordinary – in fact I can barely remember her back in the baby classes – but *this* year she's making out she's all grown up. She's always giggling about boys and sex and pop stars. Judy giggles too. She looks as babyish as me but she's got an older brother who tells her all these really rude jokes. I don't understand most of them. I'm not sure Judy does either.

I was determined to take my time, smoothing the satin ribbon, feeling the little knobs of my present under the pink tissue, trying to guess what it was, but Rhiannon was getting impatient too.

'Hurry up, Floss. I want to see if you like it!'

So I pulled the ribbon off and tore the tissue paper and held my present in my hand. It was a beautiful bracelet made of shiny pink beads.

'They're real rose quartz,' said Rhiannon proudly.

'They're really really lovely,' I whispered.

I was scared they must have cost a lot of money. I'd given Rhiannon a bracelet for *her* birthday, but it was just a pink and blue and purple friendship bracelet that I'd made myself. I'd also given her a friendship bracelet braiding set and hoped she'd make one specially for me, but she hadn't got round to it yet.

'It's like . . . awesome,' said Margot. 'Let's try it on, Floss.'

She snatched it straight out of my hand and wound it round her own wrist.

'It's *my* bracelet!' I said.

'OK then, baby – I'm not *taking* it, I'm just trying it on,' said Margot.

'You're trying it on all right,' I said grimly.

'You've got like the most amazing taste, Rhiannon,' said Margot. 'Where did you get the bracelet? I wish I had one like that.'

Rhiannon started going on about this jewellery shop in some arcade, not really trying to help me get my bracelet back. I knew if I asked, Margot would just muck around, making fun of me. I wanted to grab it right back off her horrible bony wrist, but I was frightened of breaking it.

Susan shook her head at me sympathetically. She was standing right at the back, away from the others. She was new and hadn't really made any friends yet. People teased her because she kept coming top of the class and she had a silly surname, Potts. Well, Rhiannon said it was silly. She teased her too. Rhiannon was very good at teasing. (Or very *bad*.) I wished she wouldn't. I begged her not to, but she wouldn't listen. Rhiannon bosses me about but you can't *ever* boss her. But she *is* my best friend.

'Rhiannon,' I said desperately.

Rhiannon held out her hand to Margot. 'Give us the bracelet back then, Margot.'

Margot handed it over reluctantly.

'There,' said Rhiannon, winding it round my wrist and doing up the clasp. Her cheeks were the delicate pink of the rose quartz. She was obviously pleased her bracelet had been so admired. 'What other presents did you get, Floss? What did your mum give you?'

'Clothes and one of those pull-along case thingies and a kangaroo cuddly toy,' I said.

'A cuddly toy! How gross!' said Margot. 'Imagine, still playing with teddies! What about *dolls*?'

16

I blushed, holding my b[...] seen my Barbie dolls when s[...] prayed she wouldn't tell on me.

'Come on, Rhiannon,' I said, ta[...] arm. 'I want to tell you this huge se[...] you hear what my mum told me.'

'What?' said Rhiannon, licking a litt[...] icing off her finger.

'Yeah, what secret?' said Margot. 'You always have to create, like, a drama, Floss.'

'Well, I guess this *is* pretty dramatic,' I said, stung. I decided to show her. I took a deep breath. 'We're only going to Australia,' I said.

They all stared at me. Rhiannon looked particularly impressed. 'Wow, you're going on holiday to *Australia*!'

'Well, *I'm* going on holiday to Orlando,' said Margot. 'It's got Disneyland. Australia hasn't got Disneyland.'

'It's got the Great Barrier Reef and Bondi Beach and Ayers Rock,' said Susan, who had crept to the edge of the group. 'Though actually we should call it by its Aboriginal name, Uluru.'

'Nobody asked *your* opinion, Swotty Potty,' said Rhiannon. She turned to me. 'So when are you going on this holiday, Floss? Any chance I can come too?'

'I wish you could,' I said. I was regretting telling

now. It made it seem too real. I had to
plain properly. 'It's not a holiday. We're going to
stay there for six whole months.'

'*Really?*'

'Yes,' I said miserably. 'Only I don't think I want
to. I like it here. I'll miss my dad so much. And I'll
miss *you*, Rhiannon.'

'I'll miss you too!' she said, and she hugged me
tight.

I hugged her back.

Margot and Judy made silly noises and stupid
comments but I didn't care. Susan hitched her
glasses higher up her nose, gave me a wan smile
and wandered off. I felt bad that Rhiannon had
called her names, but I couldn't help it. I *liked*
Susan. I wanted to be kind to her but I knew if I
started speaking to her properly people would start
teasing me too.

I started to think about the Australian school
during lesson time. I would be the new girl. What
if everyone started picking on me? I was *quite* clever
but I didn't ever come top, so they wouldn't tease
me for being swotty, would they? I had a perfectly
ordinary kind of name, Flora Barnes. My initials
didn't spell anything silly or rude. I didn't mind
being called Floss or Flossie for a nickname.
Rhiannon once or twice called me Flopsy Bunny but
that was when she was making a big fuss of me.

18

I'd never ever find a friend in Australia like Rhiannon.

'You will stay my friend when I'm out in Australia, won't you?' I begged her at lunch time. 'And still be best friends when I come back?'

'Yes, of course,' said Rhiannon.

She wasn't really concentrating. She was looking over at Margot and Judy, who were huddled up looking at some stupid pop magazine. They were giggling and kissing their fingers and stroking all their favourite boy bands. Rhiannon giggled too, watching them.

'You won't make friends with Margot when I'm gone, will you?' I said anxiously.

'Give it a rest, Floss! Which part of Australia are you going to, anyway?'

'Sydney.'

'Is that near Brisbane? That's where they make *Neighbours*.'

We went to the library and found a big book about Australia.

'Wow!' said Rhiannon, flipping through pictures of bush and beaches and orange rocks and weird white buildings. 'You are so lucky, Floss, it looks fantastic.'

It didn't seem like a *real* place. It was all too bright and highly coloured and bizarre, like a cartoon. I looked down at the parquet pattern on the library floor and tried to imagine myself going down down down for thousands of miles and then bobbing out in Australia.

I'd never quite got to grips with geography. I knew the people in Australia weren't *really* upside down, but it still seemed a little odd all the same.

We read a ballad about an Australian called Ned Kelly in our English lesson that afternoon. He was a sheep thief and he ended up getting hanged.

'You'd better not steal any little lambs out in Australia, Floss!' said Rhiannon.

Mrs Horsefield asked me to read a ballad about a Tragic Maiden out loud. I read it dramatically, making the Tragic Maiden weep and wail. Margot and Judy started snorting with laughter. Even Rhiannon smirked a little. I could feel myself blushing.

'That was very good, Floss,' said Mrs Horsefield kindly. 'You're very good at reading aloud.'

I'd always liked reading to my mum when she did the ironing or started cooking, but now she chatted to Steve instead. I'd tried reading aloud to Tiger, but he fussed and fidgeted and kept wanting to turn the page before I'd finished reading all the words.

'Now I want you to have a go at making up your own ballads,' said Mrs Horsefield.

'Does it have to be all daft and old fashioned and tragic?' said Rhiannon.

'It can be about anything at all, as long as it's in ballad form and tells a story,' said Mrs Horsefield.

Everyone started groaning and scratching their heads and mumbling. Everyone except Susan, sitting by herself in front of us. She was scribbling away like anything.

'Look at Swotty Potty,' said Rhiannon. 'Trust her. Oh yuck, I hate this ballad lark. What have you put so far, Floss?'

> *'The girl sat in an aeroplane,*
> *Watching the clouds with wonder,*
> *Worrying how she'd get on*
> *In her new life Down Under.'*

'Down Under what?' said Rhiannon. 'That sounds stupid.'

'Well, I know. I want to say "In Australia" but I can't find a word for it.'

'What about . . . *wailier*?' Rhiannon suggested. *'The girl went ever more weepier and wailier because she was missing her best friend Rhiannon now she was in Australia.* There!'

'It doesn't fit, Rhiannon. It's too long.'

'Well, say it very quickly then. Now help me,

21

Floss. So far I've got, *There was a pretty young girl called Rhiannon, who joined a circus and got shot out of a cannon.* Hang on, inspiration! *It hurt a lot when she got shot, that poor pretty young girl called Rhiannon.* There! Maybe I'm not such pants at ballads after all. Even though I don't show off in a swotty way like *some* people.' Rhiannon put her foot up and kicked Susan's chair.

Susan jumped and her pen squiggled right across her page. She sighed and tore it out of her exercise book. Then she turned round. 'If you were a little bit swottier you'd realize that you've written a limerick, *not* a ballad.'

'Who cares what you think, Swotty Potty? You think you're it just because you like writing this poetry rubbish. What have you put anyway?' Rhiannon reached out and snatched Susan's spoiled page.

'Oh yuck, what kind of daft drivel is that? What's she on about? Listen, Floss.

> *'She walked along the corridors,*
> *Pacing each floorboard with care.*
> *She didn't step on a single crack*
> *But no one knew she was there.*
> *She edged around the wooden fence,*
> *Tapping each post in turn,*
> *She counted each one attentively*

But she had a lot to learn.
She tried to do maths magic,
Adding all the sums in her head,
But all the figures multiplied
Her loneliness and dread . . .

'What kind of weirdo nonsense is that? And it's not a ballad either because it doesn't tell a story, it's just a lot of rubbish about nothing, so ya boo sucks to you, Swotty.'

Rhiannon crumpled the page up and threw it at Susan's head.

Susan turned round and chopped her hand quick on Rhiannon's shins.

'Get off! That *hurt*,' said Rhiannon.

'Good,' Susan muttered. 'Now get your feet off my chair.'

'Don't you tell me what to do, Swotty Potty,' said Rhiannon. She leaned right forward on the edge of her seat, ready to kick Susan hard in the back. But Susan grabbed her by the ankles and pulled. Rhiannon lost her balance. She shot straight off her chair and landed with a thump on the floor. She shrieked.

'Rhiannon! Whatever are you doing! Get up and stop clowning around,' said Mrs Horsefield.

'Ouch!' said Rhiannon. 'I think I've broken my elbow. *And* my wrist. And my bum hurts horribly.'

23

'I think you'll live,' said Mrs Horsefield. 'It serves you right for messing about.'

'It wasn't *my* fault, Mrs Horsefield,' said Rhiannon. She paused. We had a strict code about telling tales. '*Someone* pulled me right off my chair.'

Susan kept very still.

'Hmm,' said Mrs Horsefield. She came over and felt Rhiannon's arm carefully. Rhiannon moaned and whimpered.

'I think you're making a fuss about nothing, Rhiannon,' said Mrs Horsefield briskly. Then she paused. She was looking at Susan now. 'However, it's very silly and very dangerous to pull anyone off their chair – even if they're being incredibly provoking. I'm surprised at you, Susan.'

Susan said nothing but her face went very red.

I felt terrible. We'd got poor Susan into trouble.

I couldn't concentrate on my ballad any more. I kept thinking about Susan's. I wondered if she really went round counting things in her head to make everything turn out all right. Only they didn't ever turn out right. We were all horrible to her. Especially Rhiannon.

I edged closer to Rhiannon. 'Do you think we should maybe tell Mrs Horsefield it was our fault, because we snatched Susan's ballad and made fun of her?' I said. I delicately said 'we' instead of 'you' – but Rhiannon was still outraged.

'Are you *joking*?' she hissed. 'She really hurt me! My arm aches awfully. I bet it *is* broken, or at the very least badly sprained. Swotty Potty deserves to get into trouble. She's turned into mad Psycho Girl, out to get me.'

'Oh Rhiannon, you know that's not true,' I said anxiously.

'Are you calling me a liar?' said Rhiannon. She sat up properly and looked me straight in the eyes. 'Whose side are you on, Floss? Do you want to break friends and go off with Swotty Potty and write soppy poems together?'

'No! No, of course not. You're my best friend, you know that.'

'Yes, and I gave you the bracelet with real rose-quartz stones even though I really wanted it for myself. But I gave it to you because that's what best friends are for. Even though you're not even going to *be* here soon, as you'll be flying off to Australia.'

'But I don't want to go! You know I don't. I'd give anything to stay,' I said.

'Well, why don't you then?' said Rhiannon.

'Why don't I what?' I said, muddled.

'Stay here. Kick up such a big fuss that they have to change their minds.'

I thought about it. 'I'm not really very good at making a big fuss,' I said.

25

'Yes, I know, you're hopeless.' Rhiannon sighed irritably. 'You're so gutless, Floss. You just try to be nice to everyone.'

I felt wounded but I reached out and hooked my little finger round Rhiannon's.

'Ouch, watch out, that's my sore arm! What are you doing?'

'Trying to make friends properly. Because you're my best friend in all the world and I love my beautiful bracelet and I really will try not to go to Australia. Anyway, we probably won't be going until the summer holidays and that's ages away, so don't let's even think about it now.' I hung onto Rhiannon's finger and she grinned at last and hooked her own little finger properly round mine and we vowed to make friends, make friends, never ever break friends.

Susan had her head bent over her exercise book, writing her ballad out all over again. Her soft brown hair fell forward, showing the white nape of her neck. She sniffed once or twice, as if she might be trying not to cry.

I still felt very bad about her, but there was no way I could comfort her, not in front of Rhiannon.

I showed off my rose-quartz bracelet to Mum when I got home from school. She was clearing out the kitchen cupboards, while Tiger bashed saucepans at her feet.

'Oh, trust Rhiannon and her mother. They always have to show off how much money they've got,' said Mum. 'Hey, did you tell Rhiannon about Australia? I bet she was envious.'

'Yes, she was. Ever so. Oh Mum, I'm going to miss her so much.'

'You soppy old thing,' said Mum, giving me a hug. 'I think it'll do you good to make some new friends. You let Rhiannon boss you around too much.'

'I'd quite like to be friends with Susan, this new girl, but Rhiannon hates her. What do you think I should do, Mum? Shall I try to be nice to Susan even if it makes Rhiannon mad at me?'

'I don't know, lovey. It's all a bit pointless, isn't it, seeing as we'll be in Sydney in two weeks' time.'

I stared at Mum. 'In two *weeks*?' I said. 'Why didn't you tell me we were going that *quick*?'

'Quick*ly*, Flora – do speak properly. There didn't seem any point in telling you earlier, you'd have just got all worked up and excited and rushed round telling everyone.'

I thought hard. 'Telling *Dad*,' I said.

'Yes, well, it's not really anything to do with him.'

'He's my *dad*!'

'Yes, I know. Calm down. Don't shout like that. Honestly! If you must know, I was trying to be tactful to your dad. Steve's done so brilliantly to be given the chance to get the Australian branch up and running. He'll be earning twice the money – I just can't believe it! It felt like rubbing your dad's face in it because he's such a failure.'

'Dad's not a failure,' I said fiercely.

Mum cupped my face with her hands. 'Oh come on, Floss. I know you love your dad and he's a *good* dad in lots of ways. He's a very sweet kind man, and I'd never deliberately badmouth him to anyone – but he's useless when it comes to business, even you must admit that. He's in debt up to his eyeballs and that awful café is fast running out of customers. I don't know why he doesn't call it a day and sell up altogether.'

'Dad wouldn't *ever* sell the café!' I said.

'Yes. Well. Goodness knows what else he could do! Anyway, I just thank God *I* don't have to slave there any more,' said Mum. 'Oh Floss, isn't it wonderful!' She kissed me on the tip of my nose. 'Aren't we lucky girls! In two weeks' time we'll be stepping out of that plane into glorious sunshine.' She threw old rice packets and sauce bottles and jam jars with a *thump thump thump* into the rubbish bin as she spoke. Tiger accompanied her on saucepan percussion.

'You've got some serious sorting out to do yourself, Floss,' said Mum. 'We're going to put most

28

of our stuff in storage. There's no point keeping any old rubbish though. It's time you chucked a lot of your old toys out.'

'I suppose I could throw away my Barbies,' I said.

'That's the spirit! *And* some of those old teddies. We'll make a start on your room tomorrow.'

'I'll be at Dad's.'

'Well, I'll do it for you. Now, you'd better get dressed up for our meal out. You can wear your new birthday clothes if you like. You get in the bathroom while I change Tiger.'

'He's not coming too, is he?' I said.

Mum looked at me. 'What do you think we're going to do with him, Floss? Leave him here and tell him to heat up his own milk and tuck himself up in bed?'

'Oh ha ha, Mum. Why can't he have a babysitter like when you and Steve go out?'

'Because this is a family outing, silly. Now go and get shifted, Birthday Girl.'

I thought about Mum's words as I wriggled out of my school uniform and put on my new jeans and T-shirt. I couldn't ever have a *real* family outing any more. It was all so easy-peasy when we were just *our* family, Mum and Dad and me. But now when I went out with Dad, Mum was missing – and when I went out with Mum, Dad was missing and I was stuck with Steve and Tiger instead.

I stared out of my bedroom window down into the garden. Steve had landscaped it himself and made all these pretty flowerbeds and a pergola and a pond with goldfish, but now Tiger was old enough to climb out of his pram it was more like his own personal adventure park. OK, I had my lovely swing in one corner, but Tiger had his own small swing *and* his slide *and* his pedal car *and* his sandpit *and* his baby bouncer *and* his toddler gym climbing frame.

It was more like Tiger's birthday celebration than mine at TGI Friday's. He sat in lordly fashion in his highchair, giggling and kicking his legs whenever any of the waitresses went by. They all ruffled his silly sticking-up hair and tickled him under his chin, cooing and clucking. No one told him off when he ate his chips with his fingers or spilled his drink.

Mum ordered a special birthday pudding for me with sparklers. Tiger screamed and squirmed so desperately to see them that they held them in front of him for ages. The sparklers had stopped sparkling by the time they put the plate on the table. I felt as if all my sparkles had gone out too.

I knew I shouldn't be jealous of my little baby

brother. He didn't commandeer all the attention *deliberately*. It was very annoying all the same.

That was what was so great about my weekends with Dad. It was just Dad and me. He treated me like his very special little princess.

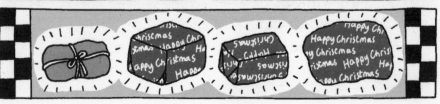

3

My second birthday was on Saturday.

I went to my dad's. Mum always took me. She usually stayed a little while and had a cup of coffee in the café. Dad often put a whole plate of cakes in front of her – jam doughnuts, apple turnovers, apricot Danish pastries, all her old favourites.

Mum could never be tempted to have so much as a mouthful. She'd just shake her head and pat her flat tummy. Sometimes she couldn't help looking at *Dad*'s tummy and shaking her head. She often gave Dad lectures about my food, saying she didn't want me eating any greasy café fry-ups, especially not chip butties, and I had to have lots of fresh fruit and vegetables and only one small cake at tea time. Dad and I would nod solemnly – and then wink at each other when she was gone.

Mum didn't drive me over to Dad's this Saturday. Steve did.

'Why can't you take me, Mum?' I said.

'I've got too much to do, Floss. I'm busy busy busy,' said Mum.

She was rushing around in her jeans and an old check shirt of Steve's, sorting our things into three big piles: TAKE, STORE and CHUCK. Tiger was crawling around on his hands and knees, playing with the piles, draping old tights round his shoulders like a feather boa and waving a saucepan as a hat.

'Let's put Tiger on the CHUCK pile,' I said.

'Oh ha ha, very droll,' said Mum. 'Go on then, off you go to your dad's.'

'I still don't see why you can't take me, same as usual,' I muttered, trailing after Steve.

But it wasn't the same as usual. I knew perfectly well why Mum didn't want to take me. She didn't want to face my dad when he found out about Australia. It was so mean of her. I sat in the back of Steve's posh company car and glared at the back of his pink neck. He had a very short haircut. Mum said it was cute and loved running her fingers through it. I thought it looked plain silly. Who wants designer stubble on their *head*? Steve was wearing one of his special weekend sport shirts with very short sleeves, showing off his big muscles. He worked out at the gym most mornings before work.

Mum had joined the gym now too. She even took Tiger to a baby gym class, which was *totally* mad.

Tiger crawled around at way too rapid a pace as it was. He was learning to climb up onto beds and wriggle right into corners. He needed to be restrained, not encouraged.

Steve started making general chit-chat in the car. He never knows quite what to say to me. Ditto me him. He asked if I was looking forward to going to Australia. I said, 'Mmm.' He said wouldn't it be fabulous living in an exciting city like Sydney. I said, 'Mmm.' We gave up after that. Steve switched the radio on and we both listened to music. Steve hummed along. I kept quiet. I only do sing-songs with my dad.

They played a Kylie song on the radio.

'*She's* Australian,' said Steve.

'Mmm,' I said.

'Maybe we'll all start talking Australian. *Isn't that right, cobber?*' said Steve, in the most truly terrible Australian accent.

I didn't respond with so much as an 'Mmm'.

I needed to concentrate on what I was going to say to my dad. When should I tell him? I tried rehearsing the right words inside my head but it was like when your computer screen freezes. I couldn't think up anything at all.

Steve turned into our road and drew up outside the café. I looked up at the sign: HARLIE'S CAFÉ. It's named after my dad. It isn't called Harlie like the big motorbikes; he's Charlie, but the big C fell off ages ago. Mum always calls Dad a Right Charlie, like it's some kind of insult.

The café used to get lots of customers. My dad's chip butties were especially famous. Everyone came to eat them. Lots and lots of guys came from the big building site. The café was always crowded out at lunch time because all the high school students spent their dinner money at our place. But then everyone got into this Healthy Eating and the students had to stay at school and eat salads. The guys finished building the big offices and moved on. The office workers had sandwiches and wraps sent in. They didn't want fry-ups and chip butties. We still had a few lunchtime regulars, but then a big pizza takeaway opened up just down the street and they started going there instead.

Dad had lots of spare time to spruce up the café now but he never seemed to get round to it. The paint was peeling and the window was dirty. Some boy had written a rude word on it with his finger. The menu had slipped sideways and one of the limp curtains was drooping off its rail and someone had thrown their takeaway pizza cartons right by the doorstep.

'Poor old Charlie,' said Steve. 'The café's starting to look a right dump. Is he still getting any customers?'

'He's getting heaps and heaps,' I said. 'My dad's the greatest cook in the world. He's going to get his own big restaurant one day. I bet he'll get to be one of those famous chefs on television, with his own programme and his own cookery books.'

'Mmm,' said Steve.

'You wait. He's going to be *heaps* more successful than you are, Steve,' I said, and I grabbed my bag and shot out of the car.

I hoped he wouldn't tell Mum I'd been cheeky. I dashed into the café, the bell ringing wildly. It was almost empty, the place settings undisturbed on the blue and white check tablecloths. There were just the three regulars.

Billy the Chip was eating a chip butty, hunched up over the table listening intently to the sports channel on his crackly little transistor radio. Billy the Chip came and had a chip butty every single day, though he made his own chip butties every evening in his chip van outside the railway station. Dad used to go to his chip van when he was a little boy. Dad's *dad* went to his chip van when *he* was a boy. Billy the Chip had had his chip van for ever. He was very old and very thin and very grey and he walked very slowly because he had to take it easy. He'd sleep late, eat his butty at my dad's, spend his afternoon in the betting shop, tow his van to the station and then fry his chips all evening until the pubs were closed and the last train had gone.

Old Ron sat at the next table eating his bacon and eggs, still in his raincoat and cap even though it was boiling hot in the café. Old Ron was old, but nowhere near as old as Billy the Chip. He nodded and winked at me, but as he had a nervous tic and nodded and winked continuously, I wasn't sure whether he was greeting me or not.

Miss Davis sat right at the other end, as far away from the two old men as she could manage. She saw them nearly every day in the café but she never spoke to them, or even glanced in their direction. She sat with her back to them, sipping her cup of tea. She had her pull-along bag by her side. She kept one hand on it, as if she was scared it would wheel itself off independently. It was lumpy with stale bread and birdseed. She fed all the pigeons in the town every morning, stopping off at my dad's café for refreshment halfway round.

'Hey, Dad!' I called.

He peered out of the little hatch in the kitchen and then came running. 'How's my little birthday sweetheart?' he said, giving me a great big chip-smelling hug. He whirled me round and round so that my legs flew out behind me.

'Mind my trolley,' Miss Davis snapped, though we weren't anywhere near it.

'There's a horse called Birthday Girl in the big race at three thirty,' said Billy the Chip. 'I'll have a little bet and if I get lucky I'll buy you a special birthday present, Flossie.'

'Birthday, is it? Can't even remember when mine is,' said Old Ron.

I wasn't sure whether he was joking or not. Old Ron didn't seem too sure either. Still, he gave me a very fluffy toffee out of his mackintosh pocket as a birthday treat. Dad thanked him very much but mouthed *Don't eat it!* at me. I said I'd save it for later.

'Oh well, I suppose I'd better find you something too,' said Miss Davis, scrabbling inside her trolley.

I wondered if she was going to give me a packet of birdseed, but she found her purse and gave me twenty pence. I thanked her very politely because I knew weird old ladies like Miss Davis think twenty pence is a lot of money.

Dad smiled at me gratefully and then led me into the kitchen. He'd manoeuvred one of the café tables into the corner and decorated it with tinsel and balloons and hung the Christmas fairy lights up above. There was a silver place mat, and little silver bows on the knife and fork, and a banner with HAPPY BIRTHDAY PRINCESS in Dad's wobbly printing.

'Oh Dad!' I said, and I started crying.

'Hey, hey, hey! No tears, sweetheart!' said Dad. 'Now, sit yourself down on your special throne and open your presents.'

He thrust three big red parcels at me, and one little limp brown paper parcel tied with string.

'That one's from Grandma,' said Dad. He rubbed his lip. 'Don't get too excited.'

I squeezed the soft brown paper. 'I think she's knitted me something again,' I said.

Grandma's presents were generally hand-knitted. They were made specially for me but she couldn't quite keep up with how old I was. She knitted me weeny toddler-size pink cardies with rabbits and ducks and teddies on the dinky pockets.

'It feels even littler this time,' I said, sighing.

'Maybe it's a vest and knicker set!' said Dad. 'Don't worry, I promise I won't make you wear them.'

Grandma's present wasn't a vest and knickers. It was almost as bad. She'd knitted me two droopy woolly animals, one grey, one sludge, with little blobby sewn eyes. It was hard working out which species they were. The grey one had big ears and a very long droopy nose. The sludge one had small ears and a tail.

'I think this one's an elephant,' I said, fingering the grey one. Then I looked at the sludge creature. 'Do you think this one's a dog or a cat?'

'Looks like it could be either,' said Dad. 'Perhaps it's a dat or a cog.'

'Dad! What am I going to say to Grandma when I write a thank-you letter?'

'Just say thank you for the lovely woolly cuddly toys,' said Dad. 'It doesn't do to specify. I once thanked her for a stripy scarf, though privately I thought it was much too small. It turned out it was a special knitted tie. Oh well. She means well, bless her. Now, open your other presents, Princess.'

The three red parcels all said *Happy Christmas* in curly gold writing.

'Sorry, pet, I didn't have any proper birthday wrapping paper,' said Dad. 'Come on then, open them up. I'm dying to see what you think of them!'

The first parcel contained a home-made silver paper crown studded with Rowntree's fruit gum jewels. Silver glitter sprinkled my curls when I put it on, but Dad said it just made my hair look extra specially sparkly.

'You look like a real birthday princess with your crown on,' said Dad. He bowed to me. Then he curtsied too, which made me giggle.

The second parcel contained a pair of silver high-heeled shoes.

'Real high heels, Dad! Wow!' I said.

They were second-hand ladies' shoes, much too big for me, but I didn't care. I kicked off my new trainers and stuck my feet in my special silver shoes.

'Oh dear, they don't really fit. Don't twist your ankle, for God's sake,' said Dad. 'You'd better just wear them indoors until you grow into them. Open the big parcel then.'

It was a long pink satin dress with puff sleeves and rosebuds round the bodice. It had once been somebody's bridesmaid's dress. They were quite a big somebody. The dress hung off me and trailed down onto the floor, even when I was wearing my new high heels.

'Oh dear, it's much too big,' said Dad.

'No, it isn't. It's lovely! I've always wanted a really long special dress,' I said quickly.

'And the shoes are too big too,' said Dad.

'But you don't get high heels my size. I can always stuff them with socks or something. I feel like a real princess in them, Dad,' I said.

'You're *my* princess,' said Dad, grinning at me. 'Right, I'd better prepare a royal feast for my little mini-queen.'

I hadn't been able to eat any breakfast at Mum's. I wasn't sure I had the appetite for one of my dad's famous fry-ups either. My tummy was still so tense because I had to tell him about Australia. I decided I should do it there and then, the minute he made me my breakfast, so it was all over and done with, and then Dad would understand why I didn't feel like eating.

But Dad was so sweet serving me a plate with a funny food face – chips for hair, two mushrooms for eyes, a sausage for a nose, a curly piece of bacon for a smiley mouth and a spoonful of baked beans either side as rosy cheeks. I couldn't spoil his fun. I shut up and ate my face as best I could, vowing to myself I'd tell him at lunch time.

But at lunch time a whole crowd of football fans came barging into the café for chip butties before the match. Dad was kept so busy that I couldn't stop him in his tracks with my news. He fried the chips and buttered the rolls and I served them and took the money. Lots of the guys were in a good mood and left a big tip for the 'weeny waitress'.

I tried to give Dad the money but he wouldn't hear of it.

'It's yours, Floss. You've earned it fair and square. We make a great little team, you and me.'

'When I leave school we'll have our own fancy restaurant, you and me, eh, Dad? Chez Charlie and Floss, yeah?'

It was one of our favourite games, but today Dad just shook his head sadly.

'I don't think you should tie yourself down to your old dad, little Floss,' he said. 'I think I'd just cramp your style. I'm hardly a success story.'

'Yes you *are*, Dad. Look, I'm sure the café will pick up soon. Look how busy we've been this lunch time.'

'Ten chip butties aren't going to change my luck, sweetheart,' said Dad. He took a deep breath. 'Floss, maybe I should tell you something . . .'

I took a deep breath too. 'Dad, maybe I should tell *you* something . . .'

We looked at each other.

'Is it bad news?' said Dad.

'Yes,' I said.

'Mine's bad news too. But we can't have bad news on a birthday! We'll tell our sorry tales tomorrow, OK, sweetheart? We've got more important things to do today – like making your birthday cake!'

We only had a couple of customers for cups of tea all afternoon so we could concentrate on the cake. Dad let me take a turn mixing it, with a tea towel tucked round me so my princess dress wouldn't get spattered. He let me scrape out the bowl afterwards. I even *licked* it. Dad just laughed.

The cake made the whole café smell beautiful when it was baking in the oven. Dad and I played catch with my birthday balloons and then he played loud rock music and we did a birthday dance. I kept falling out of my silver high heels so I took them off my feet and put them on my hands and made them do a tap dance on each tabletop.

Then the cake came out of the oven all golden brown and beautiful. We mixed up the buttercream in a bowl while the cake was cooking, and then spread it in the middle like a sandwich, with a layer of raspberry jam.

'Now we'll do the icing on the top,' said Dad. 'What decoration do you fancy? Rainbow sprinkles? Little silver balls? Smarties? Glacé cherries? Crystallized roses?'

I thought hard, pondering each choice.

'*All* of them?' said Dad, grinning.

'Yes *please!*' I said.

'OK, Bob's your uncle and Fanny's your aunt,' said Dad. 'R-i-g-h-t! The Cake Decorator Extraordinaire will get cracking, assisted by the Birthday Princess herself.'

We studded the cake with silver balls and sweets, sprinkling and dabbing and daubing until the entire cake was covered, with scarcely any room for candles.

'Shall we light your candles now and have a slice?' said Dad eagerly.

'You bet,' I said.

Dad lit each candle, singing *Happy Birthday* very loudly and off-key. Then I closed my eyes and wished as hard as I could. *Please please please let me stay seeing Dad somehow!* I blew so hard I felt my chest would collapse. I opened my eyes – and every snuffed candle burst into flames again.

I blinked at them, bewildered. I blew again. They flickered, they faded – and then flamed.

'Blow a bit harder, Floss,' said Dad.

'I *am*,' I said, struggling, nearly in tears. I so wanted my wish to come true.

'Hey, hey, don't get upset, pet. It's only silly old Dad having a bit of fun. They're just joke candles, look.' Dad blew them out too, and they instantly relit themselves.

'It's so you can have *lots* of birthday wishes,' he said. 'I'll make a wish too.' He shut his eyes and muttered under his breath.

'What are you wishing for, Dad?'

'I can't tell you or it won't come true,' said Dad, giving my nose a tiny flick. 'Come on, here's the cake knife. Let's have a huge chunk each, eh?'

We chomped our cake. Whenever one of Dad's customers drifted in we gave them a slice too. There was still a semicircle of cake left when Dad locked up the shop.

We usually cuddled up on the sofa and watched an old video on the telly. Dad hadn't got round to buying a DVD player yet. In fact the television itself was on the blink. You often had to hit it before it would work. It didn't really matter if it went into a terminal sulk. Dad read to me and I read to him or we played funny paper games like Noughts and Crosses and Hangman and Battleships.

'We'll sofa-slouch tomorrow,' said Dad. 'We've got a hot date tonight, birthday girl. Get your jacket.'

'Where are we going, Dad?'

He winked at me. 'There's a travelling funfair up on the common this week.'

'Oh wow!'

Mum never let me go to fairs. She said they were horrible noisy rough places. She said she couldn't stand all the fried-onion food smells, they were a horrible reminder of the café. Mum and Steve took me to Chessington World of Adventures and Thorpe Park and Alton Towers. They all cost a lot of money so Mum said you didn't get riffraff. But I wasn't with Mum, I was with Dad. We both *loved* fairs.

'Better change out of your fancy silver shoes, sweetheart. Fairs can be muddy places,' said Dad.

I knew it would be sensible to change out of my princess dress too, but Dad said quickly, 'No, no, you can still stay a birthday princess in your frock, sweetie.'

I knew perfectly well I looked an idiot in my second-hand bridesmaid gown, my denim jacket and my new trainers. Still, I knew Dad wanted me to act like I couldn't bear to take my dress off because it was so special. So I wore the entire bizarre outfit, silver paper crown and all.

I prayed I wouldn't meet anyone from school at the fair. Especially Margot and Judy!

The fair was crowded. There were quite a lot of big boys milling about, the sort Mum would call riffraff. Dad put his arm round me.

'You stick close to your old dad, sweetheart,' he said. 'Now, what shall we go on first?'

'The roundabout!' I said.

'Good choice!' said Dad. 'Come along then, Princess, select your steed.'

Dad let me take my time, circling the roundabout so that I could see every single horse and work out which one I liked the best. I spotted a snow-white horse with a pink mane and tail and a big pink smiley mouth. Her name was written in magenta around her neck. She was called Pearl.

I ran for her the minute the roundabout slowed down, but it was difficult in my long bridesmaid dress. Another girl elbowed me out of the way and clambered on first.

'Never mind,' said Dad. 'We'll wait.'

So we waited, and at long last the roundabout slowed down again and this time *Dad* ran too, and he got to Pearl and saved her for me.

'You ride with me, Dad,' I said.

I hitched up my skirts and sat in front of the golden barley-sugar rail coming out of Pearl's back, and Dad sat behind me, his arms round my waist. We paid our money and the lovely old music started up and we rode round and round until the whole fairground was just a mosaic of coloured lights. I wished Pearl would kick her silver hooves and rear up off her stand and gallop away with us for ever.

'Would you like another ride on Pearl, Princess?' Dad asked.

'Oh please!'

So we went round and round and round again, and when we at last got off Dad let me pat Pearl's nose and stroke her long mane.

'She's so pretty,' I said. 'I just love her pink mane. It matches my dress, Dad, look.'

'We'd better make sure our refreshments match your dress too,' said Dad. 'Candy for my Floss!'

He led me to a candyfloss stall. It was decorated with roses, and a great pink teddy bear in a frilly dress dangled from the awning.

'Mum never ever lets me have candyfloss

because it's so bad for my teeth,' I said.

'You can give your teeth an extra thorough brush tonight,' said Dad, and he nodded at the big blonde lady in the candyfloss van. 'We'll have one each please. *My* teeth are pretty duff already.'

'I wouldn't say that,' said the candyfloss lady. 'You've got a lovely smile, sir.'

Dad gave her a big grin then. I grinned too. I love it when people like my dad.

'You take after your dad, darling,' said the candyfloss lady. 'You're looking very gorgeous in that pretty pink frock. Have you been a bridesmaid?'

'No, it's her birthday. She's my birthday princess,' said Dad.

'*Dad!*' I said, feeling daft.

'Aah, isn't that lovely. Well, we'd better make you an extra big birthday special.'

I watched, fascinated, as she poured sugar into the middle of her metal cauldron and then set it spinning. Wisps of candyfloss formed as if by magic. She took a stick and twirled it round and round until it bore an enormous pink fluffy cloud of candyfloss.

'Here you are, sweetheart,' she said, handing it over.

'Oh yum!' I said.

I held it in awe, approaching it gingerly, not

quite sure how to bite into it. Then someone behind jostled me and my nose went deep into the pink fluffy cloud and stuck there.

'Watch out, mate! Mind my little girl,' said Dad, turning round.

It wasn't just one mate. There were six or seven big lads, all of them holding cans of beer. They were strutting around, saying stupid things. Very very rude things. They didn't take any notice of Dad at all.

'Give us one of them big scoops of peanuts,' the biggest guy said to the candyfloss lady.

'Yeah, one for me too, I've got the munchies.'

'I'll have popcorn – the big carton,' said another.

'You wait your turn, boys. I'm serving this gentleman,' said the candyfloss lady.

'Here, we don't wait turns. We tell you, you serve us – *get it*?' said the biggest.

'This is my stall, and I don't have to serve anyone, so you can all push off sharpish – *get it*?' said the candyfloss lady.

They paused, taking it in.

'You don't talk to me like that,' said the big guy. Then he called her a terribly rude word.

'Don't you dare badmouth the lady,' said Dad. 'You need your mouth washing out with soap, lad.'

'You need your mouth shutting, you fat berk,'

said the boy, and he punched Dad straight in the face.

Dad hit him back, but then all his mates got stuck in. I screamed and someone shoved me and I ended up flat on my face in the mud. I lay there, stunned. There was a lot of shouting, a lot of struggling.

I lifted my head. 'Help! They're hurting my dad!' I yelled.

'It's OK, sweetheart. Your dad's OK now. Here, let me help you up, you poor little darling.' It was the candyfloss lady herself, sitting me up gently and wiping my sticky face. My silver crown fell off, all torn and crumpled.

I peered round desperately for my dad. I saw a lot of figures in the distance – big burly guys dragging the horrible drunk lads away from the fair.

'They're not taking my dad away too, are they?' I said.

'No, no, of course not. He's over there, by my stall, see?'

Dad was leaning against the stall, with a big fairground guy offering him a cloth for his bleeding lip.

'Don't give him that dirty old rag, Saul! Here, mind the stall for ten minutes while I get these two properly cleaned up in my caravan,' said the candyfloss lady.

She helped me stand up, tutting sympathetically when she saw the state of my dress.

'Dear oh dear! Still, it's not ripped – I wish I could say the same for your poor dad's jeans! I'm sure all that mud will wash off easily enough. Did those idiots hurt you, lovey?'

'I don't *think* so,' I said. I still couldn't understand what had happened. One minute they'd all been hitting my dad, and then the next they were all limping away, escorted by the fairground guys.

'Dad! Dad!' I said, stumbling over to him. 'Dad, did you beat them all up, those horrible lads?'

Dad laughed and then winced, because it stretched his sore lip. '*Me?*' he said. 'I was blooming useless, Floss.'

'No, you weren't. You were wonderful, sticking up for me like that,' said the candyfloss lady.

'He stuck up for me too,' I said.

'Yes, he's very gallant and brave, your dad,' said the candyfloss lady. 'Now, you two come with me and we'll get you cleaned up properly.'

'So how come they all stopped fighting?' I asked, as we followed her in and out of the stalls and trailers to the circle of caravans.

'Our guys keep an eye out for hassle,' said the candyfloss lady. 'One hint of trouble and they all come running. And they're tough lads too.'

'I'll say,' said Dad. 'Especially the one with the fair hair and all the skull rings, the one who gave me the rag for my nose. He felled three of the boys with one blow!'

'Ah, Saul. He's *my* lad,' said the candyfloss lady. 'He's a right softie, especially with the girls, but you don't want to get on the wrong side of him.'

'I'm certainly glad he was on *my* side,' said Dad.

'Right, this is my van,' said the candyfloss lady.

It was a beautiful bright pink, with red roses carefully painted above the door.

'I love the roses,' said Dad.

'That's my name. Rose. It was my mum's name and my gran's. They claimed we were related to the fortune-teller Gypsy Rose. They used to read palms and peer into the crystal ball and all that lark.'

'Can you tell fortunes?' I asked excitedly.

'Oh, I can read the tea leaves with the best of them,' she said, smiling at me. 'Come on, up the steps.'

We climbed the neat golden ladder and went through the pink door.

'Ooooh!' I said.

It was the most wonderful magical strange room ever. The inside walls were bright pink too, with lots of paintings of flowers and country cottages and little children in nighties. Great glittery glass mirrors doubled and tripled all the images, so you weren't quite sure what was real and what was reflection. There was a big red velvet sofa with needlework cushions, and a polished table with a lace cloth, and a cabinet in one corner containing lots of china crinolined ladies. A gold clock ticked and tocked on a sideboard, with a big china dog on either side.

'It's so beautiful!' I said.

'I'm glad you like it, duckie,' said Rose, going into her tiny kitchen and running water into a red bowl.

'How come you've got running water?' said Dad.

'Oh, we get it piped wherever we pitch up.'

'So do you travel all over the country?'

'Well – just the south-east. We fetch up at a new site each week during the summer.' She got a cloth and started washing my face and hands. She did it very gently, going carefully round my eyes and nose and mouth, not scrubbing splish-splash the way some grown-ups do. Then she started dabbing at the stains on my dress.

I had another peer around the beautiful red room while she was mopping me.

'How come all your lovely ornaments and pictures don't get broken when you move on to the

56

next site?' I asked.

'I'm magic. I just go *zap!*' – she waved her long silver fingernails – 'and fix them to the walls with my occult powers.'

I blinked at her. So did Dad.

Rose burst out laughing. 'No, of course I don't! I bundle them all up carefully in bubble wrap each time,' she said.

'And where do you sleep? I can't see a bed anywhere,' I said.

'Floss, stop being so nosy,' said Dad. 'It's rude to ask so many questions.'

'I don't mind a bit,' said Rose. 'See that sofa. You lift the seat part – and there's my bed, all lovely and cosy, neatly stowed out of sight.'

'What about Saul? Where's his bed?'

'He's got his own trailer now. He's way too big to share with his old mum.'

'What about Saul's dad?' said my dad.

Rose chuckled. 'Now who's being nosy!' she said. 'Oh, he cleared off a long time ago. Last spotted with a tassel-twirling circus girl half his age.'

'Oh. Right. I'm sorry,' said Dad, going a bit pink.

'Don't be sorry, dear. I like my independence. There!' She held out my pink skirts. They were wet, but nearly all the mud had come out.

'You've done an expert job there,' said Dad.

'I've had enough practice! My Saul used to come

back covered in mud every single time he went out to play,' said Rose.

She rinsed out the bowl and got a clean cloth. 'Now, sir, let's sort you out.'

'I'm not a sir! I'm Charlie,' said Dad. 'And this is my little girl Floss.'

'How do you do, Charlie. OK, let's get you cleaned up properly. That little toerag gave you a nasty split lip as well as a bloody nose. No kissing for you for a day or two!'

'Chance would be a fine thing,' said Dad.

She mopped Dad *very* gently. Dad can be a bit of a baby when he cuts himself, but he didn't wince once, not even when she dabbed his cuts with antiseptic.

'Now, what about your legs? Are they cut too?' she said, peering at the great rips in the knees of Dad's jeans.

'Just skinned. They're fine,' said Dad.

'Oh, you're such a stoical chap,' said Rose. 'Still, it must have been a nasty shock. I think we could both do with a nip of brandy, don't you?'

She poured two drinks in pretty crimson glasses, and she gave me a lovely lemonade in a green glass goblet.

'White wine, madam?' she said, serving it with a flourish.

'Delicious!' I said. 'But I couldn't possibly have

58

a cup of tea too?'

'You don't like tea, Floss!' said Dad.

'No – but I want Rose to read the tea leaves.'

'Well, to tell you the truth, lovey, I've only got tea bags in my caddy. But I'll read your palm, how about that?'

'Oh yes, please!'

I thrust it at her eagerly. She sat down beside me and took my palm in hers, looking at it intently.

'Aaah!' she said.

'What? Oh please, what is it?'

'Rose is going to tell you that you bite your nails and you've just had a birthday and you're the apple of your dad's eye!' said Dad, laughing.

'Oh, *Dad*,' I said.

'Yes, shush, Dad,' said Rose. She delicately traced the lines on my hand. 'Now, this line is broken – which tells me you've had a little heartache, and you've felt torn in two – is that right?'

'Oh yes!'

'Don't worry though, darling, I can see very happy times ahead. Yes, there are going to be a few changes in store.'

'I don't think I like changes,' I said. 'I've had too many.'

'No, no, these are good changes, you wait and see.'

'What are they?' I said warily.

'Ah, that's for you to find out in the future!'

'Can't you give me a hint or two?'

'They're changes to do with your home, your family, your friends—'

'Oh no! Is Rhiannon going to break friends with me and go off with Margot?'

'You wait and see.' She gently chucked me under the chin. 'Don't look so worried. You wait – there are all sorts of signs and portents. This is your lucky break, Floss.'

'Is it mine too? I could certainly do with my luck changing,' said Dad.

'Do you want me to read your palm too?'

'Mmm, maybe not! I'm not sure I'd like what I heard,' said Dad, downing his drink. 'Well, you've been so kind to us, Rose. We'd better not keep you away from your candyfloss stall any longer. Come on, Floss, it's ages past your bed time.'

'Well, if you change your mind, come back and find me,' said Rose, smiling at him. 'Now, the least we can do is give you both a free ride on something. What do you fancy? The Big Wheel? The Waltzer? The Rotunda?'

Dad looked at me. I looked at him.

'Another go on Pearl?' said Dad.

'Oh please!'

So we had one more magical ride on the roundabout. Pearl galloped round and round on her

60

silver hooves, pink mane and tail flying. We flew with her, and as the hurdy-gurdy music played, I sang in my head, *Our luck is changing, our luck is changing, our luck is changing!*

I decided to tell Dad that night, but I was too tired to do more than scrub candyfloss off my face, brush my teeth and then collapse into bed.

I decided to tell Dad over breakfast instead, but he made special croissants, putting a funny black beret on his head and hanging a string of plastic onions round his neck, pretending to be French. I couldn't tell him when he was prancing around singing *Frère Jacques* and calling me his little cabbage.

I decided I'd tell Dad before lunch, but we went to the park and fed the ducks all the stale bread left over from the café. There was so much, the ducks had a veritable banquet, quacking appreciatively whenever I shook the bags and it started snowing chunks of bread. I didn't want to spoil their fun – or ours.

I decided to tell Dad during lunch, but he sat me down in the café and pretended I was a very special customer. He served me a funny little salad in the shape of a clown's face – lettuce hair, boiled egg eyes, and a cherry tomato nose.

'There! Tell your mum I give you ultra-healthy nosh,' said Dad. 'OK, now for pudding.'

It wasn't quite as healthy. Dad garnished big slices of birthday cake with cream and ice cream and raspberry sauce, making a totally heavenly birthday pudding. I couldn't possibly spoil it by blurting out my news.

We were so full afterwards we flopped at either end of the sofa and watched our ancient old video of *The Railway Children*. It jumps around a lot and sometimes gets stuck but we know it so well it's not a problem. We chanted along with it half the time. At the very end, Bobbie goes to the station and she sees her father and goes running to him, calling, 'Daddy, oh my daddy.'

My dad is a big silly softie. He always cries at this bit and I tease him rotten. Only this time I thought what it must really have been like to be poor Bobbie, parted from her father all that time – and I was the one who burst out crying.

'Hey! No blubbing allowed! That's *my* job,' said Dad, giving me a little loving poke. Then he looked at me properly. 'You're not *really* crying, are you, Flossie? What's the matter, eh? You can tell your old dad, can't you?'

That was just the trouble. I *couldn't* tell my dad, it was just too awful. I wound my arms round his neck and clung to him tightly.

'I'm going to miss you so, Dad,' I sobbed into his old grey jersey.

'I'm going to miss you all week too, sweetheart. I just live for our weekends together, especially now . . . Well, I've got in a bit of a muddle with money, and things are a bit dodgy at the café. Still, as long as I've got you, that's all that matters,' said Dad, rubbing his bristly cheek against the top of my head.

I sobbed harder.

'Hey, hey, don't cry so, little Floss. Your curly mop feels so silky. You're like my own special candyfloss. Watch out I don't eat you all up.' He made funny golloping noises, pretending to nibble my curls.

I couldn't help giggling, even though I was still crying hard.

'That's it, start cheering up, my darling. Wonderboy Steve will be calling for you soon in his flash car and I don't want him telling your mum you've been miserable with me. You've got to be the all-singing, all-dancing happy little girl who thinks her parents splitting up is a piece of cake. And *talking* of cakes, better not tell your mum we scoffed a whole birthday cake between us or we'll really be for it!'

'Dad? Oh, Dad!'

'What is it, little pal? Spit it out.'

'I don't know *how*,' I wailed.

Then I heard a car draw up outside. I reared up off the sofa. It was Steve, far too early. Steve and Mum and Tiger, all come to collect me.

I had to spit it out now. It torrented out like a waterfall.

'Dad, I can't bear it, but we're going to Australia, Steve's got this new job and we're moving there next month, they've only just told me and I've been trying to tell you all weekend and I haven't been able to and they say it's not for ever, just six months, but it will *feel* like for ever and I feel like I'm being cut in half because I love you so, Dad.'

The doorbell rang. Dad shook his head, looking dazed. For one terrible moment his face crumpled up. Then he took a deep breath and tried to smile.

'That's really exciting news, Floss,' he said. 'Australia, eh? Well, sport, we'll have to buy you one of them funny hats with corks on.'

'Do you mind terribly, Dad? Are you cross with me?'

'Of course I'm not cross with you, silly girl. I do *mind*, obviously. I'll miss you dreadfully. Just you make sure you don't forget your old dad.'

'Oh Dad, as if!' I said.

The bell went again. Someone knocked loudly with their knuckles on the café door.

'Come on, sounds like your mum's getting impatient,' said Dad.

I clung to him like a baby monkey, unable to let him go. He staggered with me to the door and opened it with difficulty.

'What are you playing at, Charlie? We've been ringing and knocking for ages,' said Mum. She looked at me. 'Oh Floss, you've got yourself in a silly state!' Then she looked properly. 'What on earth's that pink thing you're wearing? And whose silver shoes are those? They're *way* too big for you!'

Dad gently put me down. I wobbled on my high heels.

'They're my birthday princess clothes,' I sobbed. 'I think they're beautiful.'

'Yes. Well. Get your things together then, we've got to be off. We're going to Steve's mum for tea.' Mum caught Tiger's fist. He was trying to pick peeling paint off the café door. 'Don't, pet! Dirty! Yes, we're off to see Granny, aren't we?'

'She's not *my* granny,' I said. 'I want to stay with Dad.' I wound my arms as far as I could round Dad's large waist and leaned my head against his chest. I could hear his heart going *thump-thump-thump* underneath his jersey.

'Don't start behaving like a baby, Floss. You'll be able to see your dad again before . . . before . . .'

'Before you all go to Australia,' said Dad, patting me on the shoulder.

'Yes, Australia!' said Mum, looking Dad in the eyes for the first time. 'So Flossie's told you?'

'Yes, she has. She's a bit upset about it, as you can see,' said Dad.

'Well, you've obviously been stirring her up. She's really thrilled to bits. It's a fantastic opportunity,' said Mum. 'Steve's done so well, getting this job.'

'I'm *not* thrilled,' I mumbled to Dad. 'I wish she'd just shut up about Steve.'

'What was that?' said Mum.

'Why didn't you tell me before?' said Dad.

'Well, we're telling you now,' said Mum. 'Steve's going to be in charge of this whole new Australian branch at double his current salary, and—'

'Yeah, yeah,' said Dad. He obviously wanted Mum to shut up about Steve too. 'What I mean is, how is it going to affect Floss? And me, for that matter. It's going to kill me not seeing my little girl.'

'Sorry about that, pal,' said Steve. He's *not* Dad's pal, not in a million years. 'It wasn't deliberate, you know. I didn't even put in for the job in Sydney, they simply offered it to me.' He shrugged and smirked to show us he couldn't *help* being so brilliant and clever and in demand.

'It's all very well saying sorry,' said Dad. He looked at Mum. 'What about my right to see Floss? I've got joint custody, you know that.'

'You can come and see her any time you want,' Mum said calmly.

'How am I going to get there? Walk?' said Dad.

'I can't help it if you can't afford it,' said Mum. 'We can't miss this golden opportunity. There's nothing you can do about it, Charlie.'

I felt Dad sag a little.

'I don't suppose there is,' he said, so sadly. 'Well, I hope it all works out for you. And don't you worry, little Floss, we'll write lots. You never know, I might win the lottery and then I'll come flying over to see you straight away . . . or I'll put on my Superman pants and soar all the way to Sydney under my own steam.'

He was trying to make me laugh but it just made me cry harder.

'Come on, Flora, don't be such a little drama queen,' said Mum. 'Change out of those silly shoes, take that frock off and let's get going.'

I unhooked myself from Dad. I wiped my eyes and took a step backwards. I looked at him. He had tears in his eyes too, though his mouth was stretched into a clown smile-shape. Then I looked at Mum and Steve and Tiger. My two families.

I suddenly knew where I belonged.

'I'm not going,' I said.

Mum sighed. 'Look, Granny Westwood's expecting us, and Tiger's getting restless. I want to give him his bottle in the car and settle him off to sleep.'

'I'm not going *at all*,' I said. I took a deep breath. 'I'm not going to Australia. I've decided. There's nothing you can do to change my mind. I'm staying with my dad.'

It was as if I'd thrown a bomb at Mum. She exploded. She told me I was being ridiculous. She insisted I had to go with her. I was part of her family.

'I'm part of Dad's family too,' I said.

Dad gave me this great big hug – but then he held me at arm's length and looked into my eyes. 'Are you sure you know what you're saying, Floss? I think maybe you'd be much better off in Australia with your mum. You don't have to stay with your old dad, you know. I'll miss you heaps and heaps but I'll manage fine, I promise.'

'*I* won't manage, Dad,' I said. 'I want to stay with you.'

'Well you *can't*, so you can stop this silly act right now,' Mum said. 'You're my daughter and you're coming to live with me.'

'No I'm not.'

'Yes you are.'

'No I'm *not.*'

'Yes you *are.*'

'Oh no I'm NOT.'

'Hey hey hey, you two! You sound like a bad pantomime act,' said Dad.

'Don't you tell me what to do,' said Mum. 'I'm sure this is all your fault. You put Floss up to this. I tell you, she was absolutely thrilled to be going to Australia, as anyone in their right mind would be.'

'Well, she seems in her right mind now to me – and it's clear what she wants to do,' said Dad. 'She wants to stay with me.'

'She can't! A daughter's place is with her mother,' Mum insisted. She turned to me. 'Floss?' Her voice cracked as if she was going to cry. 'You do really want to be with me, don't you, darling?'

She waited. Dad waited. I waited too.

I didn't *know* what I really wanted.

Yes I did. I wanted Steve and Tiger to disappear in a puff of smoke. I wanted our family to be just Mum and Dad and me. It would be like it used to be long ago, when Dad called Mum his big princess and she laughed at all his silly jokes and we had breakfast in bed on Sunday mornings and cuddles all together on the big sofa in the living room.

I shut my eyes for a second and wished for what I wanted.

I knew my wish couldn't possibly come true. I opened my eyes again. There was Mum, her forehead pinched with two sharp lines above her nose, her carefully outlined shiny lips pressed hard together in a straight line. There was Dad, gnawing at a piece of loose skin on his thumb, his hair sticking up sideways, his sweatshirt too tight over his tummy. I could wish and wish until I blew up like a giant balloon, but Mum and Dad weren't ever going to get back together.

Tiger started grizzling because Mum was holding him too tightly. Steve reached over and took him, swinging him up onto his broad shoulders. Tiger chuckled with delight. He loved his dad.

I loved *my* dad. I loved him even more because he wasn't tall and fit and handsome and clever like Steve. Mum had Steve and Tiger. Dad didn't have anyone but me.

'I really want to stay here with Dad,' I said quietly to Mum. 'Please please please let me.'

Mum's face screwed up. Her glossy lips disappeared as her mouth contorted. Tears started rolling down her cheeks. 'All right,' she whispered. She clutched her stomach as if she'd just been punched.

Steve pulled her close, Tiger still perching on his shoulders.

Dad put his arms right round me. I could feel him shaking. I think he was crying too.

It would have been easier if we could have all split up there and then, but I stayed with Mum and Steve and Tiger until they went to Australia.

It was awful. Mum and I didn't know how to act with each other. One day Mum would act all cold and distant, and whenever I looked up she'd be staring at me reproachfully. The next day she would be brisk and bossy, telling me she was damned if I was going to mess up all their plans and if I didn't want to go to Australia it was my loss, not hers. But the day after that she suddenly burst into floods of tears and I did too. I sat on Mum's lap and cuddled in close and she rocked me as if I was as tiny as Tiger.

'I'm going to miss you so, my baby,' said Mum.

'I'm going to miss you too, Mum,' I said.

'*Please* come with us,' she murmured into my curls.

I wanted to so much. Mum looked like she'd really really miss me, maybe even as much as Dad. I didn't see how I could *bear* to be without my mum. I thought of all our cuddles, all our girly talk, all our shopping trips, all the secrets she told me about growing up and girls-and-boys.

As the days wore on I got so cast down that I

even started to feel I was going to miss Tiger. Whenever I went near him he held out his chubby arms to be picked up. When I whirled him around or blew a raspberry on his fat little tummy he chuckled and snorted and kicked his bendy legs like a little frog. He was even starting to say my name, though he couldn't quite manage the 'l' so I was his Fossie.

I suddenly got into the whole big sister thing. I sat him on my lap and read him all his boring little books about tractors and tank engines. I drew him pictures of dogs and cats and cows so that he could *woof-woof* and *mew-mew* and *moo-moo* for hours. I fed him his chopped-up chicken and carrots, pretending the spoon was an aeroplane flying through the air and docking in his drooly little mouth. I gave him his bath, making all his plastic ducks bob up and down and nibble his tummy with their orange beaks. I tucked him up at night with his dummy and his stripy teddy and my baby kangaroo.

'You can have Baby Kangaroo if you like, Tiger,' I whispered. 'Seeing as you've taken such a shine to him.'

Tiger clasped Baby Kangaroo happily.

'Maybe you'd better have Mother Kangaroo too,' I said. 'I don't think they'd like being separated.'

I knew I wasn't going to like being separated

from *my* mum. I couldn't help hoping that she'd suddenly change her mind and decide she couldn't bear to go to Australia without me. Steve didn't *have* to take this new job. We could all go on living in our house and I could go on staying with Dad at weekends and we could still be a kind of family even if Mum and Dad weren't living together.

But Steve brought home lots of cardboard boxes and started packing everything up. Tiger played happily in this new cardboard city, plumping himself down on sheets of bubble wrap and squealing with laughter when they went pop.

Mum started packing her stuff too, selecting all her favourite clothes, consigning her fun fur coat and big boots to the boxes going into storage, as it wasn't really cold in Australia even in their winter. She started going through all my things too, packing all the good stuff to be taken to Dad's and putting all my old clothes and toys in a big bag for the hospice shop.

I stared at all my special dolls and cuddly teddies. I loved them so – but Rhiannon now said they were just for silly babies. I rounded up all my Barbie girls, twirled each one round on her tippy toes, and then made them jump one after the other into the plastic bag.

'Are you sure about your dolls, Floss? Won't you want to play with them at your dad's?'

'They're just for babies,' I said firmly.

'Well, at least they look attractive. Why chuck them and keep all these moth-eaten old teddies?'

'I'm not,' I said, and I tumbled them all into the bag too, until it was bulging with soft yellow and fawn fur.

'Good for you, Floss,' said Mum. 'But you'd better keep Kanga and Baby Kanga for yourself, as your best toys. They were actually very expensive. Tiger will just mess them up.'

'No, I want him to have them, Mum. As a special present from his big sister.'

'Well, that's very sweet of you, dear. You're right, you're getting too grown up for cuddly toys.'

But then Mum suddenly seized hold of a droopy pink poodle with the embarrassing name of PP huddling at the bottom of my old toy box. (I'd simply shortened Pink Poodle to her initials, but I knew her name would make Margot and Judy chortle – and maybe Rhiannon.)

'Chuck her, Mum,' I said.

'No, we have to keep PP,' Mum said, stroking her.

'Mum! PP's *ancient*.' She was more grey than pink nowadays, her fur was very matted and she only had one glass eye, which gave her face a baleful, lopsided expression.

'You used to lug her around everywhere with

79

you when you were little,' said Mum. She looked at me. 'You're *still* little,' she said, and she started crying.

I'd seen Mum cry lots of times before, but never like this. She sat back on her heels and sobbed, her mouth like a letter box because she was howling so hard. It was so scary that Tiger stopped crawling round her wardrobe playing with shoes, and huddled down into her pashmina pile, sobbing too.

I wanted to cry as well, but Steve was out playing a farewell round of golf with all his boring buddies so he wasn't around to comfort Mum. I had to be the grown-up. I put my arms round Mum and I rocked her and she clutched me tight and wept against my chest until my T-shirt was sodden.

'Please don't cry so, Mum,' I begged. 'I'm not little, I'm big now. I'll be fine with Dad while you're away, and then when you come back from Australia we'll go back to me living with you during the week and we'll get back to normal again, you'll see.'

'Oh darling,' Mum sobbed. 'I think I've gone crazy. What am I *doing*? I *can't* leave you behind, I simply can't.'

I started to hope that she'd really changed her mind. She'd stay in this country after all and forget about Australia.

The next day she stopped all her frantic packing and consulted a solicitor. I wasn't allowed to go into his office with her. I had to stay in the reception room minding Tiger. He wouldn't stay on my lap. He prowled around on his hands and knees, his sticky hands scrabbling at all the leather-bound law books on the shelves. The receptionist tried cooing and clucking at him, but Tiger wasn't in a mood to be charmed. He was yelling his head off when Mum came out of the solicitor's office. She looked in a yelling mood too.

'As if I'm going to hang around and let the courts sort it out!' she exploded the moment we got outside. 'We've got the tickets, we're all set to go. We can't hang around now! Steve has got to start working at the Sydney branch this month. I can't

let him go off on his own. He needs my support –
and if I'm not careful some silly young thing will
bat her eyes at him and turn his head. What am I
going to *do*?'

Mum glared at me as if it was all my fault. 'Why
can't you jump at this fantastic chance, Floss? I
was mad to let you dictate to me. Look, you're
coming with us, whether you like it or not!'

'What are you going to do, Mum? Kidnap me?
I'm a bit big to bundle under your arm. Are you
going to lock me in one of the suitcases?'

'Stop being so cheeky!' Mum said, giving me a
shake.

'Well, you stop bossing me about! Ouch, you're
hurting. I've told you and told you, I'm not coming,
I'm staying with Dad.'

'*Why* do you want to stay with him?'

'I love him.'

'More than you love me?'

'I love you *both*,' I said, crying. 'Mum, he needs
me.'

'So you care more about his feelings than mine?
All right then, stay with him. I won't try and
persuade you any more. Happy now?' Mum snapped.

Of course I wasn't happy – and neither was she.
It was exhausting. It looked like we were going to
be chopping and changing for ever, best friends one
day and snarling enemies the next.

The day before Mum and Steve and Tiger flew off we were all at sixes and sevens – and eights and nines and tens. Mum and I were hugging one minute and shouting the next. But that night Mum left Steve alone in his big bed, edged her way round the last of the packing cases, and came and clambered into my single bed beside me. She held me tight and I nestled in to her. Neither of us slept much. Mum told me stories about when I was a very little girl. I told Mum stories about what I planned to do when I was a big girl. We held onto each other, Mum's hands gripping my arms fiercely, as if she could never bear to let me go.

Dad came to collect me in his van, so that he could carry all my extra stuff. It's a big white van and I'd always loved riding in it, feeling so special strapped up high beside my dad, but I saw the way Steve shook his head at the dents and scratches on the paintwork. Dad saw too, and must have minded, but he shook Steve's hand nevertheless and wished him luck with his new job. He patted Tiger on the head. Then he gave Mum a great clumsy hug.

'Let's stay friends, Sal. I swear I'll take the greatest care of our Floss. You enjoy Australia and your new life, but don't forget to come back home, babe.'

Mum always twitched with irritation when Dad

called her babe, but now she sniffled tearfully and give him a big hug back.

I held my breath as my parents embraced. Maybe now, at the very very last minute, they would realize that they really loved each other after all. Then Mum moved away and the moment was over.

It was our turn to hug, Mum and me. We hugged and hugged and hugged. It hurt so much. It seemed like I was making the biggest mistake of my life.

'I want you to have this, Floss,' said Mum, handing me an envelope. 'It's an open airline ticket to Sydney. You can use it any time in the next six months. It'll be strange travelling such a long way on your own, but the stewardess will look after you. Or of course you can change your mind now and come with us after all.'

I wanted to cling to Mum and say *Yes yes yes!*

But I saw Dad's face. He was nodding and trying to smile. I *couldn't* say yes. I just shook my head sadly, but promised I'd take great care of the ticket.

Dad opened the van door. Steve lifted me in. Mum gave me one last kiss. Then we were driving away from my mum, my home, my whole family . . .

I waved and waved and waved long after we'd turned the corner and were out of sight. Then I hunched down in my seat, my hands over my mouth to stop any sound coming out.

'It's OK to cry, darling. Cry as much as you want,' said Dad. 'I know it must be so awful for you. You're going to miss your mum so. *I'll* miss her, in spite of everything. But she'll be coming back in six months, and the time will simply whizz by. If I can only win the lottery we'll both jet out to Sydney for a month's holiday, just like that. Yeah, if I could win the lottery *all* our problems would be solved.' Dad sighed heavily. 'I feel so bad, little Floss. I should have insisted you go with your mum.'

'I want to be with you, Dad,' I murmured, though I wasn't sure it was true now.

We went back to the café. Dad opened it up and got the tea and coffee brewing. There wasn't much point. We had no customers at all, not even Billy the Chip or Old Ron or Miss Davis.

'I might as well shut it up again. I doubt anyone will be in until lunch time, if then,' said Dad. 'Come on, kiddo, let's go out for a bit. What would you like to do?'

That was the trouble. I didn't really want to do *anything*. We mooched around the town for a bit, peering in some of the shops. There wasn't much point getting excited about anything because I knew Dad didn't have any money. He tried to start up this game of what we'd buy if we won the lottery. I didn't feel like joining in much.

'I suppose your mum's Steve could buy you any of this stuff with a flash of his credit card,' Dad said.

'I don't want any of it,' I said.

'That's my girl. The simple things in life are best, eh?' Dad said eagerly. 'Come on, let's go to the park and feed the ducks. You like that, don't you?'

I wondered if I was getting too old for feeding the ducks, but we picked up a bag of stale sliced bread back at the café and trundled down to the park, even though it had started raining.

'It's only a spot of drizzle,' said Dad.

By the time we reached the duckpond we were both wet through and shivering because we hadn't bothered with our proper coats.

'Still, nice weather for the ducks,' said Dad.

They were swimming round in circles, quacking away. Mother ducks and ducklings.

I threw them some bread, large chunks for the mothers and dainty bite-sized morsels for the duck-lings, but they seemed full to bursting already. There were large chunks of bread bobbing all around them but they couldn't be bothered to open their beaks. They'd already had so many visitors. Mothers and toddlers.

'Never mind, let's take the bread back home and make chip butties, eh?' said Dad. 'Two for you and two for me. Yum yum in the tum!'

I wasn't listening properly. I was looking up at an aeroplane flying high in the sky, as small as a silver bird.

'Your mum won't be on her plane yet,' Dad said softly. 'They aren't going to the airport till this evening. It's a night flight.'

I had mad thoughts about packing my case, running like crazy to Mum's and begging her to take me after all.

Maybe that was why I was so fidgety when I got home. I heaved around on the sofa, I lolled about the floor, I watched ten minutes of one video, five of another, I read two pages of my book, I got out my felt pens and started a drawing and then crumpled up the paper. I ended up rolling the pens all over the floor, flicking them moodily from one side of the room to the other.

One went right under the sofa. I had to scrabble for it with my fingers. I found little balls of fluff, some old crisps, a tissue and a screwed-up letter. I opened it up and saw the word *debt* and the word *court* and the word *bailiffs* before Dad snatched it away.

'Hey, hey, that's *my* letter, Floss,' he said. He crumpled it up again, screwing it tighter and tighter in his hand until it was like a hard little bullet.

'What is it, Dad?'

'Nothing,' said Dad.

'But I thought it said . . . ?'

'It was just a silly letter sent to try to scare me. It's not going to, OK?' said Dad. 'Now, you just forget all about it, there's a good girl. Come on, let's have our chip butties!'

Dad made two each, and one for luck. I could only eat half of one, and that was a great big effort. It turned out Dad didn't have much appetite either. We looked at the chip butties left on the plate. It was as if Dad had made enough for both my families. I wasn't sure I could stand to be in this very small family of two now. I wasn't sure how we were going to manage.

The Apple Café

I was swimming in an enormous duckpond, gigantic birds with beaks as big as bayonets swooping towards me. I opened my mouth to scream for help and started choking in the murky green water. I coughed and coughed and went under. I got tangled in long slimy ropes of weed. I couldn't struggle free. The vast ducks swam above my head, their great webbed feet batting me. I was trapped down there, my lungs bursting. No one knew, no one cared, no one came to rescue me . . .

I woke up gasping, soaked through. I thought for one terrible moment I might have wet myself – but it was only a night sweat. I staggered up out of my damp bed, mumbling, 'Mum, Mum' – and then I remembered.

I stopped, shivering on the dark landing. I couldn't run to Mum for a cuddle. She was six miles up in the air, halfway across the world.

I started crying like a baby, huddled down on the carpet.

'Floss?'

Dad came stumbling out of his bedroom in his pyjamas and very nearly tripped over me. 'What are you doing *here*, pet? Don't cry. Come on, I'll take you back to bed. It's all right, Dad's here. You've just had a bad dream.'

It seemed as if I was stuck in the bad dream. Dad tucked me in gently but he didn't know how to plump up my pillow properly and smooth my sheet. He didn't find me a big tissue for my runny nose. He didn't comb my hair with his fingers. He did kiss me softly on the cheek, but his face was scratchy with stubble and he didn't smell sweet and powdery like Mum.

I tried to cuddle down under the duvet but it smelled wrong too, of old house and chip fat. I wanted to go to *Mum's* house, but it was all changed. Our stuff was all packed up. Soon there would be strangers renting it. I imagined another girl my age in my white bedroom with the cherry-red carpet and the cherries on the curtains. I saw her looking out of my window at my garden and my special swing and I couldn't bear it.

Three months ago Steve had fixed up the baby swing for Tiger, all colours and bobbles and flashing lights. I'd done the big sister bit and patiently pushed him backwards and forwards, but I couldn't help remarking that I wished *I'd* had a swing when I was little.

I didn't think Mum and Steve had taken much notice, but the next weekend when I was at Dad's Steve rigged up this amazing proper traditional wooden swing, big enough for an adult – certainly big enough for *me*.

'My swing!' I sobbed now.

'What? Please don't cry so, Floss, I can't make out what you're saying,' said Dad, sounding really worried. 'Listen, I know how badly you're missing your mum. I've got your airline ticket safe in the kitchen drawer. We can book you onto a flight and you can join up with them. It will be like a big adventure flying all that way.'

'No, no. I want my *swing*,' I said.

Dad missed a beat before he understood. 'Well, that's easy-peasy,' he said. 'We'll nip round to your mum's place tomorrow and take your swing. Don't upset yourself, darling. Your old dad will sort things for you.'

We went round to the house early Sunday morning, before Dad opened up the café. Dad parked the van outside the house. It looked so absolutely normal I couldn't believe Mum and Steve and Tiger weren't lurking behind Mum's ruched blinds.

We didn't have a key, but we didn't need one to wiggle open the bolt of the side gate and walk round into the back garden. Tiger's swing wasn't there. It had been dismantled and packed up. The only trace of it was the four square marks in the grass where the legs had been.

My swing still stood there sturdily. Too sturdily. Dad tried and tried to take it down. He even broke into the garden shed and bashed at the swing's supports with Steve's tools. The swing didn't budge but Steve's stainless-steel spade got horribly dented.

'Oh bum,' said Dad. 'Now I suppose I'll have to pay for a new blooming spade on top of everything else.'

'Never mind, Dad.'

'But I *do* mind. Why am I so useless? Look, I'm going to collapse that swing if it's the last thing I do.'

Dad battered and bashed a lot more. He tugged and tussled with the swing. He even tried digging around it with the bent spade, but the supports went way way down – almost to Australia.

Dad stood still, wiping his brow, his face damp and scarlet.

'It doesn't matter, Dad, honestly,' I said.

'It matters to me,' said Dad grimly.

I peered up at the swing, wishing I hadn't said

a word. Dad stared too, his brow furrowed, as if he was trying to fell the swing by sheer willpower. Then he suddenly clapped his hands and ran and got Steve's scary long pruning shears.

'Dad! What are you going to do?'

'It's OK, Floss. I've just worked it out. We'll liberate your swing. We just need the rope and the seat. We don't *need* the stupid supports. It's going to be a *portable* swing now, you'll see.'

Dad reached up and snipped at the top of each rope. They came thumping down with the wooden seat attached. 'There!' he said, as if he'd perfected the most astonishing trick.

I blinked doubtfully at the severed swing and said nothing.

When we got back home Dad took the swing out in the back yard. He's never actually got round to turning it into a proper garden. There's not really room, anyway. There are big wheelie bins for taking the rubbish from the café, and all the cardboard boxes of old stuff that Dad's going to sort one day lurking under tarpaulin, and bits and pieces of very old bikes, and an electric scooter that never worked properly.

There's a tiny flowerbed of pansies because Dad says they've got smiley faces, and an old sandpit I used to play Beaches in when I was very little, and an ancient gnarled apple tree that's too old to produce any fruit, although it was the reason Dad bought the café long ago. He was going to make our own apple pies and apple cake and apple chutney and apple sauce. He painted a big new sign to go above the door – THE APPLE CAFÉ – and he painted the walls and windowpanes bright apple-green.

He changed the name to Charlie's Café long ago, but the apple-green paint's still there, though it's faded to a yellowy-lime and it's peeling everywhere. Mum always nagged Dad to chop the apple tree down because it wasn't doing anything useful, just causing shadows in the yard, but Dad reacted as if Mum had asked him to chop *me* down.

'We'll hang your swing on the apple tree!' Dad said now.

He spent all afternoon putting it up. He tested the branches first, swinging on them himself, yelling like Tarzan to make me laugh. I still didn't feel a bit like laughing but I giggled politely.

Then Dad went up and down a ladder, fixing one end of the swing rope here and the other end there. He had to take an hour's break hunting down an ancient encyclopaedia in a box of books in the attic to find out how to do the safest knots.

When at last he had the swing hanging we found it was too low, so that my bottom nearly bumped the ground. Dad had to start all over again, shortening the ropes. But *eventually*, late afternoon, the swing was ready.

'There you are, Princess! Your throne awaits,' Dad said, ultra proudly.

I put on my birthday princess gown over my jeans to please him and sat on my swing. Dad beamed at me and then went pottering off again to find his old camera to commemorate the moment. He didn't come back for a long time.

I had to stay swinging. I didn't *feel* like swinging somehow. I wouldn't have told Dad for the world, but you couldn't really swing properly now it was attached to the apple tree. The swing juddered about too abruptly and hung slightly lopsided, so you started to feel queasy very quickly. It wasn't very pretty out in the back yard staring at the tarpaulins and bits of bikes, and the wheelie bins were very smelly.

I sat there and sat there and sat there, and when Dad came back eventually clutching his Polaroid I had a short burst of swinging and smiled at the camera.

'It's a great swing, isn't it!' said Dad proudly, as if he had made it all himself. 'Hey, why don't you phone Rhiannon and see if she wants to come round and play on it too?'

I hesitated. I'd asked Rhiannon round to play heaps of times, but always at Mum's. I'd wanted to keep my time at the weekend specially for Dad. But now *all* my time was with Dad.

'Go on, phone her,' said Dad. 'Ask her round to tea. Does she like chip butties?'

I wasn't sure. We always ate salads and chicken and fruit at Rhiannon's. Her school packed lunches were also ultra-healthy options: wholemeal rolls and carrot sticks and apples and weeny boxes of raisins. But maybe chip butties would be a wonderful wicked treat?

I knew I was kidding myself. I suspected it would be a big big big mistake to invite her round. But I felt so weird and lonely stuck here with Dad with nothing to do. If Rhiannon was here we could muck about and do silly stuff and maybe I'd start to feel normal again.

I phoned her up. I got her mum first.

'Oh Flora, I'm so glad you called! How *are* you?' she asked in hushed tones. 'I was so shocked when Rhiannon told me about your mother.'

She was acting as if Mum had *died*.

'I'm fine,' I lied. 'Please can Rhiannon come round to tea?'

'What, today? Well, her grandma and grandpa are here. Tell me, Flora, do you see your grandma a lot?'

'My grandma?' I said, surprised. 'Well, she sends me birthday presents, but she doesn't always remember how old I am. Dad says she gets muddled.'

'What about your mum's mum?'

'She died when I was a baby. There's Steve's mum, but I don't think she likes me much.'

'You poor little mite. Well, listen to me, sweetheart. Any time you need to discuss anything girly, you come and have a word with me, all right? I know your dad will do his best, but it's not the same, not the same at all. A growing girl needs her mother. I just can't understand how *your* mother . . .' She let her voice tail away.

I clutched the phone so tightly it was a wonder the plastic didn't buckle. I couldn't stand her going on like that, as if Mum had deliberately abandoned me. I decided I didn't want Rhiannon to come round after all, but her mum was busy calling to her and asking for details of the address.

I heard Rhiannon saying stuff in the background. It didn't sound as if she wanted to come round.

'You've got to go! It's the least you can do. Poor little Flora will be feeling so lonely,' Rhiannon's mother hissed.

'I'm fine, really,' I said.

'Yes dear, I'm sure you are,' she said, in a *don't-think-you-can-fool-me* tone of voice.

I couldn't fool Rhiannon either when she came

round. She was wearing a lacy blue top and white jeans. She had one little plait tied with blue and white thread in her long glossy black hair. She looked beautiful. She seemed so out of place in our café.

'Oh Floss, you poor thing, your eyes look so sore, all red and puffy,' she said.

'It's an allergy,' I said quickly.

Rhiannon sighed at me. She turned to Dad. 'My mum says you must phone her if you've got any problems.'

Dad blinked. 'Problems?'

'You know. Over Flossie,' said Rhiannon. She was acting like she was my social worker or something. Even Dad looked a bit irritated.

'We haven't got any problems, Floss and me, have we, doll-baby? But it's very kind of your mum to offer all the same, so thank her very much. Now, would you two girls like to go and play on Floss's swing?'

He led the way through the café, out into the kitchen, and opened the door to the back yard dramatically, as if Disneyland beckoned.

Rhiannon stepped warily into the back yard, walking as if she was wading through mud. She peered at the wheelie bins, the tarpaulins, the bits of bike. It was definitely a mistake inviting her round. I suddenly saw Rhiannon telling her mother all about our dismal back yard. Worse, I saw her telling Margot and Judy and all the girls at school.

I looked at her anxiously.

'Oh, there's your swing. How . . . lovely,' she said.

'I know it's not lovely,' I whispered. 'But Dad's fixed it all up for me specially.'

'Sure. OK. I understand,' said Rhiannon. She raised her voice so that Dad could hear in the kitchen. 'Oh Floss, your swing looks great hanging on the apple tree,' she said, enunciating very clearly, as if Dad was deaf or daft.

She hopped on it, had one token swing, then hopped off again. 'So, shall we go up to your bedroom and play?' she said.

'Maybe we should swing a bit more,' I said.

'But it's, like, boring,' said Rhiannon. 'Come on, Floss, I've been nice to your dad. Now let's go and do stuff.'

'OK.'

We went back indoors. Dad had started peeling potatoes in the kitchen. He looked baffled to see us back so quickly.

'What's up, girls?' he said.

'Nothing's up, Dad. I – I just want to show Rhiannon my bedroom,' I said.

I didn't didn't didn't want to show her my bedroom.

She looked round it, sucking in her breath. 'Is *this* your bedroom?' she said. She wrinkled her brow. 'But I don't get it. Your bedroom's lovely, all red and white and clean and pretty.'

'That's my bedroom at my mum's, you know it is,' I said.

I sat on my old saggy bed and stroked the limp duvet, as if I was comforting it.

'So OK, where's all your stuff? The cherry curtains and the red velvet cushions and your special dressing table with the velvet stool?'

'I've got all my clothes and books and art stuff here. The curtains are still at Mum's and the other things have been put into storage. They wouldn't fit in my bedroom here.'

I scarcely fitted in my bedroom at Dad's. It was not much bigger than a cupboard. There was just room for the bed and an old chest of drawers. Dad had started to paint it with some special silver paint, but it was a very small tin and it ran out before he could cover the last drawer. He'd propped a mirror on top of the chest and I'd laid out my brush-and-comb set and my china ballet dancer and my little cherry-red glass vase from my dressing table at home. They didn't make the chest look much prettier.

'Dad's going to finish painting the chest when he can find some more silver paint,' I said. 'And he's going to put up bookshelves and we're going to get a new duvet – midnight-blue with silver stars – and I'm going to have those luminous stars stuck on the ceiling *and* one of those glitter balls like you get at dances – and fairy lights – and – and—' I was running out of ideas.

Rhiannon looked at me pityingly. 'What sort of house is your mum going to have in Australia?' she asked.

'They're just renting. It's just some little flat,' I said.

I was lying. Mum had shown me a brochure showing beautiful modern flats with balconies and a sea view. They'd deliberately chosen a flat with three big bedrooms so that I could have the room of my dreams.

'It couldn't be littler than this flat,' said Rhiannon. 'You must be a bit nuts to want to stay here rather than go to Australia.'

'I want to be with my *dad*,' I said.

'Do you love your dad much more than your mum then?'

'No, I love them both the same. But Dad needs me more,' I said.

'Well, it still seems crazy, if you ask me,' said Rhiannon, sitting down on the bed beside me. It creaked in protest. She peered down at it, shaking her head in disgust.

'Well I'm *not* asking you,' I said. 'And anyway, *you* were the one who said I didn't have to go. I thought you wanted me to stay so we could be best friends for ever. Don't you want to be my best friend now, Rhiannon?'

'Of course I do.'

'We're best friends for ever?'

'Yes, like for ever and ever, dummy,' said Rhiannon, sighing and shaking her long hair over her shoulders.

She was saying all the right words but she was saying them in this silly American accent.

I had more bad dreams that night. I wished I'd kept my great big Kanga to cuddle in bed. I couldn't believe I'd actually thrown away all my old teddies. All I had was the limp lopsided elephant and dog that Grandma had knitted me. I reached out of bed and tucked one on either side of my head. They didn't look very fetching but they *felt* warm and soft, like a special scarf.

I lay awake worrying that the bad dreams would come back the minute I closed my eyes. It helped that every time I wriggled round on my pillow a soft little knitted paw patted me.

I fell asleep just as it was starting to get light – and then woke with a start. Something was ringing and ringing and ringing. The telephone! I stumbled out of bed and ran to answer it. Dad lumbered behind me in his pyjamas, huffing and puffing.

'Hello?' I said into the phone.

'Oh, *there* you are, Floss! I've been ringing for

ages!' said Mum. 'I thought you and Dad must have left for school already. What are you doing, having breakfast?'

'Um – yes,' I said, not wanting to tell Mum we'd slept in. She sounded so *close*, as if she was back in our house across town. 'Oh Mum, have you come back?' I said breathlessly.

'What? Don't be silly, darling, we've only just got here. My Lord, what a journey! Do you know, Tiger didn't sleep a wink the entire flight. Steve and I were just about going demented.'

'I can imagine,' I said.

'But never mind, we're here now, and you should just see the apartment, Floss. I feel like a film star! We've got a fantastic sea view and even though it's winter here it's so bright and sunny. I just can't believe how beautiful it all is. It would all be so perfect if only you were here too. Oh Floss, I miss you so!'

'I miss you too, Mum. So so much,' I whispered. I didn't want to be tactless to Dad, but he patted my shoulder reassuringly to show me he understood.

'I just *know* you'd love it here. If you could just see for yourself how lovely everything is you'd jump on a plane tomorrow, I know you would. Oh darling, are you all right? Is Dad looking after you OK?'

'Yes, Mum, I'm fine, really.'

'He's giving you proper food, not endless fry-ups and cakes and chip butties?'

'Yes, Mum,' I said.

I was still feeling queasy from last night's chip butties. Rhiannon had been a little bit rude about them when Dad served them up for our tea. *Very* rude, actually. I'd felt so sorry for Dad I'd said quickly, 'Well goody-goody, if you don't like them that means there's all the more for me.' I'd ended up eating all my chip butties *and* Rhiannon's.

Dad boiled eggs and ran down to the corner shop and bought tomatoes and cucumber and lettuce to make Rhiannon her own special salad, but she only ate two mouthfuls, and she didn't appreciate him turning them into a funny face for her.

'Does your dad think I'm, like, a baby?' she said.

'Dad's bought special salad stuff,' I told Mum truthfully. 'And he's fixed up a new swing in the garden and I've had Rhiannon round to play.'

'That's good,' said Mum. 'Well, I don't want to make you late for school, sweetheart. You take care now. I'm going to send you lots of photos of our flat and the beaches and the parks and the opera house. Once you see them I just know you'll be dying to come and join us.'

I swallowed. I didn't know what to say. Most of me *ached* to be in Australia with Mum. But not without Dad.

'Do you want to speak to Dad, Mum?'

'Well, I'll have a little word, yes please. Goodbye then, Floss. I love you so much.'

'Goodbye, Mum. I love you too,' I said.

I leaned against Dad while Mum questioned him. She sounded like a nurse taking a full medical history. She asked:

1. Is Floss looking mopey?
2. Has she cried much?
3. Is she sucking her thumb a lot?
4. Is she as chatty as usual?
5. Is she really eating properly?
6. Is she having trouble getting to sleep?
7. Did she wake up at all in the night?
8. Is she having bad dreams?

I started to expect her to ask how many times I'd been to the toilet.

'She's *fine*,' Dad kept saying. 'For pity's sake, you've only been gone five minutes. She's not likely to have gone into a nervous decline already. Now, we'd better be leaving for school. What? Of course she's had breakfast,' said Dad, crossing his fingers in front of my face. He said goodbye and then put the phone down.

'Phew!' he said. 'Oh dear, Floss, let's shove some breakfast down you quick. I'm not sure there's time for egg and bacon—'

'I don't want breakfast, Dad, there's not *time*. I'm going to be late.'

'No, no, you've got to have something inside you. Cornflakes? I'll shove my jeans on and sort something out while you run and get washed and dressed.'

I hadn't properly unpacked my pink pull-along case or my cardboard boxes of clothes. My school blouses were horribly screwed up and my skirt was creased so much it looked as if it was pleated.

'Dad, can you iron these?' I said.

'What? Oh God, I'm not sure my old iron works any more. I don't really bother with my stuff, I just drip them dry.'

I had to go to school all crumpled. I couldn't find my good white socks so I had to wear an old pair of navy woolly winter ones, and my trainers were all muddy from the garden. I couldn't even get my hair to go right. I'd been tossing and turning all through the night and now all my curls stuck straight up in the air as if I was plugged into an electric socket.

Dad didn't seem to notice as he drove me to school. We arrived at the exact time Rhiannon was jumping out of her mum's Range Rover. *They* noticed.

'Floss! Oh dear!' said Rhiannon's mum. 'You look a bit bedraggled, darling.'

'I'm fine,' I said.

'Why have you got those funny socks on? Like,

navy?' said Rhiannon. 'And yuck, what's that on your *shoes*? It's not dog poo, is it?'

'No, it's just a bit of mud,' I said, blushing.

Dad was peering out of the van anxiously, biting his lip. He frowned as Rhiannon's mum leaped out of her Range Rover and went over to him.

'Look, Mr Barnes, I know it's difficult for you now you're a one-parent family—'

'Flossie's got two parents,' said Dad. 'I'm simply the one currently in charge.'

'Whatever. I was wondering . . . You could always pop a bag of laundry into my house once a week. My cleaning lady often irons for me, I'm sure she wouldn't mind—'

'It's very kind of you, but we'll do our own washing and ironing,' said Dad.

'Well, if you think you can cope!' said Rhiannon's mum, making it plain by her tone that she didn't feel Dad could cope at all.

'Bye, Dad,' I said, waving, so he had an excuse to escape.

He waved back worriedly, obviously seeing now how scruffy I looked. I gave him a big beaming smile to show him I didn't care, stretching my mouth unnaturally wide, as if I was at the dentist's.

'You look like you're going to take a bite out of someone, Floss,' said Rhiannon.

Margot and Judy were sitting on the wall. They

heard what Rhiannon said and started snorting with laughter. Then they took in my appearance and laughed all over again.

'Oh. My. God,' said Margot. 'What do you look like, Floss? Has there been some major disaster so you've been, like, buried alive? Even your hair's exploded! Look at it, all fluffed out and standing on end.'

'And what's that funny smell?' said Judy, wrinkling her nose. 'It's like . . . chip fat!'

'Well, that figures,' said Margot. 'Her dad runs this greasy spoon caff.'

'It's *not* greasy,' I said fiercely. 'It's very special. My dad's chip butties are *famous*.'

Margot and Judy cackled so much they very nearly fell off the wall. Rhiannon got the giggles too. She put her hands over her mouth but I could still see she was sniggering.

'Don't laugh at me!' I said.

'Well, you do look funny. But I know it's not your fault,' said Rhiannon. 'Mum said I've got to make special allowances for you.'

'Why have you got to make special allowances for old Smelly Chip?' asked Margot.

'Because her mum's walked out on her.'

'No she hasn't! Don't say that!' I protested.

'OK, OK, don't get all touchy. I'm trying to be extra *nice* to you.'

115

She might *say* she was being extra nice but she certainly wasn't acting it. I was scared I was going to start crying in front of them so I ran into school.

I hoped Rhiannon would run after me. I wanted her to put her arms round me and tell me I didn't really look funny and she didn't care what I looked like anyway because she was my best friend.

She didn't run after me. She stayed smirking in the playground with Margot and Judy.

I locked myself in a lavatory and had a little private cry. Then I heard someone else come in. I clamped my hand over my nose and mouth to stop all the little snorty-snuffly sounds leaking out. I sat very still. Someone seemed to be standing there, waiting. Waiting for me?

'Rhiannon?' I called hopefully.

'It's Susan.'

'Oh!' I blew my nose as best I could on school toilet paper, flushed the loo and emerged, feeling foolish.

Susan looked at me. I glanced at myself in the mirror above the wash-hand basins. I looked even worse than I imagined – and now I had red eyes and a runny nose too.

'I've got a cold,' I said, splashing water on my face.

'Yes,' said Susan solemnly, although we both knew I was fibbing.

I tried wetting my hair while I was at it, to smooth it down. It went obstinately fluffier, springing up all over the place.

I sighed.

'What?' said Susan.

'I hate my hair,' I mumbled.

'I think you've got lovely hair. I'd give anything to have fair curls.'

'It's not pretty yellow fair. It's practically snow-white and much too curly. I can't grow it. It grows *up* instead of down.'

'I'm trying to grow mine, but it's taking for ever,' said Susan, tugging at her soft brown hair. 'I'd love it to grow down past my shoulders but I'm going to have to wait two whole years, because hair grows only a quarter of an inch each month. Vitamin E is meant to be good for healthy growth so I'm eating lots of eggs and wholemeal bread and apricots and spinach, but it doesn't seem to be having any noticeable effect so far.'

'You know such a lot of stuff, Susan.'

'No I don't.'

'You do – you know about the rate hair grows and vitamin E and all that.'

'I don't know how to make friends,' said Susan.

We looked at each other.

'I want to be your friend, Susan,' I said. 'It's just . . .'

117

'I know,' said Susan. 'Rhiannon.'

'I'm sorry she's so mean to you. Susan, your ballad – I thought it was so good.'

'Oh no. Rhiannon was right about that. It was rubbish.'

'Maybe . . . maybe you could come round and play some time, over at my dad's?' I said. 'It's not posh or anything. It's just a funny café and we live over the top. I haven't got a very nice bedroom but—'

'I'd *love* to come,' said Susan.

She smiled at me. I smiled back. I thought hard. Rhiannon would see if Susan came home with me after school.

'What about Saturday?' I said, glancing over my shoulder, scared that Rhiannon had crept up somehow and was standing right behind me, listening.

'Saturday would be wonderful,' said Susan.

'Great!' I swallowed. 'The only thing is . . .'

'Don't worry, I won't tell Rhiannon,' said Susan.

I blushed. '*This* Saturday?' I said.

'Yep, this Saturday.'

'You could come for tea. Only it might not be very . . . Do you like chip butties?'

Susan considered. 'What are they?' she said.

I stared at her in surprise. How could she know a million and one facts and figures and yet be so clueless about chip butties?

'I know what a chip is,' said Susan. 'Fried potato.'

'Well, you put a whole wodge of chips in a big soft white buttered roll – that's a chip butty.'

'Chips in a roll?' said Susan.

'It's not exactly healthy eating,' I said humbly. 'But my dad specializes in *un*healthy eating, I'm afraid.'

'It sounds a delicious idea,' said Susan.

Then Margot and Judy came barging into the toilets. My heart started thudding. But it was all right: Rhiannon wasn't with them.

Margot narrowed her eyes at me. 'Were you, like, talking to Swotty Potty?' she asked.

'What are you, the Rhiannon private police force?' said Susan. 'No, she wasn't talking to me. No one talks to me, you know that.'

She marched out of the toilets, with Margot and Judy making silly whistling noises after her. Then they turned to me. Margot still looked suspicious.

'So what are you, like, doing here? Rhiannon's looking for you.'

'Is she?'

I ran past them. Susan was halfway down the corridor. I ran past her too. I ran all the way to our classroom and there was Rhiannon, sitting on her desk, swinging her legs impatiently. She had such lovely slender lightly tanned legs. Mine were like spindly white matchsticks.

119

'There you are! What did you run off for? You are so *moody* now, Floss.' Rhiannon sighed. 'And if you don't mind my saying so, you really do look awful. I bet Mrs Horsefield tells you off. You know how fussy she is, always going on about the boys not tucking their shirts in and telling all the girls off for rolling up their sleeves. You won't be her special teacher's pet today.'

'Don't be horrid!'

'I'm not. I'm just pointing out the truth. You are, like, *so* paranoid.'

And you are, like, so stupid talking like Margot, I thought inside my head, but I didn't dare say it.

When Mrs Horsefield came into the classroom I hunched low at my desk, desperately smoothing my blouse and skirt, as if my hands were little irons. I was fine until halfway through maths, when Mrs Horsefield asked me to come up to the front of the class to do a sum on the board.

I stared at her, agonized, slumping so far down in my seat my chin was almost on the table.

'Come on, Floss, don't look so bashful,' she said.

'I – I can't do the sum, Mrs Horsefield. Can't you pick someone else?' I suggested desperately.

'I know maths isn't your strong point but let's see what you can do. It's really quite simple if you work through it logically. Up you get!'

I had no option. I walked up to the board in my

120

crumpled clothes and navy socks and muddy trainers. Mrs Horsefield looked startled. Margot and Judy giggled. I felt my cheeks flaming. I waited for Mrs Horsefield to start shouting at me. Astonishingly, she simply handed me the chalk and said quietly, 'OK?'

I was anything but OK. I tried to do the stupid sum, my hand shaking so that the chalk stuttered on the board. I kept getting stuck. Mrs Horsefield gently prompted me, but I was in such a state I couldn't think of the simplest answer.

I looked round helplessly – and there was Susan, mouthing the numbers at me. I wrote them quickly and then rushed back to my seat. Mrs Horsefield let me go, but when the bell went for break she beckoned me.

'Can we have a word, Floss?'

'Uh-oh,' said Rhiannon.

'Wait for me?' I said.

'Yeah, yeah,' said Rhiannon, but she was drifting off as she spoke.

I stood at Mrs Horsefield's desk. She waited until the last child had left the classroom. Then she put her head on one side, looking at me.

'So why are you in such a sorry state? Dear oh dear! Did your mum sleep in this morning?'

'Mum's not here any more,' I said, and I burst into tears.

'Oh Floss!' said Mrs Horsefield. She put her arm round me. 'Come on, sweetheart, tell me all about it.'

'Mum's gone to Australia for six months. She *hasn't* walked out on me, she's coming back, she badly wanted me to go with her but I said I wanted to stay with my dad and I *do*, but I want Mum too!' I sobbed like a silly baby.

Mrs Horsefield didn't seem to mind. She reached into her handbag and found me a couple of tissues, one to wipe my eyes and one to blow my nose.

'We could do with a whole handful of tissues for your shoes too,' said Mrs Horsefield. 'So you and Dad are finding it a bit difficult just now?'

'Dad's going to get an iron. We didn't have time to clean my shoes. And I've lost all my white school socks,' I wailed.

'I'm sure you'll get into a routine soon enough. Try to get your school things ready and waiting the night before. Don't just rely on Dad. You're a sensible girl, you can sort yourself out. It's really quite simple – like the maths sum! You worked it out eventually, didn't you? Well, with a little help from Susan.'

I blinked.

'Susan's such a nice girl,' said Mrs Horsefield. 'She could do with a friend right now.'

'I know,' I said. 'I want to be her friend.' I lowered my voice in case anyone was hanging round the classroom door. 'We *are* friends in secret. She's coming round to my place this weekend. It's just we can't be friends at school because . . .'

Mrs Horsefield raised her eyebrows, but didn't comment. 'Oh well, I'm sure you girls will sort yourselves out, given time. Do come and have a little chat with me whenever you're feeling upset or there's some little problem at home. I'm not just here to teach you lessons, you know. I'm here to help you in any way I can.'

She paused, and then opened her desk drawer. There was a big paper bag inside. She opened it up and offered it to me. I saw one of her special pink iced buns with a big cherry on the top.

'Go on, take it,' she said.

'But it's not my birthday.'

'It's an *un*birthday bun for a little mid-morning snack.'

'Isn't it *your* mid-morning snack, Mrs Horsefield?'

'I think I've been having far too many snacks, mid-morning or otherwise,' said Mrs Horsefield, patting her tummy. 'Go on, off you go.'

I took the bun and went out into the corridor. Rhiannon had said she'd wait but there was no sign of her. So I took my pink bun out of the paper bag and ate it all up myself. I especially savoured the cherry.

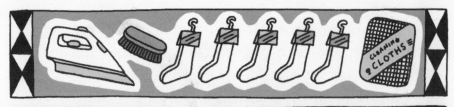

10

Dad was waiting for me when we got out of school. Rhiannon's mum was standing next to him, obviously giving him advice. He was nodding politely, but when he saw me running across the playground he rolled his eyes, pulling a secret funny face at me.

'Thank goodness,' he said, giving me a big hug. 'That woman's been bending my ear for the last ten minutes. The stuff she was saying! Blooming cheek! She even suggested I try Internet dating to get myself a girlfriend!'

'Oh Dad, you're not going to, are you?' I asked anxiously.

'There's only one girl in my life, sweetheart. She's very little and she's got masses of curly hair and big blue eyes and she goes under the name of Princess,' said Dad, whirling me around. 'Come on, let's get home. I've been shopping!'

'I thought we were short of money, Dad.'

'We are. Desperately. But we might as well spend what little we've got.'

'Who's looking after the café?'

'Billy the Chip is meant to be keeping an eye on things.' Dad paused. 'Though I doubt he'll be run off his feet.'

There wasn't a single customer in the café. Billy the Chip was glued to his radio, listening to the races at Newmarket.

'Is Birthday Girl running again, Mr Chip?' I asked.

'Don't talk to me about that silly filly! She went all flighty and finished second to last,' said Billy the Chip. 'Still, let's see if you can bring me luck on the last race, sweetheart. Here are the runners. What do you fancy?'

I peered at the list in his newspaper and then stabbed my finger at a name. 'Iced Bun! That's the one. I had a lovely iced bun today, with a cherry on the top. Bet on Iced Bun, Mr Chip.'

'It's a complete outsider, but I suppose I could risk a fiver if you're feeling lucky.'

'Put a fiver on for me too,' said Dad.

'All right, I'll nip down to the betting shop right this minute.'

Billy the Chip was so old and skinny and frail he couldn't really *nip*. He crept in slow motion, having a rest and mopping his brow every few seconds.

Dad shook his head. 'Poor old Billy. I don't know how he keeps going. I worry about him still running that chip van. There are so many yobs in town now, especially late at night. He needs someone there if any of them cut up rough. He's got a son but he's in Australia.'

We looked at each other.

'It's obviously the *in* place, Floss,' Dad said, sighing.

'Who wants to be one of the *in* crowd?' I said, taking his hand. 'I'd sooner be us.'

Dad squeezed my hand back. 'You mean all the world to me, little Floss. Now listen here, lovey, I've bought a brand-new iron from Argos and five pairs of white socks from the market and a shoebrush and some j-cloths too, so tomorrow we'll send you off to school super spick and span, I promise. And I've got a *salad* for your tea, and oranges and apples. You'll be absolutely vibrating with vitamins, the picture of health and beauty! I don't need that Rhiannon's mum muscling in. I'm going to be a brilliant dad from now on.'

'You've always been a brilliant dad, silly,' I said.

'No, darling, I've been a rubbish dad, in all sorts of ways.' He took a deep breath. 'I'm in a bit of a pickle with the café, Floss.'

'I know, Dad. Don't worry. I'm sure business will pick up soon. And you've got me to help you now.

I can be the waitress at the weekend. I promise you can keep all my tips.'

'Oh Floss, you're such a sweet kid. If only it was that simple. No, darling, I'm afraid I'm down and almost done for. I didn't spell it out before because I needed to sort out what I was going to do. Only I still haven't got a clue and time's running out.'

'Don't worry, Dad. Maybe Iced Bun will win its race and we'll make a fortune!'

'The odds would have to be ten thousand to one to sort things out for me, pet,' said Dad.

I tried to work out in my head how much we'd win at those odds. I needed Susan to help me with the maths.

It was a waste of effort anyway. Iced Bun came in last. Billy the Chip trailed back from the betting shop looking defeated.

'Well, that was a waste of time and money,' he said.

'I'm ever so sorry, Mr Chip,' I said, feeling responsible. 'Let me get you another cup of tea.'

Billy the Chip smiled at me, patting me on the head with his shaky old fingers. 'Little Miss Curlymop. You're a dear girl. No wonder your dad's so fond of you. Here, I still owe you a birthday present.'

'No you don't. Birthday Girl came second to last.

I'm rubbish at choosing horses, Mr Chip. Take absolutely no notice of me in the future!'

Dad fixed me my special salad for my tea and then spent hours ironing all my clothes with the brand-new iron. He wasn't very good at it. The collars kept rumpling up and he pressed odd sideways lines in the sleeves.

'Maybe I could have a go, Dad?' I suggested, but he wouldn't let me in case I burned myself.

He sent me to bed early so I wouldn't oversleep in the morning. He sat beside me, one arm round me, while he read me a chapter of a story about a girl and a magic toad. The girl didn't have a mum; she just lived with her dad.

'Maybe *we* need a magic toad,' said Dad. '*And* a magic iron that does the ironing all by itself. *And* a magic money box that's always stuffed full of fifty-pound notes.'

'Dad, what *is* going to happen about the café? Will we have to sell it?'

Dad swallowed. He closed his eyes. His lips puckered up. I thought for one terrible moment he was going to start crying.

'The café isn't really mine to sell now, Floss. I had to borrow money on it. Lots of money, just to keep things going. And try as I might I haven't been able to keep up with the payments. So – so it looks as if they might close us down.'

'Will someone else come and run our café?' I asked.

'I'm not sure, pet. Maybe.'

'But – but will they come and live upstairs in the flat with us?'

'The thing is, Floss, the flat is all part of the café. And if I'm pushed out of the café I'll be pushed out of the flat too.'

I saw us both being shoved into the street by a giant bulldozer. 'Oh Dad!' I said, clutching him.

'Oh Lordy, I shouldn't have told you, especially now, when you're just going to sleep. I am so *stupid*. I've kept quiet for months, mostly because I couldn't face up to it myself. I've just kept hoping something will turn up, that they'll give me another loan – *anything*. I just can't believe they'll make us homeless.'

'But what will we *do*, Dad?' I thought about the homeless people I'd seen on a trip to London. 'Will we . . . will we live in a cardboard box?'

'Oh Floss!' Dad spluttered. I didn't know whether he was laughing or crying. Maybe he didn't know either. 'Of course we won't be living in cardboard boxes. No, love, you'll be fine. I'll get in touch with your mum and pop you on the plane to Australia. I should have made you go in the first place. It was so bad of me, but it meant so much to me that you wanted to stay with your old dad.

I kept desperately hoping that business would somehow pick up – but no such luck.'

'I'm not going to Australia, Dad! I'm staying with you, no matter what. Even in a cardboard box.' I put my arms tight round his neck. 'Anyway, I *like* cardboard-box houses. Remember, I used to sit in one when I was little, with all my dolls and teddies squashed in beside me, playing Mothers and Fathers.'

'You were such a sweet little kid,' said Dad, kissing the top of my curls. 'Now, you'd better settle down. Night-night, darling. You're not to worry, promise me?'

Of course I worried. I didn't sleep for ages and ages, and when I did I dreamed that our café and flat had turned into cardboard. It started to rain and all the walls sagged and the floor split and I barged through the cardboard door yelling for Dad. When I found him he looked so old and frail, and when I hugged him he bent in half and crumpled in my arms as if he was cardboard too.

I woke up crying and ran to Dad. But he wasn't in his bedroom even though it was now the middle of the night. I peered under his duvet, I lifted his pillow, I even looked under his bed. Then I heard little creaking sounds coming from the kitchen.

I found Dad ironing away, my school blouses all round the room, hanging off doors and pegs and racks as if a flock of weird white birds were roosting in our kitchen.

'*Dad?*'

'Hello, little sweetheart,' said Dad, as if it was the most normal thing in the world to be up ironing at three in the morning.

'What are you doing? You've already ironed all my school blouses.'

'Yes, and I made a right muck-up of them, so I've damped them all down and I'm doing them again. And *again*. This is my third time and they're *still* a bit sad and crumpled.'

'They're fine, Dad. Leave it. Come back to bed, please!'

'I can't seem to sleep when I do, yet I'm knackered in the day time. I'm keeping Australian time. Maybe I should go and live there too!'

I thought about it, my heart thumping. 'Well, if we have to leave the café why can't we *both* go to Australia? Maybe Steve would lend you the money for the fare? You could pay him back once you'd started working. And I could still live with you but I could see Mum too. Maybe we could all stay there!'

'You're being so brave, Floss, about missing your mum,' said Dad. 'There's no chance of me going to Australia though, pet. I'd never take a penny off old Steve for starters. And I'd not be allowed into the country to work because I've no money and no skills.'

'Yes you have, Dad! You're great at running the café.'

'Come off it, pet! I doubt I'd even get a job as a washing-up guy. I'd *certainly* not get a job in a laundry. Look, I've scorched your blouse!' He held it up despairingly and showed me the brown mark.

'Never mind, Dad. Please. Stop ironing.'

'Maybe the mark will come out if I wash it again,' said Dad. Then he saw my face. 'Sorry, pet! Your old dad's gone a bit nuts, that's all. Right. I'll stop ironing.' He switched the iron off and stood in the middle of the kitchen in his old stripy pyjamas. 'Shall I tuck you up in bed, Floss?'

'I'm not sleepy now either.'

'So . . . what shall we do?' said Dad. He shifted his weight from one bare foot to the other, considering. 'I know!' he said suddenly. 'Let's go and have a swing!'

'But it's the middle of the night, Dad,' I said, wondering if he really *had* gone mad.

'There's no law says you can't have a night-time swing in your own garden,' said Dad. 'Put your coat on, sweetheart, and stick your feet in your welly boots.'

Dad put a thick jersey over his pyjamas and pulled on his own boots. Then we went downstairs, through the sad silent café and out into the back yard. I thought it would be dark and scary, but there was a bright full moon making the yard look silvery and magical. We threaded our way through the bits of bike and all the other junk. The rubbish bins had been emptied that day so they hardly smelled at all. A little cat circled them wistfully, mewing for food.

'Oh Dad, look, isn't she sweet?' I said. I bent down, a little clumsy in my boots. 'Here, puss.'

She looked at me, considered, and then approached me cautiously.

'Come on then. I won't hurt you.'

I reached out my hand and she came right up to me. She sniffed my palm hopefully for titbits but seemed happy enough when I stroked her instead.

'She's a very thin little cat. Can we feed her, Dad?' I asked.

Dad was peering at her. 'She's black, isn't she? Black cats are meant to be lucky, aren't they? Even skinny little stray ones! OK, if she hangs around a while I'll see if I can find a can of tuna.'

'There, puss! You're so clever, coming calling to a café. That's my dad over there. He's going to fix you a perfectly lovely meal in a minute. Purr-fectly. Hey, Dad, purrfectly – do you get it?'

'Oh, ha ha, funny Floss,' said Dad. He sat

himself down on the swing, kicking at the ground with the heel of his boot.

The cat rubbed against me, nuzzling in and purring when I stroked the side of her neck. Her bones felt so tiny and delicate underneath her soft fur.

'I wonder if you belong to anyone, little cat?' I said. 'You haven't got a collar on, have you? You don't look as if you've been fed for days. Dad, if she's really a stray can we keep her?'

'We can't even keep ourselves, Floss,' said Dad.

'Well, we can all three be strays, you, me and the cat,' I said. 'We can call her Lucky. You never know, Dad, maybe our luck is changing right this minute.'

'Yes. Whoops! What was that? A big pink pig just flew past my head, flapping its wings.'

'You wait and see, Dad,' I said, gently lifting Lucky up in my arms. She nestled in to me as if she'd known me since she was a kitten.

'*We should be so lucky – lucky lucky lucky*,' Dad sang, kicking off and swinging. 'Hey, this swing's lopsided! Oh Floss, why didn't you say?'

'It's fine, Dad, really.'

'No it's not – but I'll fix it for you tomorrow. Oh dear, did Rhiannon remark on it when she came round?'

'Not really,' I hedged.

'I'm sorry I let you down with Rhiannon. I know she's your best friend.'

'She *is*, but I've got another friend too now. Dad, can my new friend Susan come round on Saturday?'

'Is she very posh and pernickety like Rhiannon?' said Dad, swinging wildly, waving his boots.

'No, she's very clever but she's quiet, not a bit fussy or bossy,' I said.

'I like her already!' said Dad.

It was lovely having Susan as my secret friend at school. We smiled and nodded at each other whenever Rhiannon wasn't looking. Most days we managed to meet up in the girls' cloakroom for a minute or two. We fixed it that she'd come at three o'clock on Saturday and stay for tea.

'Chip butties! Promise?' said Susan.

I promised.

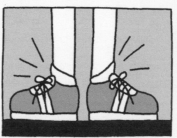

11

I was so looking forward to Susan coming on Saturday. Then on Friday Rhiannon ruined everything.

She'd been hanging around with Margot and Judy a lot of the time. They often looked in my direction and whispered and giggled.

'What's the joke?' I asked.

'You're the joke,' said Margot 'Like – your socks!'

Dad had tried hard with my new white socks. He was worried my birthday-present dress and shoes were far too big, so he'd bought extra small children's socks. They were so extra small they were Tiger-size. It took me ages to prise them over my toes, and the heel came uncomfortably under my instep. The top of the sock kept getting sucked under my shoes each time I took a step, so every few seconds I had to bend down to pull them up. I'd have been much better off in my old navy socks but I didn't want to hurt Dad's feelings.

He'd mastered the ironing now, but our laundering system was a bit of a problem. We didn't have a tumble dryer so Dad hung all my clothes on a rail in the kitchen.

'Yuck! Chip fat!' said Margot, pretending to sniff me and then holding her nose.

Judy held her nose too. Rhiannon didn't, but she smirked and spluttered.

I knew my clothes *did* smell of café cooking. I didn't know what to do about it. I tried sprinkling my school blouses with a little leftover bottle of Mum's special perfume, but that made them hold their noses even more. They wafted their hands in the air and went 'Pooh' and 'Phew'.

I felt like twisting their noses right off their faces.

I also wanted to cry because the perfume made me miss Mum so much. I ran away, and this time Rhiannon came after me.

'For goodness' sake, don't be such a baby, Floss. They're just *teasing*,' she said.

'I'm tired of being teased. I can't stick Margot and Judy,' I said.

'Oh don't be daft. They're good fun, so long as you don't take them seriously. Margot's soooo cool. Do you know, she's got a diamond stud in her belly button! I wish my mum would let me get my tummy pierced.'

'I bet she's just stuck it on,' I said. 'And it won't be a *real* diamond.'

'Well, so what? It still looks great. And she's got, like, *such* a flat tummy too. I wish *my* tummy didn't stick out so. Still, I'm going to stay on this special diet and get super slim, you wait and see.'

'You're super slim now, you know you are. Anyway, dieting's stupid at our age.'

'You're just saying that because you're still so skinny. But you carry on eating all those chips and fry-ups at your dad's café and you'll be, like, ginormous.' Rhiannon waved her arms in the air to demonstrate.

'No I won't,' I said – though I knew my dad was a *little* bit ginormous.

'Still, my mum's got this special Healthy Eating recipe book. She'll give it to your dad when he comes round to collect you on Saturday,' said Rhiannon.

I blinked at her. 'Collect me from where?' I said.

Rhiannon sighed impatiently. 'From my place, stupid.'

'But you haven't asked me round to your house on Saturday,' I said, my heart thumping.

'Well, I'm asking you now,' said Rhiannon. 'Mum says you've to come for lunch and tea *and* bring a bag of all your clothes and she'll put them in the washing machine and iron them for you. Don't look like that, Floss. There's no need to feel embarrassed. Mum doesn't mind, really.'

'I – I can't come, not this Saturday,' I stammered.

'Why can't you come? It's all fixed,' said Rhiannon.

'I've got to help my dad in the café,' I fibbed.

'You're not supposed to work in the café. That's child labour. He can't make you.'

'He doesn't *make* me do anything. I want to help.'

'Well, you'll have to help some other time, because my mum's specially cancelled her new highlights appointment at the hairdresser's just so she can be at home to look after you. Like I said, it's all fixed.'

I didn't know what to do. I couldn't possibly tell Rhiannon the truth. She'd never forgive me if she knew I'd invited Susan home.

I mulled it over miserably during the next lesson. I couldn't concentrate during history, and when Mrs Horsefield suddenly asked me a question I didn't have a clue what she was on about. She called me up to her desk when the bell went.

'You're a little Dolly Daydream today, Floss. What's the matter, dear?' She was smiling at me sympathetically, not a bit cross.

I hung my head and made one foot do a tiny little pointy dance on the floor.

'Missing your mum?' Mrs Horsefield said softly.

'Mmm,' I said, because I *was* missing her dreadfully. Sometimes when Dad wasn't around I went and looked at the ticket in the kitchen drawer. I was determined not to use it – but it was good to know it was there.

'But you're getting on well together, you and your dad?' said Mrs Horsefield.

'Oh *yes*. Dad's being lovely. He always is,' I said.

'That's good. Well, you certainly look a lot smarter today,' said Mrs Horsefield, looking at my newly washed hair, my clean blouse, my pressed skirt, my very small white socks and my spotless shoes.

I made the other shoe do a little dance, trying to pluck up the courage to ask Mrs Horsefield what I should do about seeing Rhiannon on Saturday.

'Yes?' Mrs Horsefield prompted.

I swallowed. I couldn't. I asked her something else instead.

'Mrs Horsefield, do I smell?'

Mrs Horsefield looked startled. 'Oh Floss! You're as clean as clean. You look as if you've just jumped out of a bath today.'

'Yes, but do I *smell*?'

'Not of anything unpleasant,' she said evasively.

I sighed deeply.

'Has someone been saying nasty things?' said Mrs Horsefield, sounding angry.

'No. Well. They were just teasing,' I said quickly.

'Teasing can be horribly cruel. I don't suppose you're going to tell me who it was?'

I shook my head, gazing at my feet.

'You don't need to tell me. I'm sure I can guess. Don't you take any notice of them.' She paused. 'Oh well. You'd better run out into the sunshine. I love sunny days like this. I put my washing out on a line and it dries beautifully and smells of fresh air.'

I nodded gratefully and walked to the door.

'Will you watch out for Susan for me, Floss? I think she's still a bit lonely. She could really do with a kind girl like you to be her friend.'

'Yes Mrs Horsefield,' I said.

I so so so wanted to be Susan's friend. But I was too scared to be a kind girl.

I ran to the girls' cloakroom. Susan was standing in a corner, counting the tiles up and the tiles down, muttering each number. Then she saw me and her mouth stretched into a smile.

'Hi, Floss!' she said happily. 'I can't wait till Saturday.'

I took a deep breath. 'Oh Susan, I'm ever so sorry, but I can't make Saturday after all.'

Susan stared at me. It was as if I'd taken the

smelly floor mop in the corner and shoved it in her face, smearing the smile away.

'Did Rhiannon find out?' she said, her voice wobbling a little.

'No! No, it's nothing to do with Rhiannon,' I lied. 'No, it's just I've got to do stuff with my dad, that's all. But you can come the Saturday *after*. That will be OK, won't it?'

'Yes, probably,' said Susan, but her voice still sounded funny.

'We'll still have chip butties,' I said.

'Yes. Great,' said Susan flatly.

It was as if she knew. I told myself she couldn't possibly know. I pretended that everything was still perfectly fine. I would go to Rhiannon's on Saturday. She was my best friend after all. I'd wear my rose-quartz bracelet and play in Rhiannon's beautiful blue bedroom and maybe I'd teach her how to make a friendship bracelet. Then the *next* Saturday I'd see Susan at my house and we'd play on my swing and eat chip butties and maybe she'd do all the things Rhiannon thought babyish or boring, like playing pretend imaginary games or drawing pictures or making tiny doll's houses in cardboard boxes.

Rhiannon was busy planning Saturday too. *This* Saturday.

'My mum's going to take us shopping at Green

Glades when you come this Saturday, Floss,' she said loudly.

'Ssh!' I hissed.

Susan sat right in front of us. She was writing her comprehension – but her pen paused in mid-air.

'It's OK. Mrs Horsefield's over there helping Dumbo Diana,' Rhiannon said. 'Anyway, she won't pick on us. You're total teacher's pet now. *Anyway*, Mum's going to get you some new socks and stuff, seeing as yours are, like, so weeny and weird.'

'Please ssh!' I whispered.

'It's OK. We all know it's not *your* fault. Mum's going to do it very tactfully. She's going to pretend *I* need new stuff and then she's going to say, "Oh look, why don't I get a jumbo pack or whatever, and then they'll do for both of you." She's got it all sussed. We're probably going to do shoe shopping too. I told her you just have those crazy silver high heels to wear at home and she says you'll ruin your feet.'

Susan hadn't restarted her comprehension. She was too busy comprehending the situation.

'We're going to this fabulous new restaurant for lunch. I'm going to have a mango smoothie, yum, and then you get to choose all these different salads – it's, like, soooo delicious. Mum says she owes it to *your* mum to help you eat healthily, seeing as you have to live on those chip butties most of the time.'

Susan's head bent low when Rhiannon said chip butties. Her hair fell forward. The nape of her neck looked white and forlorn.

I wanted to reach right forward and pat her on the shoulder, maybe put my arm round her. I stayed stuck beside Rhiannon. She went on and on and on about seeing me on Saturday.

There was still a tiny little bit of me that somehow hoped Susan couldn't *quite* hear.

The bell went for the end of lessons. Susan stood up, starting to pack her bag. Rhiannon jumped up, barging past her, scattering her books on the floor. She didn't try to pick them up or even say sorry.

'See you tomorrow, Floss,' she bellowed, right in Susan's face.

Susan dodged down, gathered her books and hurried out of the classroom. She clicked her fingers as she went, counting under her breath.

'That Swotty Potty doesn't half give me the creeps,' said Rhiannon. 'She's totally nuts, isn't she, Floss?'

I stared after Susan until my eyes blurred.

'*Floss?*' said Rhiannon. 'What's up *now*? Don't you go all wimpy and weepy on me tomorrow – it's got to be a fun day, right?'

It didn't feel like it was going to be a fun day

at all. I told Dad about the change of plan. He raised his eyebrows when I said I was going to Rhiannon's.

'I'll deliver you there and I'll pick you up whenever you want, but *please* don't make me come and talk to that wretched woman!' said Dad. 'So what about your new little friend Susan? Is she going to Rhiannon's too?'

I sighed at the impossibility of ever being able to explain to Dad the complications of the situation. I didn't really want him to know all the ins and outs anyway. He probably wouldn't say anything, let alone tell me off, but I'd feel bad anyway. I was feeling very very very bad as it was.

I hung my pink birthday T-shirt and special jeans over my swing seat as we didn't have a washing line in the back yard. I hoped the cool night air would make them smell fresh and beautiful the next morning.

When I woke up I heard pattering on my window. It was raining hard.

'Oh no!' I threw my mac over my nightie, stuck my feet in my wellies and rushed out to the back yard.

My clothes were sodden. My jeans had fallen right off the seat and were all muddy on the ground. My T-shirt had curled itself round and round like a Swiss roll, as if some little night creature had used it as a duvet.

'Lucky?' I called hopefully, momentarily distracted from the Wet Clothes Disaster.

I had *so* wanted her to stay with us. When she turned up in the middle of the night I'd fed her a whole tin of tuna and given her a saucer of milk to lap. She'd mewed at me gratefully. She'd even given me a little lick of appreciation. I'd squatted beside her and stroked her from her neat little head to the tip of her tail, and she'd wriggled happily and started purring. I thought she was making it as plain as could be that she wanted to live with me. But when I tried to pick her up gently and carry her indoors she cried and struggled, scratching me. I had to let her go. She flew away from me, back behind the wheelie bins.

I'd tried to wheel one out of the way so I could get at her, but she mewed at me indignantly and crammed herself into the furthest corner behind the biggest bin.

'Don't fuss her, Floss.' said Dad. 'It looks like she wants to stay outside.'

'But it's all dark and smelly by the bins. She'd be so much happier indoors. She could share my bedroom. I could make it so safe and cosy for her,' I said.

'You can't force her in if she doesn't want to

come,' said Dad. 'She's not our cat.'

'I so want her to be ours, Dad.'

'Well, leave her be for now. She'll hang around if she feels like it. *She'll* decide whether she's going to be our cat or not.'

'Our Lucky,' I said.

I'd checked up on her ten minutes later. I peered behind every wheelie bin. I peeped under every tarpaulin. I scoured the entire back yard. There was no sign of Lucky.

'She'll have gone for a little prowl around, Floss. That's what cats do,' said Dad.

'But she will come back?'

'Well. Probably,' said Dad. 'In her own good time.'

'Probably isn't definite enough!' I wailed. 'Oh Lucky, where are you? You will come back, won't you? You really badly want to be our little lucky black cat, don't you?'

I listened hard for a tiny mew. If Lucky could hear me she kept quiet.

I'd paced the back yard all the following evening, but there was still no sign of her. I got Dad to open a fresh tin of tuna and I poured out another saucer of milk and waited tensely, hour after hour.

A big ginger tom came prowling past but I hid Lucky's gourmet tea from him. Lucky herself didn't come near. I left her food out overnight and it was nearly all gone in the morning – but I couldn't tell if Lucky herself had eaten it, or whether the ginger tom had come back.

On Friday Dad had said gently that maybe we couldn't count on Lucky returning.

'Maybe she's gone back home to her real owners. Or maybe she's happy fending for herself, being a little street cat.'

'She'd be much happier with us,' I said. 'She'll come back, Dad, in her own good time, like you said.'

If she *had* come back during the night and had a nap cuddled up in my T-shirt, she hadn't hung around to say hello this morning.

I picked up my sodden jeans and T-shirt and squished my way back into the house. Dad was in the kitchen in his dressing gown, yawning and scratching.

'Floss? Have you been out to play in the pouring rain?' he said. He held up my clothes. 'For goodness' sake! We'll have to put them straight back in the wash. You should have kept them clean for visiting Rhiannon.'

I leaned against the kitchen table, helping myself to cornflakes straight from the packet. 'Lucky might just have been in the back yard last night,' I said.

'Hmm. Well, we could do with some luck right

151

this minute,' said Dad, looking through his post.

There was a handful of bills and one scary white envelope with IMPORTANT stamped in big red letters. Dad opened it up, read it quickly, shoved it in his dressing-gown pocket and then slumped beside me. He reached in the cornflakes packet for a snack. His hand was trembling and cornflakes spilled over the kitchen floor.

'What's the matter, Dad?' My voice sounded croaky because my throat was so dry. I swallowed hard but the cornflakes in my mouth wouldn't go away.

'It's our notice to quit,' said Dad. He breathed out, so hard that the cornflakes packet wavered and nearly fell over. 'I wrote to them begging for more time, explaining I'm now looking after my daughter full time. I thought that might just sway them. I mean, what sort of heartless monsters would render an innocent little kid homeless? Well, now I've found out. We've got two weeks, Floss. Two flipping weeks and then we have to hand over the keys or they'll send in the heavies.' Dad bent forward, resting his head on the table.

'Dad?' I whispered.

I lowered my own head, staring at him. His eyes were closed.

'Please, Dad! Sit up. It'll be all right,' I said,

stroking his head.

Dad groaned. 'I've let you down, darling.'

'No you haven't! Here, Dad, let me make you a cup of tea.'

I bustled around boiling the kettle and fetching a mug and milk and tea bags. I knew Dad would look up when it came to me pouring the boiling water, just in case I wasn't doing it safely enough. Just as I'd thought, he sat up straight the second the kettle switched off.

'Here, I'll do it,' Dad said, sighing.

He made us both a cup of tea and then sat sipping his, staring all around the kitchen. He looked at the greasy walls and the ancient cooker and the higgledy-piggledy cupboards and the cracked lino tiles on the floor. He stood up and stroked some silly old paintings I'd done at nursery school, each a red blobby figure with a big smiley mouth, all bearing the same title: *My Dad*. He picked up my plasticine rabbit models on the windowsill and my lopsided plaster ashtray and the plate I'd painted with big purple pansies because Dad said they were his favourite flower.

'All my treasures,' Dad mumbled, as if the kitchen was crammed with wondrous antiques.

'We'll pack everything and take it with us, Dad,' I said.

'To decorate our cardboard box?' said Dad. He

153

shook his head. 'Sorry, sorry, I'm getting maudlin. No, I'll manage. Maybe one of my old biker mates will let me kip in a corner of his living room for a bit, just till I get myself sorted.'

'Will they let me have a corner too, Dad?' I asked anxiously.

'You're not sleeping on floors, darling. No, I'll wait till this evening, when it's morning in Australia, and then I'll phone your mum. We'll whizz you over to Sydney.'

'No, Dad!'

'Yes, Floss,' said Dad firmly. 'Now, you go and find yourself some decent dry clothes and forget all this bother for the moment. You're going to have a lovely day with Rhiannon.'

I wasn't at all sure about that. I dressed myself in my old jeans and my old stripy T-shirt, after burying my head in them to see if they smelled. It was so difficult to tell at home in the café because it *all* smelled so cosily of cooking.

I brushed my hair and I brushed my teeth and I brushed my shoes. I did this varied brushing ultra thoroughly, and at each stroke of the brush I made a wish that our luck would change and that somehow or other Dad could stay cooking his chip butties for ever.

Billy the Chip came in to mind the café while Dad was taking me to Rhiannon's. He was clutching his *Racing Post*.

'Come on, young Flossie, pick me a winner,' he said.

'Oh Mr Chip, I'm rubbish at picking winners. Birthday Girl was hopeless, and Iced Bun was worse.'

'Have another go, darling.'

'What, you think it'll be third time lucky?' I said.

'Yes!' said Billy the Chip. 'Look! Third Time Lucky is running at Doncaster! We've got to back it now. What about you, Charlie? Shall I put something on for you?'

'I haven't got anything left to bet with, mate. I think it might be a bit of a waste anyway. Look at the odds. It hasn't got a chance.'

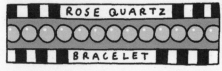

ROSE QUARTZ

BRACELET

FRIENDSHIP

BRACELET

12

Rhiannon was especially sweet to me. She was almost like the *old* Rhiannon, before she started thinking Margot wonderful. And I felt almost like the old Floss, when I still had two homes and I could see Mum whenever I wanted.

We went to play in Rhiannon's beautiful blue bedroom, and it was so *peaceful* lying back on her soft flowery duvet and seeing the clean white paint and fresh blue ruffles. It felt as if we were floating up into the sky. Rhiannon let me shake all her snowdomes and wind up her Cinderella musical box and flick from channel to channel on her own little white television.

She let me try on all her coolest clothes. She even let me try walking in her brand-new boots with pointy toes and real heels. She didn't want to try on my jeans and T-shirt, so I let her wear my birthday-present rose-quartz bracelet. It looked very pretty on her slim white wrist. I asked her where her friendship bracelet was.

'I don't know,' she said, shrugging. 'Think I must have lost it.'

'Oh. Well. Never mind,' I said. 'I'll make you another if you like. Tell you what, we could use that kit I gave you and make each other a friendship bracelet now.'

Rhiannon wrinkled her forehead. 'Like, boring!' she said. 'No, we're going shopping – I *said*. Mum's taking us to Green Glades.'

Rhiannon's mum drove us there in her big Range Rover. Rhiannon and I knelt up at the back and made faces at people in the cars behind.

'I bet you wish you had a big car like our Range Rover,' said Rhiannon.

'It's lovely – but actually my dad's van is just as big,' I said.

'Yeah, but, like, that's just a transit van,' said Rhiannon.

They obviously didn't compare so I kept my mouth shut. I was starting to feel a bit sick. I hadn't realized Green Glades was so far away. I wriggled round in my seat and stared straight ahead. My jeans were starting to be a bit too small for me. They pressed uncomfortably into my tummy. I closed my eyes, praying that I wasn't going to disgrace myself.

'Hey, don't go to sleep on me, Floss!' said Rhiannon.

'No, no, leave her be, darling,' said Rhiannon's mother. 'She looks as if she could do with a good sleep. She's looking so peaky, poor lamb. I know her dad is doing his best but I bet he doesn't get her to bed on time.'

I wanted to argue, but I knew if I sat up and opened my mouth I would actually start spouting vomit. I stayed still as a statue, eyes shut, tummy clenched, sweat trickling down inside my T-shirt with the effort of keeping my breakfast in place.

Seemingly many many years later we got to Green Glades and parked the car. I rushed to the nearest ladies, and when the cubicle door shut me away from Rhiannon and her mum I threw up as silently as possible.

'Oh darling, you do look weak and feeble,' Rhiannon's mother cooed, when I staggered out. 'You haven't been sick, have you?'

'No!' I said emphatically, because she'd only start on about my dad's chip butties. I suddenly soooo wanted my mum, who would know exactly how to deal with Rhiannon's mother. I hated being the poor sad sickly girl, especially when I was *feeling* so poor and sad and sickly.

I wanted to talk to her on the phone. Dad was going to phone her tonight to tell her that he thought I should go to Australia. My stomach started churning again. I wanted Mum but I wanted Dad too. I couldn't bear the thought of leaving him. He'd said the heavies would move in. I didn't really know what a heavy was. I pictured an army of huge red-faced prickly-headed guys, all of them punching my poor dad and then kicking him out of our café with their big heavy boots as if he was a bag of rubbish. I saw him sitting in the gutter, crawling inside his cardboard box.

I had to run right back to the ladies' loo and throw up all over again. I didn't even have anything to be sick with any more; it was just horrible bile stuff. I couldn't fool Rhiannon and her mother this time. I suffered a lecture about suitable diet for the next half-hour, though I told them truthfully I'd simply had a small bowl of cornflakes for my breakfast.

'Margot has the most amazing mango and pineapple smoothies for her breakfast. We made them ourselves. It was *so* cool,' said Rhiannon.

'When were you having breakfast with Margot?' I said.

'When she had this sleepover,' Rhiannon said airily.

I was stunned. I had been so scared of upsetting Rhiannon by having Susan over for tea, and yet here she was casually telling me that she had actually *stayed the night* at Margot's.

'What?' said Rhiannon, seeing my expression.

'Oh Floss, lighten up. It's *OK*. You don't have to be, like, *jealous*.' She actually laughed at me.

'I'm *not* jealous,' I mumbled foolishly.

'Don't worry, dear. You're still Rhiannon's special friend,' said Rhiannon's mum.

She didn't say 'best' friend. 'Special' made me sound embarrassing and needy, the poor little saddo you had to be nice to because you felt so sorry for her.

I felt my cheeks burning. I didn't *want* Rhiannon as my friend any more, best or special. I wished wished wished I'd made real friends with Susan.

I was stuck with Rhiannon and her mother. We went up and down every single arcade and walkway of the Green Glades shopping centre. I'd have liked it if I was there with *my* mum. We'd look at things together and try on different stuff and strike mad poses like fashion models and tell each other we looked drop-dead gorgeous.

Rhiannon and her mother took their shopping *seriously*. They tried on outfit after outfit, reciting the designer labels as if they were magic charms.

'You must try on anything you fancy too, Floss,' said Rhiannon's mum. 'I'm determined to treat you, darling. We can't have you wandering about like a sad little scarecrow.'

She bought me new white socks. She wanted to buy me new shoes too, but I said that my trainers

161

had been a special birthday present from my mum and I wanted to wear them all the time.

'They're starting to look a bit shabby already, dear,' said Rhiannon's mum, but she didn't press it.

She *did* press me to choose some new clothes. She didn't *say* anything disparaging about my jeans and T-shirt, but she shook her head and sighed, so it was plain what she thought of them.

I didn't want her to buy me anything. I didn't even want the socks, though I needed them badly. But there was no way I could keep saying no without seeming rude and ungrateful. I tried picking out the cheapest top and jeans I could find on the bargain rails so that they would cost as little as possible, but this didn't please Rhiannon or her mother.

'Oh God, Floss, you can't possibly like that tacky old T-shirt. It looks like something off a market stall,' said Rhiannon. 'And those jeans! I wouldn't be seen dead in them. Look at the cut of the leg. They are, like, *so* old-fashioned.'

'You're not really into fashion, are you, dear?' said Rhiannon's mother. 'Don't worry, Rhiannon's always been a bit forward – she could suss out a designer label when she was still in her buggy. We'll help you, darling. You don't need to dress in those little girly-wirly togs just because you're so small. We'll find you an outfit with a bit of oomph.'

162

I didn't know what oomph was. I didn't much like the sound of it.

I was right to be wary.

Rhiannon went rushing round collecting armfuls of clothes, including a denim outfit studded with rhinestones, with a matching cap.

'Oh darling, that's so cute. Hey, pick one out for Floss in a smaller size. I'm sure she'll look wonderful in it.'

Rhiannon looked *sort of* wonderful in the tiny tight skirt and little studded bomber jacket and the sparkly skimpy vest that showed her tummy. She slipped the cap on at a jaunty angle and struck a pose, as if a million cameras were flashing.

I didn't look at all wonderful. The little skirt looked weird way up my spindly legs and I hardly dared move in it in case my knickers showed. The bomber jacket hung on me oddly and the vest looked as if it had shrunk in the wash. The cap wouldn't stay on unless I clamped it down hard over my curls.

'You look so sweet, Floss,' said Rhiannon's mother, tugging at the cap and twitching the jacket. 'There, that's the ticket. You and Rhiannon look just like sisters. We have to buy it for you.'

'No, please. It's very kind of you but it's much too expensive,' I protested, truthfully enough. The price of each outfit would have clothed an entire

163

orphanage of children from head to foot in ordinary non-designer denim. Besides, I hated the whole outfit, only I couldn't really say so when Rhiannon and her mum thought it so wonderful.

I let them buy it for me. I said thank you over and over again. Rhiannon and I wore our brand-new outfits there and then. Rhiannon swished and strutted around the shopping centre and nearly everyone turned and smiled and stared at her. They stared and smiled at me too, but they also raised their eyebrows. It was like they had thought bubbles over their heads. They thought, *What a beautiful child* when they looked at Rhiannon. They thought, *What a sad little weirdo* when they looked at me.

I hoped we were done. We weren't. We went in heaps *more* shops before we went for lunch in the Green Glade Grotto. It had grass-green velvet chairs and fake grass carpet and rocks instead of walls, with real trickly waterfalls. Rhiannon's mother ordered Rhiannon and me a Green Glade Super Special Drink (lemonade and lime juice with slices of real lime and little green flowers cut out of cucumber and tiny green umbrellas).

'You can eat the lime and the cucumber, but not the umbrella!' said Rhiannon's mother, as if I was Tiger's age. 'Now, what would you like to eat, dear? I know you love your chips, and they *do* do very nice French fries here, but I think Rhiannon and

I will be having a Green Glade Super Special Salad. Would you like to try one too?'

So I tried one. It came on a green glass plate patterned like a lettuce. The food was very prettily set out like a flower, with strawberries in the centre, pink grapefruit petals and rocket leaves.

'There! You're really enjoying it, aren't you?' said Rhiannon's mother, as if she was introducing me to the concept of salad for the very first time.

'It's delicious,' I said, as limply as the lettuce.

'What's *up* with you?' said Rhiannon, kicking me under the table.

I didn't really know. If I'd been spending the day with my best friend Rhiannon last month, being treated to new clothes and lovely meals, I'd have been over the moon, the stars, orbiting in outer space. But now I wanted to be anywhere else. I wanted to be in Australia with Mum and Steve and Tiger. I wanted to be back home in the café with Dad and Billy the Chip and Old Ron and Miss Davis. I wanted to be playing on my swing with Susan.

Oh, Susan.

I looked at Rhiannon. I realized I really didn't like her any more.

'What?' said Rhiannon, tipping her cap at an even cuter angle. My rose-quartz bracelet slid prettily up and down her arm. 'Why are you looking

165

at me like that? Honestly, Floss, you are, like, soooo moody at times.'

'Now now, Rhiannon,' said Rhiannon's mum. 'What did I say about being kind to Flossie? Imagine how you'd feel if I went off and left you.'

'My mum *didn't* leave me. She's coming back in six months – just over *five* months – and I feel *fine*. I've got my dad,' I said.

'Yes, dear,' said Rhiannon's mother, but the expression on her face made it obvious she didn't believe a word of it.

Rhiannon yawned and picked up a magazine. 'Oh wow! Look! It's Purple!' she said.

'Purple what?' I said.

'Purple! They're just the coolest boy band ever, especially Danny. He is, like, fantastic,' said Rhiannon, kissing her fingertip and pressing it to Danny's pouty photo mouth.

'I bet Margot likes him,' I said.

'She's only got tickets for their latest tour! Her dad's taking her, and she can choose a friend to come too and she said she wants me to come instead of Judy.'

'Can't Flossie come too?' said Rhiannon's mother.

'Floss isn't into cool bands like Purple. She'd never even *heard* of them,' said Rhiannon. 'Hey, can we go to HMV, Mum? Can I get their latest album? *Please!*'

'What sort of music do *you* like, Flossie?' said Rhiannon's mother.

I shrugged. I liked all the Golden Oldies Dad played on the van radio, and we sang them together. Dad often sang the women's songs, making his voice very high-pitched, putting in lots of oohs and coos. I sang the guy parts in a deep growl. We could rarely reach the end of any song because we kept cracking up laughing.

Rhiannon would *certainly* crack up laughing if I said I liked *Crazy Little Thing Called Love* and *Stand by Your Man* and *Dancing Queen*. So I just kept shrugging, like I was doing shoulder exercises.

'Rhiannon, you should tell Flossie all about these boy bands,' said Rhiannon's mum. 'Don't worry, Floss, we'll take you in hand.'

I felt I was growing smaller and smaller and smaller and they were scrunching me up in their hands. I didn't *want* to be turned into a little replica of Rhiannon.

'Now, dear, what would you like to do most of all?' said Rhiannon's mother.

Go home! I longed to say, but I knew that would sound very rude indeed, especially as she was trying to be so kind to me. So I said I'd like to go to HMV too and Rhiannon smiled at me and went 'Yay!'

We spent the rest of the afternoon at Green Glades doing Rhiannon things. I was good at suggesting all the right places. We went to heaps more clothes shops and a special scent shop, spraying on samples until we reeked, and then we spent hours trying all the testers on Boots' make-up counters.

All the time I played a game in my head choosing the places that Susan and I might like. We'd both want to spend ages in the bookshop, and we'd maybe like the art shop too, and *perhaps* Susan wouldn't laugh if I wanted to go to the Bear Factory. We wouldn't necessarily have to spend any money. We could have fun choosing our best books and our favourite set of colouring crayons, and we could each decide on a factory bear and name it and choose different outfits for it.

I could list our choice of books and crayons and little bear clothes and Susan could count them all up in her head. We'd wander off to the swankiest restaurant and pretend to choose a special meal in celebration. But before we ordered Susan would say, 'I don't know, this all sounds totally delicious but do you know what I *really* fancy?' and I'd say, 'Mm, yes, I think there's only one possible choice,' and then we'd both laugh and shout, 'CHIP BUTTIES!'

But Susan wouldn't ever want to come back to the café with me to have chip butties because I'd betrayed her. Dad was being thrown out of the café anyway. He wouldn't be able to make his special chip butties.

I couldn't stop the tears welling in my eyes. I kept my head bent and blinked hard but Rhiannon still saw. She edged up very close so that her mother wouldn't hear.

'*Baby!*' she hissed in my ear.

I sniffed and tried to stop crying. It didn't work.

'Oh Floss, don't cry,' said Rhiannon's mother. 'Come here, you poor little thing.' She put her arms round me and gave me a powdery hug. She used the same perfume as my mum. I cried harder.

'Oh dear, oh dear. Maybe we'd better take you home now,' she said.

I was still a bit sniffly when we got back. I rubbed my eyes hard and straightened my stupid cap.

'Thank you very much indeed for the lovely day out,' I said as politely as I could. 'And thank you for the green meal and the socks and the fantastic outfit too.'

'You're very welcome, dear. I just wish you'd let me do more for you.'

We drew up outside the café. Rhiannon's mum looked at the HARLIE'S CAFÉ sign and sighed.

'I think I'll come in and have a little word with Dad,' she said.

'Oh no, don't, please. He'll be too busy serving all his customers,' I said quickly, though I knew there'd only be Billy the Chip, Old Ron and Miss Davis sitting there, stirring their tea at separate tables.

'Oh, well . . .' said Rhiannon's mum doubtfully.

'Bye, Rhiannon,' I said, climbing out of the car.

Rhiannon waved her arm. The rose-quartz bracelet slid up underneath the sleeve of her denim jacket.

'My bracelet—' I said, and then I stopped.

'Oh Rhiannon, give poor little Floss her birthday bracelet back,' said Rhiannon's mother.

'No, it's all right. I'd like her to have it,' I said.

'But we gave it to you,' said Rhiannon's mother, sounding faintly irritated.

'You've given me much too much. Rhiannon can keep it now. She lost the other bracelet I gave her.'

'Which bracelet?' Rhiannon's mother asked. 'I didn't know you gave Rhiannon a bracelet.'

'Just some old thready thing,' said Rhiannon. 'Are you *sure* I can keep the rose-quartz bracelet?'

'Yes,' I said.

I didn't want it any more. I didn't even care that Rhiannon obviously hadn't liked my friendship bracelet, even though it had taken me hours to

170

make it, and I'd chosen Rhiannon's favourite colours, pink and blue and purple, and fastened it with a little silver heart. There was no point having a friendship bracelet if you didn't want to be friends any more.

13

I walked into the café. I knew at once that something strange had happened. We didn't have any new customers, but Billy the Chip, Old Ron and Miss Davis were all sitting at the same table. They weren't drinking tea. They were drinking from dinky little glasses, filling them from a big green bottle. Champagne!

Dad had a glassful too. He raised his glass at me, and then nearly spilled his champagne when he saw what I was wearing.

'Oh Floss, what has that woman done to you! Here, darling, come and have your first weeny little sip of champagne.'

'What are we celebrating, Dad?' I asked.

'It's our dear old Billy. He's the one who's celebrating!' said Dad, raising his glass to Billy the Chip.

'Is it your birthday, Mr Chip?' I asked, taking a small sip out of Dad's glass. The bubbles fizzed up my nose and made me giggle.

173

'You can't give alcoholic liquor to the child. Look at her, she's drunk already!' said Miss Davis.

'Oh liven up, you old biddy. It would do you good to get drunk yourself for once,' said Old Ron.

'It's not my birthday, sweetheart,' said Billy the Chip. 'But it feels like it. I backed Third Time Lucky in the four thirty at Doncaster – a fifty-to-one outsider, no less – and guess what, the darling little filly grew wings and flew home, first past the finishing post!'

'Oh well done!' I said, clapping my hands. 'Oh Dad, *did* you have a bet too?'

'I thought I was being so sensible,' said Dad, shaking his head. 'Still, I'm thrilled for Billy, and very grateful too.'

'It's me that should be grateful to little Flossie here. I'll buy you a big dolly or teddy for a belated birthday present – and do your dad a little favour into the bargain.'

'Mr Chip's doing us a great big favour, Floss,' said Dad, sipping champagne. He took my cap off and ruffled my curls back into place. 'There! Call me old-fashioned, but I don't really care for the trendy outfit on you, pet.'

'I hate it, Dad. I didn't want her to buy it for me. Don't worry, I won't ever ever ever wear it again. *But what's the big favour?*'

174

'Well, you know the whole sad situation about the café—' Dad started.

'Oh Dad, oh Dad! Is Mr Chip going to give you some of his winnings so we can keep the café?' I burst out.

'Of course not, Floss! We owe far too much. No, I'm afraid we've got to go by Monday week. But I've got somewhere to go now. *And* I've got a job for the next few weeks!' Dad beamed at Billy the Chip. 'It's so good of you, Billy. You're a great mate.'

'Think nothing of it, Charlie. You're the one doing me a favour, taking over the van and keeping an eye on my gaff while I'm off gallivanting.' Billy the Chip nodded at me. 'I'm off to Australia, young Floss. I'm going to spend my winnings on a ticket to go and see my boy. I can't wait!'

'Isn't that great, Floss! You can travel with Billy, keep each other company.'

'I'm staying with you, Dad,' I said firmly, though inside I was as wobbly as a jelly.

'No, Floss, that's completely mad and we both know it.'

'Then I'm completely mad,' I said, pulling a funny face.

They all chuckled, while Dad shook his head.

'So you're going to run Mr Chip's chip van, Dad?'

'That's right, little darling.'

'And is that where we're going to live . . . in the

chip van?' I said. I tried to say it casually, but my voice came out all squeaky as I said it.

Dad burst out laughing. Billy the Chip laughed too, his pale potato face flushing pink. Old Ron roared. Even Miss Davis chirruped and cooed, sounding like her birdy friends.

'It might be a bit of a squash, sweetheart,' said Billy the Chip. 'I don't think you could squeeze even your little bed inside my old van. No, you and your dad can stay at my house. You can be my house-sitters – and feed my cats too. Your dad says you like cats. Is that right, Flossie?'

'Yes, especially little skinny black ones,' I said wistfully.

Dad wouldn't let me have any more champagne, but he poured lemonade into a special glass for me so that I could join in the party too.

'I'm a bit peckish with all the excitement,' said Billy the Chip. 'How about a chip butty, Charlie?'

'They're on the house, pal,' said Dad. 'Hey, little Floss, come and be my Number One Kitchen Assistant.'

When we were out in the kitchen and Dad had set the chips sizzling, he bent down till our faces were on a level and cupped my cheeks with his big hands.

'Are you sure you're serious about staying with me, darling? I truly think you'd be so much better off joining up with your mum. Billy's offer is a godsend but he's only going for a month. He says we can still stay at his place after he comes back but that doesn't seem very fair. I've no idea what his house is like, though I shouldn't think it's very big.'

'It'll be bigger than a cardboard box, Dad,' I said. 'I'm staying.'

Dad laughed, but his eyes went all watery. 'You're a great little kid, our Floss,' he said. 'So, we'll have to get your toys all packed up again. We'll take your swing with us too. Let's hope we can tie it up in Billy's garden somewhere, though I can't promise. Run and have a little swing now, sweetie, make the most of it. I'll call you when the chips are done.'

I went into the back yard even though I didn't really feel like swinging. I felt as if I'd been on a giant swing for far too long as it was. I was dizzy with all the changes in my life. Rose was wrong. All the changes that had happened so far had been horrible. She'd got her good luck signs wrong too. My lovely little lucky black cat had sloped off to live somewhere else. She probably hadn't been snacking on the plates of tuna. I was fattening up that ginger tom, or a stray squirrel or fox was licking its chops and coming back for more at this newly opened animal annexe to the café.

I leaned over the swing seat, moodily propelling myself backwards and forwards with my toe-tips. The seat was hard against my tummy. I hung my head right down, staring at the scrubby grass. I sent messages through the earth all the way down to Australia.

'*I miss you so, Mum,*' I whispered.

I shut my eyes and thought about the airline ticket. Everyone thought I was mad not to go to Australia, even Dad. He'd be all right now. He had a job and a place to live. It wasn't as if I'd be leaving him for *ever*. In five months I'd be back.

I could have my own bedroom in Australia, not a camp bed in a corner of some funny old man's house. I could have fresh clean comfy clothes, not creased smelly stuff or embarrassing designer denim. I could make new friends and I could be a proper friend back. I could play on the beaches and swim in the sea, I could go into the bush and see all the animals, jump with the kangaroos, cuddle the koalas . . .

'Mew!'

I opened my eyes. Lucky was sitting right in front of me, her green eyes shining, her little mouth open wide.

'Mew mew mew!' she said, for all the world as if she was saying hello.

'Oh Lucky!' I nearly fell right off the swing, onto

my head. I caught hold of the rope, wriggled free and then bent down in front of Lucky, holding out my hand.

'Hello, darling,' I whispered. 'You've come back!'

'Mew!' she said, padding softly towards me until her lovely little head was right by my palm. She let me tickle her chin, arching her neck and stretching her whole body. She wasn't quite as skinny now, and her fur seemed softer and thicker.

'Have you been eating all the food I've left for you?'

Lucky gazed at me with her beautiful emerald eyes, a *wouldn't-you-like-to-know!* expression on her face.

'Would you like something to eat now? Some nice brown slurpy slimy specially bought cat food?'

'Mew,' said Lucky. It was a definite yes.

'So what am I going to do? If I go and get your food will you promise promise promise to stay here? Or will you come indoors with me? We've got a lovely café with lots of milk. Won't you come and see it while we still live here? Please?'

Lucky stretched, considering. Then she leaned against me docilely. I slipped my hands gently round her. This time she let me lift her up, her whole body relaxed.

'Oh Lucky, Lucky, Lucky,' I said, rubbing my

cheek against her silky fur. Then I walked very carefully into the house, Lucky clasped to my chest.

Dad was concentrating on lifting the golden chips out of the sizzling pan. 'Good swing, sweetheart?' he said.

'Yep. Dad, *look*!'

Dad looked – and nearly dropped the chips. 'Oh Floss, your little cat! She's come back!'

'She doesn't mind coming in this time, does she, Dad? She wants her tea!'

'OK, you give her something to eat while I make us all chip butties.'

I had to put Lucky down to fill one little bowl with cat food and another with water. I was worried she'd try to scoot straight out of the back door but she waited patiently, licking her lips at the smell of the food.

'Eat up, little Lucky,' I said.

'You eat up too, little Floss,' said Dad, giving me a chip butty.

Dad went off with a big plateful of butties for Billy the Chip and Old Ron and Miss Davis. I stayed in the kitchen, sitting cross-legged beside Lucky. When we'd both finished eating she went to the back door, looking at me expectantly.

'You want to go away already?' I said. 'Look, I know this is a café, but you don't have to rush off the minute you've finished your meal.'

Lucky took no notice. She lifted one paw, pointing it at the door as if she could zap it open by magic.

'OK,' I said, sighing. 'But you'll come back? Promise?'

I opened the door. Lucky shot out . . . to the nearest bush. She squatted in the earth, concentrated, then carefully scattered earth with her paws, covering everything up.

'Did you just want to go to the *toilet*?' I said.

Lucky looked at me coyly, as if she didn't really want to talk about it. She let me pick her up and carry her back indoors. I showed her to Billy the Chip and Old Ron and Miss Davis.

'There we go! A lucky black cat. This is a day and a half all right,' said Billy the Chip. He smacked his lips appreciatively after eating his last bite of butty. 'I don't know how you do it, Charlie. You make tip-top chips. I've been in the business all my life, and my dad before me, but my chips pale into insignificance beside yours.'

'When's my luck going to change, then?' said Old Ron. 'Here, Flossie, let's have a stroke of that little cat and see if some of her luck will rub off on me.'

I let him stroke Lucky a few times with his gnarled old fingers.

'Would you like a stroke too, Miss Davis?' I said, out of politeness.

'I'm not very keen on pussycats. They're bird killers,' said Miss Davis, but she reached out and gingerly touched the tip of Lucky's tail with one finger. 'Don't you go near any of my pigeons, little cat.'

'You've fattened those pesky birds up so much I should think Flossie's little moggy would turn tail and run for her life if they flew anywhere near her,' said Old Ron.

'She isn't Flossie's cat,' Dad said gently. 'She's just a visitor.'

'She wants to stay, Dad. Look at her!' I said.

Lucky was still snuggled up in my arms, her head resting comfortably on my shoulder. If I carefully turned my head to one side I could see her expression. She was smiling like the Cheshire cat in *Alice*.

'Well, we'll see if she wants to stick around this time.'

'She will, she will!'

'Uh-uh, hang on. *Then* we have to go round the neighbourhood, making sure no one's lost a cat. We'll ask at the police station too.'

'But if no one's reported her missing, can we keep her then, Dad? *Please?*'

'Well, we're not going to be here, are we, sweetheart,' Dad said sadly.

'You can keep her round at my place. I've got

two cats, Whisky and Soda. One more won't make any difference. A little nipper like Lucky might liven my old ladies up,' said Billy the Chip.

'It's so good of you to let us stay at your place, Billy.'

'Well, it's a bit old-fashioned, like. I think it needs one of them makeovers. I haven't had the heart to do anything, not since I lost my Marian.'

'Ah. Well. Tell me about it,' said Dad. 'I know just how you feel, Billy.'

'Yes, but you're still young, mate, not an old geezer like me. Why don't you think about getting yourself another woman, Charlie?'

'Oh, ha ha. Who'd want to lumber themselves with a loser like me?' said Dad.

'I would!' I said.

'Yes, but you're my special princess – and totally prejudiced,' said Dad. 'No, I don't want another woman anyway. We're fine just the way we are, Floss and me, aren't we, lovey?'

'Your Floss will grow up and be off before you know where you are,' said Billy the Chip. 'Life can get lonely by yourself, Charlie.'

'I'll second that,' said Old Ron. 'Isn't that right, Miss D?'

'Miss Davis. And I'm never lonely. I keep myself far too busy,' said Miss Davis. 'In fact I must be off on my bird trail right this minute.' She stood up and started manoeuvring her bag of birdseed. She sniffed suddenly. 'I shall miss my cup of tea and my little sit-down when the café closes. I've done a little tour of Starbucks and Costa Coffee and Caffé Nero and they're all *much* more expensive.'

'And you can't get a decent chip butty in any of them,' said Old Ron. 'No, we'll have to turn into nightbirds, Miss D, and visit Charlie in Billy's chip van.'

'Miss *Davis*. And I'm not going anywhere after dark, thank you very much. It's too dangerous – yobbos all over the town.'

'I could always escort you, Miss D,' said Old Ron.

Miss Davis snorted, not sure whether to take him seriously or not – but she didn't snub his suggestion, and she didn't correct him about her name this time.

Dad cleaned up the café after the party was over while I made Lucky a very soft bed out of my duvet, folded up on the floor of my bedroom.

'So what are *you* going to sleep under?' said Dad, ruffling my curls.

'Oh, I'll be fine with an old blanket or your dressing gown,' I said.

'How about giving the cat the blanket or the dressing gown?' said Dad. 'You need your duvet, pet.'

'Yes, but Lucky's *my* pet. Well, I hope she will be. Dad, what else would she like in her bedroom? She's still quite a little cat. Would she like a cuddly toy, do you think? I could give her Grandma's dog or elephant to snuggle up with. Hey, maybe I could ask Grandma to knit me a mouse. Lucky would like that.'

'Knowing your grandma's little problem with sizes she'd probably knit a giant mouse as big as a moose and scare little Lucky to death. I think we'll leave your grandma out of it. Lucky doesn't need any cuddly toys – she's got you, sweetheart.'

We watched as Lucky tried out her duvet, playing with it for a minute, rolling around like a frisky kitten. Then she gave herself a little wash, yawned, stretched and lay on her side, paws stretched out. I stroked her back very gently and she started purring. Her purrs got a little louder, a little slower – sweet little snorty sounds.

'Dad? Is she *snoring*?' I whispered.

'She certainly is, bless her,' said Dad. 'Come on, let's leave her in peace. All the attention has tired her out. Are you tired too, Floss?'

'I'm not a *bit* tired. It's way too early for me to go to bed, Dad.'

'That's what I was thinking. So, now you've got Lucky settled, how about us going out for a little while? I think we both need a little fun tonight. Let's go to the fair, eh?'

'Oh yes! Can I go on Pearl again?'

'Of course you can.'

'And can I have another candyfloss?'

'You bet.'

'Bought from Rose's stall?'

'Naturally.'

I paused. 'Dad, do you like Rose?'

'Of course I do. She's a very kind lady.'

'I think she likes you a lot, Dad.'

'Rubbish,' said Dad, but he looked at me hopefully. 'Do you really think so?'

'Definitely!'

'You're kidding me,' said Dad, but he was looking down at his old jersey and jogging bottoms. 'Hey, I look a terrible scruffbag. I'd better change out of these old togs.'

'Well, I'm going to change *into* my old togs,' I said. 'I look stupid in this outfit, don't I, Dad?'

'You look very glam and gorgeous, my darling, but not quite *my* little girl. So yes, you get changed too.'

Dad got dressed up in his best jeans and blue shirt and I got dressed down in my old jeans and stripy T-shirt. I checked on Lucky – several times – and left a bowl of food near her and a box of torn-up newspaper as a makeshift litter tray.

Then Dad and I set off for the fair.

It wasn't there!

186

There was just an empty field with some muddy tracks and litter blowing in the wind. We both stood staring, madly waiting for it to materialize in front of our eyes. But there were no vans, no rides, no roundabout, no candyfloss stall.

Dad blinked and shook his head. 'Oh dear. Of course. It's moved on somewhere else. As fairs do. I am a fool. Sorry, Floss.'

'Where's it gone, Dad?'

'Search me. There aren't any posters or anything. Poor poppet, you've missed out on your ride on Pearl.'

'And my candyfloss.'

'Yes. Sorry.'

'Can't we . . . can't we go and look for it someplace else?'

'Well, where, pet?' Dad said helplessly. He looked all round and then spotted the pub on the corner. 'Let's see if they've got any idea.'

We hurried to the pub. I hung around the doorway while Dad went in and asked. He came out sadly shaking his head.

'No one has a clue. Oh well. Can't be helped. Look, they've got a pub garden. Would you care to join me for a glass of something fizzy, sweetheart?'

Dad had a beer and I had a lemonade sitting huddled up on the wooden furniture. There was a little plastic slide and a Wendy house in the garden,

Tiger-size. I wondered what he was up to in Australia. Maybe he'd forget all about me in six months. Steve probably *wanted* to forget about me. But I knew Mum was missing me. She kept phoning me, and once or twice it sounded as if she might be crying.

'Dad, what are we going to do about Mum phoning? Will we give her Billy the Chip's number?'

'Oh dear, I don't know. I – I wasn't actually going to tell her we were moving, as it were. I know she'll think it's not suitable, our living at Billy's.' Dad put his pint mug down, sighing. 'Who am I kidding? It's *not* suitable, dragging you off to some funny old man's house. Goodness knows what state it's in. He seemed a bit fussed about it, didn't he? Oh Lordy, Floss, I hope this works out.'

'Of course it'll work out, Dad.' I put my glass down too and felt in my jeans for my pocket-money purse. 'Right, it's my round now, Dad. What are you having, another beer?'

Dad laughed and ruffled my curls but wouldn't let me pay. He bought another pint for himself, another lemonade for me, and a packet of crisps each.

We walked home holding hands. Lucky greeted us sleepily when we came in, giving us little mews of welcome, as if she'd been our cat ever since she was a newborn kitten.

14

When I got to school on Monday Rhiannon was strolling round the playground with Margot and Judy. They had their arms linked, their heads close together. I hovered, not sure whether to run up to them or not.

'She's like *so* boring now,' said Rhiannon. 'But Mum says I've got to be kind to her, though I don't see *why*. We bought her, like, *the* most exquisite outfit because her clothes are, like, so pathetic.'

'And babyish,' said Margot.

'And smelly,' said Judy.

They all tittered.

'But it was, like, a waste of time because she barely said thank you!'

I started trembling. I ran right round them and shouted, 'Thank you thank you thank you!' right in Rhiannon's startled face.

'Hey, cool it, Floss!' said Rhiannon, giggling uneasily.

'I didn't want the denim outfit. I didn't want to go out with you on Saturday! I wanted to see Susan and I wish wish wish I had!' I shouted.

Rhiannon stopped laughing. Her face hardened, the delicate arches of her eyebrows nearly meeting in the middle. 'Yeah, it figures. You and Swotty Potty. You're a right pair. You deserve each other. You be friends with her then, Smelly Chip.'

I *wanted* to be friends with Susan, but I wasn't sure she still wanted to be friends with me. I saw her way over at the other end of the playground, walking by herself, tapping each slat of the fence. I hurried towards her but she saw me coming and ran into school.

'Susan! Wait! Please, I want to talk to you,' I shouted, but she didn't even turn round.

I ran to the school entrance and rushed to the girls' cloakrooms, where we'd always met before. I barged straight through two girls giggling together.

'What's up with Floss?'

'Maybe she's got galloping diarrhoea?'

They cackled with laughter while I ran up and down the toilets. They were all empty. There was no sign of Susan.

I set off down the corridor, charged round the corner and ran right into Mrs Horsefield, nearly knocking her flying.

'Oh! I'm so sorry, Mrs Horsefield,' I gabbled.

'It's good you're in such a hurry to come to school on Monday morning, Floss,' said Mrs Horsefield. She held me at arm's length. 'But you don't look too happy, my dear. You're not running away from someone, are you?'

'No, no, I'm trying to run *to* someone,' I said.

'Well, I hope you find them,' said Mrs Horsefield. She paused. 'If that someone's Susan, I think I saw her going into the library.'

'Oh *thank* you, Mrs Horsefield.'

'Don't be too long finding her now. Registration's in five minutes.'

I set off for the library. Susan was standing by the shelves, fingering her way along the first row of books as if she was playing them like a piano.

'Susan!'

She jumped, and dodged round the other side of the bookshelves.

'Susan, you can't keep running away from me like this! You'll be sitting in front of me in five minutes. Please listen to me. I'm so so sorry I wasn't completely honest about Saturday. I was just so stupid and I feel awful now. I don't know why I went to Rhiannon's. I didn't have a good time at all. I don't want to be friends with her any more. I want to be friends with you. Please say you forgive me. Will you come to my place next Saturday and we'll have fun together and eat Dad's chip butties?'

Susan blinked at me as I spoke, twitching her fingers. There was a little pause when I stopped.

'Do you know, you said exactly one hundred words,' she said in a matter-of-fact way.

'Susan, please, did you *listen* to what I was saying?'

'Yes, I listened. You want to be my friend now because Rhiannon's gone off with Margot and Judy.'

'No! Well, yes, she *has*, but *I* broke friends with her, I truly did.'

'Yes, well, whatever. Only the thing is, Floss, I don't really want to be your second-best friend.'

'No, I want you to be my *first*-best friend. *Will* you come next Saturday?'

Susan shrugged. 'I think I've probably got something on next Saturday.' She paused. 'I have to go to this conference thing with my parents. Maybe the Saturday after?'

'That won't be any *use*. Oh Susan, we won't have the café any more. Please don't tell anyone, but my dad hasn't kept up all his payments and we have to move out and we're going to stay at Billy the Chip's place but it sounds like it's going to be really weird and Dad's going to run his van outside the station and that's going to be weird too and what am I going to do when Dad's out working and I'm a bit scared about it but I haven't

194

liked to say because Dad's so fussed about everything.'

'Oh Floss!' said Susan, and she put her arms round me.

I started crying and she patted me on the back.

'You *won't* tell anyone, will you?'

'Of *course* not! I won't say a word. I'm sure I'll be able to come on Saturday. I don't *want* to go to my parents' conference one bit – they just haven't got anyone to leave me with. Hey, Floss, did you know you said *another* exact hundred words. It's like you've got this weird gift! One hundred is my all-time lucky number too.'

'So we're friends now?'

'Best friends,' said Susan, giving me a squeeze. 'I've wanted to be your best friend ever since I came to this school. Are you sure you're OK about it though? Rhiannon might start being your worst enemy now.'

'I don't care,' I said, though my heart began thudding at the thought. 'I wish I didn't still have to sit next to her.'

'Don't worry,' said Susan. 'If she tries any funny business I'll turn round and yank her off her chair again.'

'Yes, she looked so *surprised* when she landed on her bum,' I said, and we both giggled.

'She'll be even more nasty and totally mean

when she finds out about Dad and me leaving the café and going to live with Billy the Chip. And I don't know what will happen when he comes back from seeing his son. Dad says I should go to Australia to be with Mum, and there's a bit of me that wants to, but I can't leave Dad, I'm all he's got. Well, he's got Lucky too, but she's really my cat. OK, we'll have to see if she belongs to anyone else but I'm hoping like anything she'll be mine.'

Susan was counting on her fingers as I spoke. She stared at me in awe. 'That's *another* hundred! You are a total phenomenon, Floss.'

'A what?'

'A phenomenon. It means you've done something utterly extraordinary.'

'A phenonion?' I tried hard but I couldn't say it.

I started mixing Susan up too, so that neither of us could say it without spluttering with laughter.

'Seriously though,' I said, wiping my eyes. 'Would you say it's a good omen?'

'I'll say!'

'Dad and I keep waiting for our luck to change. Well, *some* good things happen, but most of all I'd like Dad to keep his café. No, *most* most of all I'd like my mum and dad to get back together, but there's no chance of that. I wish there wasn't such a thing as divorce. Why can't people stay together and be happy?'

'Well, people change,' said Susan. 'Like friends. My parents are divorced.'

'*Are* they? So do you live with your mum or your dad?'

'Both. No, they're married to each other now, my mum and dad, but they used to be married to different people. I've got all these stepbrothers and stepsisters. My family's pretty complicated.'

'But suppose your mum and dad did split up. Who would you live with then?'

Susan thought about it. I could see her brain trying to puzzle it out, as if it was a complicated sum. She frowned. 'I don't know! It must be so difficult for you, Floss.'

'I got used to having two homes, but now my mum's house is let out to strangers and my dad's café is going to be taken over so I haven't got *any* real home. Dad and I have this joke about living in a cardboard box like street people. I used to sit in a cardboard box when I was little and pretend it was my Wendy house. It was my best ever game for ages. I used to cram a cushion into the box and a little plastic cooking stove and my dolls' teaset and all my favourite teddies.' I saw Susan was counting again and I caught hold of her fingers. 'Don't count my words, it makes me feel weird.'

'OK, I won't. Sorry. Tell me more about the cardboard box house.'

'In my mind it had a proper red roof with a chimney, and honeysuckle grew up the walls. I tried crayoning it on the box but it just looked like scribble. There was a blue front door with a proper knocker. If Dad was playing with me I'd make him pretend to knock on this imaginary knocker when he came calling. He was too big to get in the box with me – the walls would have collapsed – so he always said he'd like to sit in the garden on a deckchair. I'd get this stripy towel and put it just beside the box and he'd lie on it. I'd make him a cup of tea. Not *really*: I'd just put some water in my plastic teacup, and I'd colour it a bit with brown smarties. It probably tasted disgusting but he always drank it right up, his little finger sticking up in the air to make me laugh. I *loved* playing house with my dad.'

'I can see why you'd want to stay with him now. My dad didn't ever play with me like that, not in a fun way. He played cards and taught me chess and read to me, but he didn't ever muck about. I played by myself mostly. I didn't make things up like you, my mind doesn't seem to do that, but I *did* play with cardboard boxes, little ones. I made a row of shoebox houses in my bedroom once, and then I started making whole streets with boxes of bricks, and lots of books too – they make very good buildings.'

'Show me,' I said, thrusting an armful of library books at her.

We sat cross-legged on the library floor while Susan built me a book house. I copied her, and then started making an elaborate tall block of flats. We turned our fingers into people and made them walk in between the houses and climb all the stairs to the high rooftop of the flats. Then the library door opened suddenly and we both got such a fright that we jumped, and the book block of flats juddered and fell to the ground with a great clatter and crash.

Miss Van Dyke stood glaring at us. Miss Van Dyke, the deputy head and the scariest strictest old bat teacher in the entire school!

'What on *earth* are you doing, you two girls! This is a library, not a nursery playroom. What a way to treat books! Why aren't you in your classroom? First lesson started twenty minutes ago! Now put those books back this minute – carefully! – and then come with me. You're in Mrs Horsefield's class, aren't you?'

We nodded, too scared to say a word. Miss Van Dyke marched us briskly along the corridors and then prodded us into our classroom as if we were cattle. Everyone looked up at us, mouths open. Rhiannon's eyes glittered triumphantly. I peeped shame-faced at Mrs Horsefield. She had given me a gentle warning and I'd let her down horribly.

'These are your pupils, I believe, Mrs Horsefield,' said Miss Van Dyke. 'I discovered them in the library building houses with the books, if you please! I wonder why you didn't send someone to look for them. They've been missing from your lesson for nearly half an hour!'

Oh no, now I'd got Mrs Horsefield into trouble too. Maybe we'd all have to stand outside Miss Van Dyke's office in disgrace, with our hands on our heads, Susan, Mrs Horsefield and me.

But Mrs Horsefield was smiling calmly. 'I knew where the girls were, Miss Van Dyke. They were taking part in my special bonding project.'

Miss Van Dyke frowned. 'There's nothing about bonding projects in the national curriculum for Key Stage Two.'

'I know that, Miss Van Dyke, but sometimes one simply has to use one's initiative to improve classroom dynamics.'

I didn't have a clue what Mrs Horsefield meant. Maybe Miss Van Dyke didn't either. She glared at Susan and me.

'Why didn't you explain, you silly girls?' she said. She marched off, *stamp stamp stamp*, as if she wished we were bugs she could squash with her sensible shoes.

Susan and I stared in awe at Mrs Horsefield. She raised her eyebrows at us and made shooing gestures with her hands, so we scurried to our seats.

'What are you *playing* at, Smelly Chip?' Rhiannon hissed.

I ignored her. She poked me hard with her bony elbow. I shuffled to the edge of my seat, as far away from her as possible. Susan turned round and gave me a sympathetic grin. I grinned back. Rhiannon could poke a hole right through me and I wouldn't care, just so long as Susan stayed my friend.

PHEW!

Smelly Chip
and
Swotty Potty

Pongy Twit
and
Spotty Botty

THWACK!

OOPS!

15

Mum rang early the next morning. I sat cross-legged stroking Lucky while she told me that:

1. She had a lovely tan already.
2. The shops in the Victoria Arcade were incredible.
3. They'd been to a concert at the opera house.
4. They'd walked over the Harbour Bridge.
5. They'd seen koalas and kangaroos (but only in Sydney Zoo).
6. Steve was working wonders at the new branch and getting a great team together.
7. Tiger had taken his first staggering steps and had learned to say 'G'day.'

'So much has happened, Floss!' said Mum. 'So, darling, what about you? What's your news?'

I took a deep breath. I didn't quite know where to start.

'Are you all right, Floss? Oh God, what is it? Is Dad looking after you OK?'

Dad was looking at me anxiously as she spoke. I gave him a big smile and a thumbs-up.

'Dad's looking after me splendidly, Mum,' I said.

'Then what is it? How's everything at school? Are you up to speed with all your lessons? Is Rhiannon still being friendly?'

'Everything's fine at school. Mrs Horsefield's being especially nice. Rhiannon's being especially *nasty*, but I don't care because Susan and I are best friends now. She's coming over to play on Saturday.'

'How will your dad look after you both when he's got the café to run? How *is* the café? Are you getting any more customers?'

I thought hard. I didn't want to lie to Mum but I didn't want to tell her the whole truth either. 'Dad's coping,' I said. 'And he's expecting lots more customers soon.'

'That'll be the day,' Mum said unkindly. 'Oh well, Flossie, take care, my little love. I'll ring you next week, OK?'

I covered the phone with my hand and mouthed at Dad, 'How can Mum ring next week? We won't be here!'

Dad took the phone from me. 'Hi, Sal. I'm glad

everything's working out for you. Now listen, I'm making a few changes at the café. We're going to have a different phone number. I'll let you know. What? Oh, just general changes, keeping up with the times, aiming at different customers. Yeah yeah. Yes, of course Floss wears clean socks every day – and yes, she washes her hair. What hairdresser? I think she looks cute all curly. Listen, Sal, we've got to go now, she'll be late for school. Bye now.'

He put the phone down and mopped his brow. 'Phew!' he said, flopping back in his chair as if someone had let all the air out of him. I came and climbed on his lap. He went 'Ph-e-e-e-e-w' again, acting it out, while I giggled.

'I am so bad,' said Dad. 'I should tell your mum exactly what's happening. But if I do she'll insist you join her in Australia. Of course *I* should insist that's what you do. In fact I *am* insisting. We'll phone your mum back and come clean and tell her.'

'No no no no no! Insist all you like, Dad, but I'm staying, OK?' I looked at the clock. 'Though I'd better be off right this minute or I'll be late for school. Mrs Horsefield was so kind to Susan and me yesterday and I don't want to let her down.'

Dad let me slide off his lap but he kept hold of me by the shoulders. 'What's all this about Rhiannon being nasty to you?'

I shrugged my shoulders under Dad's hands. 'Oh, she's just being a bit mean,' I said.
Understatement of the Century!

Examples of Rhiannon's Extremely Unkind, Unfair and Mean Behaviour (in just one day!):

1. She sat at the extreme edge of her seat and held her nose whenever I moved.
2. She called me Smelly Chip over and over again, and got half the class calling me that too.
3. She called my dad Smelly Belly Chip.
4. She told everyone my mum's walked out on me for ever.
5. She said I begged her mum to buy me new clothes when we went to Green Glades and said I didn't even say thank you when she spent a fortune on me.
6. She wrote *Smelly Chip and Swotty Potty/Pongy Twit and Spotty Botty* all over the walls of the girls' toilets. She wrote other stuff too – too rude to include in this list!
7. She jogged the desk whenever I started writing.
8. She snatched my best felt-tip pen and stabbed the point on the desktop, ruining it.

9. She tipped my packed lunch onto the floor, accidentally on *total* purpose.
10. She tore the cover right off my maths book and scribbled inside it.

I could continue my list, easily reaching 50. Make that 100!

But here's another *lovely* list:

Examples of Susan's Incredibly Sweet and Comforting and Kind Behaviour:
1. She kept turning round and smiling at me all through lessons.
2. She said Rhiannon was a pathetic parrot repeating the same stupid words over and over.
3. She said she couldn't wait to meet my dad next Saturday.
4. She said she wanted to meet my mum when she came back from Australia.
5. I told her about the designer denim outfit and she said it sounded embarrassingly awful.
6. She tried to rub out all the 'Smelly Chip and Swotty Potty' rhymes in the girls' toilets. They remained clearly visible because Rhiannon had used biro, so Susan got her thickest black marker

207

pen and scribbled right over them.

7. She pushed her chair right back against our desk to steady it.

8. She lent me her own felt tips.

9. We salvaged my banana and my apple and my Kit-Kat, but my special cheese salad sandwiches (Dad was trying hard to think Healthy Eating) spattered all over the floor, grated cheese and tomato slices and little leaves of lettuce covered in dirt. Susan shared her tuna and sweetcorn sandwiches with me, and they were delicious. She also gave me half her apricot yoghurt (taking turns with the spoon) and a little bunch of black grapes. I insisted she have half my Kit-Kat and half my banana and half my apple. We ended up having a total feast.

10. After lunch Susan mended my maths book with sellotape while I drew a picture of two girls, one serious with specs and shiny brown hair, one smiling with crazy yellow curls. They were writing an elementary sum on a giant piece of paper: $1 + 1 = 2$ BEST FRIENDS. I stuck my picture over Rhiannon's scribbles and my maths book was as good as new. *Better.*

When I had to hand in my maths classwork for marking, Mrs Horsefield smiled and shook her head at the picture. This gave me courage.

'Mrs Horsefield, I was thinking,' I said earnestly.

'I wish you'd think more about your maths, Floss,' said Mrs Horsefield, going *cross cross cross* against each sum.

'Oh dear,' I said. 'No, the thing is, Mrs Horsefield, I wonder if I could move desks so I could sit next to Susan? It wouldn't cause any major disruption, seeing as Susan doesn't have anyone sitting next to her.'

'What about Rhiannon?' said Mrs Horsefield.

'I think she'll be very very pleased *not* to have me sitting next to her,' I said.

'Yes, I gathered you two have fallen out big time,' said Mrs Horsefield. 'You girls! You have more dramas than a soap opera.'

'So . . . is that a yes?' I said.

'I'm going to have to think about it. If I let you change desks I'm going to have a whole posse of little girls wanting to swap places. Probably half the boys will start too.'

'Oh *please*, Mrs Horsefield.'

'Look, I've already done you and Susan an immense favour yesterday. You can't trade on being my special favourites, you know.'

'*Are* we?'

'I'm a very good teacher and we all know very

good teachers don't have class favourites, but if I did, you two *might* be contenders. Now, run along. I'll have a little think about you and Susan and your seating arrangements. Meanwhile, see if she's any better at teaching you maths than I am!'

Susan did try and show me stuff but my mind wouldn't stay still and concentrate properly. We'd start on this sum about six men digging a hole in a field. I'd wonder *why* they were digging this hole. Was it going to be a swimming pool? I saw them in dusty jeans, digging like crazy, and then one of them got a hosepipe and filled up the pool with sparkly water and they all stripped off and jumped in, splashing each other and spouting water like whales . . .

'So what do you think the answer is, Floss?' Susan asked.

I stared at her, because I'd forgotten all about the question.

Susan sighed and rolled her eyes, imitating Mrs Horsefield. 'Could you just concentrate, Floss?'

'I'd much sooner concentrate on you coming round next Saturday, Susan. We'll be in a bit of a mess because Dad and I are moving out on Sunday.'

It still didn't seem *real*. Nowadays I kept getting this weird feeling that my home life had turned into the longest oddest dream. I felt like a boat that had lost its anchor, and now I was bobbing out to sea and the waves were getting bigger and bigger.

It felt much safer when I was at school, because that mostly stayed the same.

I *was* late for school that morning. Ten whole minutes. I crept into the classroom and whispered to Mrs Horsefield that I was very sorry. She wasn't really *cross*, but she did shake her head and sigh at me. It made me feel really bad.

'You're such a teacher's pet, Smelly Chip,' Rhiannon hissed. 'Anyone else would have got *really* told off. It's just because old Horsey's *sorry* for you. That's the reason anyone's ever nice to you. That's why my mum made me invite you round last Saturday. I didn't *want* you to come. You're no fun. You're a total *loser*, just like your sad fat Smelly Belly Chip dad.'

'You shut up about my dad,' I hissed.

She didn't shut up. She said it again. She added bits, poking at me with her ruler. I suddenly snapped. I grabbed the ruler and poked her back hard, right in the ribs.

'Ooow!' Rhiannon screamed.

Mrs Horsefield got to her feet. 'For goodness' sake! Stop that screaming, Rhiannon!'

'I've been *stabbed*,' Rhiannon shrieked.

'Let me have a look,' said Mrs Horsefield, sighing. She came over to our desk and looked at Rhiannon's front. She pressed gently all round Rhiannon's waist.

211

'I think you'll survive this savage attack, Rhiannon,' she said. She picked up the ruler. 'I take it this was the weapon involved?'

'It hurt!' said Rhiannon.

'I'm sure it did,' said Mrs Horsefield. She looked at me. 'Were you the culprit, Floss?'

I nodded. I thought Mrs Horsefield would shake her head and sigh at me and maybe tell us both off a little bit, but it wouldn't be *serious*. But she didn't shake her head or sigh. She put her hands on her hips and looked very very very serious.

'Flora Barnes, I'm ashamed of you,' she said coldly. 'I'm very disappointed that you're behaving so badly nowadays.'

'I'm sorry, Mrs Horsefield,' I whispered.

'Sorry isn't good enough. I can't keep making excuses for you. You waltz into the classroom ten minutes late, and you don't concentrate properly when you are here. I'm going to have to think of a serious punishment.'

I bent my head, burning all over. I wanted to lay my head on my desk and weep. I felt so awful. I couldn't understand why Mrs Horsefield was so very angry with me.

'Please, Mrs Horsefield, I have a strong feeling Floss was provoked,' said Susan.

'You be quiet, Susan. Nobody asked your opinion,' said Mrs Horsefield, totally snubbing her.

Rhiannon was still groaning theatrically, rubbing her ribs, but her eyes were glittering. She was hugely enjoying our humiliation.

'Poor Rhiannon,' said Mrs Horsefield. 'I won't have you teasing and tormenting her any longer, Flora. Gather up all your books and pens and pencils, please. Put them all in your school bag and stand up.'

I stared at Mrs Horsefield. Was she sending me to the head for the whole day? Was she *suspending* me? Was she EXPELLING me?

The whole class was silent, stunned. Even Rhiannon looked startled. I shoved my stuff in my school bag, my hands fumbling. I stood up, shocked and shaking.

'Right. I'm going to move you away from Rhiannon, seeing as you can't behave nicely sitting next to her. Now, where can I put you?' Mrs Horsefield seemed to be looking all round the classroom for a spare seat. There was only one empty chair. Mrs Horsefield looked at Susan's desk. She pointed to it.

'Well, Flora, you'd better sit here for now. Susan, move the desk forward as far as it will go, right away from Rhiannon. That's it, I'll have you both beside my desk, where I can keep on eye on you. There now. Sit beside Susan, Flora.'

I collapsed onto the seat next to Susan – and Mrs Horsefield gave me the tiniest private wink.

Galileo

Ellerina

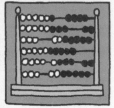

SUSAN
13116
FLORA
63691

$9\overline{)30^36}$ 34

Dimble

126.00

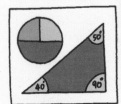

90°
40° 90°

One, two

Buckle my shoe

POLKA
THEATRE

16

School was heavenly now I was sitting next to Susan. I even enjoyed maths. Well, I didn't exactly *enjoy* it, but it was quite companionable having Susan go through each sum with me and tell me what to do.

We also started a numbers project together in a notebook exactly a hundred pages long. Susan wrote about famous mathematicians like Galileo and Pythagoras. I found out about numerology, and wrote out my name and Susan's name and checked off all the vowels and consonants and found out we were deeply compatible (but we knew that anyway). Susan wrote out neat examples of addition, subtraction, multiplication and division. She even did really difficult stuff her dad had taught her like algebra and geometry. I coloured in all her circles and triangles. Susan wrote about the abacus. I invented my own join-the-numbered-dots puzzle. Susan did a wonderful diagram of a calculator. I copied out counting rhymes like *One, Two, Buckle My Shoe.*

Mrs Horsefield said it was excellent and she'd definitely mark it ten out of ten. Rhiannon muttered behind us, '*One, two, don't they make you spew? Three, four, they're such a bore. Five, six, up to nerdy tricks.*'

As if we cared! I started making a list of all the things Susan might want to do on Saturday. The café was closing for good on Friday so Dad would be free to take us anywhere. I thought about all the special treat days I'd had with Mum and Steve. On Saturday Susan and I could:

1.   Go to Chessington World of Adventures in Dad's van and go on all the rides, even the scary ones.
2.   Go to the seaside in Dad's van and have ice creams on the pier and make a ginormous sand castle and go on a boat trip.
3.   Go to the country in Dad's van and walk up to the top of a big hill and have a picnic and paddle in a stream.
4.   Go up to town in Dad's van and go on the London Eye and Dad can row us on the Serpentine and we can play in Princess Diana's park.

216

5. Go to Bethnal Green toy museum in Dad's van and we can count all the dolls and look at the dolls' houses and play Giant Draughts.
6. Go to Greenwich in Dad's van and run all the way through the tunnel under the river and go to the market and see the *Cutty Sark*.
7. Go to London Zoo in Dad's van and see all the monkeys and the elephants and the penguins and watch them being fed.
8. Go to the National Gallery in Dad's van and choose our top ten favourite paintings and then climb on the lions in Trafalgar Square.
9. Go to the Polka Theatre in Dad's van and ride on the rocking horse and see a play and then have a pizza afterwards.
10. Go to the Natural History Museum in Dad's van and see all the dinosaurs and then have tea in the shop over the road and be allowed two cakes each.

Memo: We *don't* want to go to the Green Glades shopping centre.

I showed Dad the list when he tucked me up in bed that night.

'What about going to Disneyland in Dad's van?'

he said. 'Going for a world tour in Dad's van? Flying to the moon in Dad's van?'

'I suppose I got a bit carried away,' I said, wanting to kick myself. I'd forgotten just how much most of those days out would cost.

'I wasn't being *serious*, Dad. I was just making a silly list. You know what I'm like. No, we could just go for a little drive out in the van, maybe for a picnic. Or we could just go to the park. Maybe we'll skip feeding the ducks – Susan might feel she's a little too old, though of course *I* love feeding them. Oh Dad, if only the fair was still here! Wouldn't that be great! We could go on the roundabout. Susan and I could squash up on Pearl together and we could both have a candyfloss from Rose's stall. Maybe she'd invite us all back to her lovely caravan. That would be sooo fantastic.'

'Yes, it would be,' said Dad. 'Only the fair's not here. And I'm afraid I just don't have the cash for the other outings. I've got to be careful with petrol too. I reckon we might need a couple of trips to Billy's house with all our stuff, and then I've promised to drive him to the airport.' Dad paused. 'I went round to Billy's today, Floss. It's . . . it's a bit . . .'

I looked at Dad. 'It's a bit what, Dad?'

Dad gestured vaguely, his arms stretched wide. 'Well, you'll see for yourself. I'll do my level best to make you a pretty little bedroom somehow.

Everything will be OK. Touch wood.' He tapped his head and then glanced around my bedroom. He looked at the faded fairy wallpaper I'd had ever since I was a baby, the curtains falling off the rail, the wonky chest of drawers half painted silver, the pale pink carpet, which was now sludge-grey with age.

I sighed. I thought about the time when it was all new and clean and fresh, and Mum and Dad tucked me up in bed together and took turns telling me stories about the fairies flying up the wall.

Dad sighed too. 'I'm not much cop at the decorating lark, am I, Floss?'

'Never mind, Dad.'

'I'm not much cop at *anything*, am I?'

'*Don't*, Dad. You're fine. *We'll* be fine, you, me and Lucky.' I picked her up and held her close. 'Did you meet Billy the Chip's cats, Dad? What are they like?'

'Well, they're huge compared with our little Lucky.'

'Oh no! Do you think they'll bully her?'

'No, no, I think they're too old and tubby to do anything much but sleep.' Dad yawned. 'Like your old dad. I'm totally knackered, Floss, and yet I've still got to get to grips with all this packing. I'm so sorry, darling, but I'm going to be busy most of Saturday. I think you and Susan will just have to amuse yourselves.'

'But you'll make chip butties, won't you, Dad?'

'I'll make you chip butties fit for a queen. Well, two little princesses.'

Dad gave me a big kiss on my curls and he gave Lucky a big kiss on her fur, and then he tucked us both up, me in bed, Lucky in her duvet nest. I snuggled down with Dog and Elephant. I twiddled Elephant's trunk round my fingers and tucked Dog's limp ear over my nose like a little cuddle blanket. I was becoming very fond of them. I didn't exactly *play* with them, but they were starting to develop personalities. Elephant was called Ellarina, and was a bit flighty. She liked to show off and twirl her trunk in the air. Dog was called Dimble. He quivered at any sudden movement or loud noise. He did his best not to look at all mouse-like whenever Lucky was near him.

I couldn't decide whether to introduce them to Susan. She wouldn't tease me like Rhiannon but she might *privately* think me a total baby.

'Do you have any cuddly toys, Susan?' I asked as casually as I could on Friday morning.

'You mean teddy bears? No, I think I had one in my cot when I was very little but I don't have any now.'

'Oh,' I said, resolving to hide Ellarina and Dimble under my bed.

'I'm not *anti*-teddy. I just don't like the feel of their fur very much. I've got uncuddly toys though.

I've got eleven little wooden elephants, one wooden giraffe, one pair of crocodiles with jaws that snap open and shut, and three china rabbits – one pink, one blue and one big green one who towers over all the other animals, even the elephants.'

'But they're like ornaments. Do you actually play with them?'

'Exactly how could I play with them?' Susan asked.

'You could give them names and make them funny or naughty or shy, and maybe take them out into the garden and play jungles. You could turn your mum's washing-up bowl into a watering hole and make a big earth mountain for them to trek up and down.'

'That sounds a lot more fun than just dusting them,' said Susan. 'You do get good ideas, Floss.' She paused. 'Would you mind terribly if we didn't go on one of those special outings on your list this Saturday? I mean, they all sound lovely, and if that's what you really want to do that's fine with me, but I'd sooner make the most of our time together just playing. Is that OK?'

'Of course!' I said, deeply relieved.

Susan paused again. 'Look, Floss, this is terribly rude of me, but . . . I couldn't come in the morning too, could I? I so want to have a proper long time together – and also my mum and dad are supposed to be going to this education conference all day. They're both giving papers and I was going to have to trail along too and lurk in a corner somewhere reading a book, but if you're kind enough to invite me I could be with you.'

'Education? Are your mum and dad teachers?'

'Kind of. They teach teachers how to be teachers. They used to be at Oxford but now they've both got jobs near here.'

'Are they posh?' I said, and then I blushed because it sounded so stupid.

'They'd die if anyone thought they were posh,' said Susan. 'They *are* posh though – my mum even went to boarding school – but they try to act just ordinary.'

I didn't quite get this. Rhiannon's mum and maybe even *my* mum were just ordinary and yet they tried hard to pretend they were posh. It was a novelty to think Susan's mum and dad pretended the other way round.

'Well, Dad and I definitely *aren't* posh,' I said. 'And I'd love you to come as early as you want – that would be brilliant – but the whole place is going to be in an awful mess. Dad and I will be packing everything. We wanted to try to get it all done before you came.'

'Can't I help? I'm absolutely ace at packing because we've moved heaps and heaps of times.'

'OK then, if you really don't mind.'

'That's what friends are for,' said Susan.

'Did you have a best friend at your old school?'

222

'Not really,' said Susan. 'It's always horrible starting at a new school because you stick out so, and I seem to be the sort of person that gets picked on. Rhiannon thinks she's *so* original, but they used to call me Swotty Potty at my old school too. Maybe I ought to change my name by deed poll!'

'My mum wanted me to change my name when she split up with Dad. She wanted me to add Steve's name on with a hyphen but I wouldn't. *He's* not my dad, he's not anything to do with me, he's just my mum's new partner.'

'All these partners!' said Susan. 'I tried to do a family tree on this big wallchart but it got so complicated. I did it all in my best italic handwriting, in red ink, but then I had to keep crossing bits out because people kept splitting up. Then my mum's ex-partner kept having new babies with each new lady, so that side of the family tree got much too crowded. It ended up looking such a mess I crumpled it all up and threw it away. That's why I like maths so. The numbers don't wriggle about and change; you can just add them up or subtract them or multiply or divide them, whatever, but you always get the answer you want.'

'Only if you're you. *My* numbers wriggle all over the place and I never get the right answer unless I copy off you,' I said. 'OK then, Susan, you come as early as you like on Saturday.'

17

My 'early' wasn't quite the same as Susan's. Dad and I weren't even up when the doorbell rang. We stumbled downstairs, me in my nightie, Dad in his old pyjama bottoms with a T-shirt on his top. We opened the door. There was Susan and *her* dad.

We peered at them, mortified. Dad frantically combed his sticking-up hair with his fingers. I rubbed my eyes and pulled the hem of my nightie down as far as it would go, hoping it *might* just look like a dress.

We didn't convince Susan's dad.

'I'm so sorry. We've obviously got you out of bed. How awful!' he said.

He was much older than my dad, more like a grandad, but he was dressed sort of young, in a black T-shirt and jeans and a denim jacket with the sleeves rolled up to try to look casual. His own hair looked as if it needed a good brush. He seemed what Mum would call dead scruffy, but try as he might he couldn't make his voice sound anything but ultra posh and plummy.

'Yes, I agree, it *is* awful of us. I think I must have slept through the alarm. I've been at sixes and sevens recently. You know what it's like, mate,' Dad blurted.

'No, no, I meant *we're* awful, arriving so horrendously early . . . mate,' said Mr Potts. 'It's so good of you to say you'll have Susan for the day. I gather she rather invited herself. But I can see it's the worst possible time for you.' He waved vaguely at the cardboard boxes scattered all over the hall, like a giant toddler's building blocks.

'Susan's *very* welcome,' said Dad, smiling at her. 'Just so long as she doesn't mind a bit of chaos.'

'Oh, she's used to that in her own home,' said Mr Potts, and he gave Susan's shoulder a little squeeze. 'You know my mobile number and Mum's, don't you? Ring if there's any problem. Otherwise we'll come and pick you up about sevenish. Is that really OK?'

He was looking at Dad. He nodded and smiled. Susan nodded and smiled. I nodded and smiled too.

'Thanks again. We owe you big time. Maybe your Floss might like to come to us next Saturday.'

'Oh yes please!' Susan and I said in unison, while the dads laughed.

226

Then Mr Potts waved and walked to his car, neatly kicking two Coke cans into the gutter. I could see Mrs Potts sitting in the front of their car. She had grey hair piled up in an untidy bun and little round glasses just like Susan's. She was wearing a dark red peasant blouse and a big yellow bead necklace. She waved too. I waved back shyly.

'Right!' said Dad. 'I'd better get myself washed and dressed pronto, and then see about breakfast. Have you had breakfast, Susan? I'm sure you can manage another, anyway.'

'Oh good! Can we have chip butties?' Susan asked eagerly.

Dad laughed. 'You can have a chip butty for your lunch. You might *even* have another for your tea. But I think we'll draw the line at butties for breakfast. How about cornflakes?'

Lucky came sidling down the stairs, not sure who this new visitor was.

'Oooh, she's so lovely,' said Susan, crouching down and holding out her hand. Lucky hesitated and then took two steps forward on her dainty paws, prepared to make friends.

'You are so lucky to have a cat,' said Susan. 'My dad is allergic to cat's fur. Well, he *says* he is. And Mum fusses about their claws. We've got all these leather-bound books and she says they'd use them like a scratching post.'

'Well, we like Lucky's fur. I might well wrap her round my neck in the winter instead of a scarf; she'll keep me nice and cosy. And all our stuff is scratched to bits anyway,' said Dad. 'I'm a bit of a scratcher myself, come to think of it.' He bowed his legs in a chimp stance and scratched his chest.

'Dad!' I said.

'Oops! Sorry. I'd better go and have my shower now. Wash the fleas off.'

'*Dad!*' I said.

Dad ran up the stairs making monkey noises. I rolled my eyes and Susan giggled.

'Let's give Lucky her breakfast,' I said.

Lucky's cat food looked pretty disgusting – lumpy brown slurp – but she seemed enthusiastic. She ate it up, she had a crunch of her dry biscuits and she sipped from her water bowl while we hovered over her admiringly. Then she used her new litter tray while we turned our backs discreetly.

I showed Susan how to deal with it.

'It's a little bit disgusting, but nowhere near as bad as changing Tiger's nappies,' I said. 'Oh dear, it's weird, I even miss Tiger, though I *don't* miss changing him. Maybe he'll be potty trained when he comes back from Australia!'

We washed our hands and Lucky licked her paws, and then I set out breakfast on the table when Dad joined us, his hair all wet and sticking up from his shower. He was wearing his silliest smiley-face T-shirt and his jogging bottoms. I'd have died if he wore them in front of Rhiannon, but I felt safe with Susan.

We both had a big bowl of cornflakes for our breakfast. Susan tipped hers into her bowl and then started touching each one with the tip of her spoon.

'What are you up to?' said Dad.

Susan went pink. 'I'm just seeing how many I've got,' she mumbled.

'We've got plenty of cornflakes, sweetheart. There's another packet in the cupboard,' said Dad.

'No, Dad, Susan just likes to count things.' I smiled at Susan. 'I bet you're looking to see if you've got an exact hundred.'

'I bet *you* have,' said Susan.

'Well, why don't you two daft girls tip your cornflakes onto a plate? They'll be much easier to count then. Do you want a cup of tea, Susan? Do you take sugar? I hope you're not going to count the grains of sugar – you'll go cross-eyed.' Dad crossed his own eyes, pulling a funny face. Susan laughed and pulled a funny face back.

'I do *like* your dad,' she whispered when we went upstairs.

'I like *your* dad,' I said politely.

'Yours is much more fun. And he doesn't mind my numbers thing. It drives my dad nuts. He says

229

it's obsessive-compulsive behaviour and I should have therapy.' Susan paused. 'Do you think I'm a bit nuts, Floss?'

'Not at all. Your dad might be ever so clever but he doesn't know everything. You just like numbers. Same as I like making lists. *Right*, let's make a list of all the things we've got to do today,' I said, going into my bedroom.

I made a big thing of looking for my notebook and a pen. I didn't want Susan to be floundering for something nice to say about my bedroom. It looked smaller and shabbier than ever with cardboard boxes everywhere. Susan curled up on the duvet in the corner.

'It might be a bit furry. I'm letting Lucky sleep on it at the moment,' I said.

'I shall get as furry as possible and then see if I make my dad sneeze,' said Susan.

She reached up to my pillow. Ellarina and Dimble were lurking bashfully underneath, but their little woolly paws were protruding.

'Who are they?' she said, tweaking them.

I made Ellarina pirouette, waving her trunk. Dimble became very shy and hid for a long time, but we gradually lured him out.

'They are so sweet,' said Susan. 'But they're naked! Let's make them some clothes later on. Put that on your list, Floss.'

'Oh yes! Can you sew properly then, Susan?'

'Well, sort of.'

'Did your mum show you?' I asked wistfully.

'No, Mum can't even sew buttons on. My dad sews a bit. I worked out how to do different stitches and I can join bits together, though I don't always do it properly.'

'You are *clever*, Susan.'

'I'm not clever at making things up like you are,' she said. 'You're the one who's so good at pretending that things seem real. Like Ellarina and Dimble. Have you got any other dolls and teddies?'

'No,' I said mournfully. 'I was such an idiot. I threw them all out because Rhiannon made me feel such a baby. I wish I still had them. I hate it that they're just mouldering and sad in some stinky rubbish pile. I wish I'd at least given them a proper funeral. Hey, that would have been really cool in a creepy kind of way – a doll funeral! I could have given them each a shoebox as a coffin. It would have been like there'd been a mega-disaster in doll-land. Maybe some crazy robot toy ran amok with a machine gun and butchered all my Barbies!'

'We could have a memorial service. That happens a couple of months after the funeral. My mum went to one for the principal of her college. You sing hymns and say poems about the dead person. We could do that for your dolls.'

231

'I'll put that on my list! We'll have a memorial service and we'll make clothes for Ellarina and Dimble. And I know what I'd also really like to do. Have you ever made a friendship bracelet, Susan?'

'No, but I'd love to. I'll make you one, shall I?'

'And I'll make one for you. I've made one for my dad; blue to match his jeans.'

We heard Dad thumping up and down the stairs, shifting boxes.

'Shall we help him?' said Susan.

'Yes, let's. We'll put that first on our list. NUMBER ONE: PACK UP THE HOUSE.'

I wrote it in capital letters. It wasn't as easy as it sounded. My own things were easy enough because they'd been pared down to the barest minimum by Mum. Susan and I filled one box with my shoes, my underwear, my night things and my washing things. We filled another box with my home clothes and my school clothes and my princess dress. I was wearing my newly washed and ironed birthday jeans and top. I left the rhinestone designer denim outfit in the wardrobe till last.

'What is *this*?' said Susan, trying the cap on.

It looked comfortingly ridiculous on her too. I reminded her about Rhiannon's mother.

'I suppose it was very kind of her – but I hate it. I look such a fool,' I said.

'Well, you don't have to wear it,' said Susan.

'Maybe we should put it on the hottest wash in your washing machine and shrink it right down till it fits Ellarina.'

'Yes, she'd look really cute in it, and the cap would balance her big ears.' I crumpled the outfit up and stuffed it in the box. It felt good, as if it was Rhiannon and I was stuffing her in the box too.

'I can't stick Rhiannon now,' I said. 'How come I had her as my best friend when really she's my worst enemy? Her and Margot.'

Rhiannon couldn't get at us in the classroom now because we'd moved our front desk out of her reach. However, she and Margot and Judy lurked in the corridors at lunch time and called us stupid names and said rude things and then cackled with laughter. Margot wore the rose-quartz bracelet now. Rhiannon must have given it to her. As if I cared!

It looked as if Rhiannon and Margot were definitely best friends now. Judy still trailed round with them, telling ruder and ruder jokes, but Rhiannon and Margot simply sniggered and then ignored her.

'I feel a bit sorry for Judy now,' I said. 'She's the one who's ended up without a real best friend.'

'Don't feel sorry for her. She's been horrible to you and me,' said Susan. 'She was the one who started up the whole Swotty Potty lark – *and* the Smelly Chip bit.'

I paused. I bent my head, surreptitiously sniffing the clothes in the box. Then I buried my head in my chest and breathed deeply, trying to sniff *me*.

'Are you doing *yoga*, Floss?' Susan said.

'No, no, I'm . . . Look, Susan, *do* I smell of chips? Mrs Horsefield said I should hang my clothes in the fresh air but that's a bit of a problem, unless I find some way of pegging them to my swing. That's my best thing. I'm going to have to get Dad to untie it even though it took him *ages* to get it fixed up.'

'I *love* swings. Shall we put swinging on your list?' Susan suggested.

'Well, you can't really swing *properly*. It goes kind of lopsided. Still, of course we can swing. You ever so tactfully changed the subject. I *do* smell of chips, don't I?'

'Yes, you do. You smell absolutely delicious, and if you don't watch out I shall eat you all up,' said Susan. She seized Ellarina and Dimble. 'Yum yum yum!' she said, making their little woolly mouths nibble me.

I doubled up laughing because they were all tickling me. Then I gave Susan a quick hug. 'You're the best friend in all the world, Susan,' I said. 'Let's stay friends for ever and ever.'

'Yes, for ever and ever,' said Susan, solemn now. 'Can we stay friends right through the summer holidays?'

'Of course we can. We can play together all the time.'

'That would be lovely – only some of the time we have to go to our house in France. But I'll write and phone you heaps, OK? You will stay friends?'

'You bet. And even if Dad and I move on somewhere else after staying at Billy the Chip's house, will you still stay friends?'

'Absolutely. Even if you end up going to Australia to live with your mum. In fact I'll come and visit you and play with the koalas.'

'And what about if I go to the moon? Will you come and visit me in your spacesuit and do a dance with me in your moonboots?'

I did a slow, bouncy moon dance. Susan joined in. We danced in and out and round about the cardboard boxes.

Dad put his head round the door and laughed at us. He put an empty cardboard box on each foot and lumbered about doing his own crazy moon dance – and then we all collapsed, laughing.

'I don't know what I'm doing clowning around. There's still so much to be done,' said Dad.

'I've just got to pack up my books and crayons

and stuff in my pink pull-along case, and then we can help you, Dad,' I said.

'We can number each box and write on it what's inside,' said Susan.

'You're obviously a girl with a system,' said Dad.

Susan was great at getting both of us organized. She found some old brown sticky tape and sealed each box so we could balance one on top of the other.

We finished my room, though we left out clean clothes for tomorrow, and Ellarina and Dimble and my sewing set and Lucky's duvet. She didn't like all this sudden activity and burrowed right underneath the duvet, just her nose and whiskers peeping out.

Dad started to tackle his bedroom while we got started on the living room. There wasn't really much to take. We packed:

1. The cuckoo clock (though it didn't work). It had been Mum and Dad's wedding present from Grandma, and for as long as I can remember the hands had been stuck at four o'clock and the cuckoo sulked inside his house, though you could still see him if you opened the little doors.
2. The motorbike calendar. Dad had inked stars and smiley faces every weekend

with *Floss* written in curly writing. Last month he'd written *Floss! Floss! Floss!* in every single box.

3. The photo of Mum and Dad and a baby me at the seaside, all sitting on the sand and licking ice cream. I remembered that day and the heat of the gritty sand and the coldness of the ice cream dripping onto my tummy.

'You were such a cute little toddler, Floss. Look at all your fluffy curls,' said Susan. 'Your mum's ever so pretty too. She looks so young!'

Mum was cuddled up to Dad in the photo, licking his ice cream instead of her own. Dad was pretending to be cross with her but you could still see just how much he loved her.

I sighed. 'I wish I could rewind to when we were all happy together,' I said. I sniffed hard.

Susan patted my shoulder sympathetically. 'We could really do with some bubble wrap,' she said. 'Never mind, we'll have to make do with newspaper.'

We were leaving the television because it didn't work properly anyway. I packed all my favourite films (number 4 on the list), hoping that Billy the Chip might have a video recorder, though if his crackly old transistor radio was anything to go by he didn't seem up to speed with his electrical equipment.

We were leaving the table and chairs. The tabletop was patterned with coffee-mug rings and the woven seats of the chairs were coming unravelled and scratched your bottom. Even so, I sat down on each one, remembering when we were Mum and Dad and me, with one leftover chair for all my teddies and Barbies. They were forever falling off, the teddies too limp to sit up properly, and at the slightest nudge the Barbies jackknifed onto the floor with their legs in the air. Mum would get cross but Dad always helped me get them back on their chair. He'd sometimes put a baked bean or a chip on each of my doll's house plates for my fidgety family.

'Did your dad really never play pretend games with you when you were little, Susan?' I asked.

'He read to me and did funny voices. And he played weighing and measuring games and guessing words on pieces of card, but that was like baby lessons. My mum played music to me and I had to act it out. Sometimes we played I was a little French girl called Suzanne, but that was so I could count up to a hundred in French.'

'You're such a brainybox, Susan,' I said.

'Don't!' said Susan, as if I'd insulted her.

'I'm paying you a compliment! You're heaps and heaps brainier than me.'

'It's not that great a deal being brainy,' said Susan. She sat down on the sofa, sighing.

I went to sit beside her. The sofa sagged badly and the corduroy was shiny with age. There were several big dark stains where Dad had spilt his coffee or his can of beer. We were leaving the sofa too. I wished we could somehow take it with us. It wasn't just because it was where Dad and I cuddled up and watched the telly. When I was little it had been a fairytale castle and a wagon train across the prairie and a bridge over the man-eating crocodiles crawling across the carpet.

'I wonder if we could just take one of the sofa cushions?' I said, tugging at it.

'It's a bit . . . tired looking,' Susan said, as tactfully as she could. 'And it would take up a whole cardboard box all by itself.'

'Yeah, I suppose,' I said, stroking the sofa as if it was my giant pet.

'Shall we go and see how your dad's getting on with his packing?' Susan said, going for diversionary tactics.

Dad was having similar problems. He was slumped on the edge of his bed, his clothes scattered all over the duvet, so it looked as if there were twenty Dads sprawled beside him. There were Mum things too, clothes I'd completely forgotten about – an old pink towelling dressing gown, a sparkly evening frock with one strap drooping, a worn woollen jacket with a furry collar, even some old

239

Chinese slippers, embroidered satin, with one of the butterflies unravelling.

'Dad?' I said, and I went and sat beside him while Susan hovered tactfully in the doorway. 'Where did all Mum's stuff come from?' I picked up one of the slippers, rubbing my finger across the satin. I remembered sitting watching television long ago, leaning back against Mum's legs, stroking her satin slippers, feeling the little ridges of embroidery with my fingertip.

'Your mum left them in her half of the wardrobe when she went off with Steve. She didn't want them. I was supposed to get rid of them but I couldn't.' Dad sighed, shaking his head at himself. 'Daft, aren't I, Floss?'

'You're not daft, Dad.'

'I suppose it's time to deal with them now.'

'You can still keep them. We can pack them all up in a cardboard box.'

'No, no. It's time to chuck them out. Time to chuck half of my stuff too.' Dad picked up the jeans that had got torn at the fair and flapped the tattered legs at us.

'I thought you were going to keep them as decorating trousers.'

'Who am I kidding? When was the last time I did any decorating, for heaven's sake?'

'You painted my chest of drawers silver.'

240

'And left it half finished.'

'I still love it. Can I take it to Mr Chip's house, Dad? It won't take up much room.'

'OK OK. Definitely, little darling. So how are you two girls getting on with packing up your bedroom, Floss?'

'We're finished, Dad. Susan's absolutely ace at getting everything sorted.'

'Well, aren't we lucky! Thank you so much, Susan, you're a sweetheart. I wish *I* had a smashing friend to sort me out,' said Dad.

'I'd like to be your friend too, Mr Barnes,' said Susan. 'We can start sorting your clothes for you, if you like.'

'That's very kind of you, Miss Potts,' said Dad. 'And *I* could sort out a tasty snack, seeing as you've both worked so hard. Now let me see . . . would you like chip butties – or chip butties – or indeed, chip butties?'

We both put our heads on one side, pretending to consider, and then yelled simultaneously, *'Chip butties!'*

It was a joy to see Susan eating her very first chip butty. Dad served it to her on our best blue china willow-pattern plate, garnished with tomato and lettuce and cucumber. Susan ignored the plate and the little salad. She didn't use the knife and fork Dad had set out beside the plate.

241

She picked up the chip butty in both hands, staring in awe at the big soft roll split in half and crammed with hot golden chips. She opened her mouth as wide as possible and took a big bite. She shut her eyes as she chewed. Then she swallowed and smiled.

'Oh thank you, Mr Barnes! It's even better than I hoped it would be. You make the most wonderful chip butties in the whole world!'

After we'd eaten every mouthful of our chip butties we sorted Dad's clothes into GOOD, NOT TOO BAD and CHUCK. Susan counted and I made a list.

Dad's clothes:

GOOD – 12 items of clothing, including one tie and socks and shoes and underwear.
NOT TOO BAD – 20 items of clothing
CHUCK – 52 $^1/_2$ items (the half was an ancient pair of pyjama bottoms – we couldn't find the top).

Dad laughed ruefully and started obediently chucking his stuff into a big plastic bag. He took Mum's old clothes, hesitated, and then started chucking them too.

'Maybe we don't have to chuck all of them, Mr Barnes,' said Susan. 'We couldn't have them, could we?'

'Do we want to dress up in them?' I asked a little doubtfully.

'No, we want to make them into clothes for Ellarina and Dimble,' said Susan.

We borrowed Dad's sharp kitchen scissors and some greaseproof paper to make patterns. It took a *lot* longer than I'd realized, but after two extremely hard-working hours Ellarina had a sparkly strapless dance dress, Dimble had a fur coat and they both had pink dressing gowns, and tiny embroidered slippers tied to each of their four paws with sewing thread.

'We'll cut the legs right off your dad's ripped jeans and make them little denim jackets and Ellarina can have a skirt and Dimble can have dungarees – he'd look so cute!'

'And caps?' I asked.

'Well, I could give it a go. Just so long as you don't ever ever ever wear yours,' said Susan. She waggled her fingers. 'They *ache* now.'

'Mine too. Yet I wanted to work on our friendship bracelets.'

'We can do them another time,' said Susan. 'We're going to have lots and lots of times. You will come to my house, won't you, Floss?'

'And I'm sure Billy the Chip won't mind you coming to his place. And then . . .' My voice tailed away. I didn't have any idea where we'd be after that. It was so scary not knowing. 'Let's go and have a swing,' I said quickly. 'It goes a bit wonky but you can still swing quite high if you really kick your legs.'

We went out to the back yard. Lucky came with us and circled the wheelie bins. I always worried whenever she slipped out of sight, but she bobbed back each time.

I let Susan have first go on the swing, but she wasn't really any good at it, so I stood on the seat behind her and pulled on the ropes and bent my knees and got the swing going. We didn't really go *that* high, but we pretended we were swooping right up in the air, over the treetops, flying far over the tallest tower, up and up and up.

'Wheee! We're right over the sea now,' I shouted. 'And there's land again! See all those skyscrapers? We're over America!'

'I think it's more likely France,' Susan said breathlessly.

'No, no, look, more sea, we're swooping r-o-u-n-d and d-o-w-n and here's Australia! See all the kangaroos? Whoops, there's a boomerang. Who's that waving? It's my mum! Hey there, it's me, Floss. Meet my best friend Susan.'

We both let go of the swing with one hand and waved wildly into thin air.

18

On Sunday morning Dad and I loaded all the neatly labelled cardboard boxes into the van. Then Dad struggled with my silver chest of drawers and my swing. He crammed in his old CD player and all our pots and pans and crockery and a box of vital tools I'd never seen him actually use.

He dithered for a long time out in the yard, shifting all the bits of motorbike under the tarpaulins. He laid them all out on the concrete, as if they were parts of a jigsaw puzzle and if he could only sort them all out systematically he'd be able to construct a splendid Harley Davidson there and then. He actually moved pieces around as if he was looking for a piece of sky or a flat edge. Then he sighed.

'What am I going to do with it all, Floss?' he said. 'I've been collecting all this stuff for years and years, right from when I was in my teens.'

'Take it with us, Dad.'

'Yes, but what am I going to *do* with it?'

'Make your own custom-built motorbike, Dad. How cool would that be?'

'Yeah, yeah, if I were still twenty years old – but I'm pushing forty, Floss. I'm a tubby old dad. I doubt I've got the bottle for roaring round the roads on a bike, even if I had one. No, I might as well leave the lot here. Maybe someone else will find all the spare parts useful, eh?'

'But you like them so, Dad. They're part of you.'

'You're the only part of me I want to keep for ever, Flossie. It's time to move on. It's goodbye to Charlie's Café.'

'Let's go round and say goodbye to every room, Dad. Would that be totally nuts?'

'OK, darling, let's go on a little tour of the premises.'

We said goodbye to the kitchen and tried to count up how many chip butties Dad might have made, right from the opening day. It was as if thousands of phantom chip butties were whirling all round us like galaxies in outer space.

Then we said goodbye to the café itself. We sat at every single table and we toasted our very special customers in lemonade, our dear Billy the Chip and Old Ron and Miss Davis, but also people we'd remembered for years: the man with a red face who ordered ten chip butties and ate every single one, gollop gollop gollop; the couple who held hands and ordered a big mixed grill to share and then shyly confided that it was their wedding breakfast; the lady who came in with her labrador and ordered one chip butty for herself and one for the dog.

Then we went back upstairs and said goodbye to my bedroom, and Dad told me how he and Mum had taken me home from the hospital when I was born and tucked me up in a little Moses basket. They spent hours and hours trying to get me to go to sleep, and then when I finally nodded off they were so worried they woke me up again just to make sure I was still breathing.

'Do you know, I still sometimes creep in when you're asleep and check you're breathing,' said Dad.

We said goodbye to Dad's bedroom and the bathroom and the loo, and then we said the saddest goodbye to the living room.

'Let's have one last cuddle on the sofa, Floss,' said Dad.

We curled up together and traded memories as we stared at the blank television screen. It was as if films of our family life flickered there – long-ago happy Mum-and-Dad-and-Floss times.

We both sighed. Then Dad kissed the top of my head and said gently, 'Let's get on our way, little darling.'

Lucky was hiding in her duvet, sensing something was definitely up. She'd taken her time deciding she wanted to come and live in our house, and now we were expecting her to leave before she'd even settled in. She didn't want to be lifted up, and I had to hang on hard to her, duvet and all. She mewed indignantly for me to put her down.

'I've got to hang onto you this time, Lucky. We're going to a new house now. You'll like it just as much, you'll see,' I said, though I wasn't sure that was very likely.

Dad drove us very slowly and carefully out of the town to Billy the Chip's house. It was on a big mock-Tudor housing estate, row after row of identical semi-detached houses with black and white panels and crazy paving and clipped privet hedges. I was sure I was going to get muddled as every single street looked the same. I clutched Lucky tightly.

'We're here, pet,' said Dad, drawing up outside number four Oak Crescent.

We peered out at the house. The privet hedge was wavering out of control and the crazy paving was sprouting weeds from every crack.

'Poor old Billy. It's obviously got a bit much for him,' said Dad. 'We'll do our best to tidy it up for him, won't we, Floss?'

'Yes Dad,' I said, in a small voice.

I felt like Lucky, who was still mewing piteously in her duvet. I didn't want to start living in this shabby old house. It didn't seem to have anything to do with me.

I thought of the airline ticket. Dad had taken it out of the kitchen drawer and given it to me to look after. I had smoothed it out carefully and tucked it inside the plastic case of the *Railway Children* video. I'd opened up the case twenty or thirty times over the last couple of days, just to check the ticket was still safe.

I wasn't going to use it. I couldn't leave Dad. I couldn't leave Susan. I couldn't leave Lucky – though I had asked Mrs Horsefield privately if you were allowed to take animals on aeroplanes.

Dad reached out and took hold of my hand. 'OK, little Floss?' he said.

I took a deep breath. 'OK, big Dad,' I said.

We got out of the van. I held on tightly to Lucky. She was so keen to be put down now we were out of the noisy scary van and on firm ground again that she scrabbled frantically with her paws and scratched my neck. I knew it was an accident but it hurt quite a lot, and it hurt my feelings too. I had to blink hard and clamp my lips together to stop myself crying. I knew Dad was peering at me anxiously. I tried hard to make my mouth smile. Dad's own smile was pretty forced too.

We knocked on Billy's door. The knocker was tarnished and the black paint blistered, but there was a lovely stained-glass window set into the door, a big round sun with long slanting rays – the sort I used to paint when I was in the infants.

The door opened and there was Billy squinting in the daylight, looking paler and frailer than ever, but he was proudly wearing a strange new nylon tracksuit and he had a moneybag strapped round his old saggy tummy.

'I'm all set for my trip,' he said, patting his purse and holding his nylon arms out for inspection. 'What do you think of the new gear? I wanted to be comfy travelling.'

'You look dead trendy, Billy. Those air hostesses will be buzzing round you like bees round a honeypot,' said Dad.

'Oh, very droll,' said Billy, but he looked pleased. 'Well, come in, then. Welcome to your new home. I'm afraid it's a bit lacking in mod cons. I'm rather set in my ways.' He opened the door wider and we stepped inside.

We stayed standing still, blinking in the gloom, staring all round us. It didn't seem as if we'd stepped into someone's home. It was as if we'd moved into a museum. The hall had a little table and an umbrella stand and one of those fat old-fashioned cream phones with a round dial. There was a crocheted mat underneath the telephone, yellow with age.

There were many more crochet mats in Billy the Chip's living room. They were on the back of his shabby olive-green sofa and on each arm too. There was a matching set on both green armchairs. There were more mats on the nest of tables and yet more under the china vases on the mantelpiece over the tiled fireplace.

There was a big woollen semicircular mat in front of this fireplace. Two vastly fat tabby cats lay symmetrically either side, paws outstretched, heads raised, staring at us like sphinxes. Lucky gave an anxious mew in my arms. I held onto her protectively. Mr Chip's cats were great tigers compared to tiny Lucky.

More mats were laid out like a card game on the big sideboard, each covered with a photograph. There were old wedding photos. I stared at a strange stiff couple, the man with a little moustache and a wing collar tickling his chin, the lady with her wedding veil right down over her forehead.

'That's Mother and that's Father,' said Billy the Chip, gesturing, as if they were real and standing six centimetres tall on his sideboard. He pointed to another wedding couple, a thin awkward young man and a plump woman with her hand tucked in his arm. 'And that's me and my Marian.' He stroked the glass on the photo over Marian's rounded cheeks.

There were baby photos too; a bare little boy lying on that same semicircular rug.

'That's my boy. He's another Billy, like his dad and grandad, but he calls himself Will nowadays,' said Billy, shaking his head.

'Does he have a chip van in Australia, Mr Chip?' I asked.

'No, he swore he was never going into the fried chip business. Couldn't persuade him. He did bar-tending, and now he's got his own wine bar out in Sydney, though I dare say he serves up chips as a bar snack. French fries or potato wedges or whatever fancy name they call them now.' Billy sniffed.

'I wonder if Mum and Steve ever go there now?' I said.

'Sydney's a very big city, Floss,' Dad said gently. 'Your Billy's moved with the times, mate,' he said to Billy 'That makes him a smart guy. Much smarter than you and me.'

Time had certainly stood still in Billy's house. He *did* have a television, but it was even older than our telly at the café. There was a wind-up gramophone beside it, with a pile of old black records in brown paper sleeves.

254

'Good God, Billy, have you kept these from your courting days?' said Dad, looking through them. 'Hey, these are even before your time, surely?'

'They were Mum and Dad's,' said Billy. He gestured with his trembly old fingers. 'They moved in here right from their honeymoon. Spanking new, the house was, my mum's dream home. It was considered dead modern in those days.'

It was hard trying to imagine this musty old house as *modern*. I tried picturing a couple dancing to the gramophone, a baby crowing on the rug, laughter and shouting and doors banging – but the house stayed still and silent.

'I'll show you to your rooms,' said Billy.

He led the way up the threadbare carpet and then showed us each room along the landing. The bathroom had an old bath with rust stains under the big taps and black chips in the enamel.

'It doesn't look too grand, but I clean it regularly,' Billy said, sounding embarrassed.

'It's fine, Billy, and obviously spotless,' said Dad, patting Mr Chip's nylon sleeve. 'You're much better at housekeeping than we are. He puts us to shame, doesn't he, Floss?'

There was a main bedroom that had once been Billy's mum and dad's, and then Billy and Marian's, and now it was just Billy's. There was something about that sad big empty bed that reminded me of Dad's bedroom back at the café.

Dad looked relieved when Billy suggested he sleep in the second bedroom, which had always been a spare room with a single bed. It had fraying pink ribbons on the net curtains, and the mats all over the dressing table were pale pink to match. There was a firescreen with an embroidered thatched cottage and a faded pink ruffly bedspread. It looked like a room for an old old lady. My dad looked too big and too fat and too rough for such a room, but he told Billy it was lovely and he was very grateful.

'Now I thought we'd put little Flossie in young Billy's room,' said Old Billy.

It was the only room in the house that wasn't stuck in a 1930s timewarp. It was a strange boy mixture. There were old footballer posters on the walls and rock music tapes piled up like building blocks, and an elderly Paddington Bear stood in a corner in his duffel coat and wellingtons. Oddly, right in the middle of the carpet, there was a doll's house. It was a 1930s doll's house – *two* houses: two semi-detached homes making one whole house with a sloping red-tiled roof, black and white panelling and two front doors.

I squatted down beside it, still hanging onto Lucky, but I was so distracted that she squeezed herself out of one end of the duvet and stood alert, her back arched, her tail outstretched, not sure where she was off to now she was free at last.

'Look at the doll's house, Dad!' I said.

There was a hook at one end so I edged it open and the front of the house swung forward. It was fully furnished inside, with little carved wooden replicas of sofas and chairs, tables, baths and beds. One half house had small green cushions on the chairs and little crochet mats as small as a penny piece.

'It's *your* house, Mr Chip! Yours and the matching one next door!' I exclaimed. 'Where did you *get* it?'

'I made it myself, love,' said Billy. 'It was rather a daft notion. I'd always whittled away at the potatoes in odd moments, carving out a face here, a monkey there, a clown – whatever took my fancy. I'd fry them for the customers just for a laugh, but then when our Billy was on the way I fancied making something more permanent. I took it into my head that he'd be a girl, so I started in on a doll's house. Daft idea, really. I mean, it's not the sort of thing modern kiddies want to play with anyway.'

'*I* would, Mr Chip,' I said.

'Then you play with it all you want while you're here, sweetheart,' said Billy.

'Are you sure, Billy? It's a totally awesome work of art,' said Dad, kneeling in front of it. 'Floss is a

257

very careful girl but I'm not sure she should be allowed to touch it.'

'No, no, it's *meant* to be played with. I'd always hoped for a little girl but we only had our Billy—Will. I wondered if *he'd* have a daughter, but Will's not what you'd call the marrying kind, so if little Floss here would like it, then the house is hers.'

'Oh Mr Chip! I couldn't possibly keep it,' I said – though I wanted it desperately.

'Yes, you have it, darling. I promised you a birthday present and here it is. You can carry on furnishing it if you fancy doing so. I made a few bits and bobs and my Marian did the mats, but we felt a bit daft, like, when there was no one to play with them. It's yours, Floss.'

'Thank you, thank you, thank you!' I said, and I reached up and gave him a big hug round his wrinkled tortoise neck.

'You've got to stop doing us all these favours, Billy,' said Dad. 'You've been so good to us.'

'You're the ones being good to me, watching over the house and cats while I gallivant off.' Billy paused. 'I'm not really sure I know what I'm doing, going all the way to Australia. Maybe my lad doesn't want me visiting. We didn't always see eye to eye when he lived here. We didn't part on the best of terms.'

'He'll be thrilled to see you, Billy. Lads row with

their dads and leave home to make their own way in life. It's only human nature. But he's a man now and he'll be thrilled at this chance of seeing you.'

'Do you really think so?' said Billy, still sounding doubtful.

'Mr Chip, if I hadn't seen my dad for years and years I'd be jumping right over the moon,' I said.

'If you could jump that far you could propel yourself and save on the air fare,' said Billy, ruffling my curls.

I don't like it when people do that. It even annoys me when *Dad* does it. But I stood my ground and smiled politely. Mr Chip said I was a sweet kid and Dad was lucky to have me, and he went all watery eyed. Dad said he knew that, and he had to dab his own eyes with a hanky. I fidgeted from foot to foot, feeling foolish.

Billy insisted on cooking us Sunday dinner.

'I've got a roast chicken in the oven, and roast potatoes. I'm not cooking you chips, because you're the bee's knees when it comes to chips and there's no point competing,' said Billy.

'Chip Master of the Universe,' said Dad, beating his plump tummy and flexing his muscles.

Mr Chip's cats had their own lunch out in the kitchen. I got Lucky's special bowl and sprinkled a few dried biscuit balls in it. Whisky and Soda looked up from their own mashed fish bits and eyed

Lucky's bowl. Whisky ambled over to it. Soda followed. They licked their lips and mewed greedily.

Lucky barely came up to their furry shoulders. It looked as if one swot of a Whisky or Soda paw would send her flying.

I needn't have worried. Lucky had lived on the streets. She knew how to defend her territory. She gave a ferocious *'Mew!'*, darted forward, wriggling right under their noses, and buried her head in her bowl. She flicked her delicate tail in Whisky and Soda's surprised faces. They slunk back to their own bowls, trying to look nonchalant.

When they'd all nibbled lunch, first Whisky, then Soda squeezed out of the cat flap for a saunter round the garden. Lucky experimented, poking her little head after them curiously. She gathered courage, nudged hard and then hurtled out into the garden.

I ran to the window and watched her peer around in astonishment, like Alice newly arrived in Wonderland. She circled the centre flowerbed, trying to stalk a sparrow, but it flew away mockingly whenever she made a move.

'Is Lucky settling in, Floss?' said Dad, coming over to the window.

'I think so.'

'What about you, darling?'

'I think I am too, Dad,' I said, though I wasn't really sure.

I didn't *want* to live in Billy's house, although it was mean even to think it as he was being so generous and hospitable. It was so strange and old-fashioned and it smelled musty, like the clothes in charity shops. I hoped *I* wouldn't smell musty as well as chippy. Rhiannon and Margot and Judy went round holding their noses whenever they stood near me as it was.

It seemed so weird that only a month ago I'd taken it for granted that I just had an ordinary washing powder/clean clothes/shampoo smell just like everyone else. I had a mum and my own special bedroom in our pretty house. Even Rhiannon had remarked on my cherry-patterned duvet and my matching curtains. Now I didn't have *anything* ultra-clean or pretty or matching.

I knew I was being dreadful feeling sorry for myself when Dad was trying so hard and Mr Chip had been so kind giving me the beautiful doll's house – but I still couldn't stop two tears spurting down my face.

I bent my head quickly but I think Dad saw. He squeezed my shoulders tightly.

'We'll be fine, little Floss.' He lowered his voice. 'This is just a temporary measure, sweetheart. We'll find somewhere lovely just for us soon, you'll see. You never know your luck. Something will bob up out of the blue.'

I tried to imagine a beautiful home emerging out of nowhere: a coral palace out of the blue sea; a cloud castle out of the blue sky; a Swiss chalet out of a big blue mountain. I blinked and swallowed hard to stop the rest of my tears.

They seemed to stay in my throat. I couldn't swallow Billy's roast chicken dinner. He'd tried so hard to make it a lovely meal for us, but the chicken was still slimy under its skin and the roast potatoes were speckled with little black bits of grit from the oven and the cabbage looked and smelled like old stewed leaves.

I chewed and chewed and chewed. I felt myself getting red in the face.

'Is the roast OK?' Billy asked anxiously.

'It's just smashing, Billy,' said Dad.

I felt him nudging me under the table. He was passing me his big hanky. Then he started chatting to Billy about his chip van and where he stored it and the times he opened and shut of an evening – while I turned my head and discreetly spat most of my meal into the hanky, pretending to wipe round my mouth.

When Dad got up to clear the table he managed to dump the hanky quickly at the bottom of Billy's rubbish bin. I looked up at him gratefully and he wriggled his eyebrows at me.

'How about going out to play in the back garden,

Floss?' said Dad. 'See if you can spot a good tree for your swing.'

I went out of the kitchen door and walked up and down the stretch of grass at the back. There was going to be a big problem. Billy had a flowerbed on either side – although they looked more like weed beds now – but he didn't have any trees at all. He had a few shrubs and bushes but they would have barely supported a toy swing, let alone a real one.

Dad looked up eagerly when I trailed back. Then he saw the expression on my face. His own face sagged.

'It's OK, Dad. I think I'm maybe too old for swinging now anyway,' I said quickly.

We spent the afternoon watching television, although none of us were really concentrating on it. Billy kept checking his passport and his flight ticket and his Australian dollars. Dad kept looking around, yawning and sighing and stretching his arms in the air. He suggested I go and unpack my stuff, but I did that in five minutes.

I knelt down and looked at the doll's house. It was difficult to know how to play with it when it didn't have any people. I tried cramming Ellarina and Dimble into a room, but their heads hit the ceiling and their legs sprawled in every corner, so they looked like a battery elephant and dog in a very small cage.

I needed to make some proper tiny people. I had a pack of plasticine that Steve's mum had given me for a birthday present. I took it and started modelling. I made me first, rolling the yellow strip into lots of bobbles for my curls. I put me in the right-hand half of the house. I made Dad, and then a little Lucky. I had to make her purple as they don't make black plasticine. I made a Susan too, come to visit us, staying overnight in my bed on a special sleepover.

Then I made a Mum. I tried very hard to make the plasticine Mum very slim and stylish, using the bright pink for her dress. I got a bit sniffly creating her and had to stop to have a good blow of my nose with toilet paper. It hurt, because Billy had the weirdest crackly stuff in his bathroom that totally sandpapered your skin.

Then I did a Steve with a pink bullet head and huge muscles on his arms and a tiny Tiger crawling on all fours. I put them in the left-hand house. I made a thin plasticine door on either side of both adjoining living rooms so that the me-doll could run between houses whenever she wanted.

Then I sat back and sighed.

'Are you OK, Flossie?' Dad called up the stairs.

'Yes, I'm fine, Dad,' I said quickly.

'Are you all set to take Billy to the airport?'

'Course I am,' I said.

I picked up the pink plasticine Mum and gave her

a big kiss, stroking her very carefully because I didn't want her head or her arms or her legs to fall off.

'I love you, Mum,' I whispered. I thought about that airline ticket. In just one day and night I could be with her. I'd stay in a lovely apartment and live in a sunny, glamorous city and everyone I knew would envy me like crazy and no one would ever sneer at me or tease me or pity me.

'Floss?' Dad called.

I picked up the plasticine Dad and tickled his tummy with my fingernail and made him chuckle and jump about.

'I love you, Dad,' I whispered. 'Don't worry. I'm going to stay with you, no matter what.' I paused. 'You never know your luck. Something *might* bob up out of the blue.'

Dad and I took Billy to Heathrow. We packed the van and helped him negotiate his way to the check-in desk, and then we went with him as far as the Departures gate. Billy looked so old and frail that Dad asked if we could possibly walk him through to the other side of the airport, but they wouldn't let us.

'Oh well, I'm sure you'll be fine, Billy, my boy. Just find the prettiest young lady hostess, hook your arm in hers and get her to help you on your way,' said Dad.

'You're the guy who should be hooking up with someone young and pretty,' said Billy. 'Oh dear, my tummy's all butterflies! Wish me a safe flight, Flossie. You're the wee girly who brings me luck.'

'You'll be safe as safe, and have a lovely time, Mr Chip,' I said.

'Hmm. I don't know about that. If the good Lord had meant us to fly he'd have given us wings,' said Billy. 'I've lived well over three quarters of a century without venturing more than six feet in the air, and now I'm embarking on a journey that will take me six *miles* up in the sky. Keep your fingers crossed for the next twenty-four hours that I don't suddenly plummet downwards.'

'We'll keep our fingers and our toes crossed, mate,' said Dad, and he gave Billy a big hug.

I had to give him a hug too, and kiss his white whiskery cheek. Then he toddled off, trying to wave jauntily, though he was terribly tottery on his old bowed legs.

'I hope to God he makes it OK,' said Dad. 'Tell you what, Floss, if you were travelling with him it would be you looking after old Billy, bless him, not him looking after you.'

'But I'm not travelling, Dad.'

'I know you're not, darling. Remember though, we've got your ticket safe and sound.'

'You might as well tear it up, Dad. I'm not going to use it,' I said, taking his hand.

On the drive back from Heathrow Dad suddenly yelled out and pointed. There was a big field far off, all lit up. There were big wheels and roundabouts way in the distance.

'It's the fair!' said Dad.

'Oh wow! Let's go! Oh Dad, *please* can we?'

'Of course, little darling! We'll find your roundabout and you can have another ride on Pearl.'

'And we'll find the candyfloss stall and see Rose!'

'Well, that would be great,' said Dad, turning right off the main road, towards the fair.

We parked the car and then ran hand in hand, both of us skipping and dancing and whooping – but when we got to the field it suddenly looked all wrong. The vans were lined up strangely, the rides were all different, the roundabout had many brightly painted horses with long manes and tails but none of them were pink, and none of them were called Pearl.

We looked for the candyfloss stall. We found three different ones, but none of them had a big pink teddy bear tied up outside. None of them were Rose's. We were at the *wrong* fair.

We wandered around a little, but it was no use. It wasn't the same at all. We'd lost the heart for it. We just wanted to go home . . . though it was the *wrong* home too.

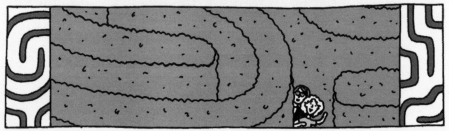

19

'What are we going to do with you while I'm working in Billy's chip van every evening?' said Dad. 'I suppose I should get a babysitter.'

'Come off it, Dad,' I said. 'I'm not a *baby*.'

'I could maybe ask Miss Davis . . .'

'*Dad!* She'd cluck her teeth at me and feed me birdseed sandwiches!'

'There's Old Ron. He's a weird old chap but he's harmless and he thinks the world of you, Floss.'

'I don't want Old Ron looking after me. He can't look after himself.'

'I suppose I could ask if you could stay at Susan's once or twice.'

'I'd like that!'

'But I can't ask them to have you *every* night.' Dad paused. 'Rhiannon's mum was on at me the other day outside the school—'

'I am not not not going to Rhiannon's, Dad.'

'OK.' Dad sighed. 'Well, what *are* we going to do with you, sugarlump?'

'We don't have to do anything. I'll stay here at Billy's.'

'I can't leave you all on your own, pet.'

'Of course you can. I'll be fine. I'll read and I'll watch Billy's telly and I'll sew clothes, and then when I get tired I'll go to bed. Simple!'

'But what if someone came to the door?'

'I won't answer it. I'm not daft, Dad.'

'I'm sure it's against the law leaving a kid your age on her own,' Dad said anxiously.

'Who's going to know? Only us,' I said. 'Dad, *please* don't worry about me. I'll be fine fine fine.'

I just about had him convinced. I thought I had myself convinced too. But when it was time for Dad to go out on Monday night I wasn't so sure.

'I'll be fine,' I kept saying.

'Yes, of course you'll be fine,' Dad kept repeating, giving me a last kiss, a last cuddle, a last ruffle of the curls.

Then he went out to work. The front door shut behind him. And I started to feel scared.

I was watching a film on television and it was meant to be funny but there were two creepy men chasing after this little kid so I had to switch it off quick. I sat in the sudden silence, ears straining, listening out for creepy men breaking into the house, coming to get me.

Billy's parents frowned out of their wedding photo at me, not liking a stranger sitting cross-legged on their faded old carpet. The house was still filled with their things. Maybe they were still here too, hiding in a dusty cupboard, whispering to each other. When it got dark they'd drift out into the room, silent on their see-through ghost feet . . .

I desperately wanted to cuddle Lucky for comfort, but she'd gone upstairs to loll on her duvet and I couldn't face those creaky stairs by myself. I tried calling her, but the thin sound of my own voice was so strange in the silent house that I clapped my hands over my mouth.

Then I heard it! The gate creaking. Someone walking up the garden path.

I sat rigid on the old sofa, waiting. I heard them outside the door. They didn't knock. There were scrambling sounds. Then I heard the door *opening*.

They were coming right in.

They were coming down the hall ready to *get* me . . .

'Floss? Flossie, love?'

'Oh Dad!' I said. I gave a shaky cartoon laugh: *Ha ha ha.* 'Hey, what are you doing back home?'

'I know it's daft, I know you're perfectly fine here by yourself.'

'Yes, Dad.'

'But I couldn't stand it. I kept imagining stuff. I know it's mad, pet, but would you mind coming in the chip van with me?'

'OK, Dad. I *am* fine here, but if it'll put your mind at rest then I'll come too. Let's go,' I said, scooting off the sofa and hanging onto his arm.

We started up a whole new routine. Every evening I set off with Dad in our van. We'd go to the big garage behind the station, hook the chip van up and tow it onto the station forecourt. Then Dad would start the generator and get the fryer heated up while I squashed up in a cramped but cosy nest in the corner of the van, out of sight of the customers. I had two cushions and Dad's old denim jacket to snuggle up in. I didn't need to wear any kind of coat. It was boiling hot in the van from the fryer, with its sizzling fat.

I did my homework first, except when it was maths, which I needed to do before school with Susan. Then I read for a bit. I started reading all these old Victorian Sunday school books from Billy's house. They were told in a strange old-fashioned way, but the stories were really good once you got into them. They were all about poor ragged children begging on the streets of London. They often had cruel drunken stepfathers and sickly little baby brothers and sisters. They sometimes coughed a lot and then said they saw angels and then they died. I read some of the best bits to Dad in between customers.

'Aren't these stories a bit morbid for you, Floss?' said Dad. 'They certainly give me the willies!'

'I *like* them, Dad,' I said.

When people started coming out of pubs it got too busy and noisy to concentrate on my books so I made things instead. I made a friendship bracelet for Susan. *Several* friendship bracelets. I made a Scoubidou keyring for Dad. I fashioned slightly wonky denim jackets for Ellarina and Dimble. I made a little blue denim mouse with a string tail for Lucky.

I tried taking Lucky to the van with us one day, but it was much too hot and cramped for her and she hated it. She seemed much happier left at home. She couldn't care less about creepy men and sad old ghosts.

Dad would give me a little paper plate of chips every now and then, or a can of Coke, but I couldn't drink too much because there was nowhere I could go to the loo. After a while I'd start to get achy and my eyes would itch, so I'd put my sewing stuff away and plump up my cushions and rub my cheek against Dad's old jacket and go to sleep. Then at midnight Dad would tow the chip van back to the garage, lift me up into our van and drive us home. I'd tumble into bed half asleep, one arm out of the covers so I could still reach down and stroke Lucky.

Dad still worried about me being in the van. 'Your mum would go mad if she knew I was keeping you up till all hours,' he said. 'It's not suitable, I know. Especially when all the lads start coming out the pubs and get a bit mouthy. The language! I think we'll have to put earmuffs on you, little Floss.'

I had learned a few amazingly awful phrases, which came in useful when Rhiannon and Margot and Judy were teasing me. They held their noses all the time when I came near. I knew I did smell chippier than ever, but I pretended not to care.

I did try very hard the next Saturday when I went to spend the day with Susan. I got up early and had a bath, although the peeling enamel scratched my bottom. I shampooed my hair as best I could and then tried to brush out all the tangles. My curls had grown a lot. They stuck up all round my head in a mad fuzz.

I wore my birthday jeans and top and I cleaned my trainers. Dad made a big effort too. He put on his blue shirt and his best jeans even though he was just going to loaf around at home for most of the day.

He drove me to Susan's house. I was worried that it was going to be a huge great mansion with beautiful polished furniture and very pale sofas and carpets, and I'd have to sit on the very edge of my seat and not eat or drink anything slurpy in case I spilled it. It was a relief to see that it was an ordinary red-brick Victorian villa.

When I got inside I saw it was gloriously untidy, with shoes all over the hall and papers and files stacked high by the phone and books *everywhere* – not just on the bookshelves but in higgledy-piggledy piles all over the carpet and climbing up the stairs and stacked halfway up each windowsill. There were books in the lavatory, books in the bathroom and books all over the kitchen, stuffed in between the saucepans and the spice jars.

The kitchen seemed to be the main Potts living room. There was a television on the dresser and fat velvet cushions scattered over the benches on either side of the long table. The actual living room was turned into a huge library study, with Mrs Potts and her computer and desk and filing cabinet one end and Mr Potts and *his* computer and desk and filing cabinet the other.

They had the big bedroom upstairs. Susan had a very little bedroom with a pine bed and a patchwork quilt and a special shelf for her elephants and giraffe and crocodiles and rabbits. The middle-sized bedroom was *Susan's* study. She had her own computer and desk and filing cabinet, and masses of books on shelves and drawings and posters and maps Blu-tacked all over the walls.

'It's so *lovely*, Susan,' I said, tiptoeing around, peering at a book here, a picture there. 'You've got so many *things*!'

'I wondered . . . would you like to make another book world like we did in the library at school?' Susan asked.

'Ooh yes,' I said.

I watched as Susan eagerly started getting books down from shelves and tipping out a stack of wooden building bricks all over the wooden floor with a great clatter.

'Won't your mum mind us making such a mess?' I asked.

'She doesn't mind a bit if we're being creative,' said Susan.

'Creative?'

'You know, making things up and being artistic.'

'I can do that,' I said.

So we were happily creative most of the morning, building a land for all Susan's animals. We made a book mountain and had the elephants plodding up it tail to trunk, led by a little Roman toy soldier that Susan called Hannibal. We made a river out of blue and green books, edged with potted ferns and ivy from the kitchen windowsill. The two crocodiles lurked in the river, jaws ready to start snapping. We made Hannibal have a paddle and then run away screaming. The giraffe came to have a drink and had a tasty fern sandwich garnished with ivy salad. The pink and blue rabbits had a frolic too, and we sat the giant green one on top of the mountain as a monument.

'We could really do with some more people,' I said. 'Do you have any plasticine?'

'No, but I've got modelling clay. Will that do?' said Susan.

It did wondrously. We made a little Roman army for Hannibal to command, and some pilgrim worshippers to kneel at the paws of the Giant Green Rabbit. We made twin giraffe babies for the big giraffe, and lots of tiny baby rabbits for Mrs Pink and Mr Blue Bunny. We made half a person screaming in the river, with a severed leg in each crocodile's jaw.

We had great fun acting it all out, but I was still a bit worried about the mess, especially as we'd accidentally smeared modelling clay all over the floorboards. However, when Susan's mum came to see what we were up to she was so pleased by our bookland that she actually took photos of it. She took photos of us two with our arms round each other and promised I could have copies of all of them.

Then we went in the kitchen with Susan's mum to watch her prepare lunch.

'Though I know I'm not as good a cook as your father, Floss,' said Mrs Potts. 'Susan adores his chip sandwiches.'

'*Butties*, Mum,' said Susan.

'My dad's butties are famous,' I said. I started talking about the café without thinking – and then suddenly shut up. It was so awful to think that it didn't exist any more. It had been my home ever since I was born.

They hadn't just closed it down. When Dad drove me past on the way to school we saw someone had taken down the HARLIE'S CAFÉ sign. There were workmen in there stripping out the kitchen, tearing everything down. I felt as if they were tearing up all my happy memories too. I didn't say anything and neither did Dad, but the next day he drove to school all round the outskirts of town so we didn't have to go past.

Susan's mum saw I looked a little bit sad. 'How about you two doing a bit of cooking too? Have you ever done any baking, Floss?'

'I've made toffee and cornflake crispies and

chocolate biscuit cake with Mum,' I said. My voice wobbled when I said her name. I think I must have looked even sadder, because Mrs Potts put her arm round me.

'I wonder if you've ever made bread,' she said.

This was a wonderful idea. It was fascinating creaming the yeast, with Mrs Potts explaining exactly how it worked. Susan helped me measure out the flour accurately. The best bit was the kneading part. I got dough right up to my elbows so it looked as if I was wearing thick white gloves.

I made one loaf and Susan made another. They started to smell utterly delicious as they were baking in the oven, and when at last it was time to take them out they looked wonderful – golden brown with a lovely crust. One had risen just a little higher out of the baking tin and was just a little bit more glossy and golden. Susan and Mrs Potts said it was *my* loaf. I rather think it was too.

'You've obviously got a real knack as a baker, Floss,' said Mrs Potts. 'Next time you come you can try making rolls.'

'If only we still had the café then I could make newly baked rolls for Dad's chips and we could be a brilliant chip butty partnership,' I said.

It wouldn't work for the chip van. There wasn't space to do anything properly. Dad's chips weren't quite the same anyway. He used the same type of potatoes, the same cooking fat, but Billy's fryer was old and unpredictable. Sometimes the chips burned to a frazzle, sometimes they swam limply like white fish in a fatty sea, taking an age to crisp up.

Dad did his best but he couldn't serve his chips with pride. He didn't care for the burgers and sausages he served up either. He didn't have any complaints though. The big lads pouring out of the pubs just wanted something hot and savoury to stuff down their throats. They covered everything in blood-red tomato sauce or bright yellow mustard anyway.

'Dad says his chip butties aren't up to scratch any more,' I said sadly.

'Well, I shall always remember mine as the most sublime culinary experience ever,' said Susan.

I didn't understand every word she said, but I knew what she meant and smiled at her gratefully.

We had our home-made bread at lunch time, with cheese and tomatoes and salad, and then Greek yoghurt and honey for pudding. Susan's mum told us all about proteins and carbohydrates and vitamins, and Susan's dad told us all about Greece and how bees make honey.

I tried hard to ask intelligent questions like

Susan and ended up giving myself hiccups. Susan's mum told me exactly what little thingy inside me had gone into a spasm and why. Susan's dad told us about some wretched man in Scotland who hiccuped for two solid years. I started to worry I might be an even more wretched girl in England, fated to hiccup her way through life for ever – but Susan suddenly leaned forward across the table and shouted, '*BOO!*'

I jumped.

'I bet you can't hiccup any more now!' Susan said – and she was *right*.

We'd have been very happy to play back in Susan's study all afternoon, but Mr and Mrs Potts felt we should go on an outing. They drove us to Hampton Court Palace because Henry the Eighth had once lived there and Susan and I were doing the Tudors in history.

Henry the Eighth had had six wives. Susan's dad told us the names and what happened to them all. Henry divorced his first wife Catherine. My dad divorced my mum. I imagined what it would be like if he got through five more wives.

There were actors dressed up as Elizabethans inside Hampton Court. They gave a talk and then you could ask them questions. Susan asked all sorts of interesting things about beheadings and religion and music. Mr and Mrs Potts pretended not to notice but I could see they were bursting with pride.

'You can ask a question too, Floss,' Mrs Potts whispered.

I couldn't think of anything intelligent to ask whatsoever.

'Go on, dear, don't be shy,' said Mr Potts.

I ended up asking the lady how she got her sticky-out skirt to stay all puffed up.

'It's called a farthingale, Floss,' Mr Potts hissed.

I think he was scared they thought I might be his daughter too. The lady didn't seem to think it too silly a question. She held up her skirts so I could see the weird hooped petticoats underneath.

We went all over the palace and Mr and Mrs Potts told us heaps of stuff about the Tudors. Susan was obviously fascinated, but I started having terrible yawning fits because it got soooo boring. I tried to keep my mouth shut when I yawned but my eyes watered. Perhaps Mrs Potts thought I was crying. She put her arm round me.

'I know what Flossie would like to see – the Tudor kitchen!' she said. 'Let's go there next.'

The kitchen *was* quite interesting, but I so wished Susan and I could have just dawdled round there by ourselves.

The very *best* bit of the Hampton Court trip was going to the maze. Susan's dad had told us this story about some monster called the Minotaur, so we pretended we were running away from this Minotaur. We ran screaming round and round the paths between the high hedges, and every time we came to a dead end and had to turn on our tracks we'd yell, *'The Minotaur! The Minotaur!'* We played we were diving between his cloven hooves or jumping high over his scaly back.

Mr Potts said we'd got the legend wrong and started to tell it to us all over again, but Mrs Potts laughed and told him to lighten up.

'The girls are just having a bit of fun,' she said, giving Susan's hand a squeeze.

'We're having lots and lots and lots of fun,' Susan shouted, her cheeks pink, her eyes shining behind her little glasses.

Mr Potts smiled at her and held her other hand. Susan jumped up and down between her mum and her dad. The back of my throat went tight. My whole head started throbbing. I'd have given anything in the whole world to hang onto *my* mum and dad's hands and for us to be a family all together.

Then Susan let go of her parents and took my hand. We ran off again, and suddenly without even trying we reached the clearing in the middle of the maze, so we danced round and round in celebration.

20

Mum phoned on Sunday morning. She wanted to know so many worrying details about the café and what was happening. I didn't know what to say. I started telling her all about Susan instead, and wonderfully she got side-tracked for a while. Then she started telling me about this outing they'd had to a special fish restaurant on the waterfront.

'I bet the chips weren't as good as Dad's chips,' I said.

'They didn't serve anything as common as chips there, Floss. This is an extremely upmarket place,' said Mum. 'But talking of chips, there was an old man at the next table who was the spitting image of that weird old man who haunts your dad's café. You know, the one who had that awful chip van. Your dad calls him Billy the Chip. It couldn't possibly have really been him, not in an ultra-stylish restaurant the other side of the world – and yet he was looking at me as if he recognized me too.'

'Gosh, Mum, how strange,' I said. 'Look, I'd better go now, I'll be late for school.'

'Floss, it's Sunday.'

'What? Oh yes. Well, my new friend Susan's coming round soon, so I must get ready. Love you. Bye, Mum,' I gabbled, and then I slammed the phone down.

'Mum saw *Billy*!' I said to Dad.

'Oh God. He didn't tell her about the café closing, did he? Oh Floss, I feel so bad putting you in this position. Maybe we should tell your mum the truth. But then she'd go spare.' Dad put his head in his hands. 'She'll go double-spare-with-knobs-on when she gets back and finds out we've been camping at Billy's. If we're still here.'

'Don't, Dad. We'll sort Mum out,' I said quickly. 'Let's have a happy Sunday. Can we go for a drive in the van?'

'Certainly, beloved daughter. We'll have a happy happy happy Sunday,' said Dad.

We drove round in the van for ages. Dad had made enough out of Billy's chip van to buy a full tank of petrol. We drove right out into the country and then round and round every little town and village. We always slowed down going past any posters and big fields and parks and recreation grounds. We didn't once say the word *fair* to each other but we both knew what we were looking for.

We didn't have any luck.

We came home feeling a bit frazzled. Of course it *wasn't* home. Still, Dad did his best. He'd bought a packet of crumpets and we stuck them on big forks and toasted them in front of Billy's old electric fire in the living room. Lucky and Whisky and Soda came and basked in the heat on the rug. Lucky lay in between Whisky and Soda. They took turns nuzzling and petting her, tying to outdo each other as foster mums. Lucky smiled to herself, happy to be the centre of attention.

All three cats eventually narrowed their eyes, lowered their heads and started napping. I was tired too, but I had to go off to the chip van with Dad. I washed my buttery-crumpet hands carefully because I wanted to make some more clothes for Ellarina and Dimble. I filled a carrier bag with material scraps and some tissues and toothpicks and some cut-up socks for stuffing. I fancied making them proper Tudor outfits, complete with petticoats and pleated ruffs. I didn't have the first idea how to go about this but I hoped inspiration would strike once I got cracking.

Dad and I set off to the station. Dad manoeuvred the chip van out onto the forecourt and got everything set up. The chip fryer was being particularly temperamental, over-heating one minute and switching itself off the next. Dad fiddled and swore at it, despairing.

'How am I supposed to cook anything halfway decent on this ropy old contraption?' he said. 'Oh Flossie, Charlie's Café was hardly the Ritz but at least I could cook *properly* back at home. Try as I might I can only manage rubbish food here.'

For a long time it didn't look as if anyone wanted any food, rubbish or otherwise. We'd been busy on Saturday night and Dad had whistled as he fried, happy that he was keeping Billy's business going and making a bit of cash for us.

But this Sunday we weren't making any cash at all. Dad sighed and fidgeted and shook the surly fryer. Then he came and squatted down beside me, his knees uncomfortably under his chin because he was so big and there was very little space.

'What's that you're doing, sweetheart?' he asked, watching me gluing bits of white tissue to the toothpicks.

'I'm trying to make one of those sticky-out hoop petticoat thingies to go under an Elizabethan gown for my woolly elephant,' I said.

Dad blinked. 'Ask a silly question,' he said. He reached out and ruffled my curls. 'You're a funny kid, Floss. Thank God you're so adaptable. Well, I'll keep the blooming fryer bubbling for another half-hour or so and then we might well call it a day. The town's dead, obviously.'

Almost as soon as Dad said that a couple fetched up at the van and started tapping their money on the counter for attention – then another couple, a little gang of girls, a rowdy mob of boys . . .

'So where have you guys all suddenly sprung from?' said Dad, heaving masses of chips into the fryer.

'There's been a green fair down by the river,' said one of the girls. 'We've been listening to the bands.'

'Oh Dad, the fair!' I said, leaping up.

'It won't be our fair, pet. Green fairs are different,' said Dad. 'You cuddle down on your cushion and try to go to sleep. It looks like it's going to be a long and busy night after all. We're not going to get home till late.'

I tried to finish Ellarina's petticoat first but it totally defeated me. I ended up with little pricks all over my fingers and bits of tissue stuck everywhere. I gave up and had a go at making those baggy knicker things that Elizabethan men wore, but it was difficult fashioning them to fit a saggy woollen dog so I stopped trying. Maybe Susan would have to be chief dressmaker in our games.

I curled up in a ball, closed my tired itchy eyes and tried to go to sleep. But it wasn't easy. It got noisier and noisier as more and more people came to the chip van on their way home from the fair.

I started dreaming a silly dream about wandering round Hampton Court with Ellarina and Dimble dressed as Tudor courtiers. I'd somehow turned into one of Henry the Eighth's six wives, only he decided he didn't like me any more and he started shouting at me. I ran away because I knew what happened to the wives who were out of favour. Then all his soldiers started pursuing me and they were all shouting too. I woke up with a start, still shaking.

I told myself that it was only a dream, that I was safe in the chip van with Dad – but I could still hear the shouting. I heard Dad shouting too. I struggled up out of my corner.

'Dad? Dad, what's happening? Are you all right?'

'Get back down, darling. It's OK. It's just some silly lads getting impatient. Pipe *down*, you guys, I'm frying as fast as I can. This isn't McDonald's – there's just me, so you'll have to *wait*.'

'Stupid idiots,' said this tall guy, who was waiting patiently, his arm round his girlfriend. 'Don't take any notice of that lot, mate. You're doing a grand job.'

I blinked, then rubbed the sleep out of my eyes. The tall guy was somehow familiar. He had long fairish hair down to his shoulders, a black vest, black jeans, a studded jacket – and large silver biker jewellery on almost every finger.

'It's Saul!' I said, bobbing up behind Dad.

'Get down, Floss! It's who?'

'Saul!'

Saul saw me and grinned. 'Yeah, I'm Saul. How did you know my name?'

'Is she an old girlfriend, Saul?' said his girl, grinning.

'Saul rescued us at the fair, Dad. *Our* fair. He's Rose's son.'

'Oh, great!' said Dad. 'Well, smashing to meet up with you again, Saul. Is the fair in our town again?'

'No, no. I'm not actually *with* the fair at the moment. I've moved in with Jenny here,' said Saul, giving her a squeeze.

'Stop the chitchat, Chip Man, and get serving!' some stupid guy yelled. His mates started chanting stuff too.

'Yobbos,' said Dad contemptuously, taking no notice of them. 'Well, I bet your mum misses you, Saul.'

'Yeah, she wasn't too pleased, but she's a tough lady, my ma, she'll cope.'

'She's a lovely lady,' said Dad, serving up a mega-huge portion of chips to Saul and Jenny. 'Here you are, have these on the house.'

'Thanks, mate, that's good of you. Fancy you working here in this chip van!'

'It's just a temporary measure. Not quite sure what the future holds. Maybe I should go and see your mum and ask her to tell my fortune,' said Dad.

'Here, Chip Man, get serving us, you useless git!' an ugly guy behind shouted.

'Keep your mouth buttoned, mate, until you learn some manners,' said Saul.

'Yeah, so who's going to make me?'

'I might,' said Saul, clenching his ringed fingers so they were bunched in a threatening fist.

'Don't come the heavy with *me*, mate! Who do you think you are, with your girly hair and your jewellery? You're asking to be sorted out good and proper!'

The ugly guy surged forward, all his gang following.

'Now cut it out, lads. Any trouble and I'm into that station and phoning the police,' said Dad.

No one was listening. They were pushing and shoving, shouting and swearing. Then the ugly guy punched Saul on the chin. Saul whacked him one straight back with his ringed fist. The ugly guy staggered, bleeding. He fumbled for something. Then I saw a sudden frightening gleam.

'He's got a knife!' I screamed.

'Oh God,' said Dad. 'Watch out, Saul! Look, you stay right here where it's safe, Floss, out of sight. Promise?'

Dad squeezed my shoulder and then went rushing out of the door at the back.

'Dad! Oh Dad, come back! Don't get hurt!'

I couldn't stay in my corner. I had to peer over the counter to see what was happening. There were people fighting everywhere. Some lads were kicking. Someone was head-butting. I couldn't even see Saul and the ugly guy now. And where was Dad? I prayed he wouldn't get into the fight himself. What if was hit or kicked? What if he was *knifed*?

I eyed the door, wondering if I dared go after him to drag him back. But I'd promised Dad to stay in the van.

It wasn't safe any more though. There were boys banging on it now, so that it rattled and shook. There were thumps and shoves. I cowered right up in the corner again, clutching Dimble and Ellarina.

More fists, more boots. The van juddered and rocked and tilted.

'Let's turn it right over!' someone shouted.

'Dad!' I yelled.

They all kicked together and the van lurched sideways. The chips sizzled furiously and fat poured out over the fryer. Then suddenly there was an enormous *whoomph!* and flames leaped high in the air.

'Dad! Dad! Dad!' I screamed.

I scrabbled for something to throw on the flames but it was too late. They were roaring right up to the ceiling, terrifyingly orange, while filthy smoke swirled all round the van, making me cough.

'Dad!' I croaked. The flames and fat were making such a noise no one would ever hear me.

I had to get out! I couldn't even see the door now. I was in a boiling burning whirl of black smoke and orange flame. My eyes smarted and stung. I couldn't breathe. I pressed my woolly toys over my nose and mouth and crouched down, crawling blindly across the floor.

'DAD!' I cried one last time.

Then the door burst open, making the fire roar and spread. There were arms fighting through the flames. Two hands grabbed me and hauled. I was out of the van, still screaming and sobbing, but safe in Dad's arms.

21

We had to go to hospital. I was completely fine but they needed to check that I hadn't inhaled too much smoke. Dad had burns on his hands where he'd fought his way forward to grab me. They were both bandaged up so that it looked as if he was wearing white boxing gloves. Dad was very brave and didn't even flinch when the nurse rubbed ointment on, but I started crying.

'Hey, hey, Floss, no tears, sweetheart, I'm fine. Look, I'm being wound up like an ancient Egyptian. Only I'm not a mummy, I'm a daddy!'

It wasn't really funny but I sniffled a little, and the nurse laughed out loud.

'Don't worry, dear, your dad's going to be as right as rain. He'll have to keep his bandages on for a bit but he should heal up nicely. It'll be a good excuse for him to sit back and have your mum wait on him for a week or so.'

'Hmm,' I said. I patted Dad's knee. '*I'll* wait

on you, Dad. You saved my life! You're a hero!'

'Rubbish, pet. I didn't do anything,' said Dad.

'Yes, you did, mate,' said Saul, poking his head round the cubicle curtain. His arm was in a sling because one of the guys had tried to knife him. 'You saved me too, grabbing that punk by the wrist so he dropped his knife,' he said.

'I wasn't really thinking straight. I just caught hold of him – and as luck would have it, that's when he dropped the knife,' said Dad.

'No, your little girl's right, you're a hero,' said Jenny, Saul's girlfriend.

Saul had had to take off all his huge silver skull rings and bangles so she was wearing them for him, jangling and clanking every time she moved her arms. She stroked Saul's sore arm tenderly.

'It's only a flesh wound but it could have been far worse,' she said.

Dad and Saul had to give statements to a policeman, though I kept dozing off while they were talking because it was the middle of the night now. I cuddled Dimble and Ellarina, who were a little singed but safe. Every time I went to sleep I heard the ugly raised voices, I felt the thuds, the shaking, I saw the sudden gold-red flare of flame and I started crying. Each time Dad held me in his arms, patting me with his big bandaged hands, soothing me.

'Come on, I've got to get my little girl home,' said Dad – and eventually they let us go.

We had no way of getting back from the hospital and Dad didn't have much cash on him, but Saul and Jenny were waiting and they shared a taxi with us, taking us all the way to Billy the Chip's house for nothing.

'If you'd like to come back tomorrow I'll give you the fare,' said Dad.

'Think nothing of it, mate. Still, I might well come back visiting,' said Saul.

They dropped us off and we staggered up the path to Billy's. I had to feel in Dad's pocket for the key and open the front door for us. Lucky and Whisky and Soda were waiting worriedly in the hall, twining themselves round our ankles like furry feather boas, wondering why we'd been out so late.

'Let's get straight to bed, little Floss,' said Dad. 'It's all right now, baby, we're safe and sound.' But as he said it he suddenly started shaking. 'Oh Floss, I can't believe how stupid I've been, dragging you off to that van night after night. You could have been burned to a crisp and it would have all been my fault.'

'No Dad! It wasn't *your* fault, silly. You rescued me. I'm fine, we're both fine,' I said, putting my arms round Dad and hugging him tight.

Dad cried a little bit while I patted him on the back. Then his nose started running and he couldn't blow it properly with his poor bandaged hands so I had to help him.

'It's like you're my big baby, Dad,' I said.

I had to help him undo all his buttons and shoe laces so he could get ready for bed. When I was in bed myself Dad lay down at the end with his pillow and blanket so that every time I dreamed about the fire and woke up he could soothe me back to sleep.

He said I could stay off school in the morning. We didn't set the alarm but we both woke up very early even so. We had to have a special long cuddle just to make sure we were both all right.

'I'll have to phone poor Billy and tell him what's happened to his van,' said Dad, sighing. 'Goodness knows how he's going to react. That old chip van has been in his family for so many years. I feel so bad. It'll probably break his heart. It seems so cruel to interrupt his holiday and tell him, but I'm worried the police will have to contact him at some stage, so I'd better let him know first.'

I carefully made Dad a cup of tea, and he managed to balance it between his bandages and sip from it. Then he dictated Billy's son's phone number and I dialled it for him.

Dad got through straight away but couldn't get

a word in edgeways at first. Billy the Chip was burbling away on the other end, telling Dad Sydney was wonderful, his son was wonderful, his son's wine bar was wonderful, the weather was wonderful – and Dad had to listen with an agonized expression, trying to wade into this wave after wave of wonder.

'I'm so glad you're enjoying yourself, Billy, mate, but I'm afraid I've got some bad news,' Dad blurted out eventually. 'Last night there was a bit of a ruckus with some yobs. They were trying to tip the van over, and the fat in the fryer caught fire. I'm afraid the van's been burned, Billy. What? No, no, I'm fine, hands got a bit singed, that's all. Thank God Floss is fine too. But I'm not quite sure how we're going to get the van back into action. Have you got proper insurance? Oh thank God, because truthfully, mate, it's a total write-off. But if you can get the insurance sorted when you're back from Oz then I'll help you buy a new van, get the business up and running again – though I'll have to make some kind of arrangement for Floss: I'm not risking her in a van at night now. What's that? Really? You truly mean that, Billy?' Dad listened. He nodded. He shook his head. He blew his breath out, his lower lip jutting.

'Yeah, yeah. Thanks, mate, but you don't have to. No, no, we'll be moving on soon anyway.

301

Definitely. Well, we've no actual concrete plans but something's bound to bob up out of the blue. OK then. You enjoy yourself, pal. Go for it. Bye then.' Dad put the phone down. He rolled his eyes at me.

'He says he wants to stay in Australia and help his son with his bar! It's a boys only bar too – not really Billy's sort of place at all – but he says he's so enjoying being with his son he wants to stick by him. I don't know whether it will work out in the long term but he seems sure that's what he wants. He's intent on giving up his chip van, whatever happens. He says he's thinking of putting this house on the market too, though we can stay in it for the time being.' Dad made to scratch his head and ended up patting it with his bandages. 'Strikes me the world's gone bonkers, Floss. Still, I suppose we should be happy for Billy.' He raised his mug of tea unsteadily. 'Here's to Billy the Chip!'

'Here's to Billy the Chip,' I repeated – and Lucky and Whisky and Soda mewed.

'Hey, Dad, what about his *cats*?'

'Well, he says maybe we can find a good home for them. He's thinking of having some firm pack up some of his stuff and ship it to Australia, but he can hardly do that to old Whisky and Soda. I doubt they'd last the journey.'

'Well, are *we* a good home, Dad?' I asked.

'We haven't got a good home for *us*, pet, let alone Billy's manky old cats.'

'*Us* meaning you, me and Lucky?'

'Us three, absolutely,' said Dad.

I made Dad and me some toast, and fed all three cats. I felt a bit weird not going to school. I was worried about Susan stuck in our classroom in front of Rhiannon without me.

'Maybe I'll go into school after all, Dad, if you feel you can cope OK.'

'Are you sure, Floss? You're probably still in a state of shock. I know I am.'

'Yes, but you're wounded, Dad,' I said, very gently stroking his bandages.

'I can't drive you at the moment, but I'll walk you there, if you like,' said Dad. 'I've got to go and sort out what's happening to the chip van anyway. And I've got to buy something too – a mobile phone! Then I feel I can always summon help straight away if we're in any more bother. I haven't much idea what they cost, and we'd better hang onto every penny now the chip van business is up the creek, but I thought about selling something. Not that I've got much left to sell, admittedly. I wondered about the cuckoo clock. I know it doesn't go any more, but it's quite old, and the carving's nice. I could take it into that antique place and see what they offer me.'

303

'But it's your wedding present, Dad!'

'Yes, I know. But your mum never really liked it. And now – well, your mum and I aren't married any more, are we?'

I swallowed. 'Sometimes I wish you and Mum *were* still married, Dad,' I said.

'I know, pet. Sometimes I still wish that too. But your mum's moved on now – literally! Maybe it's time I did too. You won't mind too much if we get rid of the cuckoo clock, will you?'

'I'd much sooner we had a mobile, Dad. Can it be half mine too? Hey, even Rhiannon hasn't got her own mobile phone yet! I'll be so cool.'

We wrapped the cuckoo clock in newspaper and Dad put it in his backpack. There was a specialist clock man in the antique centre. He sniffed at our clock a bit, but admitted it was Victorian and hand-carved. He didn't offer that much at first, but Dad argued and eventually he gave him a hundred pounds!

'Wow, Dad! We're rolling in it now!' I said.

'Not really *rolling* in it, Floss,' said Dad – but we certainly had enough to buy our mobile phone.

Then we went to the station to have a look at the chip van. It had been towed back into the shed where Billy always kept it. We peered in at it in silence. It was black all over, with half the roof actually burned off. Dad wound his arms round me tightly. We stood for a few seconds and then crept away again.

'I feel like I've let Billy down,' said Dad mournfully.

'But he doesn't want his chip van any more, Dad, he said so.'

'He might change his mind. Still, I suppose he can always buy a brand-new van with his insurance money.'

We trudged on past the station. I knew where we were going now. Dad looked at me quizzically. I nodded. It wasn't worth walking all round the moon when the direct way to school went straight past our café.

Harlie's Café didn't exist any more. It was now a Starbucks. Dad stood staring at the smart green paintwork. He stepped up to the window and looked in, past the orange lamps and all the people standing at the counter and sitting at every single table and chair and sofa. He stood still and sighed softly. Then he suddenly waved.

'Look who's in there!' he said. 'It's Old Ron and Miss Davis! Look, they're sitting *at the same table*! And getting on like a house on fire as far as I can see. Let's embarrass them terribly and go and say hello.'

We went into the café. It was just like stepping into any coffee bar anywhere. I looked up at the ceiling, wondering what was up there now. The girl cleaning the table looked up too, as if worried I'd spotted a leak.

'Yes?' she said uncertainly.

'Who lives up there?' I asked.

'No one. It's just the office and the storeroom,' she said.

'It isn't a flat any more?'

'I think it was once,' she said – like it was a hundred years ago. 'But it was in a terrible state. Goodness knows who lived there.'

I glanced nervously at Dad, who was thankfully deep in conversation with Old Ron and Miss Davis, gesturing theatrically with his bandaged hands. They were gasping appreciatively.

'Excuse me,' I said to the girl, and ran over to join my dad.

Old Ron and Miss Davis were an extremely satisfying audience. They also said how much they missed Charlie's Café.

'I'm on my beam ends, drinking Starbucks coffee,' said Old Ron. 'Talk about pricey!'

I didn't know what his beam was and where it ended, but I got the gist of what he was saying.

'And Mr Starbucks doesn't have a clue when it comes to making a good plain cup of tea from a nicely warmed pot,' said Miss Davis, sighing.

'Well, as soon as my bandages are off I'll make

306

you as many cups of tea and coffee as you can manage at my place,' said Dad, but then he bit his lip. 'Well . . . Billy's place. Whatever.'

'Is he *really* going to sell up?' said Old Ron.

'So he says. Hey, Ron, if push came to shove, you wouldn't take on his old cats, would you? Whisky and Soda, two very nice old ladyfriends.'

'Well . . .' said Old Ron. 'In the general run of things I *might* say yes, but now *I've* got this very nice old ladyfriend who isn't at all keen on cats.' He nudged Miss Davis in the ribs.

She glared at him. 'Utter nonsense! And watch what you're doing, I bruise easily,' she said, but she wasn't really cross. She leaned across the table at me. 'Do they catch birds?'

'Oh no, Miss Davis, never in a million years. They can't catch anything, they're far too lazy and plump. They don't even crunch up their cat food properly; they just suck all the juice off the fishy chunks. But they're really lovely kind cats. They've tried to be very motherly to my cat Lucky. I'm sure you'd like them if you met them.'

'Well, if there's really no other alternative I won't object if Ronald wants to give the creatures a proper home for their twilight years,' said Miss Davis.

'Old Ron and Miss Davis seem to be taking care of *their* twilight years,' said Dad, as we continued our long rambling walk to school. 'Fancy, all those years of coming into my café and they barely spoke to each other. And then there's Billy the Chip, so stuck in his ways he did the same thing every single day of his life, and yet now he's upped sticks and swanning around Australia. Your mum too, of course.' Dad sighed. 'They've all moved on. I've stayed stuck. No, I haven't even done that, I've started going backwards. One moment I've got a wife, a child, my own business, and then the next – *poof!*' But Dad was smiling at me. 'I've still got the most important little person in my life, that's all that matters. Come on then, Floss. Let's get you to school. You're astronomically late. I hope you won't get a telling-off. Do you want me to come in with you and explain?'

I didn't think this was a good idea at all. 'I'll be fine, Dad, really,' I said.

'Well, if you're sure, sweetheart. Schools do give me the heebie-jeebies. I always feel like I'm going to be told to stand in the corner with my hands on my head. What's your Mrs Horsefield like, Floss? Bit of an old bag?'

'She's lovely, Dad!'

When we approached the school I saw a class was out in the playground doing PE. *My* class, with Mrs Horsefield in her prettiest white top and shorts showing all the class how to jog on the spot.

'My goodness, is she a teacher?' Dad whispered.

'She's Mrs Horsefield, Dad. *My* teacher. See, I told you she was lovely,' I said.

'I'll say. You're a lucky girl, Floss,' said Dad. 'OK then, pet, you run and join all your friends. I'll come and collect you at going-home time.'

I gave Dad a quick kiss and started racing towards the gate into school. Dad waved with his big bandaged hand. Mrs Horsefield slowed to a standstill, panting a little.

'Floss? Is that your father? Mr Barnes!'

'Uh-oh!' said Dad. 'Looks as if I'm in trouble after all.'

He walked along by my side, his arms dangling. Everyone stopped jogging and stood still, staring. Everyone except Susan. She came flying across the playground and met me at the school gate. She flung her arms round me and gave me a great big hug.

'Hello, Susan,' said Dad. 'I know you two girls are best friends but do you always greet each other with such gusto?'

'No, no, Mr Barnes! I'm just so relieved to see Floss. I thought something awful had happened to her. One of the girls in our class said there'd been a fire in the chip van and I was so scared you'd both been burned. Oh, but you *have* been burned, Mr Barnes. Look at your poor hands!'

'They're fine, dear. I've just got the bandages on to keep them nice and clean. The nurse says they'll clear up completely in a week or so.'

'Oh, so you've just got first-degree burns. Thank goodness!' said Susan, knowledgeable as always.

Mrs Horsefield came right over to us. 'OK, Susan, you get back in line, dear,' she said. 'Are you sure you're all right, Floss? There have been all sorts of terrible rumours running round the school. I tried phoning, but your telephone number seems to be out of order, Mr Barnes.'

'Oh dear, that would be the old number, yes. Silly of me not to have let you know. I'll give the school my mobile number. We're temporarily staying at a friend's house but I expect we're moving on soon, during the school holidays.'

'Flora's had to cope with quite a few changes recently,' Mrs Horsefield said quietly, careful that the others shouldn't hear.

'Yes, yes, I'm afraid she has, but she's been a little star,' said Dad. 'She's such a good girl, my Floss. She might not always be up to speed with her lessons. I think she's a bit of a dreamer, like her old dad, but I know she tries really hard, Mrs Horsefield.'

'I know she does,' said Mrs Horsefield. 'Mr Barnes, you do know you can come in to see me any day after school? I always stay on in the classroom for a good half-hour or so. If there's anything you want to discuss, any problems, any advice – well, that's what I'm here for.'

'Thank you,' said Dad. 'I wish I'd had a smashing teacher like you when I was at school.'

'Dad!' I hissed.

Dad laughed at me and pretended to punch the tip of my chin with his bandaged fist. 'Am I embarrassing you, darling? That's what dads are for,' he said. 'I'll come and meet you after school, OK?'

He backed off across the playground. When Mrs Horsefield blew her whistle and got everyone to start jogging again, *Dad* started jogging too, arms pumping, feet pounding. We could see his head bobbing up and down all the length of the school fence. Susan laughed fondly. So did some of the others. Rhiannon and Margot and Judy laughed too, but they were standing with their hands on their hips, eyebrows raised.

'Look at Smelly Belly Chip!' said Rhiannon.

'Like, who does he think he *is*?' said Margot.

'He's so fat! See his big bum! Smelly Belly Waggle Bum!' said Judy.

They all laughed harder. I hated all three of them. When Mrs Horsefield told us to start running properly I forged ahead, kicked Rhiannon right on her own bum, then Margot, then Judy, kick kick

311

kick like a soccer star. Then I charged out of their way before they could get me back.

I couldn't keep out of their way for ever. I couldn't keep out of *anyone's* way at break time. Everyone crowded round me in the cloakroom, wanting to hear all about the fire. The story had already spread rapidly and had become wildly exaggerated. Dad and I had been besieged by thousands of yobs who had deliberately set the chip van on fire with us inside.

'No, no, it wasn't like that at all!' I said.

'So what *was* it like?'

'Tell us, Floss.'

'Yeah, come on, Floss, tell!'

So I started telling the whole story myself, and as I got into it I couldn't help doing a *little* exaggerating myself. I had my dad leaping out of the van, knocking knives out of guys' hands kung-fu style. I demonstrated enthusiastically. I had Dad snatching Saul from a serious stabbing, protecting his girlfriend, bashing all the yobs and sending them flying.

'Oh wow, Floss, your dad's fantastic!'

'That's so cool!'

'Did he *really* beat them all off?'

'Of course he didn't!' said Rhiannon. 'Old Smelly Belly Bum Chip couldn't bash so much as a baked potato. You're telling whopping great lies, Floss.'

'I am not! Well, he might not have hit them all. And maybe there was just *one* knife. But I'll tell you something, and I swear this is true. When the fryer caught fire in the van I was trapped, and I would have burned to death there and then if Dad hadn't braved the flames and fought his way over to me and carried me out,' I said.

'Your dad's truly heroic, Floss,' Susan proclaimed.

'Yes, isn't he,' I agreed proudly.

'Rubbish,' said Rhiannon.

'Yeah, like, totally gross,' said Margot.

Judy didn't say anything but she made a very rude noise.

'Take no notice of them, Floss,' said Susan. 'They're just jealous of your lovely dad.'

'Jealous!' said Rhiannon. 'My dad earns fifty thousand a year in his car business and he's always buying me heaps of stuff and taking us on fantastic holidays, and people say he looks very like Tom Cruise. *Plus* he doesn't smell, so why should I be *jealous*, Swotty Potty?'

'Floss's dad loves her tremendously and talks to her as if she's his special friend and plays with her heaps and does funny things to make her laugh and takes good care of her,' said Susan.

I squeezed Susan's hand, so moved I could barely speak.

Rhiannon still sneered. 'Takes good care of her! You must be joking! My mum says it's appalling. She's thinking about going to social services and reporting Floss.'

'*What?*' I said.

'You heard me. Or if you didn't, wash your ears out, and wash the rest of you too so you don't stink so much, Smelly Chip,' said Rhiannon.

'Your mum isn't *really* going to the social services about me, is she, Rhiannon?' I said.

'Yes, because she's truly worried about you. First your mum walks out on you—'

'She didn't! You *know* she didn't!'

'And now your dad's café's gone bust and you haven't got a proper home any more and you look a sight and you smell, and now it seems your dad's dragging you off to his chip van every night and getting into fights and you very nearly end up getting burned to death – your very own words, Smelly Chip. My mum says you need some kind lady to look after you properly. So you wait, the social services will come and get you and put you in care if you don't watch out.'

22

Rhiannon's words rang in my head all day at school. Susan kept telling me that I mustn't worry. Rhiannon was just trying to wind me up. No social worker could ever doubt that I had two parents who loved me and cared for me.

I knew she was right, but I was scared all the same. When the bell went for home time I peered round the school gates anxiously in case there were social workers lurking, ready to capture me. But there was Dad, smiling and waving his bandages at me.

'Look, there's Floss's dad!'

'Hey, Mr Barnes!'

'Hello, Mr Barnes. You're a hero!'

Dad grinned at all the kids in my class. Thank goodness he didn't seem to notice the three girls who walked straight past him, rudely holding their noses.

'How have you been today, Floss? You haven't

felt funny or had any coughing fits, have you? I've been a bit worried about you,' said Dad, cuddling me close.

'I've been a bit worried about *you*, Dad! How have *you* been today? How are your poor hands?'

'They're OK, sweetheart. I've managed fine, though it's a bit of a palaver going to the loo! It's not that easy to cook either. I think you might have to give me a hand making tea.'

'Glad to, Dad.'

'But we're not having chips! I don't want to see a chip fryer for a long long long time.'

'Are you going to give up being a chip cook, Dad?'

'Well, I've got to *work*, pet, and there's not a lot else I can do. I went down the job centre today. The girl there was quite helpful. She even filled in the forms for me, seeing as I've got my hands bandaged. Lucky that, as I'm total rubbish when it comes to spelling! But she was quite frank about my chances. They're not that great. Still, you never know . . .'

'Something might bob up out of the blue!' we said together as we turned the corner down Oak Crescent.

There was a bright pink car parked outside Billy's house. I'd once seen a caravan exactly that colour.

'Dad!' I said.

'What, pet?' said Dad. Then he saw it too. He stopped still, staring.

'Come on, Dad,' I said, starting to run.

'Hey! Hang on, wait for your old dad!'

I left him behind and rushed to the car. Saul and Jenny were squashed up in the back. Rose was in the front, her beautiful red nails tapping a tune on her white leather steering wheel. She had two red velvety roses dangling from her driving mirror.

'Hello!' I shouted.

They all saw me at once. They smiled and started getting out of the car.

'Hello, little Floss,' said Rose, and she gave me a hug.

She was wearing tight black trousers and a lovely deep pink top patterned with red roses. Her toenails were painted dark red too, peeping out of her high-heeled sandals. She even *smelled* of red roses. I wanted to hang onto her and breathe in her lovely soft warm smell.

'So where's your dad then, Flossie?' said Rose.

'Just coming! There he is,' I said, gesturing.

Dad was ambling along, his arms hanging at his side, head bent bashfully. He looked really odd, as if he was *shy*.

'Well, goodness me, this is a surprise!' he said.

His voice sounded weird too, as if he couldn't catch his breath.

He went to shake Rose's hand and then remembered his bandage. He paused awkwardly, half waving in the air.

'Come here!' said Rose, and she gave him a big hug too. 'I want to thank you for looking out for my boy.'

'I didn't really do anything, honestly,' said Dad, going bright red in the face, but looking pleased all the same.

'How are your hands, mate?' Saul asked. He waggled his sling. 'Look at us! Talk about the walking wounded!'

'You're a magnet for trouble, Saul, always have been, always will be,' said Rose, shaking her head. 'But what about you, Mr Barnes? Are your hands badly burned? Let's go into the house. I want you to show me. I don't trust you strong silent types, you don't make enough *fuss*! I'm so glad Saul remembered the right house after all. I got a bit worried when we first knocked half an hour ago and no one was in. Still, I thought you were probably meeting your little girl from school – and I was right.'

'My Floss,' said Dad. 'Well, come in, come in, all of you.'

We trooped into Billy's house. Whisky and Soda

and Lucky were waiting in the hall, tails in the air, yowling hopefully for tea. Whisky and Soda backed away and hid behind the sofa, overwhelmed by all the guests, but Lucky was perkily sociable. She gave Saul and Jenny a nod, and actually came and rubbed herself against Rose's shapely ankles.

'Hello, little cat,' said Rose, bending to give her a stroke.

'She's my cat. She's called Lucky. Oh, she *likes* you, Rose,' I said.

Lucky was daintily licking Rose's toenails as if in homage.

'And I like *her*, darling,' said Rose. She carefully stepped round Lucky into the living room. 'Oh, what a . . . nice big room,' she said uncertainly. 'Yes, you've got a lovely huge house, Mr Barnes.'

'Call me Charlie, please. And it's not *my* house. It belongs to an old pal of mine. Floss and I are only here temporarily like.'

'It's not a *huge* house, Rose,' I said, puzzled.

'All houses seem enormous to you if you've been brought up in a caravan,' said Rose.

'I love your cosy rosy caravan,' I said.

'So do I, dear. Though I know it might seem a bit cramped to some people.' She looked at Saul and raised her eyebrows at him.

He laughed at his mum. 'I want a bit more space now, Mum. And a proper roof over my head.

321

I want to live with the same girl in the same street. That's not so strange, is it?' He put his arm round Jenny, who smiled and snuggled up to him.

'Well,' said Rose, struggling. 'As long as you're happy, son.'

'So how are you coping by yourself?' said Dad.

'Oh, I get by fine. I always used to run the stall by myself when Saul was little. It's a bit of a struggle sometimes but I manage.'

'Talk to me about it!' said Dad. 'So who's looking after the stall tonight?'

'Monday's always our quiet night, when we've just set up. Liz from the Lucky Darts stall is supposed to be keeping an eye on it for me.'

'Where *is* your fair now?' I asked eagerly. 'Dad and I have looked and looked for it.'

'Have you?' said Rose, looking pleased. 'Well, we're over in Felting this week, not too far away. Are you going to come and visit us?'

'You bet!' I said. 'We can, can't we, Dad?'

'Of course, darling. Now, let's get some tea organized. Will you be a lovely helpful girl, Floss, and put the kettle on for me? Then, as I can't get at my fingers just now perhaps you'd also like to dial the pizza place?' He looked apologetically at Rose. 'I'd love to cook you a proper meal, but it's a bit awkward just now, as you can see.'

'Pizza would be lovely! It's definitely our treat though.'

Rose ordered *four* different king-size pizzas, and then ice cream for afters. I had a big slice of all four pizzas (triple cheese and spinach, chicken and mushroom, pineapple and bacon, and sausage and sweetcorn and tomato) and then a bowl of strawberry and vanilla and chocolate ice cream. Then I felt so full I had to undo the buttons on my school skirt.

Saul and Jenny stayed for a while. Saul let me try on his great big rings. I had a dragon on one finger, a snake on another, three different skulls, an eye ring, and frogs on each thumb. They looked *so* cool. But then they said they had to get going because they wanted to see some film.

'I suppose I ought to be going too,' said Rose.

'Oh no, do stay,' I said.

'Your dad probably wants some peace and quiet,' said Rose.

'I certainly don't!' said Dad. 'Please stay a bit longer, Rose.'

'Well, I've certainly still got to examine those poor sore hands,' said Rose. 'We'll take those bandages off and have a look. They've given you fresh dressings, I hope. Let's see how you're healing.'

I peered fearfully as she gently unwound the

bandages. I was terrified that Dad's fingers would have turned black and cindery like burned toast. It was a huge relief to see they were just a little swollen and shiny red – but very recognizably still my dad's dear fingers.

Rose peered at them carefully, holding his hands in hers.

'Are you reading Dad's palms, Rose?' I asked.

'I might be,' said Rose, smiling.

'What do they say? Is Dad's luck going to change?'

'I think maybe it already has,' said Dad softly.

He wasn't looking at me. He was looking at Rose.

She stayed very late that evening. Dad let me stay up but I was starting to feel very tired. I'd had hardly any sleep the night before . . . and a *lot* of excitement. I curled up in a chair with Lucky on my lap. My head started nodding. Dad tucked a cushion under my neck and covered me with his sweater.

I woke up once to wriggle round and rearrange Lucky. I saw that Dad and Rose were sitting very close together on the sofa. Billy the Chip's mother and father were frowning out of their photograph at them, but Dad and Rose didn't look as if they cared one jot.

When Dad came to meet me the next day from school he said, 'Guess where we're going!'

It didn't need much power of deduction but I played a game with Dad.

'Are we going shopping? Up to London? The seaside?' I said, trying to seem completely innocent and dumb.

Dad kept going, 'No! No! No!' Then he said, 'Come on, Floss, where would you like to go most of all?'

I took a deep breath. 'THE FAIR!' I shouted.

Dad whooped and punched the air with his bandaged fist and went, 'Yay!'

He still couldn't drive, of course, but he'd checked out how to get to Felting on the bus. He'd brought fruit juice and apples and nuts so we had a snack on the journey.

'I thought we'd eat really healthily now so that we can overdose on candyfloss when we get to the fair!' said Dad.

'Does Rose know we're coming?'

'Oh yes.'

'Dad . . . you like Rose, don't you?'

'Yes, of course I like her. You like her too, don't you, Floss? I think she's a very kind lovely lady.'

'Yeah, but I meant, do you fancy her, Dad?'

'Floss!' said Dad. His cheeks were carnation-pink.

'That means you do!' I said.

'Now then. Little girls shouldn't be talking

about fancying people, not to their dads,' said Dad. He paused. 'But say I *did* fancy Rose, would you mind?'

'I don't think I'd mind a bit,' I said. 'So, is Rose going to be your girlfriend, Dad?'

Dad flushed from carnation to peony. 'Well, it's early days, darling. I'm not sure a gorgeous lady like Rose would really want to spend much time with a dull old dad like me. We'll have to see. But whatever happens, Floss, you know you'll always come first with me. You're my little princess, and you always will be.'

I hitched right across the seat onto Dad's lap and he gave me a big cuddle.

We got off the bus at Felting Junction and found the fair on the village green. We hurried towards it, hearing the hum of the hurdy-gurdy music, smelling the fried onions and warm sugar. It was as if we were walking back into a wonderful dream. But it was all real. There was the Big Slide and the Stargazer ride, the Ghost Train and the Crooked Cottage, the Teacup Whirlies and the Tin Can Alley, the Ferris wheel and the Wacky Waltzer. There was the Victorian carousel, with Pearl galloping round and round, her pink mane and tail flying in the wind. There was Rose's candyfloss stall, with her big pink teddy waving her fat plush paw at us. There was Rose herself, looking lovely in a low-cut pink blouse with a little red enamel rose on a gold chain.

She let me go right inside her van. She even let me pour different coloured sugars into her candyfloss cauldron, and then set it spinning so that little wisps of floss started forming. I carefully wound them round and round my stick until I'd made my very own pink, lilac and blue candyfloss.

Dad and I wandered all round the fair, and I had one two *three* rides on Pearl, but every ten minutes we came back to chat to Rose. After an hour or so she got her friend Liz from the Lucky Darts to keep an eye on the candyfloss stall.

Rose took us into her magical cosy caravan for a spot of supper. She had red wine for her and Dad, and cranberry juice for me, and little savoury tarts and battered prawns and sausages in honey and chicken with peanut sauce and all sorts of crisps and olives and crunchy vegetables with dips, and then there was pink iced sponge cake with little red sugar roses and the most amazing giant strawberries dipped in white chocolate.

'Oh Rose, love, you didn't need to go to all this trouble!' said Dad, but he looked absolutely thrilled about it.

'No trouble at all, Charlie,' said Rose. 'I like fiddling with little bits. It's not often I have the opportunity, especially now I'm on my own.'

'It's like party food,' I said.

'Well, this is *our* little party, isn't it?' said Rose. 'And you and your dad could certainly do with a bit of cosseting.'

Dad found it a little difficult picking all his food up with his bandaged hands, so sometimes I popped a prawn or a sausage into his mouth, and then Rose fed him iced cake and strawberries. We ate and ate and ate, but there was still a lot left over when we were absolutely full. Rose packed all the snacks up in tinfoil and put them in a great big red plastic box.

'You can take them for your dinner at school tomorrow, Floss,' she said.

'I shall share them with my best friend Susan!' I said.

23

Susan and I had a positive feast the next day at lunch time. Everyone looked at our food enviously – especially the cake and the chocolate strawberries.

'Give us a strawberry, Floss,' said Rhiannon.

I goggled at her astonishing cheek. 'No way,' I said firmly. 'Here, Susan, have a strawberry. Aren't they delicious?'

'I didn't really want one. I bet they taste of chip fat,' said Rhiannon.

'Yeah, Smelly Chip, like we'd risk eating your dad's gross food,' said Margot.

'Smelly Belly Bum Chip,' said Judy.

They all three held their noses.

I stood up and glared at them. 'You three are so *infantile*,' I said. 'And if you'd only let go your snotty noses and take a big sniff you would see I don't don't don't smell of chips – on account of the fact that my dad's stopped frying them.'

'What's he going to do then?' said Rhiannon.

'It's none of your business,' said Susan.

'No one asked you, Swotty Potty,' said Rhiannon. 'So what sort of other work can your dad do, Smelly Chip? That's all he knows about – though he's not much use at that, is he? He lets your café go bust and he lets the chip van go up in flames. My mum says she's going to *have* to go to the social services. She says you need someone to look after you.'

I took a step closer to Rhiannon, so we were practically nose to nose. Well, she's quite a bit bigger than me, so were kind of nose to chest.

'You tell your mum she doesn't need to worry about me any more. She can send a whole *army* of social workers to see me if she wants, but it's a complete waste of time. To start with, I've got my mum, and she'll be coming back this autumn. Then I've got my dad, and he's just great at looking after me. And lastly I have my Auntie Rose.'

'You haven't *got* an Auntie Rose,' said Rhiannon.

'I have so. She came to see us on Monday and we went to see her on Tuesday and we're going to see each other heaps and heaps. *She* made me my special lunch. She's brilliant at everything. *And* she can tell fortunes. She's got all kinds of extraordinary occult powers and she says I'm highly receptive, so she's going to teach me to channel them properly, and then when I'm up to speed you three had better watch out. Now, would you and Margot and Judy just *bog off* and let Susan and me enjoy our lunch in peace!'

They did just that! They scuttled off, looking quite scared. Even Susan seemed a little disconcerted.

'You said exactly one hundred words *again*. Do you *really* have occult powers, Floss?' she whispered.

'Hey, you're meant to be the brainy one, OK? Of course not!'

'Honestly, Floss, you make things up so they sound so real! So haven't you even got an Auntie Rose?'

'Well, I have, sort of. She's not a real aunt but she's a new friend of my dad's, and she's ever so nice and she *does* tell fortunes and I'm sure she really will teach me if I ask her nicely. And she made the food for us so she is a really brilliant cook, isn't she? Susan, would you mind if I saved that biggest strawberry, the one with the most chocolate?'

'Not at all. It's your lunch, after all.'

'It's not for me.'

I wanted to save it for Mrs Horsefield. I put it on her desk at the start of afternoon school.

'This is a little present for you, Mrs Horsefield,' I said shyly.

'Oh Floss, it looks *lovely*. But I I can't eat your special strawberry, sweetheart.'

'I've chomped my way through your special iced buns with the cherry on the top. It's your turn for a treat, Mrs Horsefield,' I said.

'Well, thank you very much, Floss,' said Mrs Horsefield. She took a big bite of chocolate strawberry, breathed in and went 'Mmmm!' She rolled it round her tongue. 'It's delicious!'

'My Auntie Rose made it,' I said proudly.

'I didn't know you had an auntie!' said Mrs Horsefield, sounding delighted.

'Well, she moved away,' I said vaguely. 'But now she's moved nearer again.'

Felting wasn't really *that* near – but Dad and I caught the bus over to the fair again on Friday night. We spent most of Saturday there too. Rose let me serve candyfloss again. I even managed to give the right change to people even though I'm such rubbish at maths.

Dad hung out with us a lot of the time, but then he went off for a stroll and palled up with Jeff, the guy in charge of the Stargazer ride. He was having a spot of bother changing a dodgy wheel. Dad couldn't help much because he still had his bandages on, but he squatted down beside Jeff and peered at all the silver nuts and bolts and talked earnest engine talk.

'Look at them!' said Rose fondly. 'Does your dad know much about machinery, Floss?'

'Well, he *thinks* he does,' I said.

Rose roared with laughter. 'You're like a little old woman at times!' She paused. Then she looked me straight in the eye. 'So. What do you think about your dad and me, eh, darling?'

I shrugged shyly.

'I know it's early days yet, but your dad and me, well, we really seem to hit it off,' she said.

'Yep,' I said.

'And this time, when we move on tomorrow, we're going to make sure we stay in touch.'

'That's great,' I said.

We both paused to serve two customers with pink and lilac candyfloss. Rose went on winding a stick round and round the sugar cauldron even though she wasn't making candyfloss for anyone else.

'I know I'm quite a bit older than your dad,' she said.

'Are you?' I said, surprised. 'I didn't know that. You don't look it.'

'Oh, sweetheart, thank you!' she said. 'I also know just how close you and your dad are and that's lovely. I want you to understand, I don't want to get in the way of that. When my Saul was young I had a few boyfriends who were rather hard for

him to handle. It caused quite a lot of trouble.'
Rose stirred and stirred, her candyfloss getting bigger and bigger.

'So is Dad your boyfriend now?' I asked. 'He says you're his girlfriend.'

'Did he! Do you mind?'

I thought about it very carefully. 'I *used* to think I'd mind if Dad had a girlfriend, but I don't seem to mind a bit if it's you. Rose, that candyfloss is simply ginormous now.'

'Yeah. Well. It's a special big fluffy floss for you,' said Rose, handing it over with a flourish.

I ate it as carefully as I could, but I still ended up with sticky sugar all over my cheeks and spangling my ears and nose.

'You've even got wisps in your hair,' said Rose, picking them out carefully. 'You've got such lovely fluffy curls, darling. You're just like candyfloss yourself.' She played with my hair, fluffing it out. 'Yes, if we coloured it pale pink you'd look like perfect candyfloss.'

'Oooh, *could* we?'

'I don't know what your dad would say!'

'I can get round Dad,' I said.

'Yes, I'm sure you can, sweetie. But what would they say at school if you turned up with pink hair?'

'We've only got one more week and then it's the holidays!'

'All right then. When you've actually broken up we'll see about turning you into a real candyfloss, OK?'

I told Susan that Rose had promised to colour my hair for me.

'You lucky *thing*,' she said. 'It'll look prettier than ever. But promise it won't make you go all silly and clothes-mad and boy-crazy like Rhiannon and Margot and Judy.'

'I promise promise promise, silly!' I said, giving her a hug. 'Maybe you could come to the fair with Dad and me one day and Rose will colour your hair too.'

'My mum would go demented,' said Susan.

'Well, we could pretend it was like spraying your hair red for Comic Relief. Oh Susan, if I get my hair dyed pink I'll match Pearl! She's this horse on the roundabout. She's got a wonderful pink mane and tail, and she's snowy white with big blue eyes. She's my absolute favourite, but you can have first go on her when you come to the fair with me. Sapphire's lovely too – she's white as well but with a blue mane – and Amber's great too – he's a glossy brown with a yellow mane and tail.'

'You sound like you belong to the fair already,' said Susan.

'Oh, I wish!' I said.

I worried that we wouldn't be going to the fair so much the next week because they moved on way past Felting to a town called Bromshaw about forty miles away. But Dad went back to see the doctor on Monday morning and had his burns inspected, and she said they were healing beautifully. He could leave his bandages off and drive the van again.

'It feels so good, Floss,' said Dad, waggling his fingers at me one by one. 'It's great to have my wheels back too. Let's go for a drive, darling. How about checking out the fair at Bromshaw? I thought it would be fun to see if it looks completely different there.'

I looked at Dad. 'You think Rose will be selling burgers and Pearl will be stuck onto the Stargazer ride?' I said.

'*No!* Are you teasing me, Floss?'

'Of course I'm teasing you, Dad! We don't need any excuse. Yes, let's go to the fair.'

'You can always do your homework in the van.'

'I haven't got any homework, Dad. We break up on Friday.'

'Oh lumme, yes.' Dad sighed. 'What are we going to do with you during the holidays, sweetheart? I'll have to find *some* kind of job to keep us going, and I very much doubt I'll be able to take you with me.' Dad paused. 'Maybe it's time for you to go and join your mum, darling. We've had a lovely time together but I've been having sleepless nights, worrying about you.'

'Don't worry, Dad. I'm fine. We'll work something out for the summer.' I held my hands out in front of my face, palms up. 'Aha! Rose isn't the only one who can tell fortunes. I can see a big curvy line on each palm. They're like smiley faces. That means I'm going to be very very happy.'

'I hope so, darling. Listen, I was wondering . . . Susan's dad seems a very nice chap and he did say he owed us. Do you think you could play round at Susan's some of the time? Once I get a job I can offer to pay.'

'That would be great, Dad, though it might do my head in if they kept trying to teach me all the time! But they're going to their house in France.'

'I don't know, there's them with two houses and here we are without any.'

'Well, maybe it's good to travel light. Like Rose and all the fairground people,' I said.

We had another lovely evening at the fair. Eddie, the roundabout man, had become such an old pal by now he utterly refused to take my pound for the ride.

'In fact you can do me a favour, Floss. I need to test out all my gallopers to make sure they're all safe and solidly fixed. Perhaps you'd be an angel and ride them each in turn?'

I think he was just being sweet to me but I wasn't going to argue. While I was test-riding every horse on the roundabout Dad had another chat with the Stargazer guy, and then he bought burgers and chips from one of the vans and had a long discussion about fat and fryers and types of sauce and vinegar. But *most* of the time we hung out around Rose's stall.

Dad had several goes on Liz's Lucky Darts stall to be polite – and amazingly scored one hundred and eighty. Well, Liz insisted he had, taking the darts out of the board so quickly we couldn't really check. She gave Dad a huge blue plush teddy, the twin of Rose's pink bear.

'Here you are, Floss,' said Dad, thrusting a vast armful of bear at me.

'Thank you very much, Dad – but I think I'm maybe getting too big for bears,' I said.

'Well, who can we give it to?' said Dad.

'Tiger might like him, but he won't be back for months. Anyway, I've already given him Kanga.'

'What about Susan? Is she too big for bears too?'

'She's not really into cuddly toys, Dad.'

'Well then . . .' Dad turned to Rose with a big smile. 'You wouldn't like to hang him alongside your pink bear, would you?'

'I think that's a lovely idea,' said Rose. 'We'll

340

hook him up right this minute. Come here, Blue Ted, come and make friends with Pinkie.'

'He looks a bit of a *bare* bear compared with her,' said Dad. 'We'd better kit him out with some clothes.'

'Hey, I know an outfit that would be absolutely perfect,' I said, chuckling. 'A blue denim outfit. I can sew the skirt into shorts easy-peasy. And the denim cap will look really cute tucked over one ear!'

Dad took me on the Dodgems too. I didn't really *like* it much, especially when we got bumped, but I squealed and laughed and pretended because Mike, the owner, let us go on for free as we were friends of Rose. Mike's daughter Ella collected the money on the Dodgems. She was only a year or so older than me but she was much taller, a really tough tomboy girl who leaped lightly from car to car, her money belt tight round her slim hips. She sorted everyone out and swore cheerfully at any boys daft enough to try to cheek her or chat her up.

We went for an ice cream together while Dad and Mike were having a chat, but I hardly dared say a word to her.

'You don't *say* much, do you?' she said, licking her ice cream with her pink pointy tongue.

I just shrugged my shoulders and licked too.

'You've got a tongue, I can see it,' said Ella. 'So *speak!*'

'Have you been with the fair all your life?' I mumbled.

'Yeah, my family have always been showmen. Well, my dad used to ride the Wheel of Death, but then he saved up enough to buy his Dodgems.' She grinned. 'They're mine too.'

'That's really cool,' I said. 'I didn't know children could work at the fair.'

'I'm not like a little kid,' said Ella. 'My brothers work later on, after dark. We all help out. It's what you do at a fair.'

'Well, I always helped *my* dad,' I said. 'He used to have a café. I acted like a waitress at weekends. I even got tips.'

'So how come you're so friendly with Rose? Are your dad and Rose an item?'

I shrugged again. 'Sort of.'

'We all love Rose. She's generally useless at picking men though. They always let her down.'

'My dad never lets anyone down,' I said fiercely.

'Yeah, he seems like a nice bloke,' said Ella. 'Even though he's a flattie.'

'A *fatty*?' I said. 'He's not! Well, he's a bit plump but he's not really fat.'

'No, I said *flattie*. You're one too. Punters. Customers.'

She pretended to smoke her chocolate flake. I copied her.

'I've got real cigarettes if you want one,' she said, reaching in her jeans pocket.

'No thanks. I – I've given up,' I said quickly.

She laughed at me, but not unkindly. I decided I liked Ella even though I was a bit scared of her. I hoped we might be friends – though not of course a *best* friend like Susan.

It was so sad at school on our last day before we broke up for the summer holidays.

'I'm going to miss you so so so much, Susan,' I said, nudging up close to her at her desk.

'I'm going to miss *you*,' said Susan, giving my hand a quick squeeze.

Rhiannon made silly kissy noises behind us. We took no notice of her.

'I'll write heaps from France.'

'Yes, do! Only *not* in French. I know what you're like, Susan.'

'*Moi?*' said Susan, laughing. 'I'll text you too on my dad's mobile. And even though I'll probably see my cousins out in France, and maybe some of the stepbrothers and stepsisters too, I'll feel so lonely without you, Floss.'

Rhiannon made disgusting vomit sounds.

'Perhaps you'd better run to the toilets if you're feeling sick, Rhiannon,' said Mrs Horsefield.

'It's not fair, Mrs Horsefield, you always take *their* side. It's like they're your special favourites,' said Rhiannon. 'And they didn't even give you a proper goodbye present, just that babyish home-made thing.'

Rhiannon had given Mrs Horsefield a huge box of chocolates and a bottle of champagne.

Mrs Horsefield paused. She fingered the blue denim pencil case Susan and I had made her as a goodbye present. We'd embroidered it with pink cherry buns and written *Our very favourite teacher* in chainstitch.

'You've all given me lovely presents,' said Mrs Horsefield. 'I'm very lucky to have such sweet and delightful pupils. As a teacher I try very hard to be impartial. But do you know something, Rhiannon? I'm a human being too. Sometimes you simply can't *help* having favourites.'

Susan and I hung back at going-home time so we could both give Mrs Horsefield a big goodbye hug. Then we had to have *our* goodbye hug and that was so hard. But eventually I jumped in the van beside Dad and waved and waved until Susan was out of sight.

'I hate saying goodbye to people,' I sniffed.

'I know, pet. Still, you'll see Susan quite soon, when she gets back from her holiday.'

'I wish *we* were going on holiday, Dad,' I said, sighing. 'I know we can't help it, and I'm not really complaining, but it's going to be horrible just stuck at Billy's house all summer.'

'W-e-l-l,' said Dad. 'I've got this idea, Floss. We don't have to do it if you don't want to. It's maybe crazy, but how would you like to join up with the fair for a few weeks?'

'*What?* Really? Oh Dad, I want to, I want to!'

'Rose and I have had a long talk. She's so lovely, isn't she? I can't believe my luck. But anyway, she needs someone to help her out, for all she's so independent. And I've been talking to some of the guys, and they always need someone to help build up and pull down their rides. I'm a bit long in the tooth but they can't always get lads nowadays. I wouldn't make much money, but there's a chance I can help out at the burger stall, maybe making chip butties if there's a call for it. Only you'd stay safe in Rose's caravan, OK! How would you feel about it?'

'Oh Dad, yes yes yes!'

'So you're really up for it, Floss?'

'You bet I am!'

'It's just for the summer holidays, to see how it works out. I don't know what we'll tell your mum. She's always hated fairs.'

'We can say we're touring round the countryside for the summer. That's sort of true,' I said. 'Oh Dad, it'll be so great! I'm so lucky!' I paused. 'Oh no, what about Lucky?'

345

'She can come too. She's a streetwise little cat. I think she'll take to a travelling life OK, though Whisky and Soda will have to go to Old Ron and Miss Davis. Rose says we can rig up Saul's old caravan as a very special bedroom for you. You can have Lucky and her duvet in with you. There'll be room for your silver chest. Rose says she'll paint flowers all over it if that's what you'd like. You can have Billy's doll's house too, and space for your funny woolly toys and books and sewing stuff. And I haven't forgotten your swing. Every site we pitch up at we'll find a good tree and fix it up for you.'

'So we won't be flatties any more? We'll be fairground folk?'

'I suppose so, yes!'

'Fairground kids are expected to help out. Can I help you, Dad?'

'You always do, darling.'

'And can I help Rose with her candyfloss stall?'

'She's counting on it.'

'Dad. There's just one more thing.'

'What's that, Princess?'

'Promise you'll say yes?'

'What is it you want, darling?'

'Can I have my hair dyed pink?'

'What? Absolutely not!' said Dad.

But I'm very good at getting round him . . .

Jacqueline Wilson

Cookie

ILLUSTRATED BY NICK SHARRATT

To Martha Courtauld –
I love all your ideas

One

I turned on the television. I timed it perfectly. The music was just starting. I saw the cartoon picture of Sam and Lily spinning round, Sam waving, Lily delicately nibbling a carrot. They whirled faster and faster while a voice sang, '*Who do you want to see?*'

Little children piped up: '*Sam and Lily in the Rabbit Hutch!*'

I sang it too, but very quietly, just mouthing the words. There was only Mum at home and she was out in the kitchen. She wouldn't mind a bit if I wanted to watch a baby programme like *Rabbit Hutch* but I still felt embarrassed about it. Imagine if some of the really mean snooty girls at school, Skye Wortley or Emily Barrington or Arabella Clyde-Smith, came barging through our front door and caught me watching a programme for five-year-olds. They teased me enough anyway. I could hear them screaming with laughter over Beauty and her lickle bunny-wunny friend in the Rabbit Hutch.

I shut my eyes tight.

'Hey there!' said a soft gentle voice from the television.

1

I opened my eyes. There was Sam smiling at me, the real man, not the funny cartoon picture of him. I smiled back at him. I couldn't help it. He had such a lovely funny grin. His brown eyes shone and he ducked his head a little so his soft shiny brown hair flopped across his forehead.

'How are you doing?' Sam asked.

'I'm fine,' I whispered.

He nodded and then looked down at Lily. He was holding her close against his chest. He needed both hands because there was a lot of Lily. Her lop ears brushed the collar of Sam's checked shirt, while her back paws dangled past the belt of his jeans. Sam held her firmly so she felt safe. She relaxed against him, slowly blinking her blue eyes. She knew he would never ever drop her.

'I wonder what you've been doing today?' said Sam, looking at me.

'School,' I muttered.

'Which one?' Sam asked.

'Lady Mary Mountbank. I started there last year,' I said, sighing.

'Is it that bad?' said Sam sympathetically.

I considered. It wasn't *all* bad. Rhona Marshall had asked me to her birthday party. She'd given my arm a special squeeze as she gave me the pink invitation card and said, 'I do hope you can come.'

2

I liked Rhona a lot, even though she was best friends with Skye. Rhona never ever joined in the horrible Beauty routine. She just looked embarrassed and raised her eyebrows at me and once she whispered, 'Take no notice.' This was sweet of her, but how could I *help* noticing when they were chanting stuff right in my face.

Miss Woodhead had been kind to me too. She specially liked my Roman project. I know this sounds as if I'm showing off, but she said I was a joy to teach. She said it quietly just to me and I went bright pink I was so pleased. But one of the others heard her and by break time half the class were muttering it and then making vomit noises. Skye made such loud vomit noises she nearly made herself really sick all down her school skirt. That would have been great.

I didn't have time to gabble all this to Sam so I just shrugged my shoulders. He'd understand.

'Lily likes *her* school,' he said. 'But her lessons are easy-peasy. One lettuce plus one carrot plus one cabbage equals one big bunny snack! Just so she doesn't get *too* fat I've made her a new rabbit run in the garden. Do you want to go and do your exercises, Lily?'

She nodded.

'Shall we go and watch her?' Sam asked.

I nodded.

Sam carried Lily outside into the garden and gently lowered her into her new run. He'd put carrots and cabbages and lettuces at the very end of the run. Lily spotted them straight away and gambolled off like a greyhound, her ears flapping.

'Would you run like that if your mum put your tea at the end of the garden?' Sam joked.

Mum and I often did have tea in the garden, special picnics. Sometimes we even put our coats and scarves on and wrapped rugs round us and had *winter* picnics.

'You bet, Sam,' I said.

Mum always made us magic picnics. She didn't *cook* anything, she didn't ever really cook, but she made each picnic special. She sometimes chose a colour theme, so we'd have bananas and pineapple and cheese pasties and custard tarts and lemonade, or tomato quiche and apples and plums and Kit-Kats and raspberry juice. Sometimes she'd choose a letter of the alphabet and we'd have sausages and sandwiches and strawberries and shop-bought sponge cake carefully cut by Mum into an S shape.

When I was little she'd lay places at the picnics for my dolls and teddies, or she'd let me dress up in my Disney princess dress and she'd serve everything on the best china and curtsy every time she spoke to me.

4

I loved loved loved my mum. Sam understood. He said the word 'mum' softly, knowing it was a special word.

'I wonder if you miss your mum, Lily?' said Sam, squatting down beside her.

Lily nibbled a lettuce leaf, not really listening.

'Remember when you were really little, Lily, just a weeny newborn baby rabbit?' said Sam.

He looked at me. 'Do you know, she was only *this* big,' Sam said, cupping his hands and holding them only a little way apart.

I cupped my hands too, imagining a little fluffy baby Lily quivering under my clasp.

'Do you remember when *you* were just a weeny newborn baby person?' said Sam. 'I bet you weren't much bigger. Do you have a photo of you when you were a little baby?'

I nodded. Mum still had that photo inside her wallet, though it had got creased and crumpled. Dad had the same picture in a silver photo frame on his big desk at work. It was so embarrassing. I was big and bald and I didn't even have a nappy on. My belly button was all taped up and you could see my bottom.

'I bet you looked cute then,' said Sam, chuckling.

I didn't smile back at him. I nibbled my lip miserably. I didn't look remotely cute when I was a baby, but at least I was cuddly. Mum said she held me all day and half the night too she was so happy to hold me. She said she cried because she was so thrilled she'd got a little girl.

Dad cried too.

Most dads don't cry, especially very very very fierce dads like mine. My dad actually cries a lot. He cries at films on the television, even children's cartoon films like *The Lion King* and *Beauty and the Beast*. He cries at the news on television, when a little child is rescued in an earthquake or when a man with artificial legs runs in a race. He cries heaps whenever his favourite wins on *The X-Factor* or *Search for a Star*. He said I was his little star with that special X-factor the day I was born. He scooped the newborn baby me out of Mum's arms and cradled me close.

'Just what I wanted! A little girl at last,' he crooned. 'And such a beautiful little girl too, with those chubby cheeks and big blue eyes. Just wait till your hair grows, my darling. I bet you'll be a little blonde like your mum. You're going to turn into a perfect beauty.'

Then he let out such a yelp I started crying.

'I'll take her, Gerry,' Mum said anxiously.

'Beauty! Don't you get it? That's her name, our little sweetheart's name! We'll call her Beauty,' said Dad. 'Isn't that a great name for her, Dilly?'

Mum promised me she thought it an *awful*

name, but you didn't dare argue with Dad, even in those days.

I was christened Beauty. It's a ridiculous name. It would be a silly show-off shallow name even if I just magically happened to be beautiful. But I am so *not* beautiful. I don't take after Mum, I take after Dad. I am small and squat, with a big tummy. My blue eyes turned green as gooseberries when I was still a baby, and you can't really see them anyway because I have to wear glasses. My hair's mouse, long and lank. Mum tries to tie it up with slides and ribbons but they always fall out. You can see why Emily and Arabella and Skye tease me so. I am a laughing stock because of my name.

I wasn't laughing. I had silly baby tears in my eyes now, safe with Sam and Lily.

'Hey, don't cry,' said Sam.

I sniffed, ashamed. 'Not crying,' I mumbled.

It seemed to be raining inside my glasses. I poked my finger up and tried to make it work like a windscreen wiper.

'Why don't you clean them on the corner of your T-shirt? Your glasses will get all smeary wiping them like that,' Sam said softly. 'So what are you *not* crying about?'

'My silly name,' I sniffed. 'Beauty!'

'I think Beauty's the most special name in all the world.'

'No it's not. And it doesn't suit me,' I said tearfully. 'Skye Wortley at school says I should be renamed Plug Ugly.'

'Silly old Skye,' said Sam. 'I expect she's so mean because she's jealous of you.'

'Oh, Sam, that's the first time I've ever heard you say something stupid,' I said. 'As if someone like Skye would ever be jealous of *me*. Skye's got lovely long wavy fair hair and big blue eyes – *sky* blue – and she's clever and she's great at dancing and she's got Rhona as a best friend and – and—'

'Well, you've got sand-coloured hair and great green eyes and you're even cleverer than Skye and who cares about dancing and you've got Lily and me for your best friends,' said Sam.

'Truly? You and Lily are really my best friends?'

'Absolutely definitely, aren't we, Lily?' said Sam, bending down and scratching her head. She stopped nibbling the cabbage, looked up, and nodded her head so vigorously her ears flapped forwards.

'Well, you're my best friends for ever ever ever,' I whispered rapturously.

We smiled at each other, the three of us.

'See you tomorrow, Beauty,' Sam whispered.

Then he raised his voice.

'Nearly time to go now. Time we were getting back to the hutch, Lily. You've had enough tea now.

8

Maybe it's time for *your* tea? I wonder what you're having? Lily's favourite tea is raw cabbage, as you can see, but somehow I don't think raw cabbage is *your* favourite best-ever food. Still, maybe your pet likes it. Why don't you send me a painting or drawing of *your* pet's favourite food? Send it to Sam at the Rabbit Hutch, OK? Bye then.' He waved, then picked up Lily and helped her waggle her paw.

'Lily's waving goodbye too,' said Sam.

'Bye, Sam! Bye, Lily!' I said.

Rabbit Hutch faded, and the cartoon Sam and Lily whirled round and round and the voice said, 'Who have we just seen?'

'*Sam and Lily in the Rabbit Hutch*,' I sang.

'*Sam and Lily in the Rabbit Hutch*,' Mum sang too, coming in from the kitchen. 'Do you want a little tea-time snack, sweetheart? I've bought a couple of those little pink iced buns, the ones with jam inside.'

'But Dad said I wasn't to eat them any more,' I said.

I'd had a pink iced bun when we were all going round the Flowerfields shopping centre. I'd bitten into it and jam spurted all down the front of my best blue frilly top. Dad had knocked my hand hard so that the bun flew out onto the floor.

'Don't you ever buy her that pink jammy muck

9

again,' he'd hissed at Mum. 'Look, she's ruined her best little blouse. She didn't ought to be stuffing her face anyway, she's getting ginormous.'

Mum had meekly promised not to buy me any more buns and had whipped me into the ladies' toilets to sponge all the jam off. I'd cried a little bit and she'd given me a hug but begged me to cheer up because I'd make Dad worse if he saw me with a long face. I'd done my best, though I'd felt particularly mournful as the pink buns were my favourites.

'Dad won't know if you gobble it up now,' said Mum. 'Hang on half a tick.'

She disappeared into the kitchen and came back with two pink buns on her best little green-leaf cake plates.

'Here, I'll keep you company,' said Mum.

We both sat cross-legged on the furry white hearth rug, eating our buns.

'Yum, yum,' I said.

'Yep, yummy yummy,' said Mum.

'I'd better not spill jam all down me again,' I said.

'Me too!' said Mum, licking the icing on her bun as if it was an ice lolly.

We munched companionably.

'M-u-m?'

'Yes?'

'Mum, why do you think Dad gets so . . .' I couldn't think of the right word.

'Cross?' Mum suggested.

Dad didn't just get cross. It was way way way more scary. He was like a volcano. You never quite knew when he'd erupt and explode and engulf you in molten lava.

Mum wriggled forward on her bottom until her knees nearly touched mine.

'I don't know why he's like that,' she said. 'I used to think it was just me. I know I can be a bit silly sometimes – Silly Dilly, OK? But you're not silly, Beauty, you're the smartest little kid ever. He's got no reason whatsoever to yell at you the way he does. I wish I could figure out a way to stop him. I've tried talking to him about it but that just makes him rant even more.'

Mum looked so miserable I felt awful. I crammed the last bit of bun into my mouth and then put my arms round her.

'Don't worry about it, Mum. Dad's not cross *all* the time,' I said. 'Sometimes he can be the loveliest dad in the whole world.'

Sometimes.

Very very rarely.

Starter Happy Homes

Standard Happy Home

Deluxe Happy Home

Two

We always knew if Dad was going to be in a good mood because we could hear him whistling as he parked the car in the drive and walked to the front door.

He was whistling now, his silly 'Happy Homes' song. Mum breathed out slowly and smiled at me. I smiled back, licking my lips to make sure I hadn't left the tiniest trace of jam.

'Hello hello hello, my two best girls,' Dad called, opening the front door.

'Hello, Gerry,' Mum called quickly.

'Hello, Dad,' I echoed.

We heard Dad taking his shoes off and putting them in the special rack by the doorstep. It was one of his many rules. All outdoor shoes must be left at the front door because we mustn't risk scratching the polished parquet floor. Then he cleared his throat and started singing as he slid up the hall in his socks.

'Happy Homes, Happy Homes
Where everyone smiles
And nobody moans—'

He skidded into the living room, grinning at us, his arms outstretched.

'There's a mummy' – pointing at Mum.
'And a daddy' – pointing at himself.
'And a gorgeous little girl' – pointing at me.
'So if we're Happy in our Home
Then give us a twirl!'

He twirled around foolishly, his toe pivoting on the thick pile of the living room carpet.

He paused.

'GIVE US A TWIRL!' he shouted, wafting his hands in the air.

Mum and I stood up immediately. Even if Dad was in a very good mood like today, the slightest thing could still upset him and make him turn.

Mum twirled around, holding up her skirt prettily, pointing her toes. I twirled too. I whizzed round too fast as I was in such a hurry to get it over. I managed to trip over my own slippered feet and nearly fell headlong.

'Whoopsie!' said Dad, catching me. 'Dear goodness, Beauty! You're so clumsy! I think we'd better send you back to those dancing lessons.'

My iced bun turned a somersault inside my tummy. Dad had sent me to ballet lessons when I was six. I was the oldest in the baby class. There were some tiny girls who were only three or four. They were all much better at dancing than I was. I couldn't do bunny hops – I simply landed with a bump on my bottom. I couldn't skip – my arms and legs went all wonky. I couldn't point my toes properly – they wanted to point in, not out. And I couldn't twirl gracefully to save my life.

I stuck it out for a year, until Miss June the dancing teacher tactfully told Mum that I didn't seem to be *enjoying* my dancing classes so perhaps it might be better if I tried another hobby.

'Please don't make me do ballet again, Dad!' I said.

'Don't you want to learn to dance like a little fairy?' said Dad.

'Fairy elephant, more like,' I said.

Dad chuckled and ruffled my hair. He sat down in his big leather armchair and then pulled me onto his knee. He pulled Mum onto his other knee, as if we were both his little girls.

'Hey, Gerry darling, did you get the planning permission for the Water Meadows project?' Mum asked.

'I'm still working on it, but it looks very likely,' said Dad. 'That's what we need, two hundred spanking new, top-of-the-range Happy Homes with river views. They'll make our fortune, Dilly, you wait and see.'

'You've already made our fortune,' said Mum.

'I've worked hard for my girls, my wife, my daughter.' Dad paused. 'And my *ex*-wives and my layabout sons.'

Mum gave me a little frown. That meant, *Don't say a word!*

I was fascinated by the first Mrs Cookson and the second Mrs Cookson and my three half-brothers, Gerry Junior, Mark and Ryan. When we'd all met at Gerry Junior's wedding and Grandma's funeral I'd loved feeling part of a great big family. But Dad didn't seem to like any of them any more. He especially didn't like giving them any money, even though there seemed heaps to go round. The first two Mrs Cooksons had their own Happy Homes and now Gerry Junior and his new wife Julie had their own Happy Home too.

'So that makes them blooming lucky,' Dad said. '*I* didn't have that kind of start in life. I had to make my own way.'

Dad had started off working on a building site at sixteen. He worked his way up, until he ended up buying the building firm. Then he branched out, becoming a property developer, building lots and lots of Happy Homes. There were starter Happy Homes for young couples, standard three-bedroom Happy Homes for ordinary families, and deluxe five-bedroom, two-bathroom Happy Homes for rich families.

We used to live in a deluxe Happy Home, but now we'd moved to an even bigger, fancier home specially built for us. We had *six* bedrooms, three bathrooms *and* a special wetroom and a hot tub outside. I even had my own en suite bathroom, dusty rose to match my pink bedroom, with silver dolphin taps.

Dad said I was the luckiest little girl in the world. He didn't know of another child anywhere who had her own en suite bathroom. He kept asking me why I didn't want to invite any of my friends from Lady Mary Mountbank for a sleepover. They could sleep in one of the twin beds with the dusty-rose silk coverlets patterned with sprigs of violets, sprawl on the pink and violet velvet cushions, comb their hair at my Venetian glass dressing table and admire every inch of my en suite bathroom.

I hadn't invited anyone so far. It made *me* turn dusty rose in the face to admit it, but I didn't really *have* any proper friends. I did wonder if I dared ask Rhona to tea, but that would annoy Skye and make her meaner to me than ever. Maybe Rhona wouldn't come anyway.

I wasn't even sure I wanted her to come myself. I'd probably feel dreadfully shy and not know what to say to her. What would we play for all those hours before bedtime? I liked reading when I was by myself but you couldn't really read together. I liked painting but I had to do it in the kitchen with newspaper spread everywhere, long before Dad came home. I wasn't supposed to do any painting whatsoever in case I spilled paint on the carpets.

Dad didn't even allow felt-tip pens in case I got marks on the cream sofas. I was always very careful but Rhona was a giggly girl who never sat still. What if she flung her arm out when she was painting and accidentally spattered the wallpaper? If Dad saw he'd get into a rage whether Rhona was here or not.

I felt sick at the thought of Dad ranting in front of Rhona. I often cried because he scared me so. Perhaps he'd make Rhona cry too. Then she'd tell everyone at school. She'd definitely tell Skye because she was her best friend.

18

I kept pretending to Dad that I'd simply forgotten to ask anyone for a sleepover. He seemed to have forgotten himself for the last few weeks . . . forgotten until this very moment!

'You still haven't had any of your friends to stay, Beauty,' said Dad, jogging me on his knee as if I was a little baby.

My heart started thudding. I nibbled my lip anxiously.

'Don't *do* that,' said Dad, lightly tapping my mouth. He frowned at my teeth. 'They're sticking out *more*, Beauty. We're definitely going to have to get you fitted out with braces.'

'I don't want braces,' I mumbled.

'You don't want to end up looking like Bugs Bunny, do you?' said Dad, pulling a silly rabbit face, making his own teeth protrude.

'The dentist said to wait a year or so, darling,' Mum said. 'He's not even sure Beauty really needs a brace.'

'Nonsense! She needs perfect choppers, all girls do,' said Dad. '*Anyway*, who's your best friend at school, Beauty?'

'I like Rhona, but she's Skye's friend, not really mine,' I said.

'Can't you *all* be friends?' said Dad. 'Invite them both over. What about this Saturday?'

I breathed out thankfully.

'I can't this Saturday, Dad. That's when Rhona's having her birthday party,' I said.

'And you're going to this party?'

'Well, she's given me an invitation.'

'Lovely. Well, we'd better get cracking organizing a party for *your* birthday!'

I started nibbling my lip again.

'*Stop* it!' said Dad. 'Yes, we'll throw a really big bumper party for your birthday for every girl in your class, all your new Lady Mary Mountbank friends.'

'Do I really have to have a party, Dad?' I said desperately.

'I'm not sure about a lot of over-excited children running round the house,' Mum said quickly. She knew how Dad fussed so about the carpet and the cream sofas.

'We won't have them running riot *here*,' said Dad. 'We'll take them out somewhere swish. Leave it to me, I'll work on it. I want my Beauty to have a really fantastic birthday.'

'It's ever so kind of you, Dad,' I gabbled, though my heart was sinking.

I just had to hope he might somehow forget about it. I wasn't sure many of the girls in my class would come, especially not Skye or Emily or

Arabella. Or if they did, they'd all call me names the way they did in class.

'What does my best girl want for her birthday present, eh?' said Dad.

'I don't know,' I said.

'Well, think!' said Dad. He tapped my forehead. 'What's going on inside that little noddle of yours, eh? I bet you've got some idea of what you'd really really like for a present.'

'Well . . .'

'Ah! I thought so,' said Dad. 'Come on, what is it?'

Mum leaned forward, looking tense. Dad shifted his knee, tipping her off his lap.

'You go and make a start on tea, Dilly, I'm starving. Whack a steak under the grill. Even you can manage that.'

I tried to get up too but Dad hung onto me.

'No, no, you stay and keep your old dad company, little Beauty. I want to get to the bottom of your birthday wishes. What are you pondering? I can tell you've set your heart on something.'

I wriggled, wondering whether I dared ask.

'Come on, sweetie. No need to be shy of your old dad. What is it, eh? Have you got your eye on some outrageously expensive outfit? It's OK, baby, I'm used to your mum. I'll happily fork out for the junior designer doodahs of your choice – with a dinky little handbag and maybe your first pair of shoes with tiny heels, yes?'

'Well, actually, Dad, I wasn't really thinking about clothes.'

'Aye aye! Something more expensive, eh? It's OK, darling, the business is doing well. You heard me tell your mum I'm on the brink of the biggest deal yet. Do you fancy your very own little laptop? Or a personal flatscreen telly for your bedroom?'

'No, Dad. It's very kind of you but I truly don't want anything like that.'

'Then what *is* it? Come on, spit it out. I'll get you anything you like, my lovely.'

'Then please could I have a rabbit?' I whispered.

'What?' Dad cupped his ear.

'A rabbit,' I repeated. 'I'd really like a white one with loppy ears, but really any kind of rabbit would be . . .'

My voice tailed away when I saw the expression on Dad's face.

'Are you *thick*, Beauty?' he said.

'I – I don't know, Dad,' I said, not sure whether he wanted me to say yes or not. It didn't look as if I could win whatever I said.

'You come on like Miss Smarty Pants but I SAY YOU'RE THICK,' said Dad, jabbing me in the back at every word.

The last jab shoved me right off his lap onto the carpet. I tried to scuttle out of Dad's way but he caught hold of me by the wrist.

'Don't, Gerry!' Mum said, darting back into the room.

'I'm not hurting her,' said Dad. He deliberately loosened his fingers so that they were just like a fleshy pink bangle on my arm. '*Am* I hurting you, Beauty?'

'No, Dad,' I said.

'And *are* you thick?' he said.

'Yes, Dad,' I said.

'*Yes, Dad, certainly, Dad, as thick as* three *short planks, Dad,*' said Dad, in a horrible high squeaky imitation of my voice.

'Please let her go, Gerry,' said Mum. 'What has she done to upset you?'

'She's only gone and ignored one of the very basic rules of this household – this particularly luxurious house, custom-made by my own best craftsmen for our benefit. I don't think it's asking much to want us to take care of this lovely home. I'm not what anyone would call a finicky man, now am I?'

Mum and I didn't dare contradict him.

'I just like my house to be well looked after. No scratches on the parquet, no chips on the plaster, no dirty hairs or stains on the carpet. What *causes* scratches and chips and hairs and stains, mm, Beauty? Do you really not know the answer?'

'Pets, Dad,' I whispered.

'Yes. Full marks. And what has my view on pets always been?'

'I know I can't have a dog or a cat, but I did think a rabbit might just be OK, because it wouldn't be *in* the house, it would live in a little hutch out-side.'

'In a little hutch? Where, precisely? In the middle of my lawn? The rosebeds? The patio?'

'No, just by a wall somewhere.'

'Yes, that would really add to the classy atmos-phere, rabbits in smelly hutches. What else would you like, pigeons in cages, ferrets scrabbling in a run?'

'Not ferrets, Gerry, they'd eat the rabbits,' said Mum, trying to turn it into a joke.

'You shut your face, Dilly,' said Dad. 'No one's asking you.'

'Don't talk to me like that, Gerry, please,' said Mum. She tried to say it firmly but I could see she was trembling.

'I'll talk how I please in my own house,' said

Dad. 'Now listen to me, Beauty. I don't mind animals on a farm or in a field. I can get very fond of a winning gee-gee at a race track. I just won't have animals in the house – or surroundings, OK? When we were peasants in mud huts back in the bad old days, folk shared their homes with a cow and a goat and a guard dog, but we're not peasants now and this isn't a mud hut, this is a luxury home. Get that?'

Dad stuck his face right up close to me so that his head seemed horribly big. I could see the vein throbbing in his forehead, the blood vessels in his eyes, the hairs up his nostrils, the flecks of spit on his lips.

He looked like a story-book ogre about to eat me up. I felt tears pricking my eyes. I knew I mustn't cry in front of him. I always looked so ugly when I cried. My eyes screwed up, my nose ran, and my mouth went square. It always made Dad madder than ever.

I mustn't cry, I mustn't cry, I mustn't cry, I said inside my head, but the tears were already spurting down my cheeks.

'Go to your room right this minute, Beauty,' said Mum. 'It's naughty of you to nag at your dad for a pet, you know the rules.'

I knew Mum wasn't cross with me too. She was just trying to save me.

'Yes, get upstairs, now!' Dad thundered.

I was off like a shot. I was in such a hurry I tripped on the stairs and scraped my shins, making me cry harder. I flopped onto my rose-silk bed and hugged my old rag doll PJ. I had a shelf of big fancy china dolls in Victorian costume. They had ringlets and bonnets and parasols and long flounced dresses and tiny heeled boots. They were all collector's dolls and very beautiful but I couldn't play with them properly. They just stood on their shelves and stared straight through me with their spooky glass eyes.

I'd had PJ ever since I was a baby in a cot. Mum made her for me. Her eyes were crossed and her mouth was wonky and her arms and legs were uneven. I'd given her a drastic haircut when I was little which didn't help her appearance. PJ stood for Plain Jane but I didn't mind a bit that she wasn't very pretty. Her mouth still smiled and she felt soft and she had her own special sweet smell. When I was little I liked to suck my thumb and nuzzle my nose against her cloth cheek. It made me feel safe.

I tried sucking my thumb now, holding PJ close. I could hear Dad shouting downstairs. Poor Mum. She was getting the worst of it now.

I wanted to run downstairs, turning rapidly into SuperBeauty, my arms pumping, legs bounding a mile a minute. I'd floor Dad, seize Mum in my arms, and with one mighty bound we'd soar through the open window, up up up, away from our Happy Home.

FRANCES HODGSON BURNETT

A Little Princess

Three

I curled up in my bedroom, clutching PJ like a big baby. I smelled steak grilling. I didn't like meat much – it always made me think of the poor dead animal, but my mouth watered even so.

It didn't look as if I was going to get any tea. I sucked my thumb mournfully and then prowled round my bedroom looking for something – anything – to eat. I opened up my lunchbox. I'd finished my egg sandwiches and carrot sticks and crisps and muesli bar and apple and orange juice. I put my head right inside the plastic box, licking the crumbs. I sucked the last drop of juice from the carton and crunched up the brown apple core.

I found half a Polo mint at the bottom of my school bag and gobbled that down in a flash. The only other remotely edible object in the room was the little chocolate chicken Mum had given me at Easter. I liked it so much I said I was never going to eat it, I was going to keep it as an ornament.

That was months ago. I'd not been the slightest bit tempted up till now. I reached out, undid the yellow ribbon, and pulled the little brown chicken out of its cellophane wrapping. I held it in my hand. I made it go *cluck cluck cluck* in an anxious fashion.

'It's OK, little chicken, no need to be scared,' I whispered. 'I'm not going to eat you. I just want to look at you. Well, maybe I'll have just one little weeny lick . . .'

I stuck out my tongue and ran it along the chicken's glossy back. Soft milky chocolate glided over my taste buds. My mouth watered so that I drooled all over the little chicken. Then my teeth bit. I beheaded it, chomping the chocolate and swallowing it in seconds.

The chicken looked awful now its hollow innards were exposed. I ate the rest of it as quickly as I could, until the only sign the chocolate chicken had existed was the empty cellophane wrapper and the brown smears on my fingers.

I wished I hadn't eaten it now. I'd golloped it down so rapidly I hadn't really tasted it. It had taken the edge off my hunger but now I felt sick.

I wondered what would happen if I *was* sick. I'd once not made it to the bathroom in time and thrown up on the carpet and Dad had been so cross. I needed to distract myself quickly. I got out my schoolbooks and did my sums quickly, finishing all of them in twenty minutes, even though they were quite difficult problems. I started doodling in my rough book, making up my own problem.

Dad is a good man because
a) he loves us
b) he's given us a beautiful home
c) he works very hard for us

Dad is a bad man because
a) he gets so cross
b) he orders us around
c) he's a great big bully

So is Dad a good man or a bad man???

I had no idea how to find out the answer. I flipped over the page and started trying to draw the chocolate chicken from memory. I coloured it in with my crayons, feeling guiltier than ever. I did it very carefully, not going over my lines, even leaving little white spaces in the brown to give the illusion of glossy chocolate sheen.

I printed: *Dear Sam and Lily, This is my pet chicken*, neatly at the top of the page. *I didn't give her some tea. She was MY tea!*

A little later Mum came into my room carrying a tray.

'Dinner is served, madam,' she said, making a little curtsy, pretending to be a maid. She gave me a jaunty smile but her eyes were red.

'Oh, Mum,' I said. 'Have you been crying?'

'I'm fine, I'm fine,' she said quickly. 'Come on, pet, eat your supper.'

She'd made me a tuna-and-sweetcorn sandwich with a few oven chips and a little tomato salad. She'd cut the crusts off the sandwich and arranged the oven chips like a flower and cut the tomatoes into zig-zag shapes, trying to make it all look special. I wanted to wolf it down appreciatively but I still felt a bit sick. Maybe it was eating all the chocolate chicken.

'I'm not sure I can eat it all, Mum,' I said.

'Never mind. I'll have a little nosh, shall I?' said Mum. 'Oh chips, yummy yummy.'

'In my tummy,' I said automatically. 'Mum . . . is Dad still mad?'

'He's OK now. He's just nipped out to the office to check on something.' She paused. 'This new Water Meadows deal means a lot to him, Beauty. Maybe that's why he's so . . . tetchy at the moment.' Mum's voice sounded odd, like she was reading aloud. She wasn't looking me in the eye.

'That's rubbish, Mum,' I said. I nestled up close to her. 'I'm sorry you got shouted at when it was my fault, getting him all worked up about the rabbit. He was so angry I thought he was going to whack me one!'

'Your dad would never ever hit you, sweetheart,' said Mum. 'You're his little Beauty.'

She put her arms round me, knocking my glass

of orange juice over. 'Oh no! I'm so clumsy. We'll have to change the sheets, otherwise it'll look like you've wet the bed!' said Mum, trying to joke again. Her smile was stretched so tight it looked as if her face might split in two.

'I'm so sorry, Mum,' I said, starting to cry.

'There now, pet,' said Mum, rescuing my crayons and drawing pad from my damp bed. 'Oh, what a lovely chicken!'

'I ate it, Mum,' I confessed. 'The real chocolate chicken. I ate it. It's all gone.'

'Even its little chocolate beak and claws?' said Mum. 'Well, good for you! You had to wait long enough for your tea.'

She shook her head at the picture.

'You're so good at art, love. Can I keep it? We could frame it and hang it up in the kitchen.'

'Well, I did it for Sam. You're supposed to send your pictures in to the programme and then they show the best ones on the telly. But I think I'm a bit too old to send my picture in. It's supposed to be a programme for very little kids. Don't ever tell anyone I watch it, Mum.'

'As if I would. It's a lovely programme. *I* like it. So maybe it's a programme for little kids and little mums. I like that Sam.'

'So do I. And Lily.' I sighed.

'Oh, Beauty, I *wish* you could have your own

33

rabbit. I'd give anything to change your dad's mind. But there's no way he'll let you have any kind of pet, darling.'

I put my head on my knees.

'I hate him,' I muttered.

'No you don't. He's your dad and—'

'And he loves me very much – *not*,' I said. 'If he really loved us he wouldn't get mad and he wouldn't shout at us and he'd let me have a rabbit.'

'He doesn't *often* shout,' said Mum. 'It's just when he's really stressed out. He can't seem to help it. He doesn't always *mean* it. And I'm sure he feels sorry afterwards.'

'Yeah, like, *I'm sorry, Dilly, my mouth just opens and out come all these awful words and I swear and say dreadful things but I can't help it.* Has he *ever* said something like that, Mum? Has he ever even apologized?'

'Don't.' Mum smoothed my straggly hair, tucking it behind my ears.

'Maybe I'll ask Dad to get me boxing gloves for my birthday and then I'll bash him one if he shouts at us,' I said.

'Ha ha,' said Mum. 'How about eating one little triangle of tuna sandwich, eh? Just a little nibble.'

I tried a tiny bite. Then another. And then suddenly I was starving hungry and able to tuck into my tea. Mum had a triangle of tuna sandwich too, and we shared out the chips.

'Mum?'

'Yes, love.'

'Sometimes I wish it was just you and me.'

'Sh!' Mum looked anxiously over her shoulder even though we knew Dad was at the Happy Homes office on the other side of town.

When we'd finished our tea and I'd got ready for bed Mum stayed in my room and we read stories together. Mum's mum, my nana, never read her any stories at all, so it's fun for Mum reading them for the first time with me.

We used to read lots of stories about fairies and then another series about a princess. Mum had just bought me a new princess book.

'Oh dear, it's not the same series. I've made a mistake. Typical me! It looks a bit queer and old-fashioned. It's probably boring. We don't have to read it if you don't want to,' said Mum.

'I think it looks good,' I said. 'Look, I'll start it off, OK?'

We put the tray on the floor and Mum squashed in beside me. I started reading about this little girl, Sara Crewe. I was interested that it said right in the first paragraph that she was odd-looking. Later on she said she was one of the ugliest children she'd ever seen. I especially liked that part.

Mum liked the bit where Sara's father buys

her a whole new set of clothes, and then another elaborate set for Sara's new doll, Emily. Mum took her turn reading while I drew lots of velvet dresses and hats with feathers and fur coats and muffs and old-fashioned lace-trimmed underwear – a long row for Sara and a little row underneath for Emily.

We got so absorbed we jumped violently when we heard the car draw up outside.

'Oh, lordy, that's Dad back. Quick, chuck your crayons on the floor and settle down to sleep, pet, OK?'

Mum gave me a quick kiss, kicked my tray under the bed, switched off my light and rushed out of the room. I lay still. We'd forgotten to change my orange-juicy sheet and it felt uncomfortably damp and sticky.

I listened out for shouting. I could hear Dad talking but I couldn't make out what he was saying. Then I heard *pad pad pad* as he came up the stairs in his socks. My heart started thudding. I shut my eyes tight and tried to breathe deeply, as if I was asleep.

I heard my door creak open.

'Beauty?' Dad whispered.

I tried not to twitch. I breathed in and out, in and out, in and out . . .

'Beauty!' said Dad, very near me now. His head was so close I could feel his breath on me.

'I think you're awake,' said Dad. 'I'm sure I saw your light on when I drove up.'

Eyes shut, keep breathing, don't flinch!

'Oh, well. Never mind. You're a very naughty girl, plaguing your old dad about pets, especially when I've got a lot on my mind at the moment. No wonder I get cross! But remember this, sweetheart. Your daddy loves you. You're his special Beauty.' His voice thickened as if he was about to cry.

He gave me a kiss on my cheek. He stayed bent over me for a few seconds. I think he was hoping I'd put my arms around his neck. I kept them stiffly by my sides, my fists clenched. He sighed and then went out of my room, pulling the door to behind him.

I still didn't dare move, just in case he poked his head back in and caught me fidgeting. I stayed in exactly the same position, cramped and uncomfortable, until I heard the television downstairs. Then I dared stretch out. My arms and legs throbbed. I breathed out so deeply my nostrils quivered. My insides still hurt though, as if someone had taken my long wiggly intestines and tied knots up and down them, like a string of sausages. I clasped PJ against my sore tummy and eventually went to sleep.

Four

Dad had usually left for work by the time I got up in the morning. However, when I went downstairs for breakfast he was sitting at the kitchen table drinking coffee and reading his newspaper. My tummy squeezed back into sausages even though Mum smiled at me reassuringly. She was looking extra-pretty in her shiny peach satin nightie and dressing gown, her long blonde hair falling past her shoulders, her neck and arms as smooth and white as ice cream.

'Hi, poppet. Would you like an egg?' she said.

I shook my head, pouring myself a bowl of cornflakes.

'I've got two flaky corns on my feet. Would you like to snack on them too?' asked Dad, looking up from his paper.

I made myself giggle, though he'd made that joke hundreds of times already. It came out like a little mouse snicker. Mum poured him another cup of coffee and gave him another round of toast. Dad flicked it with his fingers.

'For God's sake, Dilly, this isn't toasted properly. It's meant to be *toast*, right? Shove it back in the toaster.' Dad raised his eyebrows at me. 'Your mother, Beauty! *Not* what you'd call a cook. Maybe it's just as well you said no to that egg, because she hasn't got a clue how to boil it.'

I smiled uncomfortably. 'There's not time, anyway, Mum,' I said, looking at the clock. 'Shall I watch Dad's toast while you go and get dressed?'

'I'm taking you to school today, Beauty,' said Dad. 'I've got to pop into the Guildhall to see about this planning malarkey so I'll drop you off on the way.'

I sat chewing my cornflakes into mush. It was a small mouthful but it seemed to be swelling right up to the roof of my mouth, swilling in and out of my teeth, coating my tongue with orangey-gold slime. I tried swallowing but my throat wouldn't work. I didn't dare spit the cornflakes out into my bowl. I was doomed to keep them multiplying in my mouth until they spurted straight out of my ears.

'Beauty? What are you pulling that silly face for? Aren't you pleased I'm giving you a lift in the Merc? Make all your little friends envious, eh?'

I nodded, incapable of speech. My nod was the biggest fib ever. I didn't want Dad to take me to school. I especially didn't want him to take me in his shiny silver Mercedes. Mercedes was my middle name. It caused almost as much hilarity as my first name. Skye suggested I should be called Ugly Skoda Cookson. This always

40

made Skye and Emily and Arabella fall about laughing.

'*Say* something, then, don't just nod your head,' said Dad.

I swallowed desperately. Some of the cornflake slurp slid down the back of my throat.

'Sorry, Dad,' I mumbled, taking a long drink of juice.

The cornflakes were still such a soggy clump that I choked. I clamped my hand over my mouth while Mum patted me on the back. I leaned against her, rubbing my cheek against the soft silkiness of her nightie. I wished I was little enough for her to pick me up and hold me safe in her arms, still way too small for school.

I cleaned my teeth and went to the toilet and stuck my arms into my brown blazer. Dad sighed when he saw me.

'I don't know! I fork out for the poshest girls' school in the whole county and they want you all to wear that ugly uniform the colour of dog's muck.'

'Gerry!' said Mum.

'Well, honestly, why can't it be pink or lilac or some pretty girly colour? She looks like Little Orphan Annie.' Dad tousled my hair in exasperation. 'At least Little Orphan Annie had curls. Can't you do something with Beauty's hair, Dilly? What about a perm?'

41

'She's still a little girl! And I think Beauty's got lovely hair just as it is,' said Mum.

'You'd like to be a little curlynob, wouldn't you, Beauty?' said Dad. 'Couldn't you put it up in those roller things at night for her, Dilly?'

'People don't use rollers any more!' said Mum. 'Not since bouffant hairdos went out of fashion.'

'Oh well, pardon me, I'm just a sad old bloke who hasn't got a clue about fashion,' said Dad.

There was an edge to his voice. I held my breath, wondering if he was going to start ranting all over again, but he just shook his head at Mum and slapped her lightly on the bottom.

'That's right, you put me in my place, Dilly,' said Dad. 'Come on, then, Beauty, let's get you to school.'

There was no way I could get out of it. I slumped down low on the soft leather back seat as Dad tooted his horn and shouted and swore his way through the traffic.

'Idiot! Call yourself a driver! Come *on*, stop dithering, I'm late already,' Dad fumed, honking at the car in front of us.

'Tell you what, Dad, I could jump out here. It would only take me two minutes to walk up the road. Then you could go straight into town to the Guildhall.'

'What? No, don't talk nonsense, darling, I'm delivering you right to the school gates,' said Dad.

42

There was no point wasting breath trying to persuade him. He drew up absolutely spit-spot in front of the school gates, even though there was an official notice on the gatepost warning parents not to park there. I didn't dare point this out to Dad, but lots of the mothers and fathers delivering their own girls to school were staring, some even raising their eyebrows and shaking their heads.

The Mercedes was always a noticeable car. Now it seemed as big as a double-decker bus. I undid my seat belt, struggled with the door handle and hurtled out of the car.

'Thanks for the lift, Dad,' I gabbled.

'Hey, don't I get a kiss from my Beauty?' Dad called loudly from his open window.

Arabella and Emily were standing watching. They nudged each other, sniggering, as I kissed Dad's cheek.

'Bye bye, Beauty!' he called.

Arabella and Emily were practically wetting themselves.

'Hello hello, Ugly!' said Arabella. 'So Big Daddy brought you to school today, eh?'

'Don't you know you're not supposed to park outside the gates? Does your dad think he's so special in that great big silver sardine tin that rules don't apply to him?' said Emily.

I tried to march past but they took an arm each,

43

hanging onto me. I craned round and saw Dad waving at me cheerily, thinking I'd met up with my two best friends – instead of my two worst enemies. No, Skye was the worst enemy of all. There she was, singing and dancing in the playground, showing off some silly routine she'd learned from the television, tossing her long blonde hair and wiggling her hips. She should have looked ridiculous but she didn't. She sounded like a *real* singer and strutted like a *real* dancer. You couldn't help watching her. It wasn't just me. We were all watching, everyone in the whole playground, and all the girls were wishing they were Skye, even me.

Skye finished with a flourish, arms up, as if expecting applause. Some of the girls started clapping as if it was a real show and Skye was the star. Rhona clapped too, begging Skye to show her how to do the little skippy strutty bit.

'Show us too, Skye!' said Arabella, dropping my arm. 'You're so good you ought to go on *Watchbox*!'

'Hey, Skye, did you see old Ugly coming to school in her dad's silver rubbish car?' said Emily, giving me a little shove.

'Oh my, the Flashmobile,' said Skye, shading her eyes, pretending to be dazzled. 'Ooh, let's all act like we're impressed.'

She pranced around, Arabella and Emily

44

copying her. Rhona went on skipping and strutting, working her way over to me.

'I'm useless at this lark,' she said cheerily. She
glanced at Skye and Emily and Arabella. 'Take no
notice, they're just being silly,' she said.

'Yeah,' I said shakily.

'You are coming to my birthday party, aren't
you, Beauty?' she asked.

I nodded shyly.

'Ooh! You haven't *really* asked Ugly, have you?'
said Skye, putting her hands on her hips. 'You are
a total ninny, Rhona. We don't want creepy old
Ugly.'

'Yes I do,' said Rhona. She reached out and
squeezed my hand. Her brown eyes looked into
mine. Her cheeks were very pink, maybe from the
dancing. 'I'm so glad you're coming, Beauty.'

She really sounded as if she meant it, as if she
wanted us to be friends. Then the bell rang and
Rhona pulled a face. 'Oh, blow. Lesson time,' she
said.

I pulled a face and sighed too, though I was
always relieved when the bell went. I *liked*
lessons. Miss Woodhead was kind but very strict,
so we weren't allowed to mess about and chat in
the classroom. We had to sit up straight at our
desks and listen carefully and put our hands up
if we wanted to say anything. I could cope with

lessons easy-peasy. It was the playtimes that were the problem, before school and mid-morning break and the endless lunch hour.

We had to play outside unless it was pouring with rain, but we were allowed in if we needed to go to the toilet. The minute I'd finished lunch I rushed to the cloakrooms and locked myself in the end cubicle in the toilets. I'd tucked my copy of *A Little Princess* inside my school blazer. I sat peacefully for more than half an hour, at Miss Minchin's Seminary with Sara. The eldest girl at the school, spiteful Lavinia, was *so* like Skye.

I wished I was more like Sara, who never seemed the slightest bit upset by Lavinia and all her catty remarks. Sara was loved by all the other girls, especially the little ones. They hung on her every word and called her a princess and begged her to tell them stories. I imagined myself sauntering next door, going into the Reception class, sitting on one of their squashy cushions and telling them one of *my* stories.

They'd think I'd gone mental. The little girls didn't seem to like me any more than the big girls.

Sudden tears prickled in my eyes and splashed the insides of my glasses. I gave a monumental sniff and wiped my glasses on my blouse.

'Don't you *dare* cry,' I told myself fiercely. 'Stop

being so stupidly sorry for yourself. Lots of people like you. Rhona likes you. She's asked you to her birthday party. She wants to be friends.'

I felt a lot better – until I heard two girls from our class, Louise and Poppy come into the toilets. I knew it was them because they kept calling out their silly nicknames, Lulu and Poo-poo. I think I'd almost sooner be called Ugly than Poo-poo, but Poppy didn't seem to mind at all. They kept up this long silly conversation, shouting to each other from their individual cubicles.

'Hey, Lulu, what are you going to give Rhona for her birthday?'

'I thought I'd maybe give her one of those special stuffed bears with a recording inside its tummy, Poo-poo. I could make it sing *Happy Birthday*.'

'*Great* idea, Lulu. Maybe we could give her *two* bears? I could give her a boy and you could give her a girl?'

'Yeah, OK, Poo-poo – thought it *was* my idea first. Don't tell anyone else or Rhona will get *heaps* of birthday bears.'

'How many of us are going, Lulu?'

'She's invited everyone, Poo-poo, the whole *class*.'

I tensed up like I had stomach-ache, bending forward so that *A Little Princess* dug into my chest uncomfortably. So Rhona hadn't singled me

47

out. She hadn't invited me to her party because she particularly liked me. She'd invited *everyone*. Maybe she didn't like me at all, but she was kind and didn't want to invite every other girl in the class, leaving me out altogether.

I waited for Louise and Poppy to stop their silly twitterings in the toilets. When they went I let myself have a two-minute howl. I timed myself by my watch, clamping my hand over my mouth and pinching my nose to make myself stop. I mopped myself dry with toilet paper but it was the shiny scratchy sort and it made my eyes redder than ever.

'Look at Ugly-Wugly! She's been *crying*! Boo-hoo, boo-hoo, little baby,' said Skye, as we went back into the classroom for afternoon school.

'Are you OK, Beauty?' said Rhona, looking concerned.

'Yes, I'm fine, thank you,' I said. I tried to say it in an airy confident way but my voice was still a bit wobbly and I gave a loud hiccup at the end of my sentence.

'Oh dear, she's got the burps now,' said Skye, spluttering. 'Someone thump Baby Ugly on the back, quick.'

'Watch out or I'll give *you* a thump,' I said fiercely and I gave her a shove right in the chest.

It wasn't a particularly hard shove but she

wasn't expecting it. She staggered, arms flailing, shrieking like a siren.

'For goodness' sake, Skye, stop making that dreadful noise!' said Miss Woodhead.

'I'm in *pain*, Miss Woodhead. Beauty Cookson punched me here and it *hurts*,' said Skye, hands clutching her front dramatically.

'*Beauty* punched you?' said Miss Woodhead, raising her eyebrows.

'Yes, she did, Miss Woodhead. I was watching,' said Arabella.

'I saw her too. Beauty just *attacked* poor Skye for no reason at all,' said Emily.

'I expect she had reason enough, but that's still no excuse for fighting, Beauty! I'm not having my girls brawling like guttersnipes. I don't particularly care for tell-tales either. Now sit down and settle down, all of you, before I get really cross. I *was* thinking of having a special story-time this afternoon but I'm not sure you're in the right mood. I think we'd better have a spelling test instead.'

Everyone groaned and glared at me, as if it was all my fault. They groaned even louder when we marked our spellings at the end of the lesson and I got twenty out of twenty.

I hurtled out of school when the bell went. Mum was waiting for me. She was wearing jeans and a pink T-shirt with a fairy on it. She'd tied her hair into two cute plaits secured with pink bobbles. She looked about fourteen, so much younger and prettier than any of the other mums.

'Hi, Mum,' I said happily, linking arms with her.

Way back in the playground I heard Skye and Arabella and Emily calling after me. I didn't look round. Mum did though.

'Is that you they're calling?' she asked.

I shrugged.

'What is it they're saying?'

'Just something stupid. *They're* stupid. Come on, Mum, let's get home quick. I don't want to miss my programme.'

'OK, OK. Sam is calling to you, is he?'

'You bet he is.'

We made it home in heaps of time. Mum gave me a glass of milk and a banana sandwich. I was starving as I'd had very little breakfast and I'd bolted my lunch. I sipped and munched as Sam waved at me and Lily nibbled her carrot.

'*Who do we want to see?*' sang the children.

'*Sam and Lily in the Rabbit Hutch,*' I sang, through a mouthful of milky banana.

'Hello there,' said Sam, smiling straight at me. 'How are you doing?'

'So so, Sam,' I said.

He gave me an understanding nod.

'Lily here is getting very excited,' he said, cuddling her.

Lily lolled sleepily against Sam's chest, her blue eyes dreamy.

'She doesn't *look* very excited, Sam,' I said.

Sam gave me a little wink. We had to keep up the pretence for all the little kids watching the programme.

'Guess how old Lily is,' said Sam. 'Go on, have a little think. How old are *you*?'

'I'm a bit embarrassed to tell you, Sam. I think I'm heaps older than most of your viewers,' I said.

'Well, Lily's a bit younger than you,' said Sam. 'She's very nearly one year old. She's very mature for a nearly one-year-old, isn't she?' He tickled her gently under her chin. 'You can toddle out into the garden and fix yourself a lovely veggie tea and you can tuck yourself up in bed and get yourself up in the morning and give yourself a good wash. Could *you* do that when you were nearly one?'

'Maybe I had a stab at it,' I said, giggling.

'I thought I'd throw a little birthday party for our Lily. Do you think she'd like that?'

'I think she might like a party,' I said. 'But not with heaps and heaps of people.'

Sam nodded. 'I don't think Lily wants a *big* party with lots and lots of friends. She's a bit shy sometimes. I think we'll give her a *little* party. Just

Lily and me – and you too, of course. You can come, can't you?'

'Of course I can come! Oh, Sam, I wish *you* could come to my birthday party. Just you and me and Lily. And Mum. And *maybe* Rhona. She's asked me to *her* birthday party but I'm not sure I want to go. Skye will be there. She's Rhona's best friend and my worst-ever enemy. She's so horrible. I don't know why Rhona wants to be her friend.'

'Maybe Rhona will get fed up with Skye and make friends with you?' said Sam.

'Oh, I wish! But it's never going to happen,' I said, sighing.

'You never know,' said Sam. 'But remember, Lily and I are still your best friends.'

'I'll always remember that,' I said.

Same gave me a special secret smile, and then he raised his voice, talking to everyone else.

'What do you think I should get Lily for a birthday present? Have you got any good ideas? How about painting me a picture of an ideal present for our birthday bunny? Send it to Sam at the Rabbit Hutch, OK? Bye then.'

I waved goodbye and then I went upstairs and drew a very special picture of Lily with a little paper crown perched on her head and a H @L NMD SNC@ X badge tied round one floppy ear. I drew her a birthday carrot cake with real baby carrots decorating the icing on top. I drew one big candle in the middle.

Then I got a new piece of paper and drew my own birthday cake. I'd seen exactly the one I wanted, with white icing and pink rosebuds. I *loved* proper birthday cake. I loved the soft sponge and the jam and the buttercream and I especially loved the sweet icing.

I looked at my paper birthday cake and then pretended to blow out my candles and make a wish.

Five

I went to Lily's birthday party of course – along with a million other little kids, all of us singing *Happy Birthday to You* into our television sets. Lily looked up and blinked her big blue eyes especially at me. Sam was wearing a fantastic new T-shirt in her honour, dark green with little white Lily-type rabbits running across his chest. Lily seemed very appreciative, cheekily poking out her little pink tongue at Sam.

'She likes my green T-shirt, doesn't she? Maybe she thinks it's a great big cabbage!'

Sam gave Lily real cabbage leaves for her tea and, *guess what*, a carrot cake with a candle, almost exactly the same as the one I'd drawn!

'You gave me the idea, Beauty,' Sam whispered. 'Lily loves her cake, though I'm not sure she's up to blowing out her candle. Will you help her? One, two, three – *blow*!'

I blew, Sam blew, children all over Britain blew – and Lily's candle went out.

'There! Now Lily has to make her special birthday wish. She'd like to share her birthday wish with you, Beauty. Close your eyes and wish hard.'

I closed my eyes and wished: *I wish I could really meet you and Lily, Sam!*

Sam gave Lily a cosy new bed for her birthday present, with a special green duvet and a straw pillow. She tried it out, looking very cute, though she lay in it the wrong way round, her head under the duvet and her big fluffy-tailed bottom on the pillow.

'Silly old Lily,' Sam said fondly. 'Out you come, sweetie. It's not bedtime yet. It's time for all your party games. We're going to play Blind Bunny Buff and Pass the Parsnip and Hunt the Carrot.'

Lily took no notice.

'Do you know something? I think she's really gone to sleep!' Sam said. 'Oh well! Maybe you'd like to invent a special party game for Lily? Would you like to paint it for me? Send your paintings to me at the Rabbit Hutch. I'm looking forward to seeing them. Bye for now – oh, just a minute!' he said, as the music started up to show it was the end of the programme. 'Beauty? I do hope you enjoy Rhona's party!'

'Thank you, Sam,' I said.

I went upstairs and drew a picture of me with Lily on my lap. I'm quite small and Lily's very big so it looked as if I was giving a polar bear a cuddle. I had my arms outstretched to cope with Lily's breadth, one hand clamped round her haunch to

56

keep her safely wedged on my lap, the other hand stroking her head.

This is a very simple but very special party game, I printed at the top of my picture. *It can be played at very small parties by one person and one pet. It's called Stroke the Rabbit.*

Then I sat cross-legged on my bed with my arms out as if I was holding an imaginary Lily. I stroked thin air until my arms ached.

I heard Dad's car draw up in the driveway. I listened hard as he came in the front door. He wasn't singing his silly Happy Homes song. He wasn't dancing down the hall in his socks. It looked like he was in a bad mood. I decided to stay in my room as long as possible. At least I couldn't hear any shouting.

After a long time Mum called up to me that supper was ready. I started down the stairs and went to go into the dining room, where Mum usually set the table.

'No, no, we're having supper on trays in the living room. Dad's a bit tired,' said Mum, taking me gently by the shoulders and turning me round. She gave me a little reassuring pat as she did so.

Dad was slumped in his chair, his shirt top buttons undone and his belt buckle loosened. He looked as if he needed to ease his head too. There were lines stretched tight across his forehead, pinching the top of his nose.

My tummy tensed but he gave me a surprisingly warm smile.

'Hello there, little Beauty. What have you been up to, eh?'

'I've just been doing my homework, Dad,' I said.

'That's my clever girl,' Dad said, sighing. 'You come and cheer your old dad up now. I've spent the whole day arguing with jobsworths who won't budge an inch and it's doing my head in. Tell me about *your* day, darling. What did you get up to with all your chums?'

I took a deep breath and launched into an utterly fictitious account of my day with my best friend Rhona. Mum served us Marks and Spencer's spaghetti bolognese while I nattered on about Rhona and me making up a dance routine together and everyone clapping. I was getting a little carried away as I couldn't dance to save my life but Dad seemed to believe me.

'That's my girly!' he said happily.

'Will Rhona be having dancing at her party tomorrow?' Mum said.

'I don't know. Maybe,' I said cautiously. 'It says wear casual clothes on the invitation. Oh, and we're supposed to take our swimming costumes too.'

'Have they got their own pool then?' said Dad. 'Where does she live, in Groveland Park? Most of the houses there have pools, but they're all the size of postage stamps. I bet you'll just sit on the edge and swish your tootsies in the water.'

'I wish they'd say exactly what they mean by "casual",' said Mum. 'Does that mean you wear your jeans?'

'Beauty's not wearing jeans to a *party*,' said Dad. 'No, she'll wear her little pink number.'

I stopped eating. Dad had taken me to one of his golf dinner and dances at Christmas. He'd insisted on buying me an elaborate bridesmaid-type satin dress with gauzy puff sleeves and ruching and frills flouncing everywhere. I looked truly terrible in it, like I was wearing an old lady's eiderdown.

I imagined the remarks that Skye and Emily and Arabella would make.

'*Not* my pink dress!' I blurted.

Dad stopped eating too. And Mum.

'What's the matter with your pink dress?' said Dad. 'It cost a small fortune from Harrods. Don't you like it?'

I forced a smile.

'Oh I love love love it, Dad,' I said. My voice went high and squeaky I was trying so hard. 'That's precisely the *problem*. It's so ultra-gorgeous and glamorous that I'm terrified of getting it spoiled at the party. I could easily spill juice all down it or tear one of the frills.'

'Not if you're *careful*,' said Dad, but he nodded approvingly all the same. 'I'm glad you want to look after it. Still, no jeans, you don't want to look like a dirty scruffy tomboy at this party. How about your pretty blue blouse and your little white pleated skirt? You look sweet in that.'

It was my second-most-hated outfit. They would still sneer and snigger at me – but it was marginally better than the pink eiderdown outfit.

'Yes, good idea, Dad,' I said.

'Mum could maybe tie blue ribbons in your hair?' said Dad. He ran his fingers through my long limp hair, sighing. 'Couldn't you *find* some rollers, Dilly, and give it a bit of a curl?'

'Beauty would hate having those uncomfy rollers prodding her head,' said Mum.

Dad wound spaghetti round and round his fork.

'You girls have to suffer a bit for your looks,' he said, chomping, his tongue and teeth coated with tomato sauce. '*I* know! Take her to the hairdresser's Saturday morning, get *them* to primp and twiddle with her hair, do it up fancy-like.'

'Well . . .' Mum saw my desperate expression. 'I don't think we'd be able to get her an appointment

60

at the hairdresser's at such short notice.'

'Oh, Dilly, why are you always so hopeless? Look, get Beauty along there when they open and *insist* on an appointment. You could do with getting your hair done yourself, it's a bit' – he made wobbly gestures with his hands – 'sort of *tired.*'

All of Mum looked tired nowadays. It was such hard work trying to keep Dad happy. She was very pale, with violet circles under her eyes. She still looked very pretty but like she hadn't had any sleep for a week.

She looked at me apologetically. 'OK, I'll take Beauty tomorrow morning and we'll both get our hair done.'

'That's the ticket,' said Dad, breaking off a piece of bread and wiping it round his plate. 'I want my girls to do me proud.'

'We know that, Gerry,' said Mum, with the tiniest edge to her voice.

Dad was up very early on Saturday to go to play golf. He crept around getting dressed and going to the bathroom, but tripped at the top of the stairs. His golf clubs made such a clatter that I shot out of bed and ran onto the landing, convinced the house was falling down.

Dad collected up his clubs, cursing furiously.

'Oops, pardon my French,' he said, when he saw me. 'Back to bed, Beauty. I'm just off to my golf. Got to keep in with the right guys. This is the way your dad sorts out all his little problems. Just call me Gerry the Fixer. Ta ta, baby. Enjoy your party.'

I didn't go back to bed. I pattered into Mum's bedroom and slid in beside her. Mum put her arms round me and cuddled me close. Both our hearts were still thudding fast because of the noise. We were just drifting back to sleep when there was another crash from downstairs, and sounds of Dad swearing.

'Oh God, that sounded like a bottle of juice. He's jerked the fridge open so violently it'll have fallen out,' Mum murmured.

'Can't you even stack the fridge properly, Dilly? I've got cranberry juice all over my cream golf trousers!' Dad yelled up the stairs.

I couldn't help giggling – and Mum started spluttering too. She covered our faces with the duvet so he couldn't hear.

'Dilly!' Dad shouted furiously. 'Get that lazy butt of yours downstairs and sort this fridge out before I get back!'

He slammed out of the house, banging the front door. We waited, listening for the thud of the car door, the hum of the engine. The gravel crunched as Dad drove off. Mum and I sighed and lay flat on our backs, limp with relief that he'd gone.

'I think he's woken all the neighbours, not just us,' said Mum.

'Do you think he'll still be cross when he gets home?' I asked.

'Not if he wins at golf,' said Mum, yawning.

'What time do you think he'll be back? Will he want to collect me from Rhona's party?' I asked anxiously.

'Maybe,' said Mum.

'So I've really got to wear my blue blouse and that pleated skirt?'

'You look lovely in it, really. And we'll get your hair all curly.'

'Mum, they're all going to laugh at me.'

'No they won't,' said Mum. 'You'll look wonderful. They'll be envious.'

'You're just saying that to make me feel better,' I said, giving her a little shake.

'Well, OK. I wish I *could* make everything better for you, Beauty.' Mum paused, gently stroking my neck and shoulders. 'Are you unhappy, pet?'

I took a deep breath. 'No, I'm fine,' I said.

'Now *you're* just saying that to make me feel better. Oh, lovey, I don't know what to *do*. Your dad's getting worse, isn't he? But if I try to stop him he gets even angrier.'

'I know.'

'And at school – do they still tease you lots?'

'Yep.'

'Does Rhona?'

'No. She's always kind to me.'

'Well, that's great. Can't you be friends with her?'

'Mum! She's Skye's best friend. And Skye is my most deadly enemy. She hates me.'

'Well, *we* hate *her*,' said Mum. 'And her horrible patronizing mother. When we got you into Lady Mary Mountbank she came up to me in the playground and welcomed me to the school like it was her own family house. And then she goes, "So are you Beauty's big sister?" and then she gives this great shriek when I said I'm your mum. "You must have had her so *young*," like I'm a child bride. Well, OK, maybe I *was* – but it's none of her business, eh?'

'I liked it better at Jenner Street Primary, Mum.'

'I know, love, but your dad set his heart on you going to Lady Mary Mountbank. It *is* a really good school. You'll go on to the Seniors, swan off to university, get a brilliant degree, have a fantastic career, whatever. I don't want you to end up like me. I've never had a proper job. I was just a receptionist at Happy Homes – and I wasn't even a *good*

64

receptionist. I was too shy to speak up properly and I kept getting muddled using the telephone switchboard. Your dad called me into his office all set to fire me only I was wearing some silly skimpy top and he got distracted and asked me out on a date instead.'

'Maybe if you weren't so pretty you'd have simply got the sack. You'd have found some other job and some other man, someone the complete opposite of Dad.' I tried to imagine him. I saw Sam, as if I had a tiny television set inside each eye. 'Someone gentle, who listens and lets you do what you want. Someone who never ever shouts. Someone who's always always always in a good mood.'

Mum lay still, holding her breath as if I was telling her a fairy story. Then she gave a long sigh.

'Yeah, right,' she said sadly. Then she tickled me under the chin. 'No, *wrong*. If I hadn't married your dad I wouldn't have had *you*, babe.'

'But you'd have had *another* girl. You could have met a dead handsome guy and then I'd maybe be a *real* beauty.'

'You're my Beauty now – and we're going to make you even more beautiful at the hairdresser's.'

Mum was trying hard to sound positive. I

65

hoped the hairdresser's would be totally booked up, maybe with a bride and her mum and six bridesmaids and a flower girl – but they were depressingly empty when we went in the door. They could fit us in with ease.

My hairdresser was called Becky. She was very blonde and very slim and very pretty, almost as pretty as Skye. I was worried she'd act like Skye too, sniggering and making faces in the mirror to her colleagues as she shampooed my straggly hair and then twisted it into spiral curls, lock by lock. But she was really sweet to me, chatting away as if we were friends. She spent ages on my hair. When she'd finally finished dabbing at it with her styling comb she stood back, smiling.

'There! Don't you look lovely!' she said.

I didn't look lovely at all. My hair twizzled this way and that in odd thin ringlets. My ears stuck out comically in between the curls. I wanted to hide my head in her wastepaper basket and weep, but she'd tried so hard to please me I politely pretended to be delighted with my new-look corkscrew head.

Mum had a similar hairstyle but it really did look lovely on her. Her little pale heart-shaped face was framed with a halo of pale gold curls. Skye's mother was actually right – she really did look like my big sister. When we went round the town shopping lots of men stared at her and a gang of boys all wolf-whistled.

'No one would laugh if *you* were called Beauty, Mum,' I said. 'Hey, let's swap names. You be Beauty and I'll be Dilly.'

'Dilly's a duff name too. Dilys! I suppose my mum thought it was posh. Let's choose different names. I'll be ... mm, what shall I be called? Something dignified and grown up and sensible.' Mum giggled. 'All the things I'm not.' She saw the sign on the front of a shop. 'How about *Claire*?'

'OK. I'll be Sara, after Sara Crewe. Let's be best friends, Claire.'

'Are we the same age then?' said Mum.

'No, I'm a couple of years older than you,' I said firmly. 'So I get to sort things out for both of us.'

Mum laughed. 'Yep, I think you'll be good at that,' she said.

We played the Claire-and-Sara game as we went round the shopping centre looking for a good birthday present for Rhona. She was our friend, but only our second-best friend. *We* were best friends, and now we'd left college we shared a flat together and we both had fabulous jobs. Claire was a television presenter and Sara was a children's book illustrator.

67

'Maybe you'll work in the same studio as the *Rabbit Hutch* show and you'll get to meet Sam and Lily, Claire,' I said.

'Oh, I know Sam already,' said Mum, acting Claire. 'Don't tell, but we're actually dating.' She looked at me a little anxiously. 'Is that OK, Sara, or do *you* want Sam as your boyfriend?'

'Maybe,' I said.

'Well, perhaps we'll have to share him,' said Mum, giggling. 'I'll go out with him one week and you can go out with him the next.'

'And I'm going to draw Lily. Yeah, I'm going to make a picture book all about her.'

'Do you think Rhona would like a book as a birthday present?' said Mum, swapping back to herself.

'I'm not sure what sort of books she likes,' I said. I thought about it. 'Do you think *she*'d like *A Little Princess*? It's my absolute favourite book.'

'Then I'm sure she'd like it too.'

So we bought her a copy in W H Smith's, and then we went into the actual Claire shop and bought her three slim silver bangles and then we went to New Look and bought her a pink T-shirt with *Princess* written in silver lettering on the front.

'There, it all goes beautifully together,' said Mum. 'She'll love her presents, Beauty.'

'Do you really think so? They're more interesting than a stuffed teddy bear, aren't they? That's what Lulu and Poo-poo are giving her.'

'She'll like your presents best, Beauty,' said Mum. 'Just you wait and see.'

Six

'There, you look lovely, Beauty,' said Mum, giving me little strokes, as if I was Lily.

'No I don't,' I said.

'Yes you *do*, darling, honestly,' said Mum.

I dodged round her to get to the long mirror in her bedroom. I knew she was simply saying that to make me feel good – but I still wondered whether somehow she could be right. I looked in the mirror, hoping for a miracle.

It hadn't happened. I stared back, a podgy, awkward girl with corkscrew curls, a frilly blue blouse and a white skirt way too tight. I looked at myself until I blurred, because my eyes filled with tears.

'I look a total berk, Mum,' I said flatly. I stuck out my tongue at my image and waddled about in my black patent shoes, turning myself into a clown.

'Stop it, darling. You look great. Well, maybe the shoes aren't quite right. They do look a bit clumpy,' said Mum. 'We should have got you some lighter party shoes. White, or maybe silver?'

She suddenly darted to her wardrobe and

rummaged at the bottom among her own shoes. She produced a pair of silver dance shoes and waved them triumphantly in the air.

I stared at her as if she'd gone mad.

'I can't wear *them*, Mum. They're yours! They'll be much too big.'

But when I sat down and put them on they very nearly fitted me. I was alarmed at the thought I had feet as big as my mum's already. They'd be totally enormous by the time I was grown up. I'd have to wear real clown's boots, those long ones as big as baguettes.

'They look great on you!' said Mum.

'But they've got high heels!'

'They're not *that* high. Anyway, it'll make all the other girls jealous if you're wearing proper heels,' said Mum.

I considered this. 'OK. So how do you walk in them?' I said, wobbling to my feet. I took one uncertain step and nearly fell over. 'The answer is, with great difficulty!' I said, clutching Mum.

'You'll be fine, Beauty. You just need to practise,' said Mum.

I staggered around the bedroom and out onto the landing. I toured my own bedroom, my bathroom, Mum and Dad's bathroom, Mum's dressing room and one of the spare bedrooms. I fell over once and twisted my ankle twice.

72

'Maybe the heels aren't such a good idea after all,' said Mum.

I begged to keep them on, knowing that none of the other girls had proper high heels, not even Skye.

Wonderfully, Dad wasn't back from his golf game when it was time to leave for the party, so Mum drove me in her little purple Ka. Dad bought it for her on their tenth wedding anniversary. It had purple velvet cushions in the back and two fluffy purple teddies with their arms wrapped round each other and silly smiles sewn on their snouts to show they were in love with each other. I knew for a fact that one colour Mum didn't care for at all was purple, but she squealed obediently when she discovered the car outside our house. It was tied up with an enormous purple satin ribbon so that it looked like a gigantic Easter egg.

I sat in the back with the canoodling teddies while Mum drove to Rhona's house. We set off in good time but we ended up arriving ten minutes late. Mum drives very slowly and cautiously. She takes ages edging out onto the main roads, not making a move until there's not another car in sight. She also got lost twice.

'I'm sorry, babes, I'm so useless,' she said, drawing up outside Rhona's house at last.

There was a big bunch of pink and blue balloons

tied to the gate to show there was a party going on. The living room glowed rose with pink fairy lights. I saw hordes of girls rushing around, waving their arms and dancing. We could hear the music from inside the car. Skye bobbed into view, flinging back her long silky hair as she step-tapped sideways.

My tummy tightened.

'I don't think I really want to go to the party,' I said.

'Oh, Beauty! Come on, darling, you'll be fine once you get inside,' said Mum, squeezing my hand tightly. 'You're going to have a lovely time.'

When I teetered up to the front path in my high heels and knocked at the front door Rhona opened it immediately. She smiled as if she'd been waiting specially for me. She was wearing a red stripy top and a short black skirt. She had red lipstick on too, though it had gone a bit wobbly at the edges.

'Happy birthday, Rhona! You look lovely,' I said.

Rhona was blinking at my new corkscrew hair.

'Wow, Beauty, you look so different,' she said. She swallowed. 'You look lovely too,' she said.

Her eyes slid down my blue frills and white pleats. When she saw my shoes her mouth widened in genuine delight.

'Oh my goodness, look at your *shoes*! Mum won't let me wear even the weeniest heels, she says I've

74

got to wait until I'm at least thirteen. Oh you're so *lucky*!'

I walked in proudly, keeping my legs rigid, willing myself not to wobble.

'Here's your present,' I said, offering it shyly.

I'd spent ages wrapping it up. Rhona didn't snatch it carelessly or shove it in a corner. She held it carefully, stroking the silver paper and pink satin ribbon.

'Rhona! Come *on*, it's the *Don't Feel Like Dancing* song!' Skye called from the party room.

'Just a minute,' said Rhona.

She undid the ribbon, smoothing it out and then winding it in a little silky ball. She slid her finger under the wrapping paper and eased it off. She slipped the three silver bangles over her wrist and waved her arms so that they jangled. She held her pink *Princess* T-shirt against her, showing that it would fit her perfectly. She opened her book and peered at it politely.

'Thank you so much, Beauty,' she said, giving me a big lipsticky grin. 'They're wonderful presents.'

'I'm so glad you like them,' I said.

We smiled at each other. I wanted to freeze-frame us so we stayed in that magic moment in her hall, on the edge of her party, Rhona and me. But then Skye shouted again and Rhona rolled her eyes at me.

'Come on,' she said. 'Just wait till they all see your gorgeous silver shoes!'

They didn't notice my high heels at first. They were too busy gawping at my hair. Skye gave an exaggerated double take when she saw me, standing still, hands on hips. She was wearing an even shorter skirt than Rhona and a little black vest top that showed her totally flat tummy. She'd inked a blue star round her belly button that looked almost like a real tattoo.

'Oh my God, who's this? Hey, it's the Corkscrew Kid! Old Ugly Curlynob!' She got started on my blouse next, pulling the pussycat bow, saying her granny had exactly the same blouse, she'd bought it for ten pence at a jumble sale. Emily and Arabella hooted with laughter.

'Shut up, Skye,' said Rhona, but no one could ever shut Skye up.

I turned my back on her and went over to the sofa. An entire *squadron* of teddy bears were squashed up together, jostling each other with their furry paws.

'Look at Beauty's fantastic shoes,' said Rhona.

'She can't walk properly in them,' said Skye. 'Wiggle-waggle wobble-bum.'

I plonked myself down in the midst of the teddies, blinking hard. The others started dancing – Rhona and Skye, Emily and Arabella, Lulu and

76

Poo-poo, everyone. Some girls danced in a little group together. I could have got up and danced with them, but I didn't. I picked two of the teddies and made them dance instead, up and down the arm of the sofa.

Then they had a singing contest. Skye had given Rhona a karaoke set for her birthday. She had first go to show us how to do it. Skye was brilliant at it of course, using the mic professionally and jigging along to the music. Rhona tried hard when it was her turn but she kept getting the giggles and losing her place. Arabella and Emily performed as a duo and were quite good, jumping up and down and shaking their hips in unison.

'Whose turn is it now?' Skye asked.

There was a general clamour of *'Me! Me! Me!'*

Skye ignored all of them. She was looking straight at me.

'You have a go, Ugly Corkscrew,' she said.

'No thanks,' I said.

'Come on, you've got to join in. Don't be a party pooper,' said Skye. 'It's your go now. Choose your song.'

I'd never even heard of most of the songs. Dad hated all modern pop music, calling it 'that waily-thumpy rubbish'. He listened to old rock bands from ages ago. I could sing those songs all right, but they weren't on offer.

I dithered helplessly. Skye raised her eyebrows.

'Get *on* with it, Ugly. Come on, come on, come on!' She turned it into a chant. The others started joining in.

'We'll sing a duet, you and me, Beauty,' said Rhona.

Skye frowned. 'No, let her sing solo. You've had a go anyway, Rhona.'

'Yes, but it's my party, so I can sing as often as I want,' said Rhona, smiling sweetly. She scanned the songs on offer. 'We'll sing *Baby Boo*.'

She took hold of me and pulled me to the mic. I squeezed her hand.

'I don't know it!' I whispered.

'You don't need to. I'll sing the main bit and you just go *Baby Boo boo boo, boo boopy do* after each line. It's easy-peasy, Beauty.'

She started the music and sang the line. I mumbled my way through the daft *Baby Boo* refrain. Rhona sang the next verse and then I went through the *Baby Boo* babble again. I realized Rhona was right. It *was* easy-peasy. She got the giggles again in the last verse because there was a whole lot of silly stuff about making you moan, obviously a reference to s-e-x. When Rhona collapsed *I* sang the lines because I knew the tune now. We sang the last line together and yelled the chorus: '*Baby Boo boo boo, boo boopy do,*' finishing with a twirl.

I wobbled wildly in Mum's heels and clutched Rhona. We both ended up on the floor, shrieking with laughter. The others laughed too, but they were laughing *with* us, not *at* us. Well, Skye wasn't laughing.

'I hope you realize what a fool you're making of yourself, Ugly,' she hissed. 'Don't think Rhona wants to be your friend. She's just being kind because she feels sorry for you.'

I tried not to take any notice but I worried that she might be right.

I got to sit on one side of Rhona at her birthday tea. Skye sat the other side of course. It was wonderful food: giant turkey-and-bacon-and-salad club sandwiches held together with toothpicks; sausages dipped in tomato sauce; potato wedges with sour cream and salsa dips; four-cheese pizza with pineapple topping; mini burgers with relish and pickles; an enormous trifle with whipped cream and cherries; fairy cupcakes with pink and lilac and baby-blue icing; chocolate fridge cake and a huge birthday cake in the shape of an R, decorated with little silver hearts and crystallized roses.

'It looks so *beautiful*,' I said in awe.

'Oh, my mum loves cooking,' said Rhona. 'Let's tuck in!'

I picked up my plate and started munching.

Rhona's mum poured us all glasses of juice – cranberry, orange or raspberry.

'Which juice would you like, dear?' she asked me.

'Cranberry, please,' I said indistinctly, my mouth full. I swallowed. 'Oh, Mrs Marshall, this is absolutely delicious.'

'Thank you, darling. I'm glad you're enjoying it,' she said, smiling at me, and then moving on.

'Good grief! Look at the way Ugly's piled her plate high,' Skye muttered. 'She's such a greedy guts, no wonder she's got such a big belly. Look, it's sticking out all the pleats in her ridiculous skirt.'

Rhona pretended not to hear but Arabella and Emily sniggered. I wanted to push Skye's head *plop* into the bowl of trifle. I tried to act as if I hadn't heard her. I ate my entire plateful – though the food tasted like cardboard now.

It was easier after tea because the grown-ups came into the living room with us and Skye was too sly to be blatantly mean to me in front of the Marshalls. Mr Marshall stuck a false moustache under his nose, balanced a silly hat sideways on his head, and said he was Bumble the Conjuror. He did a lot of tricks that didn't work properly. I wasn't sure if this was deliberate or not. I tittered uncertainly when he picked the wrong card or tapped the wrong box. Rhona roared with laughter and kept yelling, 'Oh, *Dad*, you are so so *stupid*!'

I held my breath the first time she said it, but Mr Marshall didn't turn a hair. He just pulled a funny face, sticking one finger in his mouth, looking all droopy and woebegone. Rhona laughed all the more.

I wondered what my dad would do if I called him stupid.

Mr Marshall's conjuring act went on a little too long and some of the girls started chatting amongst themselves.

'Can't we have our swim now?' Skye asked.

'You need to let your tea go down properly first,' said Mrs Marshall. 'Let's all give Mr Bumble a clap and then we'll play a nice quiet party game.'

She fetched a big tray full of twenty tiny objects and told us to look at them carefully. I stared hard, memorizing everything. There was a watch, nail varnish, lipstick, ring, rubber spider, plaster, pencil sharpener, flower, matches, bottle opener, tape measure, straw, key, nail, postcard, stamp, little scissors, thermometer, perfume and a very tiny teddy in striped pyjamas. Everyone went 'Aaah!' when they spotted the little teddy because he looked so cute.

Mrs Marshall covered the tray with a big cloth and gave us each pens and paper.

'Write down as many things on the tray as you can remember,' said Mrs Marshall.

There was a great groan.

'That's not fair! I was just looking at that little teddy,' said Skye. 'Let me have another look at the tray.'

She went to twitch the cover off.

'Certainly not, Skye!' said Mrs Marshall.

'But I don't know what else was on the wretched tray!'

'I'm afraid that's just your bad luck,' said Mrs Marshall.

She said it cheerily, but I started to wonder if *she* didn't like Skye either, even though she was Rhona's best friend.

I closed my eyes and saw a picture of the tray inside my head. I opened my eyes and started scribbling quickly on my piece of paper. Everyone else was moaning and sighing and conferring. I didn't need to. I wrote: watch, nail varnish, lipstick, ring, spider, plaster, sharpener, flower, matches, bottle opener, tape measure, straw, key, nail, postcard, stamp, scissors, thermometer, perfume . . . and tiny teddy.

'Wow, look at Beauty! She's written a huge long list,' said Rhona.

'Oh, that Ugly! It's just the sort of stupid swotty thing she *would* do. I think this is a boring game. Can't we play something else?' said Skye.

'No, let's carry on. I think this is a good game,' said Emily, who was writing rapidly too.

She ended up with twenty answers and was sure she'd won – but when Mrs Marshall checked she'd made up four items.

'Still, sixteen correct is positively brilliant,' said Arabella. 'I could only come up with five. Still, at least I'm not bottom.' She glanced at Skye, who had only written one word – teddy.

'I wasn't playing,' Skye said quickly. 'So, well done, Emily, you've won.'

'No, no,' said Mrs Marshall, running her finger down my list. '*Beauty*'s won. She's got every single item right. That's brilliant, sweetheart!'

Skye groaned and pulled a face. 'Trust Ugly,' she said.

She said it loud enough for Mrs Marshall to hear. She frowned at Skye and then turned to me.

'Well done, Beauty. You get the little teddy bear as your prize.'

'Oh, *lucky* Beauty,' they all said.

Rhona picked the tiny teddy off the tray and tucked him in the palm of my hand.

'I'm glad *you* won him, Beauty,' she said.

There was a quiz game after that. I knew all the answers in the history and literature and geography sections. I started to worry that it wouldn't be polite to win this game too – but I could only answer one question in the television section and none at all in pop music and famous celebrities, so I didn't win anything. Emily *did* win this time, though she didn't get a tiny teddy, she just won a pen and notebook.

'*Now* can we go for a swim?' Skye whined.

'Yes, dear,' said Mrs Marshall brightly. 'Change in Rhona's bedroom. The pool's outside. Take a running jump. Be my guest.'

Some of the girls were wearing their swimming costumes under their clothes so it was easy for them to get changed quickly and decently. I struggled to unbuckle Mum's shoes, wriggle out of my tights and get my knickers off without anyone looking. I wished I was a lot smaller and my white skirt more voluminous.

'Look at old Ugly showing off her bum,' said Skye. 'Wibble wobble, wibble wobble.'

She cast off her own tiny skirt and top in two shakes. She was wearing an emerald green bikini, high cut so that it made her slender legs look longer than ever. She twisted her long fair hair into a knot on top of her head and secured it with a green hair clasp.

Most of the girls had similar cool glamorous swimsuits. Arabella had a red halter-neck bikini and she looked very grown up in it, though she had to keep tugging at the top to keep it in place.

I had a silly baby costume, pale blue patterned with ice-cream cones. It was last year's costume, because I hardly ever went swimming. It clung to me, emphasizing my tummy. I sucked it in as far as I could. It felt as if they were all staring at me. I felt incredibly self-conscious padding across the carpet and out into the hall. I clutched the tiny teddy for comfort.

Mrs Marshall smiled at me.

'I don't think that teddy is really into swimming,' she said.

'I'm not sure *I* am either,' I said.

I could swim breast stroke, I'd had proper lessons, but I couldn't risk getting my new hairdo wet. I let the others jump wildly into the pool and caper about. I sat hunched on the edge, feet dang-ling in the water. I tried to keep my stomach sucked in, hanging on tight to Teeny Teddy.

Rhona came and sat beside me. She was wearing a tankini, a pink-and-white top with little shorts. Her tummy stuck out a little too but she didn't seem to care in the slightest.

'I'm so glad you got to win the little teddy, Beauty,' she said. 'I've got a twin one just like him, with those sweet little pyjamas, only mine's got red stripes instead of blue.'

'What do you call yours?'

'Teddy!'

'Oh, Rhona, he's got to have a proper name!'

'Well, I don't know. What are you going to call *your* teddy?'

I sat him in the palm of my hand, staring at his little furry face. He had a long snout and a serious expression. He might be tiny but he certainly wasn't a baby.

'I think he's quite elderly in teddy years. He's wearing the sort of pyjamas that grandpas wear. I think I'll call him . . . Nicholas Navybear.'

Rhona giggled. 'That's a great name. OK, so what can mine be called?'

'You said your teddy's got red pyjamas, so yours can be Reginald Redted.'

'Perfect!' said Rhona, giggling.

'Rhona! Get in the pool!' Skye shouted.

Rhona laughed and kicked her legs, splashing. 'In a minute,' she said cheerily.

I wished I had Rhona's happy-go-lucky knack of being friends with everyone.

'You'd better name all my other birthday bears too, Beauty,' said Rhona.

'Rhona, Rhona, Rhona! Get in the pool! We want to give you your birthday bumps,' Skye shouted.

'I'm talking to Beauty just this second,' said Rhona.

'Who wants to talk to boring old Ugly?' said Emily.

'Don't call her that,' said Rhona.

'Come on, jump in the pool,' said Arabella.

'*Rhona!* Come *here*!' Skye yelled imperiously.

Rhona raised her eyebrows. 'Watch this!' she muttered to me.

She stood up, took a running jump, tucked her knees up and landed right beside Skye, totally capsizing her. I couldn't help laughing. Skye spluttered to the surface, shaking her head. She blinked – and saw me grinning.

'Oh, so you think it's funny, do you, Ugly?' said Skye. 'Well, come and join in the fun with us then.'

She swam three strokes towards me and tugged hard on my ankles. I shrieked as I shot into the water, right over my head. When I surfaced, gasping, Skye screamed with laughter.

'Look at Ugly! Her curls are all unravelling! She's getting unscrewed!'

I put my hands up to my hair. What would Dad say now? I tried winding one of the curls quickly round my fingers but it wouldn't go back into shape.

I had both hands free.

Oh no!

Nicholas Navybear had drowned.

Seven

I dived down looking for him. Rhona dived too. Everyone dived, even Arabella and Emily.

'You dive too, Skye,' said Rhona. 'You're the best at diving and it's your fault for yanking Beauty into the water like that.'

'It was just a *joke*,' said Skye sulkily, but she dived too.

I dived until my eyes streamed and my heart thumped. I was desperate to find little Nicholas. I'd only owned him for twenty minutes but I already loved him with all my heart.

I couldn't find him. Rhona couldn't find him. Arabella and Emily and all the others couldn't find him. Skye couldn't find him, though she swam a whole length underwater looking for him.

'I think we'd better call off the teddy search, girls. You're all getting a bit blue and goose-pimply. Out you all get!' said Mrs Marshall, handing out warm towels.

I tried one last dive, holding my breath and keeping my eyes wide open, my hands scrabbling sideways across the pool tiles like pink crabs. There was no sign of Nicholas Navybear.

'Come along, Beauty, you must get out now,' said Mrs Marshall, hauling me out and wrapping a big towel round me.

Mr Marshall was in charge of the hot chocolate to warm us all up.

'Don't look so upset, sweetheart,' he said to me, popping two extra marshmallows into my mug. 'I'm sure we'll be able to find you another little teddy.'

He was so kind I felt tears pricking my eyes.

'Oh, lordy, look at old Ugly. She's blubbing just because she's lost her little teddy-weddy,' Skye muttered.

'You can be so mean sometimes, Skye,' said Rhona.

She ran off, towel wrapped round her like a toga. When Rhona came back she had something clutched in her hand. Something small and furry, in striped pyjamas.

'Rhona's found him!' said Arabella.

'No, no, this is *my* teddy,' said Rhona. She thrust him into my hand. 'But he's yours now, Beauty.'

'I can't take Reginald Redted!' I said.

'Yes, of course you can. I've just got heaps of new birthday teddies. So you have Reginald Redted.'

'Reginald Redted!' said Skye, rolling her eyes.

'What kind of mad name is that?'

'I think it's a brilliant name,' said Rhona. 'Beauty made it up.'

'Oh, well, no wonder it's so weird,' said Skye. She blew out her cheeks and stuck out her stomach, pretending to be me. 'Weginald Wedted,' she said. She was supposed to be imitating me, though I haven't got a lisp. It didn't matter so much that Skye was being horrible, not when Rhona was being so extra-specially lovely to me.

'I'll look after him so carefully, Rhona – but I won't keep him for ever. I'll give him back to you at school on Monday,' I suggested. 'We'll share him, OK?'

'Yes, that's a great idea,' said Rhona. 'We'll be co-parents. Cool!'

'We'll have to have a little teddy bear's picnic for him, with very tiny honey sandwiches.'

'Oh yes! You have such good ideas, Beauty,' said Rhona.

I beamed at her.

'I'm so glad you've cheered up, Beauty,' said Mrs Marshall. 'Now, you girls must all go and get changed out of your costumes. Your mums and dads will be here to collect you any minute now.'

I prayed hard inside my head as I struggled back into my frilly blouse and pleated skirt: *Please let Mum fetch me, don't let it be Dad!*

Wonderfully, it *was* Mum, looking shy and anxious, nibbling her lip, not really joining in any of the conversations with the other mums. Most of them didn't realize she *was* a mum.

I thanked Mr and Mrs Marshall for having me and then I thanked Rhona all over again for Reginald Redted.

'He's *our* Reggie now. He's a very lucky bear to have two mothers,' said Rhona, and she gave me a big hug.

'This is a bear hug,' I said, and we both laughed.

'Bye, Beauty,' said Rhona.

'Bye, Ugly-Wugly,' Skye called. She was collected by her Polish au pair.

'What did that girl call you?' Mum asked, as we got in the car.

'Oh, just silly stuff,' I said quickly.

'Did she call you *Ugly*?' said Mum. 'How dare she! I've a good mind to go back and slap her!'

'It's just her stupid nickname for me.'

'Do they all call you that?'

'Rhona doesn't.'

'So all the others do?' Mum sounded as if she was going to burst into tears.

I clutched Reginald Redted for courage. I tried to smile at Mum reassuringly.

'It's no big deal, Mum, honestly. We've all got

nicknames. One of the girls is called Poo-poo. It's just their idea of fun.'

'Mm,' said Mum. 'I still think Ugly is a *horrid* nickname. Can't they call you something else?'

'They do sometimes,' I said, but I knew Weirdo, Wobblybum, Brainbox and the new Corkscrew weren't necessarily any kinder than Ugly.

'I think you'll have to invent a *nice* nickname for yourself,' said Mum. 'Let me think.'

She drove slowly, humming along to the music on the car radio.

'They used to call me Dilly Daydream at school. And your dad used to be called Cookie because of his surname. *Your* surname. Can't your new nickname be Cookie?'

I thought about it. I quite liked the name Cookie. It sounded funny and bouncy and happy. Not really like me.

'I can't just get them to start calling me Cookie,' I said. 'It doesn't really work like that, Mum. *They* decide what they're going to call me.'

'Mm,' said Mum again. 'Well, we'll find a way of *encouraging* them along the Cookie route.'

She took one hand off the steering wheel and patted my shoulder sympathetically. She very gently tugged a lock of my damp hair. 'That was a bit of a waste of fifty quid,' she said.

'Will Dad be mad, do you think?' I asked.

'Maybe,' said Mum, sighing.

Dad *was* mad. He usually came home jolly after a day's golf but we knew as soon as we heard the door slam and the *thump thump* as he threw his shoes in the rack that he was furious. He stamped into the living room in his socks and poured himself a large whisky, barely looking at us.

'Oh dear,' said Mum, in her sweetest trying-to-please voice. 'Didn't you have a good game, darling?' She made a little shooing motion to me so I started sidling out of the room.

'I won both games, as a matter of fact,' said Dad, glaring at her. 'My golf swing is pretty lethal at the moment – and I was playing with a bunch of blithering idiots. I just don't *get* it. I've given them every incentive. It would be so *simple* for them to fix things for me, but they all witter on about their hands being tied. It's so frustrating sucking up to the lot of them all day long and getting nowhere, absolutely blooming nowhere.'

I dithered in the doorway.

'Is this the Water Meadows deal?' said Mum. 'I thought you said it was all sewn up.'

'Some cowardly nincompoop unstitched it all. He says there's no way they'll ever grant planning permission.'

'Oh dear,' said Mum.

'Oh dear! That's a bit of a limp reaction. Is that all you'll say when the guys I owe start clamouring for their money and I haven't got the wherewithal to pay them? Will you just say "Oh dear" when the entire business goes down the pan and we're out of this lovely house, sitting in the gutter looking stupid?'

I crept into the hall, biting my nails.

'Gerry, don't. You know you'll sort things out, you always do. Come on, put your feet up, relax a little. Shall I run you a hot bath?'

'You can get me a hot *meal*; I'm starving. Shove any old muck in the microwave, as if I care. I didn't pick you for your culinary skills, I picked you for your looks.'

I hated the way Dad talked to Mum as if she was some silly doll.

'Hot meal coming right up, darling,' said Mum.

She *sounded* like a doll too, as if someone had pulled a tab in her back to make her parrot a few silly phrases. I knew she was simply trying to sweet-talk him out of his mood but it still made me squirm.

It seemed to be working though.

'You're certainly looking good tonight, babe,' Dad said. 'Like the hair! It's perked up a treat. So what about Beauty? Let's see *her* new hairdo.'

'Oh, Beauty's upstairs,' Mum said loudly. 'She got tired out at her party.'

I scooted up the stairs two at a time but I was still wearing Mum's high heels. I tripped over, bumping my knees.

'Beauty?' said Dad, going to the door. 'Oi, Beauty, I'm talking to you. Come downstairs into the light. Let's have a proper squint at you.'

I walked down the stairs, holding my breath.

'Good God, you're a right sight!' said Dad. 'You look uglier than ever!'

I felt the tears pricking my eyes. I pressed my lips together, trying hard not to cry.

'Gerry, shut up,' said Mum.

'Don't you dare tell me to shut up in my own house!' Dad said. 'What in God's name have they done to the kid? She's all over rat's tails.'

He took hold of me and tugged my hair in disgust.

'Stop it! Don't you dare hurt her!' said Mum.

'I'm barely touching her. So did you actually pay good money – *my* good money – for this terrible hairdo, Dilly?'

'It was a silly idea to start with. Beauty's just a little girl, she doesn't need fancy hairdos. It didn't really suit her, all those curls. Then it was a swimming party, so of course she got wet.'

'I thought you were just going to paddle, Beauty?

What's the matter with you? Whatever made you dunk yourself head-first in the pool and ruin your hair? Don't you *want* to look pretty? Don't pull that silly face, nibble nibble at your lip like a blessed rabbit. Stand up *straight*, don't hunch like that, sticking out your stomach!'

'Don't say another word to our lovely daughter! Beauty, go upstairs, darling,' said Mum.

I ran upstairs to my bedroom. I put my hands over my ears so I couldn't hear them arguing about me. I saw myself in my Venetian glass mirror. I tried brushing my hair. It stuck limply to my head. I looked at my big face and my fat tummy and my ridiculous clothes. Dad was right. I did look a sight.

No wonder Skye and Arabella and Emily and all the other girls called me Ugly. It wasn't just a play on words because of my silly name. I really was ugly ugly ugly. It was like staring into one of those distorting mirrors at the fairground. My hair drooped, my face twisted like a gargoyle, and my body blew up like a balloon. My clothes shrank smaller so that my blouse barely buttoned and my skirt showed my knickers.

I seized my hairbrush and threw it at my image in the mirror. There was a terrible bang and I saw myself crack in two. I gaped in horror.

I'd smashed the mirror, the ornate Venetian glass mirror Dad had bought specially for my bedroom. A long crack zig-zagged from the top to the bottom of the glass.

I shut my eyes tight, praying that it was all a mistake, an optical illusion because I was so upset. I opened my eyes a fraction, peering through my lashes. Everything was blurry – but I could still see the ugly crack right across the mirror.

I kicked the hairbrush across the room. Then I sagged onto the carpet, down on my knees. I clenched my fists. I was still holding Reginald Redted in my left hand. Why hadn't I hurled *him*? He'd have bounced off the glass and somersaulted to the floor, no harm done. I held onto him. He looked back at me quizzically.

'I am in *such* trouble,' I whispered. 'Dad always goes totally mad if I break anything, even if it's a total accident. When he sees the mirror he'll realize I threw the brush on purpose.'

I rocked backwards and forwards. I could hear the angry buzz of his voice downstairs. He was obviously still ranting about his ugly, freaky daughter.

'I hate him,' I whispered. 'I can't *help* being ugly. He's my *dad*, he's meant to *like* the way I look. He's meant to be kind and funny and gentle, just like

98

Rhona's dad. Oh, I wish wish wish I could swap places with Rhona.'

Reginald Redted tilted his head at me. He seemed to be nodding. It looked like he longed to be back with Rhona instead of stuck with me.

FLOUR

Eight

Dad went off to golf again early the next morning. The minute he slammed the front door Mum jumped out of bed and pattered along the landing.

'Beauty? Are you awake, sweetheart? Hey, can I come and have a cuddle with you this time?'

'No, Mum! Don't come in!' I said.

'What? Why not? What is it?' said Mum, opening my bedroom door. 'Are you still sleepy? Do you want to snuggle down by yourself?'

'Yes. No. Oh, Mum!' I wailed.

Mum came right into my room and switched on the light. I looked desperately at the mirror, wondering if it could have magically mended itself during the night. The crack looked uglier than ever.

Mum's head jerked when she saw it, her hand going over her mouth.

'Oh, lordy! A broken mirror, seven years' bad luck! However did it happen?'

'Don't be cross, Mum!' I begged.

'Don't be nuts, when am I ever cross with you?' said Mum, coming over to my bed. She put her arms round me and hugged me tight. 'What did you do? Did you knock against it somehow? Don't worry, I know it was an accident.'

'No it wasn't, Mum. I did it deliberately,' I said, in a very small voice.

'Deliberately?' Mum echoed, astonished.

'I threw my hairbrush at it – at *me*, my reflection,' I said.

'Oh dear,' said Mum, and she started crying.

'I'm so sorry, Mum. I'll pay for it out of my pocket money,' I said. 'Please don't cry.'

'I'm crying because your dad was such a pig to you, making you so unhappy. He was talking stupid rubbish, sweetheart. You look *lovely*. When your hair's natural it's all soft and shiny, you've got beautiful eyes, rosy cheeks, gorgeous smooth skin. Don't you dare let him put you down, baby.'

'He puts *you* down.'

'Yes, I know. Well, I'm going to try and stand up to him more. I know he's dead worried about his work but that doesn't mean he can just be hateful and take it out on us,' said Mum. She looked at the mirror, running her finger down the long crack.

'Could we mend it somehow?' I asked.

'Don't be daft,' said Mum.

'So what are we going to *do*?'

'Simple. We'll buy another one and we'll sneak this broken one out to the dump.'

'But they cost hundreds of pounds, Mum, you know they do. I've got seven pounds left out of my pocket money after buying Rhona's birthday present.'

'*I'll* buy the new mirror, silly.'

'But you haven't got any money, Mum.'

Dad didn't want Mum to go out to work now, not even at Happy Homes. He said her job was to make *our* home a happy one. He didn't give her an allowance out of his money. She had to ask for everything. Dad didn't even let her have her own credit card.

Mum was nibbling at one of her nails, thinking about it.

'I'll sell some stuff,' she said. 'Some of my rings, or maybe a necklace.'

'But that's not fair on you, Mum. It was me that broke the mirror. Shall I sell some of *my* jewellery?'

I had a gold chain with a tiny real diamond and a silver bangle and some turquoise beads and a small gold signet ring with my initial on.

'I don't think your jewellery would fetch much, Beauty. I've got masses of stuff. I've sold one or two bits to that jeweller's near the market before when I've needed to.'

'Oh, Mum.' I knew she spent the money on me. Every so often Mum took me up to London on Saturdays to go to art galleries. We never told Dad. He hated art: he said all Old Master paintings were boring religious stuff and all modern art utter rubbish and a con. I'm not sure Mum really liked going round all the galleries either. She often yawned and rubbed her back, but she still tottered around gamely in her high heels. She bought me postcards of all my favourite paintings and I pasted them into scrapbooks so that I had my own mini-gallery to look at whenever I liked.

'If I get to be an artist when I'm grown up I'm going to treat you to so many different lovely things, Mum,' I said.

'I think artists are supposed to starve in garrets,' said Mum. 'Maybe we'll both be living on dry biscuits and water. Ah, that reminds me! Do you fancy doing some baking this morning?'

'Baking?' I stared at Mum.

'Yeah, why not?' she said. 'I thought I'd have a go at making cookies. Then you could maybe take them to school, to share them round?'

I suddenly saw where she was coming from. 'So they'll start calling me Cookie?'

'We could try it, eh?'

'Oh, Mum, you are sweet. But . . .' I hesitated. 'Do you know how to bake cookies?'

'Of course I do,' said Mum. 'Well. It can't be that difficult. Remember that time we made cakes together?'

I remembered. They weren't proper cakes, they were just made from a cake-mix packet, and even so we got them wrong, adding too many eggs because we thought it would make them taste nicer. We put them right at the top of the oven, hoping that would make them go golden. They didn't do this at all, they burned themselves black, though the insides were all sloppy and scrambled. We still iced them and I ate them all up, insisting they were delicious. Maybe this had been a mistake.

'Have you got a cookie packet mix, Mum?'

'I'm not sure they do them. We'll just have to make it all up from scratch,' said Mum.

We had breakfast first, spooning down our cornflakes. Then we rolled up our sleeves and got cracking on the cookies. Mum found an old bag of flour at the back of the cupboard. It had been there since I used flour-and-water paste when I was at nursery school. Mum cracked in an egg and stirred in some milk. Then she kneaded and I kneaded. We both got our great lumps of cookie dough and thumped them around on the table until they were lovely smooth balls.

'Hey, they look good!' I said. 'How shall we roll them out?'

We didn't have a rolling pin so Mum improvised with a bottle of wine. We didn't have any cookie cutters either but Mum twisted the lid off a jar of jam and started cutting out rounds in her flattened dough.

'I'm going to make mine into people,' I said, starting to mould my dough.

'What, like a gingerbread man?' said Mum.

'Sort of.' I made a dough woman, carefully cutting a skirt for her, then putting little dough high heels on her pale legs. I broke off pieces of dough and rolled them long, and then with my fingers I twirled them round and round, creating long curls. I stuck them on the dough woman's head. I found a safety pin and fashioned features on her dough face: two big eyes, a little nose, a cupid's-bow mouth smiling at me. I smiled back as I laid her carefully on a baking tray.

I started on another dough person, small and square. I made a dough dress for her and gave her a fancy hairdo. Her eyes went squinty when I scratched them into place, her nose went blobby and her mouth turned down. I stared at her, sighing. Then I pulled all her dough ringlets right out and gave her a radical haircut, chopping it tomboy short. It didn't look so bad now. I peeled off her party dress and made her dough dungarees. She looked much better. I rubbed at her mouth and she started smiling.

Mum peered over at the finished figure on the baking tray.

'Oh, Beauty, that's so good! Is that me?' She came and stood beside me. 'And who's this? Is it a boy? No, it's *you* with short hair! You look so cute.'

'I wish I did have short hair,' I said. 'Do you think Dad would mind terribly if I had it all cut off?'

Mum rolled her eyes. 'Don't even think about it,' she said.

I put my dough girl beside her mum. Then I got started on a dough man.

'Is that Dad?' said Mum.

I didn't answer. I made the body and then rolled the arms and the legs. I made pin marks on the dough shirt to show it was checked and gave his long legs comfy jeans. I spent ages carving his face with my pin to give it the right gentle expression. Of course it wasn't Dad.

I started on a new smaller person, very fat, with four little legs. I fashioned long loppy ears. Then I carefully picked her up and laid her on my man's checked chest. He wrapped his doughy arms around her, holding her close.

My tray was full now. I patted my special pastry people, feeling bad as I put them into the hot oven.

'I hope it doesn't hurt,' I whispered foolishly. 'I'll try hard not to let you burn.'

Mum put her tray of plain round cookies above mine and we shut them in the oven.

'Tra la!' said Mum. 'Welcome to the world, Cookie Girl.'

'Well, hi there, Cookie Mum,' I said.

Mum switched on the radio and we started dancing to the pop music in our pyjamas. We didn't disco dance like Skye; this was happy mad dancing, leaping around the room, beating a tattoo on the table top, tapping out tunes with the spoons. We sank into our seats exhausted when the music stopped.

'I can smell the cookies!' I said, my nose twitching like Lily's. 'Do you think they're ready yet?'

'We've only just put them in the oven, sweetheart. They'll be ages yet. Come on, let's go and get washed and dressed while we're waiting.'

I washed and dressed in double quick time, not quite trusting Mum's judgement. I decided to have a little peep in the oven. I just opened the door a tiny crack so as not to let the heat out. I stared. Then I opened it wide, peering at the two trays.

'Mum!' I shouted. 'Oh, Mum, something really awful's happened!'

Mum came rushing into the kitchen in her underwear.

'Have you burned yourself? Have you broken something? What *is* it, Beauty?'

'Look at the cookies!' I wailed.

Mum's neat cookies had expanded in every direction, joining up so that her baking tray contained one long flat misshapen biscuit. My lovely cookie people had expanded too. They were now great grotesque caricatures. Sam was this bloated blobby man, all head and huge stomach, and lovely Lily had blown up into a beach ball. Little Mum was a great giant. Even her careful curls were ruined. Now she looked as if she had snakes writhing right out of her head.

I was the worst, so squat I was completely square, my dungarees inflated into vast overalls, my short haircut making me look like a man. Not any old man. I looked the spitting image of my dad.

I put on an oven glove and pulled the baking tray out of the oven. I picked up the me-cookie even though it was red hot and snapped off its stupid head.

'Hey hey, stop it, Beauty! Don't burn yourself. And stop spoiling them. They might look a bit weird but I bet they taste yummy,' said Mum.

We waited until they'd cooled down a little and then nibbled. They *didn't* taste good at all. They were as flat and hard and boring as cardboard.

'Oh dear,' said Mum. She took the oven glove and pulverized her own cookie. 'They're horrible, aren't they?'

'Yep.'

'Your dad's right. I can't cook for toffee,' said Mum, drooping.

'Yes, you can,' I said. I hesitated. 'Well, maybe you could *learn*.'

'I'm useless at learning stuff. I was always bottom of the class at school,' said Mum. 'Thick as a brick, that's me.'

'No, you're not. You're . . . pretty and witty,' I said.

'OK, OK, so you're . . . cute and astute,' said Mum.

'Maybe we need a proper recipe book?' I said, scraping the cookie crumbs into the wastebin. 'I think we need to get all the ingredients right. Maybe this is the wrong sort of flour? And perhaps we've left out something important? What would make the cookies softer and sweeter?'

'Butter and sugar!' said Mum. 'OK, I'll look for a recipe book tomorrow. Number two on my shopping list. Number one will be the new Venetian glass mirror.'

I quivered.

'Sorry! Forget about it now. Shall we go and watch some telly? Don't they have a Sam and Lily omnibus edition on a Sunday morning?'

Mum and I curled up at either end of the sofa. We tucked our feet up cosily. We were never allowed to do that when Dad was around because he said

110

it marked the sofa cushions. Mum flipped through the Sunday papers while I spun round and round into Sam and Lily world in the Rabbit Hutch. I'd seen all five programmes during the week and so I could whisper all the right words. At the end of all the repeats there was a special five minutes of Sam and Lily on Sunday.

'Hey there!' said Sam.

He was holding Lily. She twitched her nose at me, but she was more interested in something down on the ground. She struggled a little in Sam's arms, not quite sure of herself.

'Hey, Lily, it's OK. It's only a little black cat come to say hello. Let me introduce you.'

Sam bent down so that Lily's face was on a level with the cat's. They regarded each other warily.

'Lily, meet Lucky. Lucky, meet Lily.' Sam looked out of the television set at me. 'And here's my very special friend, Beauty. Say meow to her, Lucky.'

Lucky obediently gave a tiny mew, lifting and licking one small paw.

'Oh, Lucky, you're so *sweet*,' I whispered.

Lily stared at me reproachfully.

'Not quite as sweet as Lily, of course,' I said.

'Lucky's come to live in the house next door. She's just popped in to meet her new neighbour,' said Sam. 'Are you going to come and say hello on a daily basis, Lucky?'

Lucky gave a demure nod.

'Well, that's just fine and dandy, because that means you'll cross our path and if a little black cat does that then we'll have a lucky day.'

'I wish you lived next door to me, Lucky,' I whispered. 'I need all the luck in the world to counteract seven whole years' *bad* luck.'

'Seven *years*?' said Sam. 'That's all the way until you're practically grown up! Whatever have you done to inflict such a curse upon yourself?'

'I broke my mirror,' I confessed.

'Oh, Beauty, is that *all*!' said Sam. 'Don't worry, you won't really get seven years' bad luck. That's just an old wives' tale.'

I glanced at Mum, who was deep in a fashion article.

'OK, a *young* wives' tale,' said Sam. 'But it's just silly superstition. I think we make our own luck, Beauty.'

'Well, I'm not very good at it,' I said, sighing. 'I wish I could come and live in the Rabbit Hutch with you and Lily, Sam.'

'We'd love that too,' said Sam.

'Do you think we'll ever meet?'

Sam looked straight into my eyes. 'Yes, we'll meet.'

'Really? Actually face to face?'

'Absolutely. Face to face. Or ear to ear in Lily's case.'

Lily made a little snorty noise as if she was laughing. Then Sam reminded everyone that he'd love to see a drawing or a painting of their pet, and said goodbye.

'Bye, Sam, bye, Lily,' I said out loud.

'Bye, Sam and Lily,' Mum said, turning her page.

The television voice said, 'Who have we just seen?'

'Sam and Lily in the Rabbit Hutch!' Mum and I said simultaneously.

I stood up. 'I think I'll go and do some drawing, Mum,' I said.

I sat cross-legged on my bed upstairs with my drawing pad and coloured pencils. I propped Reginald Redted up beside me, telling him I wanted to draw his portrait.

'You can be my pet and then I can send your picture off to Sam in the Rabbit Hutch,' I said.

Reginald Redted looked down his snout at me. He seemed offended at the idea that he was *my* pet. He wouldn't pose properly, falling forwards, flipping backwards, even tumbling head over heels over the edge of the bed onto the carpet.

'OK, *don't* co-operate then. I won't draw you. I'll draw Nicholas Navybear instead,' I said.

I divided my page into four squares. I drew myself looking at Nicholas on the tray at Rhona's party. I was smiling from ear to ear as I saw his little furry face. Then in the second square I drew my hands gently cradling Nicholas. He lounged against my fingers, using my thumbs as a footrest. He was smiling from ear to ear too.

I drew great splashes of water in the third picture, with poor Nicholas thrashing wildly through the waves, mouth wide open, screaming for help. Then I drew the poor drowned Nicholas lying in an open coffin, paws crossed on his chest, with wreaths of daisies and dandelion crosses arranged all around him.

It was hard getting all four pictures properly balanced. I had to rub out quite a lot but at last it seemed OK. I coloured it in very carefully, not going over a single line and keeping my pencil strokes as smooth as I could.

Mum came up to see how I was getting on and acted like I was an artistic genius.

'You have to send it in to Sam, Beauty,' she said.

'No, Mum, I'm too old – and my picture's too weird,' I said, closing my drawing book.

'You're *so* artistic, Beauty.' Mum hesitated. 'Shall we show it to Dad when he comes in?'

'*No!*'

'He'd be ever so proud.'

'No, he wouldn't. He'd go off on a rant.' I puffed

myself up and put on a deep Dad voice. 'Why don't you do a proper drawing of a teddy rather than this damn daft cartoon rubbish.'

Mum burst out laughing. 'Oh, stop it! Yes, that's *exactly* what he'd say. OK, we won't show him.'

Nine

I wanted to keep out of Dad's way when he came home from golf but he started bellowing for me the moment he got in the front door. I didn't dare lurk in my room. I didn't want him thudding up the stairs and bursting into my bedroom. If he saw my broken mirror he'd explode.

I went downstairs, ducking my head, fiddling with my hair, so scared of what Dad might say to me this time. But he was in one of his determinedly jolly moods.

'Hello hello hello, here's my lovely little Beauty!' he boomed. His face was very red and he smelled of drink. 'Who's my pretty girl, eh? You look lovely, darling.'

I felt my face going red too. He was trying to make up for yesterday. It didn't make me feel better, it just made me go all squirmy inside. Dad patted the top of my head and then chucked me under the chin.

'My little girl,' he repeated.

'I'm not that little, Dad,' I said.

'I know, I know, you're growing up fast. Your birthday's just around the corner.'

I held my breath. Mum came out into the hall.

'I've fixed it all up,' said Dad, and he planted a wet kiss on my cheek.

'Fixed what, Gerry?' said Mum. She'd seen the expression on my face.

'Beauty's party, Silly Dilly!'

'Are you sure about this, Gerry?' said Mum. 'Think of all those children running riot, sticky hands all over the furniture—'

'We're not going to have a party *here*. We're going to go out,' said Dad. 'I've been talking to a couple of chaps at golf. One of them is part of some theatrical management company. He reckons he can get a whole block of front stalls seats for that *Birthday Bonanza* musical. Isn't that great? It's solidly booked up for the next six months. It's always a matter of who you know, eh? And to make the day *extra*-special I've done a deal with another chap who has his own fleet of limos. You can ask all your friends, Beauty, and we'll fit them into a super-stretch white limo, how about that?'

I opened my mouth but no sound came out.

'Look at her, she's speechless!' Dad chortled. 'There, trust your old dad to turn up trumps. Gerry the Fixer, that's me!' He turned to Mum. 'I'll fix the Water Meadows deal too, just you wait and see.'

'I know you will,' Mum said mechanically.

'So, Gerry, what about Beauty's birthday tea?'

'I've thought of that. They'll have a birthday buffet when they get here. None of that cheese cubes on sticks and jelly and trifle rubbish. This is going to be a dead sophisticated buffet with canapés.' He ticked each one off on his fingers. 'Little tartlets and tiny vol au vents, chicken satay, sausages in honey sauce, crispy prawns, the works – and then instead of a birthday cake we're going to have a profiterole tower.' He smiled at me. 'Don't look so stunned, baby. You'll love it. Profiteroles are them little chocolate creamy balls – they taste just like éclairs.'

'But, Gerry, who's going to make all this stuff?' said Mum.

'You are, of course,' said Dad, and then he roared with laughter, redder than ever, wheezing and spluttering. 'Your face, Dilly! Dear lord, you're practically wetting your pants. Calm down, darling, I'm only kidding you. We're going to get caterers in. They come along and lay it all out, even provide the fancy plates, and then they serve it all too. Won't that be grand, Beauty? Fancy having a proper waiter and waitress serving all your little friends, treating you all like grown-up ladies. Won't they be impressed!'

I felt faint. I could just imagine what Skye and Emily and Arabella would say.

119

'It's ever so kind of you, Dad, but won't it all cost an awful lot of money? You said we'd maybe be poor if your Water Meadows deal doesn't go through,' I stammered.

'It will go through, one way or another. Just you leave it to your old dad. Who am I? Gerry the . . . ?' He put his hand to his ear, waiting for me to say it.

'Fixer,' I whispered.

'That's right, little Beauty. There! I bet there's not another girl in your whole school who will have such a special birthday treat. Aren't you a lucky girl?'

'Yes, I'm very lucky,' I said.

I made myself smile and bounce about though inside I was dying. I didn't *want* a party. I didn't want a posh buffet with profiteroles instead of a birthday cake. I didn't want a fancy stretch limo and front stalls seat at *Birthday Bonanza*. I especially didn't want all my class at school to come to my party.

I took a deep breath.

'Dad, it all sounds as if it's going to be wonderful but I think I'd like it just as much – maybe even more – if I just had *one* friend, say, and you and me and Mum.'

I thought of Rhona and me partying together.

We could feast on our buffet and then swan off to the show in a posh limo, playing we were celebrities. It would be such fun, just Rhona and me . . .

'Don't be daft, Beauty,' said Dad. He was still smiling but there was an edge to his voice. 'We don't want people to think you haven't got any proper friends.'

'But I *haven't*, Dad, not really,' I mumbled.

'I saw you just the other day with two lovely little girls – hanging on your arms, they were. And then there's that other gorgeous kid, the one with all the hair and the big blue eyes.'

Skye.

'But Dad—'

'Stop all this butting! You're not a little goat! How many girls are in your class?'

'Nineteen.'

'Well, you'd better get busy, little Beauty. You need to write out eighteen invitations. You can do it on my laptop or maybe hand-print them yourself, seeing as you're artistic.'

I hand-printed the first one. I used special purple card and my silver italic pen. I didn't address it to Skye or Emily or Arabella. I didn't even address it to Rhona.

I wrote:

Dear Sam and Lily,
Please come to my birthday party next Saturday.
There will be a big buffet for you, Sam, and I'll
make special lettuce sandwiches and carrot cake
for you, Lily.
Love from Beauty xx

I drew a border of little silver rabbits chasing each other all round the edge of the card, and then I put it in a purple envelope and shook little silver hearts inside.

I didn't post it. I put it in the folder where I kept all my Sam and Lily drawings. Then I sighed deeply and started on the real invitations. Eighteen of them. I used ordinary white cards and envelopes and a blue pen. I drew a birthday cake on each one, even though I wasn't going to have one. I saved Rhona's card till last. I used red card for her and a gold pen. I drew four little teddy bears in each corner. I added, *Reginald Redted is of course invited. He can feast on his very own pot of honey.*

Then I thought of everyone opening their invitations at school. They would see that Rhona's was more elaborate. If they looked at what I'd written they'd laugh at me and think I was weird. I sighed again and wrote a new invitation for Rhona on white card with a birthday cake, identical to all the others.

I gave her the invitation first, when I got to school on Monday morning. I made Reginald Redted hold it.

'He's had a good weekend but he wants to live back with you now,' I said.

'Is he giving me a letter?' said Rhona, laughing.

'It's an invitation to my party,' I said shyly.

'Oh, how lovely!' said Rhona, opening up the card.

'What's that you've got, Rhona?' said Skye, running over to her.

'Beauty's asked me to her birthday party,' said Rhona.

'Oh, *gross*. Ugly's having a party. Well, that will be total freaky funtime,' said Skye. 'So who else have you invited to your party, Ugly? You've got a whole *wad* of invitations there. Just as well, because I bet very few girls will want to go to *your* party.'

'I want to go,' said Rhona, as I handed out invitations. 'What sort of birthday cake will you be having, Beauty?'

'I'm not having a proper birthday cake,' I said apologetically. 'I'm having a profiterole tower.'

'Oh wow!' said Rhona. 'I've seen those cakes in a special shop in London. Are you *really* having one?'

'Yes. But you can't put candles on them.'

'Who needs boring old candles?' said Rhona.

123

I wanted candles so I could blow them all out in one go and have a proper birthday wish. But my wishes didn't ever come true, so maybe I didn't need candles after all.

'What else are you having to eat at your party apart from this proffy thingy,' asked Poppy. 'My mum says I can have proper pizzas when I have my party, with all different toppings.'

'I don't think there'll be pizzas,' I said. 'It's going to be like a buffet. Finger food. Canapés. Little tarts and sausages and stuff.'

'Canapés!' said Rhona. 'How *cool*, just like a real grown-up party.'

'It sounds totally weird if you ask me,' said Skye. 'Are you going to have dancing at your party, Ugly, as you're such a good dancer – *not*.'

'No, we're not having any dancing, Skye,' I said.

Skye rolled her eyes. 'So what kind of a dull party is it going to be? Are you all going to sit cross-legged and do spelling tests for fun?'

'We're going to the theatre to see *Birthday Bonanza*,' I said.

'Oh wow, wow, wow!' Rhona shrieked. 'That group McTavish are in that – and Will Forman. They are *so* cool. I've been dying to see that show for *ages* but my dad can't get tickets.'

'Well, my dad can,' I said, suddenly proud.

'So who's going to *Birthday Bonanza*?' said Skye, narrowing her eyes. 'Just you and Rhona?'

'Dad's got tickets for everyone,' I said.

There was a great whoop from all the girls standing around.

'Am *I* going?'

'Are we really *all* going?'

'Are we sitting near to the stage so we can see McTavish and Will really close up?'

'Dream on,' said Skye. 'They'll be those rubbish seats right at the back where you can't see a sausage.'

'We've got front-row stalls seats,' I said. 'My dad's fixed it.'

'So how is everyone going to get there?' Skye said. 'I suppose your famous fixer dad has hired a *coach*?'

'No, he's hiring a super-stretch limo,' I said, with a little nod of my head.

Everyone squealed and clapped their hands, even Arabella and Emily. Skye stood there, arms folded, chin jutting.

'So, is *everyone* invited?' she said.

I still had her invitation in my hand. I so wanted to tear it into tiny pieces and say 'Everyone but *you*, Skye.'

She was staring at me, her blue eyes suddenly

125

anxious. I hated her, but I still couldn't do it to her.

'Of course everyone's invited, Skye. Even you,' I said, and I pressed her invitation into her hand.

She didn't even thank me. She simply glanced at hers and then said in an off-hand manner, 'I'm not sure I can make it that Saturday anyway.' But we both knew wild horses wouldn't stop her coming.

She was still horrid to me all day long. In a way I respected her for that. Emily and Arabella still called me Ugly but they smiled at me in a new silly way and Arabella offered me some of her crisps at playtime. Louise and Poppy started up a *Did-I-like-bears?* birthday-present conversation and some of the girls who hadn't said a single word to me since I joined the class last year started chatting away as if I was their new best friend.

It felt so weird. Dad really was Gerry the Fixer. I'd longed for them to like me and now it looked as if they did. But it wasn't *real*. They hadn't really changed their minds about me, they just wanted to keep in with me so they could come to my party. I smiled and chatted back to all of them but inside I despised them.

I didn't despise Rhona, of course. She'd been kind to me all along – and she was lovely now.

'You're so *lucky*, Beauty! Imagine your dad fixing all that for your birthday!'

'Yes, Dad's like that,' I said.

126

'Can I sit next to you in the super-stretch limo, Beauty?' Rhona asked.

'Of course. And will you sit next to me in the theatre?'

'You bet.' She hesitated. 'I suppose I'll have to have Skye on my other side, seeing as she's my best friend.'

I took a deep breath.

'Is she *always* going to be your best friend, Rhona?'

Rhona shrugged awkwardly.

'Well, we've been best friends since that first day of infant school and we live in the same road so we *can't* really break up. I hate it when she's mean to you. I've begged her to stop but she won't. You know what she's like.' Rhona edged closer to me and whispered in my ear. 'I wish *we* could be best friends, Beauty.'

Ten

When I went to meet Mum after school lots of girls called goodbye to me. They said it nicely enough, but they still called me Ugly.

'I can't *stand* them calling you that,' Mum muttered. 'You wait, we'll get them calling you Cookie.'

She looked unusually red and shiny, with her hair scraped back into a quick ponytail. She had white smudges all down her shirt.

'Have you been baking more cookies, Mum?'

'Wait and see,' she said, grinning.

The whole house smelled like a baker's shop, though there was an underlying burning smell too. We went into the kitchen. I stared, open-mouthed. There were cookies everywhere, on big plates and little plates and three different baking trays. They covered the kitchen work top and spiralled round and round the table. Some were burned nearly black. Some were pale grey and sludgy. Some were great overblown monster cookies. Some were oval, some were square, some had no determinate shape at all. But the cookies on our best big green-leaf china plate looked perfect: round and smooth and golden.

'Take one,' said Mum, proudly proffering the plate.

I picked one up and held it to my face. It smelled delicious.

'Have a bite, go on!' said Mum.

I nibbled. 'Oh, Mum, it tastes so good!' I said, munching.

'They're OK, aren't they?' said Mum, whirling about the crazy kitchen. 'I've been making them all day long. I found this old American recipe book for twenty-five p in the Oxfam shop. It's got *heaps* of cookie recipes, but I thought I'd stick to the very basic one to start with – and it's worked, hasn't it! I've actually made proper cookies. Eventually. I had to do three batches before they came right.'

'You're the total Cookie Queen,' I said, savouring each mouthful. 'Can I have another one?'

'Of course you can! I'll have another too – and then we'll have to get going clearing up all this mess. Your dad will go nuts if he sees the kitchen like this.'

I went upstairs to take off my blazer and dump my school bag – and then I stared at my Venetian glass mirror. It was glittering and gorgeous, the glass shining. No crack!

'Mum! You've got me a new mirror!' I shrieked.

'Yes, it's been a very hectic day,' said Mum. 'I sold that diamond collar thingy your dad gave me for our first anniversary. I only ever wear it for

130

posh dances and I hardly ever go to them now. I didn't really like it anyway. I didn't like it being a *collar*, like I'm a little dog. Anyway, I got heaps of money for it, enough for a roomful of mirrors, only try hard not to break this one, eh, darling?'

'You are just the best mum ever,' I said.

I helped her get the kitchen spick and span. We threw away all the experimental cookies, but kept the plate of perfect ones.

Dad got home from work early. He started up his Happy Homes routine the moment he got in the front door:

'Happy *Homes*, Happy *Homes*
Where everybody smiles
And nobody moans.
There's a mummy—'

He burst into the kitchen and pointed at Mum. Then he got distracted. He sniffed.

'What's that *smell*?' he said.

'I've just been doing a little baking,' said Mum.

'A little *burning*, more like,' said Dad, laughing at her.

'I've made cookies,' said Mum.

'You're the cookie one, you daft little Dilly, you know you're hopeless in the kitchen,' said Dad.

'Mum's made lovely cookies, Dad. Try one,' I said, offering him a plate.

'I don't really like home-madey stuff,' said Dad,

131

wrinkling his nose. 'What sort of cookies are these anyway? I can't see any chocolate chips or sultanas.'

'They're plain,' said Mum.

'Plain but perfect,' I said. 'Do eat one, Dad, they're utterly delicious.'

He picked one off the plate, mimed taking a bite, smacking his lips together, the way you pretend to a baby.

'Yum yum yum,' he said, and he put the biscuit back.

'Oh well, Mum, all the more for us,' I mumbled.

'What's that?' said Dad. 'Are you being cheeky, Beauty?'

'Oh, Gerry, she's just being sweet, that's all,' said Mum. 'How are things at work? What's happening with the Water Meadows situation?'

Dad's face cheered.

'Well, we seem to be making progress at *last*. One of the chaps at the council, one of my golfing mates, got back in touch and I feel we *might* be able to get planning permission after all. I just need to put a few things in place and we're *there*. Gerry the Fixer, eh?' He looked at me. 'So, little Beauty, what did your little pals say about your birthday celebration? I bet they're thrilled, eh?'

'Yes, they are. Ever so,' I said.

'And how about my birthday girl? You're thrilled too, aren't you?'

132

Mum looked at me.

'Yes, Dad. Ever so, ever so, ever so,' I said. I whirled round and jumped up and down in a little pantomime of excitement.

'That's my girl,' said Dad. 'I spoil you rotten, don't I? I've got a little idea up my sleeve for your birthday present too. You're going to be *so* surprised, totally bowled over.'

My tummy churned, wondering what Dad had in store for me.

'What's Dad giving me?' I asked Mum later, when she was kissing me goodnight.

'I don't know. I've asked and asked, but he just taps the side of his nose and won't tell. I've suggested we get you a new outfit for your birthday. I know just how much you hate that pink dress.'

'Oh, Mum, he won't choose it for me again, will he?'

'I said he'd maybe get the size wrong and I'd need to supervise as dresses are girly things – but he didn't seem to take any notice,' said Mum, sighing.

I curled up with PJ, hugging her tight. It took me a long time to get to sleep.

Skye wasn't at school the next morning. Rhona said she had a dental appointment and wouldn't be back until the afternoon. Rhona played with *me* at lunch time. She gave me half her crisps from her packed lunch and I gave her half my chocolate from mine. I gave her half my tangerine too and she shared her apple. We took careful alternate bites until we got down to the core.

Then we went and sat on the wall together. Rhona found a piece of string and showed me how to play cat's cradle. It was so special. I hoped Skye would stay at the dentist getting every single tooth filled and filled for ever.

'I don't know what to get you for your birthday present, Beauty,' Rhona said. 'You gave me lovely presents. I especially like my T-shirt. And I wear my bangles all the time. I love the way they *clink clink clink.*'

'Have you started *A Little Princess* yet?'

'Well, I'm not really a great reader, not like you. I looked at the first chapter but it seems a bit . . . old-fashioned.'

'It's a truly lovely story when you get into it,' I said earnestly. 'Maybe I could read you a bit?'

'Maybe,' said Rhona. '*Anyway*, what can I get *you*? Do you want some books? You'll have to tell me the titles because I don't know all these weird old classics. I know what I *really* wanted to get you – another little teddy like Reginald Redted and poor Nicholas Navybear. I told Mum and she went looking for one yesterday, but the shop hasn't got any more.'

'It was ever so nice of you to think of it though,' I

said, giving her arm a little squeeze. She squeezed me back and we smiled at each other.

'Isn't there anything else you really really want for your birthday?' said Rhona. 'I know you like books but they are a bit boring.'

'No they're not!'

'Is that what your mum and dad are getting you too?'

'I don't know what I'm getting,' I said gloomily. I felt so close to Rhona I wondered if I dared confide in her. 'My dad's a bit . . . funny.'

'So's mine,' said Rhona, not understanding. 'I was so embarrassed when he told all those silly jokes at my party.'

'No, I mean my dad likes to be the boss. He likes to decide stuff, like what he's giving me for my birthday present. He went bananas when I asked him for a rabbit.'

'A *rabbit*?' said Rhona. 'I used to have a rabbit. A little grey one with blue eyes. He was so sweet.'

'A *real* rabbit? Oh, you lucky thing. What did you call him?'

'Bunny.'

'Oh, Rhona, didn't he have a proper name?'

'He *liked* being called Bunny. Mum let me have him in the house sometimes, though I had to promise to clear up after him if he did a poo. You're supposed to be able to house-train rabbits but Bunny did *heaps* of poos.'

'So what happened to him?'

'Oh, he died last winter. It was so sad. Mum and Dad said I could have another rabbit but I didn't want a new one, I just wanted Bunny back. I cried and cried whenever I saw a picture of a rabbit. I even cried when I watched some goofy baby programme on television about a rabbit.'

'*Rabbit Hutch?*' I said casually, though my heart was beating fast.

'That's the one. There's this big white rabbit with funny droopy ears.'

'That's Lily.'

Rhona grinned. 'Yeah! And then there's this smiley man—'

'Sam.'

'Do *you* watch *Rabbit Hutch?*' asked Rhona.

'Occasionally,' I said.

Rhona giggled. 'We're a pair of babies, aren't we?'

'Rhona! Rhona!'

It was Skye, running up the playground towards us.

'Don't tell Skye,' I said quickly.

'As if!' said Rhona.

Then she jumped down off the wall and left me.

When I got home after school I switched on the television straight away.

'Who do we want to see?' said the voice.

'Sam and Lily in the Rabbit Hutch!'

'Hey there!' said Sam, and Lily twitched her nose to say hello too.

'Lily's got a little friend who's come to tea,' said Sam. He squatted down and pointed to a little fat furry black-and-tan creature.

'It's Oliver the guinea pig. Hello, Oliver, how lovely to see you. Say hello to Oliver, Lily!'

Sam tried to put Lily down on the ground beside Oliver but she scrabbled her paws, trying to cling on. Sam smiled and stroked her. 'Lily's a bit shy,' he whispered to me.

'I know what she feels like. I feel ever so shy sometimes,' I whispered back.

'There now, Lily,' said Sam, easing her gently until she was nose to nose with Oliver. 'It's dear old Oliver, Lily – you like him. He's your special friend. That's right, twitch your noses at each other. Shall we twitch noses too?'

Sam twitched his nose, looking wonderfully silly. I twitched mine back, giggling.

'Do *you* have a special friend?' Sam asked.

This was my opportunity.

'Yes I do! It's Rhona! You might know her, she watches *Rabbit Hutch* too.'

'Oh, that's good,' said Sam, nodding.

'She's *my* special friend but I'm not sure she'd

say I was *her* special friend. Her absolute best friend is this girl called Skye. She is a truly *revolting* person. Why on earth Rhona stays friends with her I simply can't understand. But I think Rhona might like me second best. She sat with me at lunch time and it was *so* lovely and we chatted about all sorts of stuff and that's when she said she sometimes watches you too.'

I burbled on to Sam while he nodded and played with Lily and Oliver. He had to interrupt every now and then to talk to all the other children but I didn't mind. I knew he was still listening to every word I was saying. I wasn't through when he said goodbye. I went to talk to Mum instead.

There was a wonderful warm baking smell in the kitchen. Mum smiled at me, flour sprinkled down her front like fairy dust.

'More cookies?' I said.

'I'm having another go. I'm making oatmeal-and-raisin cookies this time. I already made two batches this morning but they didn't come out quite right. The first lot looked weird, though they didn't taste too bad. The second lot looked fine but they weren't quite *munchy* enough.' Mum patted her tiny waist ruefully. 'I'm going to put on pounds and pounds doing all this baking lark. I went to the gym at lunch time but if I keep on stuffing cookies I'll need to go to the gym twice a day. And I *hate* that blooming gym, it's so boring.'

'Maybe you could have your own personal trainer, Mum? That might make it more fun.'

'I'll say,' said Mum. 'A young hunky guy putting me through my paces, eh? I wonder what your dad would have to say about that! You know what he's like.'

I knew all too well. 'Doesn't he trust you, Mum?'

Mum shrugged. 'I don't know. He just doesn't want me getting close to anyone else but him. He'd go bananas if I got matey with any man even if it was entirely innocent. He doesn't really like me having women friends either.'

'Did you have lots of friends when you were at school, Mum?'

'Not really.'

'Did you have a best friend?'

Mum nibbled her lip. 'No, they didn't really like me much, the girls in my class.'

'But you must have been the prettiest one!'

Mum shrugged. 'They all teased me because I was a bit slow and dreamy. I was hopeless, I just let them walk all over me. I've never been able to stand up for myself.'

She opened the oven door and had a peep at the cookies.

'Hey, I think they're done. They look pretty good, don't they?'

She took the baking tray out of the oven and showed me twenty-four raisin-and-oatmeal cookies, pale gold and perfect.

I reached out eagerly.

'Hey hey, let them cool down a bit, you'll burn your mouth.'

'OK, but they smell so delicious! I can't wait!'

'We'll give all your friends cookies on your birthday and that'll be your new nickname, little Cookie Cookson.'

Mum picked up an oatmeal-and-raisin cookie and popped it into my mouth. I chewed appreciatively. They were softer than the plain cookies, much chewier, with a spicy, nutty tang.

'Well done, Mum!' I said through my mouthful. 'They're really really gorgeous. How did you do it?'

'Just call me the Cookie Fairy,' said Mum. 'I wave my magic wand' – she mimed it – 'and hey presto, cookie heaven. No, actually it's this recipe book. It told me to use cinnamon and cloves and chopped nuts as well as the oatmeal and the raisins, and then there's eggs and brown sugar and all sorts. You sift and sprinkle and stir like crazy. I think I'm getting the knack of it, Beauty!'

'You are, you are.'

'Funny if I turn out to be a good cook after all these years of being such rubbish at it,' Mum said, nibbling one of her own cookies appreciatively.

'Maybe Dad doesn't need these fancy buffet people. Maybe you could do it all, Mum?'

'Maybe *not*,' said Mum, laughing. 'I think I'd better stick to cookies.'

Eleven

'Surprise!' Dad shouted, bursting into my bedroom on Saturday morning.

I opened my eyes and screamed. An enormous shocking-pink hairy monster loomed above me, its horrible bug-eyed buck-tooth face inches from my own.

'Happy birthday to you,
Happy birthday to you,
Happy birthday, dear Beauty,
Happy birthday to yoooooou!' Dad sang.

Every time he said the word 'birthday' he made the monster nuzzle my face grotesquely.

'Careful, Gerry darling, you'll smother her,' said Mum.

'She's fine, she's fine! She's just having a happy romp with her birthday rabbit,' said Dad. 'Do you like him, Beauty? You said you wanted a rabbit, didn't you! I bet you never thought you'd get one this size. Biggest in the whole of Hamleys! I had to get a taxi all the way home. I couldn't possibly struggle on a tube with him in my arms. Isn't he the loveliest bunny you've ever seen, Beauty? Why don't you give him a big hug? What's up with you?'

143

'She's still half asleep, Gerry. Give her a chance!' said Mum. She wriggled round the dreadful giant rabbit and gave me a kiss. 'Happy birthday, darling.'

I hugged her close. Then I sat up properly and hugged Dad. And then I took a deep breath and wrapped my arms round the rabbit. Its fur was coarse and tickly and it had an overpowering smell of wool and carpet.

'Don't you just love your birthday bunny?' said Dad.

I hated hated hated the monster rabbit but I pretended to be thrilled with him.

'So what are you going to call him, eh?' Dad demanded.

I didn't want to personalize the rabbit with a proper name.

'He's called . . . Pinky,' I said.

'Pinky!' said Dad. 'All right, so be it.'

He lumbered round the room with Pinky, singing:

'My name's Pinky,
I'm not dinky,
I'll give you a winky
'Cos my eyes are blinky!'

Dad gave the rabbit a vigorous shake. His eyes revolved alarmingly.

'Come and join in the dance, Beauty!' said Dad.

I had to get up and caper in a circle with my mad dad and the worst toy rabbit in the world.

'I *told* you she'd love the rabbit,' Dad said to Mum.

'Yes, of course she loves it, Gerry. Now, Beauty, you'd better whiz along to the bathroom and then you can open the rest of your presents at breakfast.'

'Special birthday breakfast! Scrambled eggs and smoked salmon. I'd better go and do it. Your mother still can't scramble an egg to save her life. Can't even *boil* a blooming egg for that matter, can you, Silly Dilly?'

'Mum *can* cook. She makes wonderful cookies,' I mumbled, but Mum put her finger to her lips, shushing me.

Dad marched downstairs. The pink rabbit lounged on my bed, giant limbs sprawled, paws clenched like boxing gloves. Mum and I stared at it. Then I suddenly spluttered. Mum giggled too. We became helpless with laughter, our hands clamped over our mouths in case Dad heard us.

'Oh, Beauty, I'm sorry,' Mum whispered. 'I couldn't *believe* it when I saw it. You hate it, don't you?'

'Yes!'

'It completely fills up your bedroom. Dear God, it's going to give you nightmares.'

'Maybe I can stuff it in my wardrobe every night?'

I tried lifting it but I could barely drag it off the bed.

'Watch those massive arms! We don't want to break another mirror!' Mum hissed.

'It so spoils my bedroom,' I said despairingly, suddenly near tears.

'Yes, I know. Maybe we'll sit him in a corner and drape a huge wrap over him when your dad's not around. But cheer up, there's a trade-off! As your dad bought you the pink rabbit I begged him to let me buy your birthday outfit as *my* present to you. He was fed up with shopping by this time, so he said OK. He even gave me a hundred quid towards it. You go and get washed and it'll be waiting in your wardrobe when you get back.'

'Is it pink or frilly?' I asked anxiously.

'Not a single frill and it's not pink, OK?' said Mum. 'Scoot.'

I scooted – and when I got back I saw my new outfit hanging outside my wardrobe. The dress was pearly-grey with long sleeves and a full skirt with a white broderie anglaise pinafore over the top. There were grey silky tights and amazing grey laced boots with little heels.

'I know you'd much sooner wear a T-shirt and jeans but your dad would never allow it, especially when he's turned your birthday into such a big do. He said you had to wear a proper party frock. I was going bananas trying to find something you'd like. Then I saw this. I know it's very old-fashioned but I thought you wouldn't mind. It's like something Sara would wear in *A Little Princess*.'

'Oh, Mum,' I said, stroking the soft dress. 'It's beautiful – but will I look funny in it? Will it fit me? I'm getting *sooo* fat.'

'No, you're not, sweetheart. I think it'll look great. Try it on and see.'

Mum had bought me new underwear too, white pants with lace and a wonderful whirly petticoat a bit like a ballet dress.

'Maybe I'll just wear this as a party dress,' I said, doing wobbly arabesques all around my bedroom.

'Come and put your dress on, Sugar Plum Fairy,' said Mum, unbuttoning it for me.

She acted like a Victorian maid, buttoning me into my dress, tying the sash of the pinafore and kneeling in front of me lacing my boots.

'There!' she said. 'Look at yourself in the mirror!'

I went and stood in front of the Venetian glass. I looked so different. I really looked like a girl in a Victorian story book. I still didn't look *pretty* – but I didn't look hideously ugly either.

'Oh, Mum!' I said, my eyes shining.

'Oh, Beauty!' said Mum. 'You look lovely, sweetheart. Maybe I ought to get a job as a stylist!'

Dad shouted impatiently from downstairs. 'What are you two up to? The eggs are scrambling into sawdust!' he yelled.

'We're dressing Beauty in her finery. Come to

147

the bottom of the stairs, Gerry,' Mum called.

She took me by the hand and then led me downstairs. I walked down cautiously in my heeled boots, my petticoat and skirt swishing around my calves, making a lovely rustling sound.

Dad was frowning at first, still fussing about the eggs. Then he saw me – and he looked taken aback.

'Oh goodness! It's not really a *party* dress, is it? Still, you don't look bad in it, Beauty. The colour's a bit insipid, mind you. A nice bright pink might have been prettier. And I'm not sure about the apron. It's certainly unusual. What do you think, Beauty?'

'I absolutely love it!' I said, twirling round.

I ended up changing out of my beautiful grey dress and pinafore to eat my breakfast just in case I spilled scrambled eggs all down me. I sat in my new petticoat and my Tracy Beaker dressing gown opening up my birthday presents. Dad's parents were dead, but Nana, my mum's mum, sent me pink nylon baby-doll pyjamas about a hundred sizes too small.

'How lovely – *not*,' said Mum. She bent close to my ear. 'I wonder if they'd fit your new rabbit?'

We had a private snigger. There was a present from Auntie Avril, the first Mrs Cookson. She always liked Mum because she thought she'd taken Dad away from the *second* Mrs Cookson, Auntie Alysha. Auntie Avril *hated* Auntie Alysha. They couldn't even be in the same room together without starting a screaming match, but Auntie Avril and Mum were quite matey.

Auntie Avril sent very good birthday presents. This time she'd given me a large tin of fifty felt-tip pens, special Swiss ones with fine points, all the colours of the rainbow. Dad frowned when he saw them.

'You watch what you're doing with them crayons,' he said, but mercifully he didn't confiscate them.

The present that made me smile the most was one wrapped in blue paper with a white rabbit pattern. The label was carefully printed SN AD@TSX + KNUD EQNL R@L @MC KHKX.

'Oh my goodness!' said Mum. 'Fancy Sam and Lily knowing it's your birthday!'

'Who on earth are Sam and Lily?' said Dad.

'They're special friends of Beauty's,' said Mum.

Mum was my special friend. I knew her writing, even though she'd tried to disguise it. I ripped off the paper – and there was a DVD compilation of all the best *Rabbit Hutch* shows.

'Oh how *lovely*,' I said.

'Looks very babyish to me,' said Dad, glancing at it. He stood up, patting me on the head. 'Glad your birthday's got off to a good start, Beauty. What's your favourite present, eh?'

I didn't have any choice.

'The toy rabbit,' I said.

Dad chuckled triumphantly, rolling his eyes. He looked alarmingly like the rabbit himself.

'Now, girls, I've just got to dash to the office to meet up with this guy who's going to sort everything out for me.'

'But it's Beauty's birthday, Gerry! The children are coming at twelve!'

'Don't worry, don't worry, I'll be back long before then, fusspot. You two girls get the living room in spit-spot shape. The caterers are arriving at eleven. OK, my darlings. Ready to show off our Happy Home?'

Dad went off whistling his silly song. Mum and I rushed round dusting and vacuuming. The house already seemed spotless but Dad winced at the tiniest scuff or smear. When it was all utterly perfect Mum sent me off to sit on her bed and watch Sam and Lily on her DVD player.

'While you're watching could you bear to write some labels for me?' said Mum. 'You made such a lovely job of the party invitations. It would be great if you'd write this out for me, eighteen times over.'

She put the message in front of me, scribbled on her shopping-list pad:

Hears a little gift!
Cookies from Beauty Cookson!

'Is that OK?' she asked anxiously.

I wasn't going to tell her but she saw my eyes flicker. 'What is it? Have I got it wrong?'

'I think "here's" is maybe spelled differently, Mum,' I said gently.

'Oh lordy! Good job you're my little brainbox. Spell it properly for me then, sweetie, while I go and sort out all the cookies.'

I wrote out the eighteen labels with Auntie Avril's felt-tip pens while Sam and Lily chatted to me. They kept getting distracted from each little programme to wish me a happy birthday. Sam even sang the birthday song for me, making Lily's ears sway in time to the music.

'Are you having a lovely birthday, Beauty?' Sam asked.

'I *think* so,' I said. 'I'm scared it'll all go wrong when all the girls come. You know how they all tease me. It would be OK if Skye and Arabella and Emily weren't coming. Do you think they'll laugh at my new party dress? It's not a bit like the sort of stuff they wear.'

'It's much much nicer,' said Sam. 'We think you look stunning in your dress and pinafore and special boots. Your mum's chosen a wonderful outfit for you. We're not so sure about your dad's present though. You're a bit frightened of that great big pink rabbit, aren't you, Lily?'

Lily snuffled, nodding her head.

'*I* was frightened just at first,' I said. 'It's hideous, isn't it?'

We have a private chuckle together and then Sam and Lily went through their paces for their ten programmes, pottering in the garden, clearing out the rabbit hutch, coping with a cold, smelling the spring flowers, getting wet in the rain. I especially loved that episode because Sam made Lily her own little sou'wester to keep her ears dry.

I finished off the labels and ran down to give them to Mum. She had eighteen special transparent gift bags lined up on the kitchen table. I stuck a label on each one and then Mum brought out four huge tins.

'These are the oatmeal-and-raisin cookies,' said Mum, pointing. 'And these are the plain, but I've iced them with lemon frosting and stuck those little silver balls on top so they look quite pretty, don't they? Then these are cherry cookies and *these* are chocolate chip.'

'You're so clever, Mum! They look wonderful.'

'They do, don't they!' Mum agreed happily. 'We'll give each girl three of each kind, OK? You get filling and I'll tie the tops with ribbon.'

Mum had brought beautiful thin satin ribbon, all different colours. When each bag was neatly tied up Mum washed her hands and then tied one lock of my hair into a tiny plait and secured it with the last of the green ribbon.

'There, it matches your eyes!' said Mum. 'You'd better go and get into your party finery now, the caterers will be here any minute.'

I went upstairs and put on my grey dress and pinafore and my lovely boots. I looked at myself in the Venetian glass and then I went to check in the long mirror in Mum's bedroom. Sam and Lily were still talking on the television. They stopped and looked at me.

'Oh, Beauty, you look lovely!' said Sam, and Lily's eyes shone as she stared at me.

I blew them both a big kiss and then switched them off. I imagined them snuggled up together asleep in the dark of the Rabbit Hutch, waiting until I wanted to wake them up again.

Mum came running in to change into *her* party outfit – a cream dress that showed off a lot of her own creamy skin. Mum squinted sideways at herself in the mirror.

'Do you think I ought to wear a little camisole under this dress, sweetie?' she asked.

I lowered my voice, doing my best gruff Dad imitation. 'If you've got it, babe, flaunt it,' I said.

Mum cracked up laughing. 'You are a card, Beauty.' She cupped my face with her hands. 'You're going to have the happiest birthday ever, just you wait and see.'

The caterers arrived and started setting up the buffet on the dining-room table. Mum and I hovered, worried about getting in the way, but when they put the extraordinary profiterole tower in pride of place in the middle of the table Mum spoke up.

'Can we leave room for a plate of my home-made cookies, please?' she said.

She'd arranged all the left-over cookies from the tins on her best green-leaf plate. She laid them in circles, lemon iced cookies in the middle, then the cherry, then the chocolate chip, with the darker oatmeal round the edge. They looked like a beautiful biscuit flower. To make the plate even prettier Mum had scattered little white and purple freesia heads across the cookies.

'They look lovely, madam,' said the head caterer – and Mum flushed with pride.

Then we heard the front door bang and Dad came stomping into the dining room. He didn't pause to take off his shoes. It was immediately obvious he was furious about something. Mum took my hand and squeezed it.

'Hello, Gerry, darling,' she said. 'Look, doesn't Beauty's birthday buffet look wonderful?'

Dad barely glanced at it. He nodded curtly at the caterers, stretching his mouth into a grimace.

'What's the matter?' Mum murmured. 'Is the super-stretch limo still coming? The theatre has reserved the seats?'

'Oh, everything's fine and hunky-dory for Beauty's birthday,' said Dad, ruffling my hair and pulling my ribbon out of place. 'I've fixed *that* all right. I'm just stuffed when it comes to the Water Meadows development.'

'But I thought this chap was going to fix it all for you?' said Mum.

'That's what *I* thought. But he's gone and got cold feet. And not only that, he's blabbed to some-one else about a little gift I gave him.' Dad lowered his voice to a hiss so the caterers wouldn't hear. 'And now there's ridiculous talk of *bribery*.'

'Oh no!' said Mum, her hand to her mouth. 'But . . . isn't that a criminal offence?'

'Sh! Don't act as if I'm about to be frogmarched off to jail. It won't come to that, but it might mean hiring lawyers and it's all going to be horrendously expensive one way or another – and the Water Meadows deal is off now, whatever happens.'

'Oh, darling, I'm so sorry,' Mum said.

'I should think you jolly well are, because we're going to have to pull our horns in *very* smartly. No more fancy frocks and finery for either of you!'

Dad turned to me. 'Make the most of this birthday, Beauty. It looks like it'll be the last proper party you'll have in a long time.'

I knew it wasn't the moment to remind Dad I'd never asked for a proper party. I looked at his red face and his twitchy eyelid and his clenched fists, all the warning signs. He was primed like a hand grenade. He was just about keeping it together because the caterers were here but all it needed was one tiny trigger – and then he'd explode.

The girls were due to arrive in twenty minutes. I thought of Dad screaming and shouting in front of Skye and Emily and Arabella and I wanted to die.

'Don't look so tragic, Beauty!' said Dad. He forced a smile to his face, teeth bared as if ready to bite. 'Don't you worry about Daddy's little troubles. You're still going to have a grand time with your little pals. Look at this lovely spread, yum yum!' Then he frowned. 'What's the big green plate doing bang in the middle?'

Dad marched up to the table and banged the cookie plate. They all bounced out of their elaborate pattern and the freesias fell off.

'What are you doing, fobbing me off with all these arty-farty fancy biscuits? I didn't order them!'

'I know, sir. Your wife made them,' said the chief caterer. 'She asked us to put the plate there.'

'My wife? Is *she* paying your company then?

156

I think you'll find *I'm* the poor Joe Soap writing the cheque, and if that's the case you'll take your orders from me. Move that home-made rubbish off the table, pronto. Look at it, half the biscuits are broken anyway!'

They were broken because Dad had thumped them around. Mum picked up the plate and carried it into the kitchen. She kept her head held high but I saw the tears in her eyes. I followed her and gave her a big hug.

'I'm so sorry, Mum. They looked so lovely too,' I said.

'Never mind,' said Mum, swallowing hard. 'We can still give the girls their own special bags.'

'What are you two whispering about?' said Dad, following us into the kitchen. 'Beauty, stop looking at me like that! Dilly, shove all that biscuit muck in the bin where it belongs. I don't want you to start all these damn daft cooking experiments, you're useless at it. Your job is to look beautiful, so brighten up and put a smile on your face, for pity's sake. You need a bit more sparkle. Put some jewellery on. That neckline's a bit bare. I know, wear your diamond collar.'

I froze.

'Yes, good idea,' Mum said calmly. 'Or even better, my string of pearls. They'll look beautifully creamy with this dress. I'll go and put them on.'

'No, pearls are a bit mumsy and understated. I want you looking flash, girl. Go for the diamonds,' said Dad.

Mum walked out of the kitchen and went upstairs. I followed her, feeling frantic.

'Stop trotting after your mother, Beauty. You're acting like you're her little shadow. Come here, let's look at you. You're a bit *pale*. What's up with you?'

Dad didn't wait for an answer. He went to pour himself a drink and order the caterers around. Mum stayed upstairs. Then there was a ring at the door. It was only quarter to but one of the girls was here already!

'Go on then, Beauty, answer the door to your first guest,' said Dad, prodding me out into the hall. 'Dilly, what the hell are you doing? Get yourself down here!' he hissed up the stairs.

I went to the door. It was Arabella and her mother, both of them long and thin and jittery, like thoroughbred ponies.

'Happy birthday, Beauty,' Arabella neighed.

It was the first time I'd ever heard her use my real name.

'Happy birthday, Beauty,' Arabella's mother said in her high posh voice. She said my name as if it was in quotation marks, her eyebrows raised. 'Where's Mummy, dear? I'd just like to check on all the arrangements. Is it right that all

158

the girls will be delivered back to their own homes?'

'Please come in. Oh yes, they'll be delivered in a super-stretch limo,' I said.

Mum came flying down the stairs. She was wearing a big gold heart locket. Dad joined her in the hall.

'Ah, Mrs Cookson – and Mr Cookson,' said Arabella's mum. 'This is Arabella.'

'Hey, hey, Gerry and Dilly, please,' said Dad, shaking hands. 'Welcome to our Happy Home.'

My throat dried. I thought Dad was going to start his Happy Homes song and dance routine. Mum obviously thought so too because she started talking hurriedly about car times and the theatre seats and when we'd get back home.

'Dilly, Dilly, quit burbling,' said Dad.

Mum flushed. Arabella's mum blinked. She smiled pityingly at Mum.

'Bless you, dear, you're just putting my mind at rest. We can't help worrying. It's a female thing, Mr Cookson,' she said.

Dad stared at her, not liking it that she'd called him Mr Cookson again – but he managed a wintry smile. He held his glass of whisky up.

'Oh no, nothing for me, thank you,' said Arabella's mother, as if he'd offered her rat poison. She turned to Mum. 'Who's going to be driving this limousine?' she asked.

'Oh, don't worry, there's a special chauffeur,'

said Mum quickly. 'And of course Gerry and I will be there with the girls, keeping an eye on things.'

'Mmm,' said Arabella's mum. She pressed her hand on Arabella's shoulder. 'Well, I'll be off, darling. Remember, you've got the mobile if you need me at all. Have a lovely time.'

'Bye, Ma,' said Arabella. She thrust a pink parcel at me. 'This is your birthday present.'

I opened it. It was one of the *Princess* paperbacks. I'd read it last year.

'Oh, Beauty, how thoughtful. Araminta's given you one of them books you like so much,' said Dad. 'Say thank you, darling.'

'Ara*bella*,' I said. 'Thank you.'

'Dilly, can I have a word?' said Dad.

'In a minute, Gerry,' said Mum. 'Would you like some juice, Arabella?'

'That's what we've got the caterers for, Dilly. I need you.' Dad took hold of Mum by the wrist.

She had to go with him. They went into the kitchen and shut the door but I could still hear Dad clearly.

'*Why the hell aren't you wearing your diamond collar?*'

'Thank you very much for my *Princess* book,' I said loudly. 'It's very kind of you.'

'No, it's not,' said Arabella. 'Someone gave it to me at Christmas and I've never been bothered to read it.'

160

'*You're to put it on now!*'

'I love reading, I read all the time, I even read in the bath,' I burbled.

'What's your dad getting so het up about?' asked Arabella.

'Nothing. He just shouts sometimes, it doesn't mean he's really cross,' I said.

'*You've LOST it? What the hell do you mean, you dozy cow?*'

Arabella blinked. 'Your dad just called your mum a *cow*!'

'No he didn't. Shall we eat something? Or we could go out in the garden if you like?'

There was a sudden unmistakable sound from the kitchen, harsh and horrible.

'Was that a slap? Does your dad *hit* your mum?' Arabella asked, her eyes wide.

'No. No, of course not. I expect he just bumped into something. Look, do you see my profiterole tower? I wonder how they're going to cut it?'

Arabella shrugged. 'I don't know. It *was* a slap. This is kind of weird.' She fingered the mobile phone in her pocket. 'Maybe I'm going to phone my mum to come back.'

'No, don't! You've only just got here.'

'I wish Emily and the others were here,' said Arabella.

Then the doorbell rang and there was a whole

161

gang of girls on the doorstep. They all crowded into the hall. Dad came out to greet them, getting their names wrong, welcoming everyone to his Happy Home.

Mum stayed in the kitchen. She didn't come out for another ten minutes, when nearly everyone had arrived. One side of her face was still much pinker than the other and her eyes were red, but she smiled heroically at everyone and helped serve the food, even though Dad told her not to. He made himself another drink.

Arabella was huddled in a corner whispering to Emily and Skye. They kept looking round at my dad and rolling their eyes.

Emily gave me the very same *Princess* book as Arabella. Her eyes gleamed as she gave me her parcel. I knew they'd done it deliberately but I thanked her all the same.

I expected the exact same copy from Skye but her present was a different shape. It was a little child's brush-and-comb set, painted with rosebuds. There were two words in swirly writing round the edge of the mirror and across the back of the brush. *Little Beauty*.

Skye and Emily and Arabella all grinned.

'There you are, Ugly,' Skye said. 'Your very own brush to get the tangles out of your corkscrews, and a mirror specially for you.'

'I bet it cracks the minute she looks in it,' said Emily.

'She looks *especially* weird today. What *is* that you're wearing, Ugly? Some kind of historical costume?' said Arabella.

'She's got her apron on, so maybe she's the maid,' said Skye, sniggering. 'Go on, give us a curtsy, Ugly-Wugly.'

'What did you just say, Skye?' said Mum, pushing forward to stand beside us. Her voice was steely.

'Nothing,' Skye mumbled.

'You just mind that mouth of yours,' said Mum, and walked on.

Skye flushed scarlet.

'What a cheek!' Emily hissed. 'You're not allowed to tell someone else's child off!'

'Especially a s-l-a-g like her,' said Skye.

I stood still. I clenched my fists. 'You say another word about my mum and I'll drag you by your hair over to that table and shove you head first into that profiterole tower and I'll stuff profiteroles up your snobby nose and down your foul mouth until you're sick,' I said.

Skye stared at me, shocked. She took a step backward, then another. Then she recovered a little and shook her head at Emily and Arabella, rotating her finger into the side of her head.

'Watch out, she's got a screw loose,' she said shakily.

'I think I'm going to phone my mum,' said Arabella.

'Maybe I'll phone mine,' said Emily. 'Where's Rhona, Skye? Isn't she coming?'

'She *said* she was,' said Skye. 'But she's obviously thought better of it. Clever her. I *knew* she didn't really like Ugly.'

My heart started thumping. I thought she was simply trying to wind me up – but where *was* Rhona? She was half an hour late. Everyone had eaten the vol au vents and sausages and all the other buffet bits.

'Time to cut your birthday cake, Beauty,' said Dad.

'But Rhona isn't here yet,' I said.

'Which one's Rhona? I don't think she'll be coming now,' said Dad.

'Yes she will. Rhona's my friend,' I said desperately.

'Did you hear that!' said Skye. 'As if!'

'Everyone knows Rhona's *your* friend, Skye.'

'You and Rhona have been best friends for ever,' said Arabella.

'Rhona's still my friend too – and she said she was coming,' I said.

Mum put her arm round me. 'Maybe she's not

very well,' she whispered. 'Don't worry, Beauty. We'll save her some of the profiterole tower, and you can give her a bag of cookies at school on Monday.'

'I wish she'd come *now*,' I said.

There was a ring at the door.

'Rhona!' I said, and went flying.

It *was* Rhona, standing on the doorstep clutching a large box, her cheeks bright pink with excitement. Mr Marshall stood beside her, hauling what looked like a wooden crate.

'Happy birthday, Beauty! Hey, what a lovely dress! And *wonderful* boots!' said Rhona. 'I'm so sorry we're so late. We were all set to leave an hour ago but then your birthday present escaped!'

'It . . . escaped?' I said.

'It took ages and ages to catch him. Be very careful when you take the lid off! We don't want him to get away again.'

She set the box on the front doorstep. I knelt down and cautiously lifted the box lid a few inches. I peered into the darkness inside. There was a lot of soft straw. Huddled right in the middle, ears twitching anxiously, was a little grey rabbit.

Twelve

'A rabbit!' I whispered.

'It's your birthday bunny,' said Rhona. 'Dad's scrubbed out my rabbit's hutch for you, and we've got bedding and rabbit food. Mum's parcelled up some lettuce and dandelion leaves too.'

'Oh, Rhona!' I said. I shut my eyes tight but I couldn't stop two tears spilling down my cheeks.

'What's the matter, Beauty? You did *want* a rabbit, didn't you?' said Rhona.

'Yes, I wanted a rabbit more than anything else in the world,' I said.

'So there you are then!' said Rhona. 'I can't wait to hear what you're going to call him.'

'Call who?' said Dad, coming up the hall behind me. 'Can you just lift that wooden thing off of the parquet flooring?'

'Certainly, certainly,' said Mr Marshall. 'Shall I shove the hutch round the back?'

'The . . . hutch?' said Dad.

I swallowed so hard my head started spinning. I had one hand inside the box. I stroked the soft soft fur.

'Rhona's bought me a little r-r-rabbit for my birthday,' I said.

I waited. I didn't dare look round at Dad. I heard his sharp intake of breath.

'I think our Beauty's been a bit of a naughty girl asking you to give her a rabbit,' said Dad. 'She knows she's not allowed to have pets.'

'Oh, she didn't *ask*, Mr Cookson,' said Rhona, totally unfazed. 'But I *knew* just how much she'd love a rabbit. It's just a little weeny baby rabbit. He won't make any mess at all, he'll just stay neat and cosy in his hutch. You'll let Beauty keep him, won't you?'

'I certainly hope you will, pal, because I don't want to lumber this damn hutch all the way home!' said Mr Marshall.

I waited, holding my breath. We all waited, Rhona and Mr Marshall, Mum, Skye, Emily, Arabella and every other girl at my party.

'Well, in that case of course Beauty can have her little bunny,' said Dad.

'Hurray!' said Rhona.

'Cheers!' said Mr Marshall.

There was an excited babble as everyone crowded round, wanting to see my rabbit.

'No, no, careful, we mustn't frighten him,' I said firmly, feeling the poor little thing quivering.

I looked up at Dad. He was smiling at me. He even said 'Aaah!' as I lifted the little rabbit out of his box and cradled him in my arms. But I saw his narrowed eyes, his clenched jaw, the pulse beating in his forehead.

Mr Marshall carried the hutch through the house and out of the French windows into the back garden. Rhona carried the bunny box and I carried the rabbit. Everyone else crowded round, wanting to see him and stroke him.

'Get back a bit! He's getting so frightened. He's little, he's worried you might hurt him,' I said, fiercely protective.

They all moved back, even Skye. It was tricky transferring my rabbit into his hutch. He wriggled frantically and I had to hang onto him really tightly though I was terrified of hurting him. I knew how clumsy I could be – and yet somehow my hands knew how to cup and hold and soothe him.

'Let's tuck him up in bed,' said Rhona, pulling his straw out of the box.

'Watch what you're doing, dear, that stuff's going all over the patio,' said Dad. 'Come on, girls, we've still got to eat the profiterole tower, and the super-stretch limo will be here soon.'

'Hang on, Mr Cookson. We've got to feed the rabbit first!' said Rhona. 'I didn't give him any breakfast so he wouldn't do too many poos in his birthday box.'

All the girls giggled and started chatting about

what rabbits liked to eat. Dad's smile was so strained his lips disappeared.

'Buck up, then, dears,' he said.

Skye had hold of the lettuce-and-dandelion parcel.

'Here you are, Bunny, here's your yummy greens,' she said.

'No, Skye, it's not *your* rabbit. Beauty must feed him,' said Rhona.

So I fed my rabbit. My hand was shaking and my tummy in knots because of Dad, but it was still the most fantastic feeling offering the leaves and seeing my rabbit's nose twitch, his soft mouth open, his little teeth starting to chomp chomp chomp.

I'd loved Nicholas Navybear but that was nothing like having a real soft breathing little creature nuzzling my fingers.

'He's the loveliest rabbit ever, Rhona', I whispered.

'So what's his name, your little birthday bunny?' she said.

'We'll *call* him Birthday,' I said. 'Because he's the best birthday present I've ever had.'

'Apart from the gorgeous giant toy rabbit I gave you, Beauty,' said Dad. 'Come on now, they're about to cut the cake. Back in the house everyone.'

Mum made me wash my hands though I

wanted to keep the feel of Birthday's soft fur and warm tongue on my fingers. I didn't get to cut the profiterole tower myself as it was such a complicated job but I handed out the plates to everyone. Mr Marshall stayed to have a piece too.

'Yum yum, I've got lucky,' he said. 'Happy birthday, Beauty. You look an absolute picture in that lovely dress.'

I looked at him. He didn't seem to be making a joke. He was smiling as if he really meant it.

'Thank you,' I said, smiling back at him. 'It's my birthday present from Mum.'

'Oh well, your mum's got the knack of looking lovely herself,' said Mr Marshall, nudging up to Mum and giving her a little pat. He was just being silly, wiggling his eyebrows and playing about – but Dad glared at him.

'Right, we'd better start rounding up the kids, the super-stretch will be here any minute,' he said, peering at his Rolex. 'I don't want to chase you out, chum, but we need to get cracking.'

Mr Marshall took this heavy hint and said goodbye. I wished he was coming with us. He was so kind and funny. I felt nothing really bad could happen when he was around.

'Now, girls, you'd better all make a quick trip to the little girls' room. We don't want any of you taken short in the super-stretch,' said Dad.

I blushed scarlet. Some of the girls tittered, some rolled their eyes.

'Beauty, show everyone the bathroom. Don't worry, at the last count we had four loos in our Happy Home, so you shouldn't have to stand around with your legs crossed too long.'

'Honestly!' Emily muttered. 'He's so *crude*.'

'Vulgar,' Arabella agreed.

'Why go on about all his loos anyway? Does he think we don't have any at home?' said Skye.

'Oh stop it, he's just being funny,' said Rhona – but I knew she was just saying it to comfort me.

She came up to my bedroom with me. She squealed when she saw the monster pink rabbit lurking in the corner.

'Oh my goodness! It's the biggest rabbit I've ever seen!'

'It's horrible,' I said.

'What's it *called*?'

'Just Pinky. If I give it a proper name it'll start to get real.' I suddenly gave Rhona a big hug. 'Thank you so much for Birthday, Rhona. I really meant it, he's the best birthday present in the whole world.'

'He's only a little bunny from the pet shop. Your dad isn't really cross about it, is he?'

'No,' I lied. 'No, he's fine.' I sighed. 'I do like *your* dad, Rhona.'

'Oh, my dad's a silly old sausage,' said Rhona

fondly. 'That's what I call him sometimes – and he calls me his little chipolata.'

Rhona danced round my bedroom, gently touching all my Victorian doll collection and my little china animals and my musical box and all my glass snowstorms.

'You've got such a *lovely* bedroom, Beauty. And fancy having your very own bathroom! Even Skye hasn't got her own en suite bathroom and her family have got pots of money. It must be such fun to be as rich as you!'

Lulu and Poo-poo were clamouring to use my bathroom too so we let them in and then went downstairs. I heard a sudden squeaking.

'It's here! Look out the window! Oh goodness, it's *enormous*! Our own super-stretch limo!'

All the girls were dancing up and down, so excited. I had a peep too and my heart started thumping at the thought that it was *my* birthday super-stretch limo.

The caterers were starting to clear my birthday buffet already. There was no sign of Mum and Dad. I went looking for them to tell them the car was here. I opened the door of the kitchen. Dad had hold of Mum, his face contorted. I ran forward, terrified he was going to hit her again.

'Dad, Dad, the super-stretch limo is here! Come and look, it's so grand, I'm so lucky!' I blurted.

Dad didn't even seem to hear me.

'Never never let me see you flirting with that creep Marshall again,' he said, giving Mum a shake.

'She *wasn't* flirting, Dad!' I said.

'I'll thank you to mind your own business, Beauty,' Dad said. 'Did you say the car was here? Right, let's be off then.'

Mum rubbed her wrist, blinking hard. She looked at Dad as if she wanted to say something – but then looked at me instead. She tried to smile.

'Come on then, birthday girl,' she said, picking up a large carrier bag on the kitchen floor.

'What's that you've got, Dilly?' Dad asked.

'It's little going-home presents,' said Mum. 'Beauty can give one to each girl as we drop them off.'

Dad breathed a little easier. 'Nice touch,' he said grudgingly. 'So what are we giving them all? Bracelets, smelly bath stuff, cuddly toys?'

'Oh, it's just a little token,' said Mum, walking to the door. 'Come on, Beauty. A super-stretch limo, imagine! How exciting!'

But Dad grabbed at the carrier bag before she could get any further. 'Let me see!' he demanded.

He delved in and brought out a handful of the beautifully beribboned cookie bags.

'Are you *still* trying to palm them off with this muck?' he said.

174

'They're just little cookies, Gerry, so the children will start calling Beauty their little Cookie,' said Mum.

'Don't talk such nonsense. You're not shaming us by doling out these. We'll be a laughing stock – and we'll probably give them food poisoning to boot,' said Dad.

He picked up the carrier bag and bashed it to the floor. Then he stamped up and down on it dementedly, smashing all the cookies into crumbs.

We watched him silently, wincing as if he was stamping all over us. Dad slowed down a little, out of breath, half glancing towards the door, obviously wondering if anyone could hear.

Mum gave him one long look and then she took hold of my hand.

'Come on, Beauty, let's look after our guests,' she said.

They were huddled in the hall, nudging each other, looking anxious. Rhona came and slipped her arm round me.

'Come on, girls, let's get in the limo,' said Mum. She acted like nothing had happened, though her cheeks were burning and even her chest was flushed pink.

She opened the front door and the girls ran out eagerly, jostling over who was going to sit where.

'I'm sitting next to Beauty,' said Rhona.

'No, you're sitting next to *me*,' Skye insisted.

'I've got two sides, haven't I, silly?' said Rhona. 'I'll be sitting next to *both* of you.'

I looked at Mum. 'Is Dad still coming?' I whispered.

'I don't know and I don't care,' Mum whispered back.

Dad did come, rubbing his hands and humming *Happy Birthday to you* as if nothing had happened.

'Hands up who's ever been in a super-stretch limo before!' he said.

No one put their hand up. Dad nodded triumphantly. I saw Skye and Emily and Arabella roll their eyes at each other.

'He'll be telling us how much it cost to hire it next,' Arabella whispered.

'He is so awful,' said Emily.

'He's just plain nuts,' said Skye.

Rhona shifted closer to me and started talking about Birthday.

'They had six rabbits in the pet shop. They *did* have a white one like Lily but it didn't have floppy ears and it wasn't anywhere near as little and cute as Birthday.'

'He's the best rabbit ever. And you're the best friend ever,' I said.

'Hello?' said Skye. 'Rhona just happens to be *my* best friend.'

'I'm best friends with both of you,' said Rhona. 'Now shut up, Skye. It's Beauty's birthday.'

It *was* my birthday, and here I was with Rhona being lovely to me, on a fantastic birthday trip, and back home I had the present I'd been longing for. I should feel the happiest girl in the whole world – and yet every time I looked at Mum I wanted to burst into tears. She was terribly squashed up beside Louise and Poppy, trying hard to chat to them, giving barley sugar to someone who felt sick, pointing out places we were passing, being so *brave*. She smiled at me from time to time but she didn't so much as glance in Dad's direction.

He'd stopped going on and on about the super-stretch limo and had dozed off. I prayed he wouldn't start snoring.

He didn't wake up until we drew up outside the theatre. Then he sprang into action, assembling us all on the pavement, jumping around and joking. He made a great show of counting everyone, tapping each girl on her nose. He tried to tap Mum too but she ducked out of his way.

Birthday Bonanza started off wonderfully. There was a huge birthday party on stage with lots of singing and dancing. I liked McTavish, I liked Will Forman, I liked the actress playing the

Birthday Girl, a beautiful slender girl with long red hair past her waist. But then she came to the front of the stage and asked if there were any other birthday girls or boys in the auditorium.

I turned round and saw lots and lots of hands waving.

'You wave too, Beauty,' said Rhona.

So I stuck my hand up and waved feebly, thinking they were just going to sing *Happy Birthday*.

'Hey, there! You'd better come up on stage and share our birthday party,' said the red-haired girl, beckoning.

Oh no! I saw ten or twelve kids rushing forward to get on stage. The girls were all pretty skinny Skye-type girls in short skirts or tight jeans. I imagined myself standing amongst them in my prim pearl-grey dress and nearly died.

'Go on, Beauty,' said Rhona.

'No fear!' I said.

'Anyone else?' said the red-haired girl, peering in our direction.

'*Beauty!*' Dad hissed along the row. 'Get yourself up there!'

'I can't!' I said, shrinking down in my seat. 'I *won't!*'

'Well, if she's not going to, I am,' said Skye, jumping up.

'But it's not your birthday, Skye!' said Rhona.

'They're not going to ask for my birth certificate, are they?' said Skye, shoving her way along the row.

I heard Dad hollering at me but I shook my head determinedly, knowing he couldn't push his way right along past eighteen girls to physically shove me on stage.

Skye was up there like a shot, tossing her blonde hair and standing with one hand on her hip, totally at ease. They all had to join in a birthday song and then play a crazy game of musical chairs. Then disco lights started flashing and they all had to dance. I was so so so relieved I hadn't gone up on stage myself, even though Dad was madder than ever at me. He glared down the row at me when he looked back at the stage he couldn't help smiling as Skye pranced and strutted up and down, arms up, hips shaking, toes tapping. It was obvious he'd give anything to have a daughter like her. Rhona's hand found mine and she gave it a comforting squeeze.

Everyone talked like crazy in the car going back, telling their favourite parts, arguing about which was the dreamiest boy in McTavish, singing snatches of song. Skye stood up to repeat her little dance routine but the chauffeur told her to sit right down again. Dad didn't tell Skye off. He winked at her. She winked back and then

179

turned her head and sniggered at Emily and Arabella.

Dad wasn't in a winking mood with me. I knew he was furious because I wouldn't go up on the stage. I didn't want him to start ranting in front of everyone – but I was getting very scared about being left on my own with him.

We dropped Rhona off last and we gave each other a very big hug.

'Thank you so so so much for Birthday, Rhona,' I said again.

'I'm so so so glad you like him,' said Rhona. She paused and then whispered in my ear, 'We'll let Skye still think she's my best friend but really I want to be *your* best friend, Beauty.'

'Come on, girls, no need for all these grand farewells, you'll be seeing each other at school on Monday!' said Dad. 'Off you go, Rosa.'

'Rhona!' I said, giving her another hug.

Her mum and dad must have been watching out for her because her front door opened and Mr and Mrs Marshall were there on the doorstep waving to her. Rhona gave me one last hug and then ran up her garden path to her home.

'Is she the one with the swimming pool?' said Dad. 'It must be the size of a footbath because those houses haven't got any back garden to speak of. It's a tacky house too. Look at the state of the paintwork! Wouldn't you think that guy would take a bit of pride in his own house and keep it up to scratch? I don't know why you're acting so pally with that little kiddie, she isn't anything special. Why on earth don't you make friends with that little blonde poppet Skye?'

Dad remembered *her* name all right.

'I don't like Skye,' I mumbled.

'Don't be so silly! You could take a few tips from that girl. *She's* not backward in coming forward. She was off like a rocket when she got the chance to go on stage. Why wouldn't *you* go, Beauty? That's the whole blooming point of the show, to celebrate your birthday in style. Why the hell do you think I forked out a thousand quid for the tickets? You were supposed to get up there and enjoy yourself and show off to all your little friends, not sit quivering in your seat like a great fat pudding.'

'Gerry!' said Mum.

'I'm sick to death of the two of you,' Dad said, his voice raising, not caring that the chauffeur could hear every word. 'I work my butt off for both of you, flinging money at you like it was confetti and yet I never get one word of gratitude. You're both sitting there with your faces tripping you. I've spent a small fortune on your birthday, Beauty, and yet you haven't the wits to make the most of it. You stand in the corner like you're some little saddo no-friends while all the other girls bounce about and have a laugh and enjoy themselves.'

'Please don't, Gerry!'

'You're no better, Dilly. You won't chat properly with the other mums. You act like you can't say boo to a goose half the time. I buy you lovely clothes and jewellery so you can show yourself off and what do you do? Only go and lose your diamond collar! How can you *lose* it, for pity's sake? I know you're a fool but surely even you can do up the clasp of a necklace?'

'I know I'm a fool,' said Mum. 'I'm a fool to let you talk to me like this. I'm even more of a fool to let you say such unkind things to poor Beauty.'

'*Poor* Beauty!' Dad reached over and gave me a shake. 'You're a little slyboots, miss. How *dare* you suck up to that Rosa like that and ask her to bring you that wretched rabbit.'

'I didn't, Dad.'

'Don't you lie to me, I won't have it,' said Dad. 'And don't think you can get the better of me either. You've a long way to go before you can outwit your old dad.'

He had an awful gleam in his eye. I didn't understand until we got home. I went running right through the house and out of the French windows to see Birthday.

The hutch door was swinging open. I stared at it. I *knew* I'd shut it up properly. I'd carefully checked the latch to see it was secure. I held my breath, bending down to see if Birthday was still there, huddled in his bedding. I scrabbled my hands through the straw desperately but it was no use. He was gone.

I looked wildly round the patio and then started searching the garden, going down on my hands and knees to peer under every bush.

'Beauty?' Mum came out onto the patio. She saw the empty rabbit hutch. 'Oh no!'

'I left it latched up properly, Mum, I know I did,' I cried. 'I don't know how it came undone.'

'I do,' said Mum. 'Gerry? Gerry! Come here!'

Dad came out onto the patio too.

'Quite bawling at me like I'm your pet dog, Dilly!' he blustered. 'Beauty, what the hell are you doing? Stand up, you're getting your fancy new dress filthy!'

'I'm looking for Birthday,' I sobbed.

'Who? Oh, that damn rabbit. Has it escaped already?' said Dad.

'You deliberately let him out,' said Mum. 'You must have sneaked out here while Beauty and all the girls were getting into the limo.'

'I didn't *sneak*,' said Dad, putting his hands on his hips. He stuck his chin up belligerently. 'Yes,

I let the rabbit out. I've always made it plain, I'm not having animals all over the place.'

'But he's *mine*,' I wept. 'How could you let him out, Dad? He's so little. He'll be so frightened. Oh, Birthday, where *are* you?'

'Stop talking nonsense. He'll be chomping grass somewhere with all his little bunny friends,' said Dad. 'That's the place for rabbits, out in the wild. Now stop that baby crying. You look a sight with your face all screwed up like that. There's no need to make such a stupid fuss. You've got your lovely pink toy rabbit to play with.'

I barely listened to Dad. I carried on searching. Mum helped too.

'He must be here somewhere. He couldn't have burrowed all the way under the fence, could he?' I said.

'He might have squeezed out at the end, behind the shed,' said Mum. 'I think there's a bit of a gap in the fence there.' She ran to look and then gasped. She staggered backwards, her hands over her mouth.

'What? What is it, Mum?' I said, getting to my feet.

'Don't come any nearer, Beauty! Stay where you are,' Mum said.

She was shaking all over, as if she was going to fall down. I couldn't help running to her, though she shouted at me to keep away. Then I saw why. Birthday was lying limply beside the shed, his little furry body and his soft paws. But his head mostly wasn't there.

I started screaming. Mum put her arms tight round me, pushing my head against her chest so that I couldn't see poor torn Birthday any more. Dad ran over too.

'Oh God. How disgusting! A fox must have got it. That's animals for you,' he said.

'You monster,' said Mum.

'What? Look, *I* didn't tear its head off its shoulders. *I* wasn't to know a fox would get it. Still, that's what happens when you have pets. Come here, Beauty, have a cuddle with your dad.'

I shrank away from him. 'I bloody hate you!' I sobbed.

'*What?*' Dad stared at me, shaking his head. 'Don't you dare talk to me like that! I'll wash your mouth out with soap.'

'Stop your stupid threats, Gerry. You sicken me,' said Mum.

'I *sicken* you?' said Dad. 'How dare you say that to me! I dragged you out the gutter, spent a fortune on you, gave you this beautiful home—'

'It isn't a beautiful home, it's a living hell,' said Mum.

'Well, if you don't like it then get out,' said Dad.

'Go on, push off out of it, you ungrateful cow.'

'All right, I shall,' said Mum.

'Mum!' I said, clutching her.

'And you can take the kid with you,' said Dad.

'Of course,' said Mum.

Dad stared at her and then folded his arms. 'Right then. Sod off, both of you,' he said.

'We will, just as soon as we've buried poor Birthday,' said Mum.

'You're going to do *what*? You're not digging a hole in my lawn,' said Dad.

Mum took no notice. She went to the shed and got a big garden spade and a smaller one for me.

'We'll dig here, Beauty,' she said. 'Go and change out of your dress and boots. Put your jeans on and come back and help.'

I did what I was told, still sobbing. When I got back to the garden Dad was digging too, sighing and swearing. Mum carried on, digging as well, though her hands kept slipping and her spade didn't cut cleanly through the earth. She'd taken her high heels off but she couldn't put her bare foot on the spade and push down. I gently took the spade from her and started digging properly. Mum straightened up, staring over at the remains of Birthday.

'I won't be a minute,' she said, going into the house.

I hated being left alone with Dad. He was crimson in the face and sweating badly.

'This is all your fault,' he said to me. 'You would go on and on about wanting a rabbit. Maybe this will teach you a lesson.'

I didn't answer, I just went on digging. Mum came back with a pillowcase. She went up to Birthday's body.

'I'll do it,' said Dad.

'No, I will,' said Mum.

She retched as she touched Birthday, getting her hands all bloody, but she wrapped the pillowcase round him and carried him at arm's length over to us.

'Say goodbye to him, Beauty,' said Mum.

'Goodbye, darling little Birthday,' I said, touching the pillowcase.

I could feel him underneath, still and stiff. Mum let me lay him in the bottom of his grave and then we started covering him with earth.

'Let *me* do it, for God's sake. You've got to fill it in evenly so the turf fits back on top,' said Dad.

'All right, you do it, Gerry,' said Mum.

She took me by the hand and we walked into the house. Mum looked at me.

'Go and pack a suitcase, Beauty. Three or four outfits, a few of your favourite things, washing stuff, pyjamas, just as if we're going on holiday,' she said.

'So we're really leaving?' I said shakily.

'Yes, we are,' said Mum. 'You don't want to stay, do you?'

'No, I want to go with you!'

'Then that's what we'll do,' said Mum. 'Quick then!'

I chose my new grey dress and boots, my other jeans, a denim skirt, three T-shirts and a thick jumper. I packed my new felt tips and my drawing book, my Sam and Lily folder and my new DVD, and *A Little Princess*. The giant pink rabbit leered at me in a corner as I snatched things frantically and squashed them into my suitcase.

'Ready, babe?' said Mum.

She'd got her suitcase packed too. She carried them both out to her car.

'Let's go now, Mum, while Dad's still round the back.'

'No, we'll say goodbye properly,' said Mum.

We waited in the hall, both of us trembling. Dad came in from the garden at last, his shoes in his hand.

'What are you two doing, lurking there?' he said, walking down the hallway. 'Get those shoes off, you'll be walking mud all over the carpet.'

'We're going, Gerry. I'll keep in touch, obviously, as you'll want to see Beauty.'

'What? You're not really going?' said Dad. 'Because I set the damn rabbit free?'

'Because of many many things,' said Mum.

'Now, listen. I've had enough of this. Walk out of here and you're never coming back, do you understand? And if you think I'm setting you up in another Happy Home you're very much mistaken. I'll sue you for desertion and I won't pay you a penny. I won't *have* any money anyway, not if I'm done for bribery. I'll probably end up in *jail*.'

'I don't care where you end up,' said Mum. 'Don't worry, I'd sooner live in a pigsty than one of your Happy Homes. Goodbye.'

'Goodbye, Dad,' I whispered.

Dad was still shaking his head, looking utterly baffled, as we walked out of the house.

Thirteen

Mum started the car and we drove off.

'Where are we going, Mum?' I asked.

Mum didn't answer for a minute. I thought she was just concentrating on her driving. Then she gave a shaky little laugh.

'I don't know!' she said.

'Oh!' I said.

Mum carried on driving. I bit my lip, thinking hard.

'Well, there's *your* mum, my nana,' I suggested.

'No,' said Mum. 'Not if she's still with that same boyfriend. I left home at the age of sixteen on account of *him*. My mum didn't seem to care much. She certainly wouldn't welcome me back with open arms.'

'OK. Not her then,' I said quickly, because Mum was sounding like she might burst into tears any minute.

My other granny was dead. We didn't really seem to have any proper relations.

I thought about friends. I thought about my best friend Rhona. My heart started beating faster.

'We could go to the Marshalls'!' I said.

'Who?' said Mum.

'Rhona's family.'

'Oh, Beauty, we don't know them properly. I don't even know Rhona's mum's first name. I've only ever said hello to her. We can't just turn up on their doorstep,' said Mum.

'I know Rhona,' I said stubbornly. 'And Mr and Mrs Marshall are ever so kind. They really like me. I know they'd like you too.'

'No,' said Mum. 'Get real, Beauty. We can't just up sticks and go and live with the Marshalls. This isn't just for one night. This is for ever. Well, if we want it to be for ever.' Mum slowed down. 'We could go back.'

I thought hard. I was nearly crying too. It was so frightening having to make decisions. Dad had always told both of us what to do. *Should* we go back to Dad? If we went down on our knees and said sorry enough times he'd welcome us back with open arms. But then I thought of those arms swinging through the air and smashing all those cookies Mum had made so lovingly. I thought of his hands unlatching Birthday's hutch and shooing him out into the garden.

'We're not going back. We're going forward,' I said.

'Right,' said Mum, and she reached out and squeezed my hand. 'Two girls together.'

'Driving on and on and on into the sunset,' I said. 'Driving and driving and driving until . . .' I let my voice tail away. We were both silent. I took a deep breath.

'I suppose we can always sleep in the car, Mum.'

'Oh, Beauty, bless you. No, we're definitely not doing that. I'll make sure there's a proper roof over your head. I'll sell some more of my jewellery. It's just tonight and Sunday that are the problem. But don't worry, I'll think of something.'

Mum drove on, staring straight ahead. She was gripping the steering wheel so tightly her knuckles looked about to burst through her skin.

'What's that song? *Don't Worry, Be Happy!*' she said. She didn't know all the words so she sang the same line over and over again.

I stared out of the window. Everything looked so astonishingly ordinary and everyday. Street after street, shops, restaurants, houses, a Happy Homes estate . . .

'Mum! I know where we can go! Auntie Avril!'

Mum slowed down, thinking. 'But she's your dad's ex-wife,' she said.

'Well, you're going to be his ex-wife too. And she likes us. She's just sent me those lovely felt pens. Oh, Mum, let's go to Auntie Avril's. She lives on the Fruitbush estate and that's just over there, look!'

'Well, maybe we could try,' Mum said doubtfully.

She reversed into a side entrance and drove back to the Happy Homes Fruitbush estate.

'Are you sure it's this one? There are so many blessed Happy Homes estates,' said Mum.

'She lives at Seven Cherry Drive. I know it from writing her thank-you letters.' I peered out of the car window. 'That's Lime Avenue. And Grape Lane.'

'All these fruity names! I wonder what else your dad made up? Do you think there's an Apple Alley?'

'What about a Banana Bend? Or Raspberry Road?'

We started giggling hysterically as we drove round the estate.

'Hey, look! Cherry Drive!' I said.

'Well done, Beauty.'

Mum drew up outside number Seven. It was less than half the size of our own house, a small shrunken semi-detached Happy Home with a narrow strip of grass at the front, but Auntie Avril had put trellis up on her brickwork so that clematis and wisteria hung lushly, softening the red of the brick. She'd planted pansies and geraniums in her garden and there was a hanging basket of pink petunias swinging above the blue front door. Her doormat said VDKBNLD . We hoped Auntie Avril would say welcome too.

'Right, ready, steady, go!' said Mum.

She opened up her handbag and peered at herself in her mirror. 'God, I look such a mess!'

'No you don't, Mum, you look lovely,' I said. 'Come on.'

We got out of the car and went up the drive together. I rang the bell. We waited, holding hands. Then the door opened and Auntie Avril stared at us in surprise. She looked older than I remembered, and she was a lot plumper. Her hair was a very bright yellow blonde.

'Good Lord! Dilys and Beauty!' She peered behind us. 'Where's Gerry?'

Mum and I looked at each other uncertainly.

Auntie Avril put her hand to her mouth, smudging her red lipstick. 'Oh God, he hasn't *died*, has he?'

'No, no, he's fine,' said Mum. 'It's just . . .' She swallowed. 'Can we come in, Avril?'

'Yes, of course, only I'm going out in about half an hour. Still, there's plenty of time for a cup of tea. In you come.'

We trooped in after her. We automatically took our shoes off by the front door. Auntie Avril kept her high heels on and laughed at us.

'I see Gerry's got you well-trained,' she said. 'Come into the living room.'

It was a warm little room with a dark crimson carpet and a black leather sofa with furry cushions as pink as the petunias. There was a big white cat curled decoratively at one end.

'You've got a cat!' I said.

'That's my Cream Puff. Give her a gentle shove and she'll make room for you,' said Auntie Avril. 'Goodness, you're getting a big girl, Beauty. Of course, it's your birthday today, isn't it? Many happy returns.'

'Thank you ever so much for my lovely felt tips, Auntie Avril. They were just what I wanted,' I said, nestling near Cream Puff. I delicately ran my fingers down her soft fur and she sighed and quivered.

'You've brought her up very nicely, Dilys,' said Auntie Avril.

'Oh, she means it, Avril. She loves crayoning. She's ever so good at art. Well, Beauty's good at most things. Not a bit like me,' said Mum.

'Not much like Gerry either!' said Avril. 'Well, he's bright enough, no flies on him. I'll go and make us that tea then. Or would you like something stronger, Dilys? You look as if you could do with a pick-you-up. Shall we have a little gin?'

'It'll have to be a *very* little gin because I'm driving,' said Mum. 'Unless . . .' She didn't dare say the rest.

Auntie Avril bustled around, making two gin and tonics and a special lemonade for me with a couple of cherries and a weeny paper umbrella, just like a real cocktail.

Cream Puff crept right onto my lap and started purring when I stroked her.

'It's lovely to see you both,' said Auntie Avril. 'We'll have to get together more often. After all, we're family, sort of.'

I started to dare hope we might be at the start of a wonderful new life together, Auntie Avril, Mum and me. I imagined living in this cosy little house, playing with Cream Puff every day, sipping cocktails every evening, all of us dancing up and down the carpet in our outdoor shoes with no one to tell us off ever.

'Come on then,' Auntie Avril said, glancing at her watch. 'Tell me why you've popped round out of the blue. It's Gerry, isn't it?'

'Well, yes,' said Mum. 'We've split up.'

Auntie Avril sighed and downed the rest of her gin and tonic. She reached over and patted Mum's knee. 'You poor little darling. Still, you know what it feels like now. So who has he left you for? Not another little blonde?'

'No, no, Gerry hasn't left me.' Mum took a deep breath. 'I've left *him*.'

'*What?*' Auntie Avril looked astonished. 'When?'

'Just now. We packed our bags, Beauty and me, and walked out.'

'But *why*?'

'I just couldn't stand it any more,' Mum said shakily.

'What did he *do*?'

'He just kept shouting at us, belittling us, telling us what to do all the time,' Mum said, starting to cry. 'I know he's very stressed about his work, it's all going wrong, there's even some talk of bribery, I suppose he could be in really big trouble – but that's no excuse for being so mean to us.'

I eased Cream Puff off my lap and went to put my arm round Mum.

'Oh, don't you worry about our Gerry,' said Auntie Avril. 'He's always stressed, he's always in trouble, but he'll fix it, just you wait and see. I know he can be a royal pain at times. That's just the way he is. The way most men are, come to think of it. But he's not such a bad egg, Dilys. He thinks the world of you and Beauty, he's set you up in a lovely home, he's lavished money on you. What more could you want?'

'He was terrible today, humiliating me in front of Beauty's party guests. He organized this ridiculous stretch limo and tickets for *Birthday Bonanza*.'

'Oh yes? Well, that doesn't sound particularly humiliating! It sounds like he was doing his best to give Beauty a lovely birthday treat. Grow up, Dilys. Gerry's got many faults, as I know all too well, but you could do a lot worse.'

'He broke all the cookies Mum made specially and let my birthday rabbit out of his cage and a fox killed it,' I said, starting to sob too.

'Oh dear, oh dear. That's a real shame, darling – but you don't break up a happy home just for that.'

'It isn't a happy home, even though it's got that stupid name,' said Mum. 'We've not been happy there, Avril. It's getting to Beauty as well as to me. I've never been able to stand up for myself very well but I *can* stand up for my little girl. She needs a fresh start, somewhere quiet and peaceful where she's not shouted at all the time.'

'And where's that?' said Auntie Avril.

There was a silence.

'You don't mean . . . you don't mean here with *me*?' she said.

'Well, if we could just stay a few days, until we get on our feet and I've found myself a job?' Mum suggested timidly.

'You have to be joking! You can't stay here. Whatever would Gerry say? Well, I have a rough idea what he'd say, only I'm not using that sort of language in front of Beauty here. Don't forget Gerry's given me this house. I'm not risking putting his nose out of joint. I don't want to find myself shoved out on the streets, homeless.'

'But *we're* homeless now,' said Mum, snuffling. 'We haven't got anywhere else to go. What are we going to *do*, Avril?'

'*I* don't know, darling.' She looked at her watch again. 'I'm going to be late. I'm meeting three of my girlfriends in town for a pizza and then we're all going to the Gala Bingo. It's not exactly a wild night out for a Saturday but it's not likely a tall dark stranger is going to come calling at my time of life. Do yourself a favour, Dilys. Gerry's not tall and he's not dark and he's certainly not a stranger, but he's all man and if I remember rightly he can be fun to be with. Stop this nonsense and get yourself back there sharpish.'

'No,' said Mum. 'I know you mean well, Avril, but we're not going back. We'll just have to find some place else.'

'*Where*, exactly?' said Auntie Avril.

'Perhaps . . . perhaps we can go to the council on Monday and they'll find us a little flat,' Mum said desperately.

Auntie Avril laughed at her. I was starting not to like her now.

'They've got a waiting list a mile long, you silly woman. You and Beauty would never qualify in a million years. You've got a luxurious six-bedroom house. You've deliberately made yourself homeless.'

200

'Well, there are still refuges, aren't there?' said Mum.

'For battered wives. So has *Gerry* battered you?'

'He slapped my face. And he twisted my wrist.'

'Oh, get a grip, Dilys! Most of those poor women in those places have been beaten to a pulp. They'd give their right arms to swap places with you. If I'm honest *I* still would, even though I know Gerry's no angel.'

'Well, you have him then,' said Mum.

'I don't stand a chance. I'm way past my sell-by date as far as Gerry's concerned. And most men too, apart from the daft old codgers. You think twice, Dilys. It's a lonely life without a man.'

'It's a lonely life with the *wrong* man,' said Mum. She drained her glass and then stood up. 'Well, thank you very much for the drink, Avril. We must let you be off to your friends.'

'*You* don't have to go. Look, you can stay here tonight by all means, if you really won't go back. There's heaps to eat in the fridge, you just help yourselves. Have another drink or two, watch a bit of telly, whatever. I've only got one bed in my spare room, but I'm sure you won't mind squashing up together. I'll be back around half ten or eleven. Then we'll talk about things in the morning. I'm sure you'll see things differently then. You've got to consider Beauty and what's best for her. Think about it, Dilly. Ta ta then.'

She kissed Mum, she kissed me, slipped on her lilac leather jacket, and rushed off. Mum and I sat either side of Cream Puff, neither of us saying a word. Mum nibbled the edge of her fingernail, staring down at the deep red carpet.

'Are you thinking about it, Mum?' I asked in a tiny voice.

'I'm thinking so hard my flipping head's going to burst,' said Mum. She bit harder, breaking one of her lovely manicured nails.

'*Don't*, Mum!'

'What?' She hadn't even realized what she was doing.

'You'll chew right down to your knuckles if you don't watch out,' I said. 'I don't want a mum with fingers all frayed at the edges.'

I said it to make her laugh but she still looked as if she was going to cry.

'Avril thinks I'm bonkers,' she said shakily. 'Maybe I *am*. Oh, Beauty, I don't know what to *do*.'

'Let's stay here tonight. I like it here,' I said, stroking Cream Puff. She stretched herself lazily. She obviously liked it here too. 'Maybe Auntie Avril will change her mind and let us stay for a while. I could do all sorts of errands for her, feed Cream

202

Puff and make cups of tea and do the vacuuming. And you could . . .'

'Yeah, what could I do?' Mum said tearfully.

'You could make us cookies,' I said.

I was serious, but this time Mum snorted with laughter, even though the tears were still running down her face.

'A fat lot of use that is,' she said, blowing her nose. 'No, Beauty, we'll have to go somewhere else tomorrow. Avril's right, your dad would be furious. It's very kind of her to let us stay now. Come on, let's go and see what's in the fridge.'

There were lots of special ready-meals for one. We heated two in Auntie Avril's microwave and ate them at her tiny kitchen table. I'd hardly been able to eat any of my special birthday buffet. I realized I was starving now. I wolfed my meal down *and* most of Mum's, because she just stirred her food round and round with her fork. She was thinking again, frowning hard at her plate, twisting her knife and fork round and round like the hands of a clock. I leaned forward and rubbed her frown lines with my fingers.

'We'll be OK, Mum,' I whispered.

'Yes. Of course we will,' she said. 'Tell you what – shall we see if Avril's got some flour and sugar and stuff? We could make her some cookies as a thank-you present. Do you think she'd like that?'

'I think she'd love your cookies, Mum.'

'You start looking for all the ingredients, then. I'll go and get the cases. I remembered to pack my recipe book,' Mum said proudly.

We made sugar and spice cookies, raiding Auntie Avril's spice rack and sifting cinnamon and cloves into the cookie dough. We washed up carefully while the cookies were baking, looking anxiously at Auntie Avril's oven every two minutes in case it might misbehave and burn them. When we opened the oven door we breathed a great sigh of relief. The cookies looked perfect and smelled delicious.

'We could have one each, just to make sure they're all right,' said Mum.

It was getting near my bedtime now but I didn't want to go to bed and leave Mum sitting worrying all by herself.

'Oh, you might as well stay up if you're not sleepy. After all, it *is* your birthday,' said Mum.

I'd totally forgotten it was still my birthday. It seemed to have lasted for weeks already. Mum switched on Auntie Avril's television but we couldn't settle to watching anything for more than two minutes.

'I know,' said Mum. 'You packed your Sam and Lily DVD, didn't you?'

'You bet I did.'

'Well, run and fetch it then.'

I slotted Sam and Lily into the DVD player. Mum and I curled up together to watch. Cream Puff woke up to watch too.

'Who do we want to see?' said the voice, as Sam and Lily spun round and round.

The little children sang, '*Sam and Lily in the Rabbit Hutch.*' Mum and I sang it too.

'Hey there!' said Sam, directly to me.

He looked surprised to see me squashed up on a slippery leather sofa in a completely strange room. Lily blinked at Cream Puff.

'How are you doing?' asked Sam.

'I'm fine,' I said.

Sam put his head on one side.

'Well, maybe I'm telling fibs,' I whispered. I glanced at Mum. She was frowning again, nibbling at her nail, clearly not concentrating on the programme.

'Sam, Mum and I have left Dad. Something terrible happened. I can't say it in front of Lily. We're at Auntie Avril's now but we can't stay here and we haven't got anywhere else to go,' I mouthed.

'Oh dear, oh dear,' Sam said softly. 'I think you and Mum need a little break. How about a holiday?' He raised his voice, asking everyone now. 'Where do *you* go on holiday? Do you go to the seaside?'

'We don't really go anywhere on holiday,' I said. 'We went to Marbella once but Dad got all fidgety and bored on the beach and said it was a waste of time.'

'Lily doesn't like to go on holiday much,' said Sam. 'She doesn't like too much sun, she doesn't like getting her paws all sandy, she doesn't like paddling – she doesn't even like ice cream! Isn't she a funny bunny? I *love* sunbathing, I *love* building sandcastles, I *love* swimming in the sea – and I especially love ice cream!'

'So do I!' I said.

'I should have a little holiday right now,' Sam said, just to me. 'You and Mum. You'll have a lovely time. It will all work out, you'll see.'

I nodded, snuggling up to Mum and Cream Puff, suddenly soothed. My head went on nod-nod-nod-ding and then Mum was gently shaking me awake.

'Your DVD's finished, pet. You've had a little doze. Let's pop you up to bed. I think I'll go to bed too. I don't really want Avril lecturing me when she comes home.'

We had a quick wash in Auntie Avril's bright turquoise bathroom. Mum had forgotten to pack a nightie so she wore one of my T-shirts. She looked more of a little girl than ever.

The spare room was very grown up and glamorous, with a leopard-skin throw over the bed and a great china leopard baring its teeth at us in a corner.

'Watch out he doesn't bite,' said Mum.

'He looks almost as scary as that giant pink rabbit!'

We got the giggles again and tried to jump into bed quick, but Auntie Avril had sheets instead of a duvet and she'd tucked them in so firmly you had to pull for all you were worth to prise your way in. They felt icy too so Mum and I had to cuddle up close. We were both shivering though it wasn't *that* cold.

'I can't quite believe we're here,' said Mum. 'It feels so strange. I wonder what your dad's doing now.'

'He'll be ranting,' I said.

'But he's all by himself,' said Mum.

I imagined Dad stomping up and down the house in his socks, bellowing abuse. I saw him very big at first, but he started to get smaller and the empty house got bigger until he was scampering about like a mouse, squeak-squeak-squeaking to no one at all.

'Mum?'

'Yes, darling?'

'I feel kind of sorry for Dad.'

'I know. So do I.'

'But if we went back he'd just start all over again.'

'I know that too.'

We were quiet for a little. I thought of Dad bashing the cookies. I thought about Birthday.

'Beauty? Don't cry, darling.'

'Oh, Mum. Look, this sounds daft, but do you think baby rabbits go to heaven?'

'Yes, definitely,' said Mum.

'And do you think he'll be . . . whole there? His little head will be back in place?'

'Yes, of course. He'll be skipping about with all the angels. They'll be having little arguments over who gets to have him as their special pet,' said Mum.

We were quiet again. We heard the front door open and Auntie Avril come in. We heard her go into the kitchen and give a little gasp. We nudged each other, knowing she must have spotted the plate of cookies. We heard a glass clinking downstairs, and then after ten minutes or so she came upstairs. We stayed quiet until she'd been in bed a while.

Then I whispered in Mum's ear, 'Are you still awake?'

'Yes.'

'I know you're right. Auntie Avril's OK but we can't stay here,' I said.

'Mm.'

'So have you thought where we can go?'

'I've thought and thought and thought, but

208

I haven't come up with anything just yet,' said Mum.

'I think I know where we can go!'

'Where, darling?'

'The seaside!'

'But we don't know anyone at the seaside, do we?'

'It doesn't matter, does it? We could pretend we're going on holiday. We haven't had a holiday for ages. We've got a *bit* of money. Let's just go to the seaside and paddle and sunbathe and it'll all feel easy and normal. We'll just be like everyone else, on our holiday.'

I was cuddled up so close to Mum I could feel her heart beating fast.

'OK,' she said. 'That's what we'll do. For tomorrow, anyway. Well done, Beauty, it's a great idea.'

Peggy's Parlour

WELCOME TO RABBIT COVE

Bed & Breakfast

Fourteen

Auntie Avril didn't look as if she thought it was a great idea when we told her over breakfast the next morning.

'For pity's sake, this isn't a *game*, Dilys. You can't just take off with your child and play you're on holiday.'

'Why not?' said Mum. 'Beauty and I *need* a holiday. You know what Gerry's like, he'll never leave the firm for more than a couple of days and he's hopeless at relaxing anyway. We just need to chill for a bit.'

'Chill!' said Auntie Avril, shaking her head.

But when we said goodbye to her she pressed a large wad of notes into Mum's hand.

'Here, this is for you, Dilys.'

'I can't take your money!'

'Well, how else are you going to do this "chilling"? I know Gerry. I bet you're not even allowed your own credit card. You take it, my dear. Just don't ever tell Gerry I helped you out.'

'Oh, Avril, you're a star,' said Mum, giving her a hug.

'You're my all-time favourite auntie even if we're

not exactly related,' I said, giving her a hug too.

I wanted to hug Cream Puff as well but she was busy gobbling up her breakfast and wouldn't be distracted.

We lugged our cases into the car and thanked Auntie Avril for letting us stay overnight.

'Well, if you get into totally dire straits you'd better come back, Gerry or no Gerry,' she said. 'And thanks for the cookies, girls. They were a lovely surprise. They're very good, Dilys. I thought you couldn't cook!'

'Mum's the greatest cookie cook in the whole world,' I said. 'And I'm learning fast, so maybe I'm the second greatest!'

We drove off, Auntie Avril standing on her doorstep under her hanging basket of petunias, waving and waving until we turned the corner.

'So, which seaside shall we pick?' said Mum. 'Brighton's fun.'

I remembered Brighton from a day trip.

'It's too big and busy and the beach is all pebbles,' I said. 'Let's find a sandy seaside place.'

'OK,' said Mum. 'Well, we'll drive due south and see what we find. If we tip over into the sea we'll know we've gone too far.'

We couldn't go directly south all the time because the roads wiggled around and once or twice we had to stop the car and peer hard at the map. I couldn't read it when we were driving along because it made me feel sick. I wasn't much better sorting out the route when we were stopped. I kept squinting at red roads and yellow roads and little spidery black roads, trying to work out which one we were on.

'Don't worry, babes, we'll make it to the seaside somehow,' said Mum. 'Bournemouth's very sandy. And Bognor. Which one shall we aim at?'

I peered at the map. A name in tiny print suddenly swam into focus.

'Oh, Mum! Not Bournemouth, not Bognor. I've found a place here right by the sea and guess what it's called: Rabbit Cove! Oh, Mum, *please* let's go to Rabbit Cove!'

'I've never even heard of it. Let's see where it is.' Mum squinted at the map. 'It's obviously a very *small* place, not a proper town. I wonder why it's got such a funny name? You don't get rabbits at the seaside, do you?'

'I think it must be because of the shape of the cove. See those two sticking-out bits of land? They look like rabbit's ears!' I said.

'So they do! OK, OK, we'll go and have a look at Rabbit Cove if you've set your heart on it, though I'm not sure there'll be anywhere to stay there.'

I tried hard to keep us on a direct route now, peering at the map as Mum drove, though I started to feel horribly travel sick.

'Open your window a bit – and sit back and close your eyes,' said Mum.

I did as I was told because all the world outside the window had started spinning and I kept yawning and swallowing spit. It seemed to be spinning inside my own head now. I was falling down and down and down into a scary black nothingness.

I called and called for Mum but she wasn't there. And then I called for Dad and I could hear him calling back. I struggled to get closer to him, reaching out, but then a light flashed on his face and I saw it was screwed up with rage.

'You don't want me and I don't want *you*, because you're ugly ugly ugly,' he shouted.

He shoved me hard and I tumbled on downwards, mile after mile, but I could still hear him shouting *ugly*. Other voices joined in. Skye and Arabella and Emily were shouting it, all the girls in my class, even Rhona, and I started crying, my hands over my ears . . .

'Beauty! Beauty, sweetheart, wake up. It's all right, Mum's here.'

I blinked in sudden dazzling daylight. Mum leaned over and pulled my head onto her shoulder.

'Oh, Mum, I couldn't find you!' I sobbed.

'It was just a horrible nightmare, darling, that's all. You were crying out and tossing about. I had to stop driving,' said Mum.

214

'We're driving?' I said stupidly. Then everything snapped properly into place. 'Oh yes, we're going to Rabbit Cove!'

'Yes, we are – and we're nearly there! You've been asleep a long time. OK now, pet?' Mum wiped my nose with her tissue as if I was two years old.

'I'm sorry to be such a baby,' I said, feeling ashamed.

'You're not a baby, darling! You're ever so grown up, much more than me. There now, let's get cracking. Rabbit Cove, here we come. Penny for the first one to see the sea.'

I sat up properly and we edged out of the layby back onto the road. I still felt a bit weird but Mum had the window right down and I breathed in deeply. We were on one of the yellow roads now, surrounded by fields of corn and barley, gentle rolling hills purple in the distance. And then I saw a dazzle of brilliant blue . . .

'The sea, the sea! I spotted it first! You did say a *pound* for the first one to see it, didn't you?'

'No, I didn't! A penny, you cheeky baggage.'

Mum slowed down when we got to the next road sign. We could stay on the main road and go to Seahaven – or turn down a little lane marked Rabbit Cove!

'OK, OK, we'll make for Rabbit Cove,' said Mum. 'You bet!'

'Don't be too disappointed if there's nothing much there, sweetheart,' said Mum. 'We can just have a little wander and then make for Seahaven. I think that's a proper seaside town so we should be able to find a little bed-and-breakfast place there.'

We turned down the lane for Rabbit Cove. There were tall trees growing on high banks on either side of us, their branches joining to make a dark green canopy overhead. Then there was a sign to a little farm, and then driveways to houses, then a whole street of little terraced houses with pebbles stuck on the walls. Then the shops started, a small supermarket, a dress shop, a little gallery, a newsagent's, an off-licence, an antique shop with a rocking chair outside, and a tearoom called Peggy's Parlour.

'Oh, we'll definitely go and have a cup of tea in Peggy's Parlour,' said Mum, giggling. 'It all looks so old-fashioned. I do hope Peggy herself is a little old lady in a black dress with a frilly white apron, tottering around writing everybody's orders in a little notebook tied to her waist.'

'You are daft, Mum. Don't let's go there yet though. I want to see the sea.'

'OK, OK, stop bouncing around in your seat!'

We drove on past a proper restaurant, a pub, and a white hotel with a big green lawn and several swings.

'See, there *is* a hotel! Oh Mum, can we stay there?'

'Maybe. It might be a bit expensive.'

'But Auntie Avril's given us heaps of money.'

'It might have to last us a long time until I manage to get a job,' said Mum. She nibbled at her lip. 'Beauty, what can I do? Jobwise, I mean. I've only ever been a receptionist, and I was hopeless.'

'You could do *heaps* of things, Mum,' I said. 'You could . . . be a cookie baker.'

It was a little joke to make Mum laugh. She smiled at me. 'OK, that's what I'll do,' she said.

She turned down a steep little lane towards the seafront. There were more houses now with sloping gardens. Some of the houses had ADC @MC AQD@JE@RS signs.

'We *could* say in one of these,' I said.

'OK, we'll pick one later,' said Mum.

We drove downwards, round another bend, Mum's foot hard on the brakes – and then we were at the seafront.

'Oh, Mum!' I said.

'Oh, Beauty!' said Mum.

Rabbit Cove was perfect. There was a high cliff on either side (the rabbit's ears) sheltering a beautiful cove of soft golden sand. There was hardly anyone on the beach, just a few families with little kids running about trailing seaweed and sticking flags in sandcastles. An old-fashioned artist with a beard and a baggy blue shirt was sitting up on the little white wall, painting. At the other end of the wall there was a small car park, a little wooden hut for toilets, and a beach shop-cum-café festooned with buckets and spades and an old tin ice-cream sign spinning outside.

'It's just like a picture in an old story book!' I said. 'It's so lovely!'

I couldn't be sure I wasn't making it all up. I closed my eyes, counted to three, and opened them again. Rabbit Cove was still there, serenely beautiful.

'I'm so pleased it's lovely,' said Mum. 'I was hoping and hoping it would be and yet sure it would be this ropy old pebbly place, all grey and ugly.'

'Maybe I'm still dreaming?' I said. 'And you're dreaming it too, Mum.'

'Well, let's park the car and then we'll have a little run on the beach. If you can feel the sand between your toes you're definitely wide awake,' said Mum.

We put the car in the little car park. I delved into my suitcase for my drawing book and new felt tips and then we went on the beach. I kicked my shoes off and wiggled my toes in the soft powdery sand.

'I'm definitely not dreaming!' I said.

218

Mum kicked her own sandals off and did the same. 'Doesn't it feel great!' she said. 'Here, roll your jeans right up, Beauty. We'll go and have a paddle.'

We ran across the sand, slowing as it became hard and damp, and then both of us shrieking as the first wave washed round our ankles.

'It's absolutely *freezing*!' Mum said. 'I think you can be the chief paddling girl, babes. I'll sit and watch.'

Mum sat back on the soft sand looking after my felt tips for me while I waded around up to my knees, jumping waves, stooping to search for shells, walking up and down the little ridges in the wet sand. When I went back to Mum I was soaked right up to my bottom but she just laughed at me.

'They'll dry soon enough. That's what the sun's for! Are you hungry, sweetheart? Shall we have a picnic? Wait here!'

Mum sprang up and went skipping over the sands, not bothering to put her sandals on. She went into the beach shop. When she came out she was carrying two huge whippy ice creams with a big carrier bag over her arm.

'The ice creams are for pudding but we'll have to eat them first or they'll melt.'

Mum sat down cross-legged and we licked our ice creams appreciatively. Each ice had two chocolate flakes and a little blob of raspberry sauce.

'They're a Rabbit Cove special,' said Mum. 'The chocolate flakes are meant to be ears and the jam blob is a little bunny nose.'

'Yum!' I said, eating all the distinguishing features of my rabbit face.

When we'd finished our ice creams Mum produced two cheese salad rolls, two packets of salt-and-vinegar crisps, two mini chocolate rolls, two apples, two bananas and two cartons of orange juice.

'This isn't a picnic, it's a veritable feast!' I said, clapping my hands. 'There's only one thing missing – cookies!'

'We should have kept a few of Avril's cookies. I'm sure she's not going to munch her way through the whole batch,' said Mum. 'Oh well, I'll have to try and make some more some time.'

We ate all our wonderful lunch and then Mum lay back on the sand, using her handbag as a pillow. I trickled sand on her feet and she giggled sleepily, shutting her eyes. She was asleep in seconds. I wondered about burying her legs in the sand, but it was too soft and slithery to cling.

I tried to make a sandcastle, using my hands as scoops, but I needed the damp sand nearer the sea and I didn't want to leave Mum alone. I got out my drawing pad and felt tips and *drew* a sandcastle instead. I made it a huge sand palace with pinnacles and domes and towers. I had a sand princess with long golden hair peering out of her tower window, waving at the mermaids swimming in the moat around the castle. All the mermaids had very long hair right down to their scaly tails. I had a blonde, a brunette and a redhead and then experimented with emerald-green, purple and electric-blue long wavy hair. I gave them matching jewellery and fingernails and thought they looked gorgeous, if a little unusual.

I studded the mermaid moat with starfish and coral flowers and decorated the palace with sea-shells in elaborate patterns. The princess looked a little lonely even though she had the mermaids for company, so I drew more people looking out of the windows. I drew a queen mother with even longer golden hair, a best-friend princess with short black hair, and a handsome prince with a crown on his floppy brown hair. He was holding a very special royal rabbit who had a tiny padded crown wedged above her floppy ears.

Mum turned on her side, opened her eyes and yawned.

'Have you been drawing? Let's have a look. Oh, darling, that's lovely! It's so *detailed*. I must have been asleep ages.' Mum sat up and stretched. 'Shall we go and have a little walk round and explore Rabbit Cove?'

We stood up and brushed ourselves down. We didn't have a towel with us to get all the sand off our feet but when we got to the little wall Mum sat us down and rubbed our feet with the hem of her dress.

'Here,' said the artist, holding out one of his painting rags. 'Use this. I've got heaps.'

'That's very sweet of you,' said Mum. 'This is a lovely spot, isn't it?'

'Yes. I must have painted it hundreds of times but I never get sick of it,' said the artist.

He was quite old and quite fat, with a smiley face and a little soft beard. He wore a big blue shirt and old jeans dappled with paint and surprising scarlet baseball boots.

'Are you admiring my funky boots?' he said, seeing me staring.

'I'd like a pair like that,' I said shyly.

I stuck my feet in my own boring sandals and sidled towards him, keen to see his painting. It was very bright, the sky and sea a dazzling cobalt blue, the sand bright ochre yellow. I wondered if that was the way he really saw the soft grey-blue and pale primrose cove. He'd painted the children paddling, the families chatting – and right in the middle of his canvas there was a lovely blonde woman lying asleep, a plump little girl by her side, her head bent over her drawing pad.

'You've painted us!' I said.

The artist smiled.

'Oh, God, let's have a look,' said Mum, banging her sandals together and slipping them on her feet. She peered at the canvas, giggling.

'Oh dear, you've painted me fast asleep!' She squinted closely at the painting. 'You've drawn me with my mouth open, like I'm dribbling!'

'No I haven't! And anyway you looked lovely lying back like that.' He turned to me. 'You were drawing a long time.'

'Oh, Beauty *loves* drawing. She's ever so good at it,' said Mum.

'No I'm not,' I mumbled. I wished Mum hadn't told him my stupid name.

'Yes you are. I shouldn't wonder if she ends up a proper artist like you,' said Mum.

'I'm not a *proper* artist. I wish I was! No, I just *like* painting.' He looked at me. 'You've seen my work. Can I see yours?'

'Oh no, mine's silly. It's just made-up stuff,' I hedged.

'Go on, show him, Beauty,' said Mum.

I opened up my drawing pad and flashed my sand picture at him bashfully.

'Oh my goodness! Let's have a proper look.' He

took the drawing back from me and peered closely at my picture.

'I know it's silly and babyish,' I said. 'I was just sort of fooling around. I know you don't really get rabbits with crowns and mermaids with green and purple hair. Well, mermaids aren't real anyway, obviously.'

'That's the whole point of painting though. We can imagine the world the way we want it,' he said. 'I think you're very talented, Beauty. Is that your real name?'

'Poor Beauty hates her name,' said Mum. 'You can call her Cookie if you like. That's her new nickname.'

'I think Beauty's much more distinctive,' said Mike. 'What's *your* name? Total Delight? Ravishing? Gorgeous?'

Mum laughed. 'I'm Dilys – but everyone calls me Dilly.'

'I'm Mike.'

We all nodded and smiled and then stood a little foolishly, not knowing what to say next.

'So . . . are you here for a day out?' Mike asked.

'We're here on a little holiday,' said Mum.

'Oh, lovely. You're staying here in Rabbit Cove?' said Mike.

'Oh yes,' I said.

'At the hotel or a guest house?' Mike asked.

Mum and I looked at each other.

'Sorry! I didn't mean to be nosy,' said Mike.

'No, no, it's just we haven't quite decided where we're staying yet,' said Mum. 'Maybe we should go and do that straight away, Beauty? Oh heavens, I hope they're not all fully booked.'

'It's not the proper holiday season yet. You should be fine,' said Mike. 'There's just the one proper hotel in Rabbit Cove but there are lots of bed-and-breakfast guest houses.'

'That's what we'd prefer. Could you recommend a particular one, seeing as you're local?' said Mum.

'I'll do my best,' said Mike. 'There's a row of them just up the hill in Primrose Terrace. I'll come with you if you like. I've finished my painting for today.'

He let me help screw up all the tubes of oil paint and fit them carefully in their box.

'I *love* the smell of oil paint and the way it's so thick and shiny,' I said.

'Have you ever used oil paints yourself?' Mike asked.

'No. Dad doesn't let me have paints,' I said without thinking.

I wished I hadn't said Dad. It suddenly stopped being a holiday. I started to feel scared and sad all over again.

Mike was looking at me carefully.

'Tell you what – if you're around the beach tomorrow you can come and have a daub with me. I'll give you your own little bit of canvas, OK? Is that all right with you, Dilly?'

'It's very kind of you.'

We went to get the car, Mike walking with us.

'Do you think the bed-and-breakfast places will have their own car park?' said Mum.

'There's a little alleyway behind the terrace of houses. You can park the car there. I'll show you if you like.'

He got in the car beside Mum and directed her to the alleyway. It was a tight squeeze to get the car slotted in the space and Mum's always been rubbish at parking. She made one attempt. Two attempts.

'It's OK,' Mike said gently. 'How about swinging the steering wheel round, backing in – no, no, the other way!'

'Oh God, I'm hopeless!' said Mum.

'No, you're not. It's blooming difficult parking here. It takes ages to get used to it. Do you want another go – or would you like me to back it in?'

'You do it, please!'

Mike had the car properly parked in a matter of moments. He didn't crow though, he just shrugged and smiled when Mum thanked him. We got the two cases out of the boot, and Mike insisted on carrying them for us. I carried his paints and his art folder and his folding easel, feeling very important. I hoped people would look at me and think I was the real artist.

'OK, here we are, Primrose Terrace. Which guest house do you fancy?'

We gazed up and down the street. They were tall narrow Victorian houses painted in pretty pastels, pale yellow, pink, peach and white.

'Which do you think, Beauty?' said Mum. 'What about the one that's painted primrose yellow to match the name of the terrace?'

'That's *quite* a good choice,' said Mike. 'But maybe . . . ?'

'There's the pink one,' said Mum.

'Not pink,' I said, and Mike nodded in agreement.

'OK, OK, the peach one. That's got lovely roses in the garden,' said Mum.

'Mmm. Maybe,' said Mike. He was looking towards the white house at the end. I laid his art stuff down carefully and ran to have a proper look at it. It had a shiny green door and green willow-leaf curtains and there were white flowers painted on a sign above the door. I read the name – and came flying back to Mum and Mike.

'We have to stay in the white one at the end. It's called Lily Cottage!'

'*Excellent* choice,' said Mike. 'Let's see if they've got any vacancies.'

We walked up to Lily Cottage. I rang the bell. We waited. I rang again. Nothing happened.

'They're obviously not in,' said Mum. 'Maybe we'd better go next door after all.'

'Or maybe *I* can let you in?' said Mike, producing a key. He put it in the lock and opened the door with a flourish.

'It's *your* house!' said Mum, laughing.

'It's how I earn my living,' said Mike, grinning. 'I've got a double bedroom free with an en suite bathroom and a sea view. It's my best room and very cheap. Come and take a peek. I hope you like it.'

It was a lovely old-fashioned room with a patchwork quilt on the bed, a rocking chair in the corner, two comfy armchairs with flowery cushions, a scarlet Chinese storage chest – and Mike's bright paintings all round the white-washed walls.

'We'll definitely take it!' said Mum.

'Make yourself at home,' said Mike. 'I'll go and put the kettle on. I'm sure you'd like a cup of tea.'

'I wish this *was* our home,' I said to Mum, when he'd gone downstairs.

'Oh Beauty!' Mum sighed and opened her handbag, taking out her mobile. 'I think we'd better phone home.'

'What? We're not going back, are we?'

'No, no. But it's only fair to let your dad know where we are. You're his daughter. I can't just whisk you away and not let him keep in contact.'

'Not yet though, Mum. We're on *holiday*.'

'Well, I think we should just reassure him that you're all right.'

Mum switched on her phone. It immediately started beeping and beeping with many messages. Mum held it at arm's length, as if she thought it might explode. She pressed the first text message, the second, the third, so quickly that I couldn't read them. She listened to the first recorded message. She kept the phone pressed to her ear but I could still hear a few words. They were mostly rude swear words.

'Oh dear,' said Mum. 'Maybe we'll wait until tomorrow,' and she switched the phone off again.

Fifteen

I woke up to see the sun streaming through a chink in the curtains. It was going to be another lovely sunny day in Rabbit Cove! I lay quietly beside Mum, fingering the stitching on the patchwork quilt, looking at each seaside picture in turn. Then I heard a loud mewing right outside the window. I jumped up and pulled back the curtains. Two seagulls were balancing boldly on the window ledge, tapping their beaks on the glass in a jaunty fashion.

'Shoo!' I said, tapping back at them.

They flew off and I wondered what it would be like to soar effortlessly up into the sky. I spread my arms and whirled round and round the bed.

'Whatever are you doing?' Mum mumbled.

'Just having a little fly,' I said.

'You are such a funny kid,' said Mum, sitting up and stretching. 'Are you happy, babes?'

'Ever so ever so ever so. I simply love it here. Can we go on the beach again and have another picnic?'

'Of course we can.'

'And do you think Mike was serious about letting me do oil painting?'

'I think so.'

'He's so nice, isn't he?'

'Yes, he's a sweetheart. I'm sure he's not charging us the full rate for the room – but I'm not going to argue!' said Mum. She sniffed. 'Can you smell bacon? Mmm!'

We had a quick bath and then went downstairs to the breakfast room. There were two sets of couples wearing jeans and big woolly socks over their boots, obviously all set to walk along the coast path, and a family with a little boy and a toddler.

Mike rushed in and out of the room in a big navy striped apron, bringing veggie sausage breakfasts for one walking couple, bacon and egg and black pudding for the other, baked beans on toast and boiled eggs with soldiers for the family. Mum just wanted a bacon sandwich but I had a big plate of everything – and it was delicious. Mike was too busy to chat much, though he found the walkers a special map and he gave the two little boys some tiny cars to race up and down their arms and round and round their plates.

When the walkers and the family had all finished Mike came and sat down at our table and had a cup of tea with us. It made us feel special.

'What are you two ladies planning for today?' he said.

'The beach!' I said.

'Well, I've got to clean all the bedrooms and do a spot of shopping this morning,' said Mike. 'But this afternoon I'll be down on my usual patch with my paints, and you're very welcome to come and do a bit of daubing too, Beauty.'

Mum and I had another lovely lazy morning at Rabbit Cove and a picnic on the beach. The family with the two little boys were on the beach too. I built a real sandcastle down on the damp sand near the sea and they came and 'helped' me, finding shells and seaweed to decorate it and pouring water from their buckets to make a moat.

Then Mike arrived and he had a small canvas specially for me! He'd even brought me a piece of board to mix my colours on and two different brushes, one fat, one thin.

'OK, what are you going to paint?' said Mike. 'A seascape?'

'I think I'd like to do a portrait, a made-up one. Is that all right?' I asked.

'Of course it is, funny girl! You can paint what-ever you want.'

So I sketched out a big figure that nearly filled the whole canvas. I squeezed dabs of blue and black and brown and red and white paint on my palette and got started. It was such *fun* sploshing on the thick paint. It stayed obediently where I put it; it didn't slop all over the place like watercolour. If I made a mistake I could just wipe it off or decide to paint over it later.

I painted a man with shiny brown hair and lovely blue eyes. I gave him blue jeans and I fiddled around with the smaller brush, trying to give him a plaid shirt. It was tricky work, but not a lot of it showed because the man was holding a big white rabbit in his arms. It was hard making her *look* like a rabbit rather than a huge blob of marshmallow, but Mike showed me how to make a pale grey and do little dabbing strokes of the brush to look like fur. I mixed up a perfect pink for the rabbit's little nose, and I gave my man matching rosy cheeks.

'That's fantastic, Beauty,' said Mike. He hesitated. 'So . . . is that your dad?'

'No!' I said. 'It's Sam and his rabbit Lily. They're on the television. It's a little kids' programme. I'm a big baby.' I hung my head.

'Beauty, you're looking at a man who used to watch a little kids' programme called *The Magic Roundabout* every single day. In fact I have a daughter called Florence named after one of the roundabout characters. Luckily she hasn't got a funny face and very big feet like the Florence puppet.'

'I didn't see any girl at Lily Cottage,' I said shyly.

'Oh no no, she's grown up now and lives in London, near her mum,' said Mike.

'Oh,' I said, nodding.

'We split up several years ago. My wife hated it here.'

'How could you *possibly* hate Rabbit Cove?' I said, astonished.

I started doing the sky behind Sam, realizing that it might have made sense to fill it in first.

'Oh, Jenny likes city life, bright lights, lots going on, lots of shops. She found it incredibly boring when I took early retirement and we moved down here. I think she probably found *me* quite boring too,' said Mike.

'You're not a *bit* boring,' I said.

Mike laughed at me. 'You're an incredibly polite girl, Beauty. You've obviously been impeccably brought up by your mum and dad. So . . .' He hesitated again. 'Where *is* Dad?'

'Back at home,' I said. I hesitated too. 'I think maybe he and Mum have split up too. Just the day before yesterday, on my birthday, actually.'

'Oh dear! So where are you going to go after your holiday here?'

I didn't say anything, painting green grass under Sam's feet. It went a bit blobby and lumpy, but I pretended the biggest lumps were lettuces for Lily.

'I was prying again,' said Mike. 'I'm sorry, take no notice. I'm so nosy.' He tapped himself on his big cherry nose, telling himself off. I giggled, because he left a big smear of sand-yellow paint on the tip.

'I think maybe you should wipe your nose, it's all painty now. Here, shall I do it?' I said, brushing at him. 'I'm not really sure *where* we're going to go next.'

'But Mum knows?'

'Nope. We did go to Auntie Avril but she couldn't have us for more than one night.'

'I see. Well, what would you like to do, Beauty?'

I hung my head.

'Do you want to go back to Dad?' Mike asked gently.

'No! He tries to be a kind dad and he spends heaps of money on me but he gets so scary sometimes. He gets mad at Mum and me and he broke all the cookies and he let my birthday rabbit out of its hutch and it *died*,' I said, all in a rush.

236

I suddenly couldn't see my canvas any more because my eyes were blurry with tears.

'Oh, Beauty, I'm so sorry. I didn't mean to upset you,' said Mike, dabbing at my eyes with the much-used paint cloth.

I'd thought Mum was asleep down on the beach but she came dashing over the sand towards us.

'What have you said to upset her?' she demanded of Mike.

'It wasn't Mike's fault, Mum, honest,' I snivelled. 'I just thought about my *rabbit*.'

'Oh. Yes. Poor darling,' said Mum, giving me a big hug.

'It *was* my fault,' said Mike. 'I was asking stuff about her dad. I'm sorry, it was unforgivable of me. I was worried because Beauty let it slip that you haven't got anywhere to go.'

'We'll be absolutely fine,' said Mum. 'And you needn't worry about us not paying for our room and breakfast, I've got more than enough.'

'Oh Dilly, stop it. You *know* that's not what I'm worrying about.'

'You don't have to worry at all,' said Mum. 'Come on, Beauty, I think we'll go for a walk.'

'But, Mum, I haven't finished my Sam and Lily painting,' I said.

'Oh, for heaven's sake, I'm getting a bit sick of stupid Sam and his Lily,' said Mum. 'Come on. Now.'

I glanced despairingly at Mike.

'Better do what your mum says,' he said.

So I miserably followed Mum along the seafront and up a little winding chalk path to the clifftop. I walked behind her, glaring at her back. She walked faster and faster, swinging her arms, her fists clenched. I lagged behind, out of breath.

'Keep *up*, Beauty,' Mum hissed.

'I don't want to,' I said, and I suddenly sat down.

'Oh come on, don't be a silly baby,' said Mum.

'Stop bossing me about! Why are you being so *horrid* all of a sudden? You were so rude to Mike and he was just trying to be *kind*.'

'He made you cry. I'm not having that.'

'You *know* why I was crying – it was because of my rabbit.'

'Beauty, you spent five minutes maximum with that blessed rabbit,' said Mum, squatting down beside me.

'I still loved it – and it was so terrible seeing it without its poor little head,' I said, my voice going shaky again. 'I'll never forgive Dad for that, never never never.'

'Your dad didn't mean that to happen. I know he undid the hutch but I'm sure he just meant Birthday to escape. You mustn't blame him.'

'Why are you sticking up for *Dad*? Yet you were being mean to Mike who's ever so nice. And being mean to me too.'

'I'm not being mean. Don't be so childish.'

'I'm a *child*, how else am I supposed to act? And you *are* being horribly mean. Why are you being so nasty, even saying Sam and Lily are stupid.'

'Well they are. And you're stupid being so obsessed with them. You're a big baby,' said Mum.

'I am *not*,' I said, and I shoved her, hard.

She was still squatting and so she lost her balance. She fell backwards, legs in the air.

'Don't you *dare* hit me!' she said. 'Do that again and I'll hit you right back.'

'I *didn't* hit you, I just shoved. *This* is a hit,' I said, and I punched her shoulder.

It was only a token punch, a feeble little tap, but Mum smacked me hard on my leg. I stared at her, shocked. She'd never ever smacked me before.

Mum seemed stunned too. Her face suddenly crumpled and she burst into tears.

'I don't know why you're crying. *I'm* the one who should be crying – that really hurt,' I said.

'I'm sorry,' Mum sobbed, her head in her hands.

She cried and cried. I edged closer and then put

my arm round her. She cried even harder, clinging to me.

'Oh, Beauty, I'm so sorry,' she gasped. 'How could I have slapped you like that? You're right, I was being horribly mean. It's just I'm so *scared*. I don't know what to do for the best. I was awake half the night worrying about it. I think I've gone crazy, running away with you like this. I haven't got an idea in my head what we're going to do. I couldn't stand Mike looking at me like that, acting so kind and concerned, when he must think I'm the worst mother in the world.'

'He doesn't think that at all. He *likes* you. Don't you like him?'

'Of course I do. I feel dead embarrassed that I was so snotty to him. I think we'd better be on our way tomorrow.'

'Oh *no*, Mum. I love it here.'

'I know, darling, but we can't stay here for ever.'

'Why can't we?'

'This is just our little holiday, you know that. We've got to make proper plans. I've been trying so hard, but my head just goes whirling round and round. I've got so used to your dad telling me what to do I can't seem to think for myself any more.'

'So I'll think for you. We'll stay here in Rabbit

Cove and you'll get a job, right, and we'll find our own little place—'

'Oh, Beauty, we couldn't even afford a blooming beach hut.'

'Well then, I'll build us a blooming sand-castle and we'll live in that, happily ever after,' I said.

Mum burst out laughing and hugged me tight. 'Oh, thank God I've got you, babe. We'll be fine, you and me, just so long as we stick together. I'm sorry I was so crabby.'

'Are you going to say sorry to Mike too?'

'Oh, lordy. Yes, I suppose so. He *has* been sweet to us – and it was lovely him showing you how to paint.'

'I'm quite good at it, aren't I! We don't really have to go tomorrow, do we? I so want to paint some more.'

'We'll see,' said Mum.

When we walked back arm in arm we saw Mike still perched on the wall, painting away.

'I don't think we'd better disturb him just now,' said Mum.

'Oh, Mum, stop being such a coward! Let's get it over with,' I said.

I practically had to pull her over to Mike. Her cheeks went very red as we got nearer. He didn't look up, even when we were standing right next to him. He carried on dabbing paint on his canvas in determined fashion.

Mum pulled an agonized face at me. I gave her a nudge. She swallowed hard.

'Mike, I'm very sorry for being so rude and off-hand with you,' she said in a tiny voice.

Mike paused, paintbrush in mid-air. He looked up at last.

'I don't blame you. I was asking Beauty all sorts of silly questions which were none of my business,' he said stiffly.

'Not at all,' said Mum.

Mike nodded awkwardly. Mum made little shuffling movements, about to stride off again. I couldn't bear leaving it like that.

'So to make friends properly we'd like to ask you out to supper tonight,' I said.

Mum and Mike stared at me, looking equally astonished.

'*Where?*' Mum mouthed at me.

We'd discovered that Peggy's Parlour closed on the dot of six last night so we'd bought cod and chips from the fish shop and eaten them on the beach.

'That's very sweet of you, but I was actually planning a meal in tonight, with friends,' said Mike.

'Oh,' I said, drooping.

'Yes. I do a great fish pie. Fancy trying it, you two?'

'Well, we wouldn't want to intrude, not if you're having your friends round,' said Mum.

Mike looked at me. I rolled my eyes.

'*Mum!* I think *we're* the friends,' I said.

So we had supper with Mike. We did wonder if he'd invited any of the other guests, but the two walking couples drove off to some gourmet pub and the family went to try the evening meal at the hotel.

'So it's just us,' I said, smiling. 'Mum, can I wear my grey dress and pinafore and my new boots?'

'Oh, Beauty! It's just supper. Just pop a clean T-shirt on and wear it with your jeans.'

'No, I want to look lovely. Well, I know I look total rubbish no matter what, but I *feel* lovely in my grey dress.'

'Oh, sweetheart. You don't look the slightest bit rubbish. But OK, you wear your grey outfit if you like. *I'm* not going to make a big effort though.'

Mum wore her jeans – but she changed into her little pink clingy top with pearl buttons and she wore her pink strappy high heels. She even bothered to paint new nail varnish on her toes.

We went downstairs at seven as Mike had suggested but the breakfast room was empty, all the tables set ready for the morning.

'Oh goodness, maybe he's changed his mind,' Mum whispered.

But Mike came into the breakfast room, beaming at us.

'Through here, ladies. I thought we'd be cosier in the kitchen, and it won't give any of the other guests ideas if they come back early.'

Mike had on his stripy apron, but underneath he was wearing a big blue flowery shirt and clean jeans without a single paint smear, and his big baseball boots shone scarlet. He had obviously made a *big* effort.

'Oh, Beauty! *Is* it you, Beauty?' he said. 'You look so grown up. And you look even younger, Dilly. You're just like sisters.'

We were used to people saying this but it was still good to hear. We followed him into the kitchen. I'd expected it to be a big formal stainless-steel working kitchen, but it was a glorious colourful old-fashioned room with a great wooden dresser hung with willow-pattern plates. Old toby jugs jostled each other on the windowsill and there were big blue lustre vases on the wooden table, containing red asters, white daisies, yellow lilies and pink rosebuds.

244

The cooker itself was a big green Aga that spread a cosy glow throughout the kitchen. There was a red and yellow and blue rag rug on the tiled floor with a black cat stretched out, comfortably dozing.

'I didn't know you had a cat, Mike!' I said, squatting down beside it and stroking its sleek head.

'I don't. It's next door's, but she's got a sixth sense whenever I make fish pie. She comes on the scrounge for the scraps,' said Mike. 'Right, sit yourself down, girls. What would you like to drink? White wine, Dilly? And I thought you'd like a special *red* wine, Beauty.' He grinned and poured us each a glass. Mine was the most beautiful deep red. I knew it couldn't really be wine but I felt wickedly grown up sipping it all the same.

'It's wonderful!' I said. 'What *kind* of wine is this, Mike?'

'Oh, the very best. Vintage pomegranate,' said Mike. 'Now, you ladies talk among yourselves while I do the finishing touches to the meal.'

He popped some runner beans and asparagus into a pan of boiling water and then had a peer at the fish pie. It was golden brown and smelled wonderful. The cat raised her head from the mat and looked hopeful again.

'No, you've had your share, greedy-guts,' said Mike. 'It's our turn now.'

It truly was delicious – soft creamy mashed potato with a crispy cheese topping and large chunks of haddock and cod and curly pink prawns. I ate my entire plateful and then had a second helping. Mike didn't frown at me and make comments about my weight. He seemed delighted that I appreciated his pie and congratulated me on my appetite. Mum couldn't quite clear her plateful because she's got the appetite of a bird at the best of times, but she told Mike he was a brilliant cook.

'I'm not much cop when it comes to puds, I'm afraid,' he said, producing a bowl of red apples, some purple grapes and an orange cheese. 'I'm not sure I've got any sweet nibbles for you, Beauty. There might be a biscuit or two in that tartan tin.'

'Are they home-made?' I asked.

'Beauty!' said Mum.

'No, sorry, I don't do that sort of baking,' said Mike.

'Mum does,' I said proudly. 'She makes the most fantastic cookies, all different sorts, iced and chocolate chip and cherry and oatmeal-and-raisin.'

'Mm! So you're a good cook, are you, Dilly?'

'No! I've just got a very sweet daughter,' said

Mum. 'I can't cook for toffee, apart from cookies. I *can* make good cookies though.'

'What about breakfasts?' said Mike. 'I'm going to need a hand in the kitchen now the summer season's starting up, and I usually employ a student to come in and do chambermaiding. It's a bit of a boring job but you'd be finished and free by lunch time. You don't fancy trying it for a few weeks?'

Mum looked stunned. She just stared at Mike, not saying a word. So I answered for her.

'Yes, *please!*' I said.

'No, no, hang on, Beauty. Mike's just being kind, trying to be helpful,' Mum muttered.

'No, I *need* help. It's a bit of a rubbish job and I can't pay much, but it'll give you time to think out what you really want to do. The only trouble is I can't let you keep the first-floor double, not if you're here as staff. If I have a live-in girl she usually sleeps up in the attic, but it's a bit basic, I'm afraid.'

'The attic!' I said, clapping my hands. 'Oh, can we see? I've always wanted to live in an old house with a proper attic.'

So Mike led us up the three flights of stairs to his attic. It was a dark narrow little room with just one very small window, but it was still beautiful. The small bed had a navy patchwork quilt with silver stars and moons appliquéd all over it. There was a squashy ruby velvet armchair with a matching footstool and a red-and-blue tapestry curtain hiding a clothes rail.

'Oh dear, I don't think it's anywhere near big enough for you,' said Mike worriedly.

'We can easily scrunch up together. It's great!' I said.

I ran to the window, rested my elbows on the sill, and looked out over the red tile rooftops to the sea. 'I feel just like Sara Crewe in *A Little Princess. She* lived in an attic!'

I knelt down, examining the wainscoting.

'Whatever are you doing, Beauty? Get up!' said Mum.

'I'm just seeing if there are any little rat holes,' I said.

'What? There are absolutely no rats in this house, I promise,' said Mike. You won't find so much as a mouse's whisker!'

'Oh, I'd *love* my own pet rat like Sara's Melchisedec,' I said.

'You might, Beauty, but I definitely wouldn't,' said Mum. She smiled at Mike. 'We'll be great here, Mike, Beauty and me. I'll bring our stuff up here and start work in the morning, how about that?'

'No, no, you must have your little holiday first.'

'Please. I'd like to get stuck in straight away. Shall we shake on it?'

Mum stuck out her hand and they shook, sealing the deal.

Sixteen

Mum was up extra early next morning, wearing her checked shirt and jeans, her hair scraped back into a ponytail.

'Do I look like a breakfast chef?' she asked me anxiously.

'No, you need checked trousers and one of those big floppy white hats,' I said, laughing at her.

'Don't, Beauty! I'm so scared. I'm sure I'm going to mess up royally. Your dad always says I can't even boil an egg and I *can't* – they always come out rock hard or so soft they ooze everywhere. Mike's being so kind but he'll so regret it when I muck everything up for him.'

'Mum, you *can* cook.'

'I can't give folk a plate of cookies for their blooming breakfast!'

'I don't know, oatmeal-and-raisin cookies might be just the ticket.'

I went down with Mum to the kitchen, though she told me not to.

'I'm like the kitchen maid. I promise I'll be useful and not get in the way,' I said to Mike.

'You're child labour and I'll get sent to jail for

251

exploiting you,' said Mike, but he patted me on the head and told me to stay.

He sent Mum into the dining room to take the breakfast orders. She got in a terrible fluster at first and couldn't remember which walkers wanted veggie sausages and which black pudding, and whether they wanted tea or coffee, but I'd been lurking in the doorway and knew exactly. Mike asked Mum to keep an eye on the sausages and bacon while he made some porridge for a new pair of old ladies. Mum's hand shook as she tried to turn the sausages so that three of them shot straight out of the pan and skidded across the floor.

'Oh God, I'm so sorry!' she said, nearly in tears.

'They can be *your* breakfast, Dilly!' said Mike cheerily. 'Never mind, shove some more under the grill, there's a dear.'

He didn't get the slightest bit cross, dancing around the kitchen, laughing and joking. Mum was soon laughing and joking back. She had to serve up the little boys' breakfasts and she made them each a face on a plate: a sausage cut in two for the eyes, a tomato nose and a bacon-rasher mouth, which they both loved. She made a smiley golden syrup face in both bowls of porridge too and the old ladies clapped their little claw hands in delight.

Mike seemed pleased when we all had break-fast together – but Mum and I *really* came into our own when it came to making the beds and doing the cleaning. We were used to living in a home where everything had to be pin-neat perfect. I'd followed Mum around when I was a toddler, doing my own 'dusting' with a hankie and riding on the vacuum cleaner. Now I could tackle housework properly myself. We worked together in each room, making beds, cleaning the bathroom, vacuuming the carpet.

We were astonished at everyone's untidiness. We didn't like to tidy things up too thoroughly in case people thought we were meddling with their things, but we couldn't help playing little games. The walkers had left big woolly socks strewn all over the floor so we hung them in a row at the foot of the bed like Christmas stockings. The little boys had thrown their teddies every-where so I collected them up and tucked them all into the cot, the covers pulled up tight to their button noses.

Mike did a tiny tactful inspection in our wake and grinned appreciatively.

'I've got two girls for the price of one – and you've both done an excellent job. I *knew* it was my lucky day when I spotted you on the beach.'

'*Our* lucky day,' I said happily. 'Can we do some more painting together this afternoon, Mike?'

'You bet we can,' said Mike.

Mum and I went up to our little attic room to gather our things together for the beach. We were running out of clean clothes now but Mike said we could use his washing machine.

'I wish I'd packed more sensibly,' said Mum. 'I filled half my suitcase with your baby photos and all the pictures you've ever drawn for me – and yet I forgot my nightie and my good knickers and I didn't even think to take any tights. Oh well, I can always buy some more when I get my first wages. Unless we ask your dad if we can go back to collect some more stuff? No, maybe not.'

'*Definitely* not!'

'We'll have to phone him though.' Mum took a deep breath. 'Now!'

'*No*, Mum.'

'Come on, we've got to. It's only fair and responsible.'

'But he'll spoil it all.'

'Beauty, he's your *father*.'

'Yes, but I wish he wasn't.'

'Now don't be silly.'

'He wishes I wasn't his daughter.'

'Now that's totally out of order. Your dad thinks the world of you.'

'He's ashamed of me. He'd swap me for Skye quick as a wink.'

'That's crazy,' said Mum, but she was nibbling

her lip, not looking me in the eye. 'You mustn't ever think that, babes.'

'I don't just think it, Mum, I *know* it.'

'And *I* know you're just nattering away so I'll lose my bottle and put off phoning your dad. But I'm not going to!' Mum's fingers darted over the phone keypad and she pressed the green button before I could stop her.

'You're through to the desk of Gerry Cookson,' said Dad in his brightest and best Happy Homes tone.

Mum and I stared at each other. He sounded so cheerily normal, as if nothing had happened.

'He's fine, Mum! Switch off now!' I hissed – but Mum had already started talking.

'Hello, Gerry darling,' she said, and then pulled a face. The 'darling' had obviously slipped out from force of habit.

'Dilly? Dilly, what the *hell* are you playing at?' Dad's voice revved up. I could hear him; Mike all the way downstairs could hear him; even kids down on the beach could hear him.

'I'm not playing, Gerry. This isn't a game,' said Mum.

'You've been gone three *days*. You've made your point. Now pack your gear and get yourself home, pronto.'

'We're not actually coming home,' said Mum.

255

'*What?* Don't talk such total bilge. Of course you are. What sort of a mother are you, flouncing out of your lovely home and dragging poor little Beauty with you?'

I tried to take the phone to stick up for Mum but she wouldn't let me.

'You were the one who told us to get out, Gerry,' Mum said.

'Because you were bang out of order, you jumped-up little tart,' Dad bellowed.

'Well, nice to know what you think of me,' said Mum. 'Now listen, Gerry, I'm trying to be as responsible as possible. I know you need to know where Beauty is—'

'No! *No! NO!*' I said, jumping up and down.

'We're staying at a little spot on the coast called Rabbit Cove. It's lovely here. I promise you Beauty's very happy.'

'Stop burbling this nonsense! Now come back home this *instant!*'

'We're going to stay here for a while, Gerry, at least for the summer season.'

'And what exactly are you going to live on, you little fool? You needn't think I'm sending any money for you and the kid.'

'I've got a job,' said Mum proudly.

'*You've* got a job?' Dad said. 'What is it? The Useless Ageing Dumb Blonde Page Three Pin-Up job?'

Mum took the phone away from her ear, stared at it a moment, and then terminated the call.

'About time,' I said.

'Oh God,' said Mum, starting to shake.

'I *told* you so,' I said.

'Don't, Beauty,' said Mum, and her eyes went watery.

'I'm sorry. I *hate* people who say I told you so. I didn't really mean it,' I said, giving her a hug.

We stayed hugging hard, glancing anxiously at the phone. It started ringing again almost immediately. Mum switched it off quickly, keeping the phone at arm's length as if Dad could wriggle right out of it and grab her.

'OK, babes, let's go on the beach,' said Mum.

We left the phone shut up in our dressing-table drawer and went down to the sands. We were both hot and flushed. We longed to cool down by going in for a swim. We hadn't packed swimming costumes but Mum felt I'd look perfectly decent in my T-shirt and knickers.

'I can't go swimming in my *knickers*!'

'You wore them with your T-shirt on the beach the other day.'

'Yes, sitting down. I can't go gallivanting into the sea dressed like that. Everyone will stare at me and laugh.'

257

'No they won't! Don't be so daft. Look, *I'll* go in wearing my underwear. I've got my old red bra and knickers on. They look *kind* of like a bikini. OK, ready steady *strip!*'

Mum ripped her top and jeans off. I gaped at her – and then pulled my own jeans off. We went charging into the sea. It was incredibly cold but we didn't hang around shrieking. We plunged straight in and splashed around like crazy.

We saw Mike setting up his easel by the wall and called to him to come and join us. He was an old spoilsport and wouldn't even come in paddling. He painted us instead, bobbing about in the sea, Mum in her red 'bikini' and me in my big T-shirt.

When I'd dried off I went to paint with him too. I did another Sam and Lily portrait: Sam was sun-bathing in a funny long stripy costume and Lily was hunched up on a deckchair, licking a carrot-flavoured ice lolly, with sunglasses hooked onto her ears. I sang the *Rabbit Hutch* song under my breath as I painted, and I made Sam say, 'Hey there,' to me.

'Hey there,' said Mike, thinking I was talking to him.

'Hey,' I said again, giggling.

Mum put her clothes back on when she'd sunbathed herself dry. She gathered up our beach stuff and came to join us up on the wall.

'Do you want to do some painting too, Dilly?' Mike asked.

'You have to be joking!' said Mum. 'No, I'm going to nip back to Lily Cottage if that's OK. I'm planning a little surprise.'

I had an idea what Mum's surprise would be. Sure enough, when Mike and I went back to the guest house with our finished canvases there was a wonderful warm sweet cookie smell the moment we opened the door. Mike breathed in deeply.

'What's your mum been up to?' he asked.

'Cookies!'

They were the most amazing ice-cream cookies: sugar cookies for the cones with different coloured frostings on each one, white, pink and pale brown.

'Oh Mum, *ice-cream* cookies!' I said. 'How did you cut them all into such neat shapes?'

'There was this funny little sandcastle-making kit in the beach shop and they had three different cutters, starfish, mermaids and ice-cream cones!' said Mum. 'It was only one pound fifty so I thought I'd treat us. And I bought the flour and sugar and eggs myself, Mike. I wanted to give you this little present to say thank you for being so kind to us.'

'That's truly lovely of you, Dilly! They look wonderful. Gosh, you've done masses!'

'Well, I thought we could offer all the guests a cookie and a cup of tea when they come back from the beach or wherever. I thought they might like it,' said Mum.

They all *loved* Mum's cookies – and not just the children. The two very old ladies were particularly appreciative and asked Mike where he'd bought such lovely novelty biscuits.

'I didn't buy them. Dilly here made them with her own fair hands,' he said.

'My goodness! Well, they're excellent, my dear. We used to run a little teashop and we'd have been so proud to serve your cookies, Dilly,' they said earnestly.

Mum went bright pink with pride and I wanted to hug her. She practically danced up to our little attic bedroom.

'I'm good at cookies now, *really* good at them!' she said, lying back on our bed and bicycling her legs in the air. 'I've never been good at anything in my life, Beauty, but now I can say I'm an ace cookie-maker! I'm so happy!'

'So am I, Mum, so am I,' I said, leaning my arms on the windowsill and gazing out across the rooftops at the glistening sea.

Then I glanced down at our road, and saw a silver Mercedes draw up at the end. I stared, telling myself it couldn't possibly be Dad. There were hundreds and hundreds of silver Mercedes all over England. But then the door opened and a man stamped out, a small square balding man with a salmon-pink face. It *was* Dad.

I opened my mouth but no sound came out. I watched him marching up the path and hammering on the door of number one Primrose Terrace. Someone answered the door, Dad said something, waited, then stormed back up the path and tried number two. He was systematically searching for us.

'Mum!' I croaked.

'What, darling?'

'It's Dad! He's here and he's going to every guest house and he'll be knocking at our door in a minute or two! Oh quick, Mum, we've got to get out of here!'

Mum jumped up and ran to the window.

'Oh, God! Look at his face, he's *flaming*!' Mum took a deep breath. 'But we're not running, sweetheart. We're going to stay here. We'll see him and . . . we'll talk quietly and sensibly and maybe Dad will understand.'

'Are you *mad*, Mum? Dad never understands. Come on, please!' I said, shaking her, but she wouldn't be budged.

'We're not going to skulk in our room. We'll go and meet him,' she said, taking hold of my hand.

We went downstairs hand in hand, up the hallway, and opened the green front door. We stood in the porchway of Lily Cottage, waiting. We heard Dad's footsteps, his abrupt knocking, his demands. *Have you got a Mrs Cookson staying here – Mrs Cookson and her daughter Beauty?* Then he pounded back up next door's path and burst through our gate. He was so intent on finding us that he wasn't quite focusing. He stamped halfway up the path staring at us but somehow not *seeing* us. Then he stopped still, mouth open.

'Hello, Gerry,' said Mum calmly – although I could feel she was trembling.

He stared at us, his face flooding purple.

'Right. Come on. Get yourselves out of this dump *now*. You're coming back home with me.'

I hung on tight to Mum's hand. Dad looked so crazy I was scared he'd pick us both up bodily and stuff us head first into the boot of the Mercedes.

'We're not coming. This is our home now,' said Mum.

'This isn't a home, it's a tacky little B and B – and a right dump it looks too,' said Dad. 'Why didn't you stay in the hotel up in the village?'

'It's a *lovely* home, Dad,' I said.

'You shut your face, Beauty. I'm sick of you. If you hadn't started begging for that bloody rabbit then

262

none of this would have happened,' Dad shouted.

The two teashop ladies came into the hall behind us, coughing discreetly to let us know they were there.

'Come on, I haven't got time to mess around discussing the pros and cons of guest houses,' said Dad. 'Get your stuff and get cracking – *now*!'

The two old ladies gasped.

'Are you all right, dear? Shall we go and get Mike?' one enquired timidly.

'Mike? Who the hell's *Mike*?' Dad asked.

'I'm Mike,' said Mike, coming into the hallway. He put his arms round the elderly ladies.

'Don't worry, my dears. I'll look after things here. I should go up to your room,' he said. Then he walked forward and stood beside Mum and me.

'I gather you're Dilly's husband? Would you like to come in?' he said.

'No, I'm not bloody coming in! I'll thank you not to interfere, you nosy git. Just who the hell do you think you are?' Dad shouted.

'I'm Dilly and Beauty's friend,' said Mike.

'Do you think I'm stupid? Friend! Don't take the mickey out of me,' said Dad, and he punched Mike right on the nose.

'For God's sake!' said Mike thickly, blood dribbling. He felt his nose gingerly. 'Have you gone mad?'

'Oh, Mike, I'm so sorry. Here, have a tissue,' said Mum frantically.

'Do you think I was born yesterday? How long have you known her? So this was all a put-up job! I *knew* you didn't have the bottle to leave me and strike out on your own, Dilly! But is *he* the best you can do? He's a pensioner, for pity's sake – and he doesn't look like he has a bean to his name.'

'You're right on both those counts,' said Mike. 'But totally wrong when it comes to any kind of relationship between Dilly and me. We are simply friends, plus I'm technically her employer.'

'You *what*?' said Dad. 'What do you employ her *as*, might I ask?'

'She's my breakfast chef,' said Mike.

Dad stared – and then he started spluttering with laughter.

'Well, if you want to kill off all your guests then set our Dilly free in your kitchen! She can't cook to save her life. All she can make is bloody *biscuits*.'

'Very very good biscuits,' said Mike. 'Would you like to come in and calm down and have a cup of tea and one of Dilly's cookies?'

'Don't take that patronizing tone with me! This is a private conversation between me and my wife.' Dad took a step nearer Mum. Mike did too, protectively.

'Now pin back your ears, Dilly. You obviously cleared off because you thought the whole business was going down the pan, and me with it. But I've got a lot of pals in the right places. They're dropping the bribery nonsense, and now this guy's tipped me the wink about a riverside council site that's going to be pulled down. It could be even bigger than the Water Meadows deal and I'm pretty damn sure I'm going to get it. Do you understand what I'm saying?'

'Yes, you're probably going to make a lot more money,' said Mum.

'So I'm giving you one last chance, girl. Come back now and make the most of it – or I'll cut you off without a penny, you and the kid.'

'Gerry, I don't want your money,' said Mum. 'That wasn't the reason I married you. I wanted you to look after me. But I'm not that stupid little girl any more. It's time I learned to look after myself, and Beauty too, of course.'

'Well, to hell with you,' said Dad. 'I can do a lot better than you. You're already losing your looks.' Then he looked at me. 'And *you*'ve never had any looks to speak of. You're just a waste of space, both of you. I wasted my time driving all this way to find you. You can stew here in this little seaside dump for ever for all I care.'

Dad spat on the doorstep and then stamped off. Mum and I stood watching, still holding hands tightly.

'Phew,' said Mike. 'Well, come inside my little seaside dump, my dears. *We'll* have that cup of tea and another cookie – and I need to bury my poor nose in a bag of frozen peas!'

'I'm so so sorry, Mike. I feel so terrible. Do you think you need to go to hospital? It could be broken!' said Mum.

'I very much doubt it. It's been broken twice before in rugby accidents so it's no big deal even if it is. It'll be fine. We'll all be fine, once we've stopped shaking!'

We stayed chatting to Mike and eating cookies, Mum and Mike talking about anything under the sun – apart from Dad. But when Mum and I went upstairs she pulled a *'help'* face at me.

'It looks like there's no going back now,' she said.

'We'll stew here for ever, hurray, hurray, hurray!' I said. 'So, Mum, *is* this home now?'

'Yes, I suppose it is.'

'Then can I write to Rhona to let her know where I am?'

'Of course, darling.'

I got out my best card and Auntie Avril's

266

felt tips. I drew a picture of myself on the front, painting with Mike. I did a teeny weeny picture of *my* picture on Mike's easel, and a picture of Rhona holding poor dear Birthday on my canvas.

I wasn't quite sure what I was going to write to Rhona so I spent a long time colouring everything in. I even did the sea in the background all different blues and greens, leaving a little white tip on the top of each wave.

When the page was shiny and stiff with colour I had to turn over and write my letter. I'd been rehearsing what to say inside my head but it was so difficult. In the end I just scribbled:

Dear Rhona,

Oh dear, I think this card will come as a shock as Mum and I have moved to the seaside. Rabbit Cove is lovely and we are staying at Mike's guest house and he has been teaching me how to paint (see front). I am happy to be here but so sad I can't see you any more (though it would be GREAT if you ever came on holiday here!). I do hope you still want me to be best friends even though I'm here and you're there.

267

Give Reginald Redted a kiss and a spoonful of honey from me.
Love from Beauty xx

P.S. Something very very very sad happened to dear Birthday. It's so awful that I can't write it. But he will always be the best birthday present in the world.

I put Lily Cottage as my new address but I didn't really expect Rhona to write back. She wasn't really a girl for writing letters. But in two days' time I got a little *parcel* from her. It was small and soft and when I slid my little finger under the wrapping paper I felt *fur*.

I thought Rhona was sending me Reginald Redted to keep me company, but when I ripped the paper open I found a tiny droopy bear in a very wrinkled faded navy outfit.

'Nicholas Navybear!' I whispered. 'But you *drowned*!'

I opened Rhona's note.

Dear Beauty,

Oh I will miss you so! Guess what, Dad drained our swimming pool yesterday to clean it out and Nicholas Navybear was stuck in the drain!!! My mum washed him and steamed him dry but he still looks a bit weird. I hope you will still like him.

Love from your best friend, Rhona x x x

P.S. I hope nothing too dreadful happened to Birthday, but never mind.

Seventeen

'I think we'd better get you into a school here, Beauty,' said Mum, as we had a cup of tea together after serving breakfast.

I stared at Mum, appalled.

'I don't want to go to *school*!' I said. 'I can't! I've got to do my share of the guest-house work – and then I paint with Mike. I'm *working*, Mum.'

'Don't be such a noodle, you know you've got to go to school.'

'Yes, *some* day, but not *now*. It'll be the summer holidays soon anyway. I can start school in September, if I must.'

'You'll start *now*. I want to do everything properly. What if your dad starts suing for custody of you and it comes out in court I didn't send you to school. I don't want to be declared an unfit mother! No, you're going, sweetheart, and that's final. We'll ask Mike where the Rabbit Cove primary school is.'

'That's simple,' said Mike, coming in to load the dishwasher. 'There isn't one. It closed down five years ago because the numbers were dwindling.'

'Hurray!' I said. 'Then I can't go, Mum, can I?'

'Yes, you can. You'll have to go to the nearest school, that's all,' said Mum determinedly.

It turned out the nearest primary school was in Seahaven, a good six miles away.

'Then I can't go,' I said.

'Yes, you can. You have to,' said Mum. 'It's the law.'

'But how on earth could I get there?'

'I'll have to drive you.'

'You can't, not if you're serving breakfasts.'

'Well, maybe there's a bus. Although I don't want you going on a bus on your own. Oh, God, how can I be in two places at once?' said Mum.

'Don't worry, Dilly,' said Mike. 'There are kids at number two and number seventeen. They go on the bus. Beauty can go with them.'

'It's not *fair*,' I raged. 'I won't go. You can't *make* me, Mum.'

'Stop it, Beauty. You're doing my head in,' said Mum.

'Here, Beauty, leave your mum in peace,' said Mike. 'Come shopping with me. I need to stock up on heaps of flour and sugar and stuff. Your mum's cookies are getting incredibly popular. Mrs Brooke next door has got wind of them and wants to buy a batch to offer to *her* guests, if you please!'

Mike kept nattering on as we walked up the hill to the little supermarket. He kept asking for advice as we went round all the shelves, getting me stretching and bending and balancing and adding up in my head. He didn't mention the dreaded 'S' word until we were trailing home, with huge carrier bags in both hands.

'Now then,' he puffed. 'About school . . .'

'You think I've calmed down now and I'll be reasonable. But I'm still—' I tried to think of the right word. '*Adamant!*' I finished triumphantly.

'Does it not occur to you that a girl intelligent enough to use a posh word like *adamant* might be in need of a good school?'

'There's no such thing as a good school. I think they're all bad bad bad.'

'You didn't like your last school?'

'It was awful, the worst ever. It was ever so posh – and I'm not.'

'But you must do OK at most lessons?'

'That's partly the problem. If you come top that's another reason for everyone to tease you and call you Brainbox and Cleverclogs and Snotty-Swotty,' I said gloomily. 'I *did* try to act thick when I first went to Lady Mary Mountbank but the teacher got cross with me and said I wasn't trying. She got really upset and I hated that and so I worked hard and she was pleased so *then* I got called a teacher's pet too.'

'Well, they could call you worse things.'

'Oh, they did, they did! There was this one girl called Skye – she was ever so pretty and popular but the meanest girl *ever* and she invented a new nasty nickname for me nearly every day. It was just like a game to her. The worst nickname of all was . . .' I swallowed, still scarcely able to say it. 'Ugly,' I mumbled, my eyes stinging.

'What was that?' Mike said apologetically. 'I didn't quite catch it.'

'*Ugly!*' I said, shivering with the shame of it.

'Oh dear,' said Mike, but he didn't sound shocked. 'That's not very nice.'

'It's a silly take on my name, Beauty. Skye laughed and laughed at it because I'm the exact opposite of my name. I *am* Ugly,' I said.

'Oh *dear*,' said Mike, more sympathetically. 'You're not the *slightest* bit ugly, Beauty. You're not a pretty-pretty curly-wurly sort of girl, I grant you, but I think you look bright and intelligent and interesting. However, I'm not going to waste my breath trying to convince you, because I know what you women are like! And this poisonous Skye seems to have done her best to demoralize you. What about the school before this last one? Was that posh too?'

'It wasn't posh, it was quite tough, but they didn't like me there either. They all had a belly laugh at my name too.'

274

'And you're worried that's what will happen at Seahaven?'

'Yep. Unless I can make them call me something else, like Cookie.'

'Cookie's a cool nickname, but I'd stick with Beauty. It's great to have a distinctive, unusual name.'

'Oh, Mike, I do like you ever so much and I don't mean to be rude but you do talk rubbish sometimes. How would you like to be called Handsome?'

'I'd love it!' said Mike, chuckling. 'And why would that be funny, Miss? I *am* handsome!' He struck a silly pose as if he was being photographed, big belly much to the fore. I couldn't help laughing as he intended, though I was still feeling very fussed.

'I'm sure you'll like it there once you've settled in,' said Mike.

'That's what my dad said about my last school. I didn't *ever* settle.'

'Perhaps it's time to think *positive*, Beauty. I'm sure it's a great little school.'

'Did your children go to this school, Mike?'

'No, no, they were both grown up when I moved here,' said Mike.

'So how do you *know* it's a great school?'

'Sometimes you just have to take things on trust,' said Mike. 'You and your mum didn't know anything about Rabbit Cove, right – but you *knew* you'd like it here.'

I lightened up at last. 'OK, OK, you've got me now,' I said, laughing.

I didn't feel like laughing next Monday morning. Mum had phoned Seahaven Primary and they said they'd squeeze me in somehow. Mum asked about uniform and they said they didn't have one, just a sweatshirt. Mum and I had a long discussion about what I should wear.

I had very few clothes now so I didn't have much choice. I obviously wasn't going to wear the grey party dress and pinafore and my grey heeled boots – that outfit was far too grand for school. I wanted to wear my jeans and a T-shirt but Mum said they might look too scruffy. I was left with my denim skirt and the blue stripy top that went with it.

'I can't wear it every single day though, Mum,' I said.

'I know. We'll maybe go shopping in Seahaven next week and buy you another couple of outfits. I've been saving my wages,' said Mum. She ruffled my hair. And we'll have to get you to a hairdresser, you're starting to look like a Shetland pony.'

'Mum . . . Can I have it *all* cut off?'

'What? You want a crew cut? Are you *mad*?' said Mum.

'No, I'd like it just ordinary short. So I don't have to bother with stupid bows and slides and stuff. They always fall off anyway. Oh *please*, Mum.'

'But your dad won't let you—' Mum stopped herself.

'We're not *with* Dad. We're just us – and you don't really mind if I get my hair cut, do you?'

'All right. If that's what you want.'

'Whoopee! Will you do it for me? I'll go and find some scissors.'

'No, no, we'll get it cut *properly*. There's a hairdresser's card in the newsagent's window. We'll phone her up.'

The hairdresser was called Dawn. She was a lovely large lady with a plump baby who smiled and waggled her legs in her baby chair while her mum did her hairdressing. The baby had very cute hair in little dandelion tufts.

'Do you think mine would go like that?' I asked.

'Maybe *not* a good idea,' Mum said quickly. 'I think you'd suit a pageboy, Beauty. What do you think, Dawn?'

Dawn played around with my hair, draping it up and under.

'Oh *yes*! Perfect. Right, dear, hop up on a chair and we'll start snipping,' said Dawn.

Mum winced as she cut the first lock of hair, peering at me worriedly, but by the time Dawn was making the last little tidying up snippets she was smiling.

'It looks lovely! Look, Beauty!' said Mum.

She held up her powder-compact mirror so I could see for myself. I stared at the face in the mirror. I didn't look a *bit* like me. I stuck my tongue out just to make sure it *was* me, and the mirror girl stuck her tongue out too. I looked so different. My face seemed so much smaller with its smooth cap of honey-coloured hair. I didn't look especially fashionable or grown up, but for the first time ever I felt I looked like *me*.

Mum smiled, Dawn smiled, the baby smiled – and Mike mimed that he was struck dumb by this vision of beauty before him.

I wondered if I really was a new person now. Maybe this was the start of a whole new me. Cookie, cool and confident . . .

But on Monday morning I felt the old scared shaky Beauty – and I looked *awful*. Even my new hairstyle looked dreadful. I'd tossed and turned so much in the night it was all sticking up sideways, and it wouldn't lie down properly, even when I drenched it with water.

'Come *on*, Beauty. You need to get a bit of breakfast down you. You've got to leave at ten to eight. Hurry, sweetie,' Mum urged me.

I stood in front of the mirror, brushing dementedly.

'It won't go *right*,' I said, stamping my foot,
almost in tears. 'I look ridiculous!'

'Hey, hey, don't hurl that hairbrush whatever
you do. You're a menace when it comes to mirrors,'
said Mum. 'Your hair looks *fine*. Tell you what, I'll
slap some gel on it. Don't worry, I won't turn you
into a totally punky girl.'

'I look a totally *pukey* girl,' I said.

'Don't use that horrible word,' said Mum, fussing with my stupid hair.

'I *feel* like I'm going to puke. I don't want my
breakfast. I feel so *sick*.' I felt my forehead. 'And
I'm all hot. You feel, Mum. I'm sure I've got a temp-
erature. You can't send me to school when I'm *ill*,
they'll think you're a terrible mother.'

'Sweetie, you're *not* ill. You just don't want
to go to school and I understand but you *have* to
go. There! Look at your hair! It looks great now,
truly.'

I glared at my reflection. Mum had made my
hair look a lot better, admittedly, but the rest of me
still looked ultra-depressing.

'Stop scowling!' said Mum. 'You must *smile* at
everyone in your class, then they'll all want to
make friends.'

279

'I don't want to make friends with any of them,' I said. 'I've *got* a friend already, Rhona.'

'Maybe there'll be someone at your new school you'll like even more than Rhona,' said Mum.

'Don't be so *stupid*, Mum,' I said sulkily.

'Hey!' Mum caught hold of me by the shoulders. 'Don't you be so rude to me! You've been so good and grown up until now. *Please*, give this school a chance.'

'OK, I'll try, but it won't work. They won't like me, I *know* they won't.'

Mum shook me in exasperation.

'Look, get your Sam and Lily DVD, go and sit in Mike's living room and watch it for five minutes. It'll calm you down. I'll bring you a little bowl of cornflakes and some juice, OK?'

I did as I was told. Mike was busy in the kitchen so I had the living room to myself. I skipped along the Sam and Lily DVD to an episode right at the end, called *Starting School*. It was aimed at very little kids going to school for the first time, but inside I *felt* like a very little kid. I couldn't even sing the Sam and Lily song when the episode started.

'Hey there!' said Sam.

Lily looked up at me, her nose twitching.

'Are you about to start school?' said Sam.

I nodded mournfully, spooning up cornflakes.

'Are you getting excited?' Sam asked.

I stared at him. Even Sam was being stupid today.

'OK, maybe you're just a little bit scared,' said Sam softly. 'I don't blame you for feeling like that, Beauty. I wish you could go to Lily's school, you'd absolutely love it. There's just five other rabbits in her class and they have such easy-peasy lessons. They learn how to groom their fur and make a comfy bed and how to lap water delicately so it doesn't dribble down their front. They run races with each other all round the vegetable patch and they have a little snack every ten minutes.

'Lily was a little bit shy her very first day and wouldn't talk to the other rabbits in her class. She crept round by herself at playtime and sucked the tip of her ear for comfort but she soon made friends with the others. Now they're *all* best friends. When they're playing they all go into a huddle together, cosying up close, little white puffball tails in the air.'

'*How* did she make friends, Sam?' I whispered.

'She sidled up to the rabbit she liked best, a funny friendly one, and snuffled her nose at him.'

'Hmm. Well, if I sidle up to some funny friendly boy in my class and snuffle my nose he'll think I'm a total nutter,' I said.

Mike came into the room, a big paper bag in his arms. I blushed and switched off the DVD player quickly.

'Hi, Beauty. Did you finish your cornflakes? Your mum's fussing. Are you just about ready?'

'I suppose.'

'Let's have a look at you,' said Mike. 'Mm, cool hair, nice T-shirt, cute skirt. Your trainers are a bit scuffed and grubby though.'

'I know. I've tried brushing them but they still look rubbish,' I said.

'Well, see if these fit,' said Mike, throwing the paper bag at me.

I opened it up – and found a pair of scarlet baseball boots, little versions of Mike's own funky boots.

'Oh, Mike! Oh, I *love* them! Can I really wear them to school?'

'That's what they're for, kiddo. Do they fit OK? I got a half-size bigger than your trainers so that they'd last you a while.'

They fitted perfectly and looked incredible.

'There! Maybe your new nickname will be *Booty*,' said Mike, laughing.

I gave him a hug and I gave Mum a kiss. I clutched my carrier bag – my own school bag and lunchbox were at home so I had to make do for the moment. Mum wanted to go with me to call at number two and number seventeen but I was scared the kids would think me a baby so I went by myself.

A red-haired freckled boy about my own age opened the door of number seventeen. I'd seen him several times rollerblading along the terrace. He'd always pulled a hideous face at me. He pulled a hideous face now.

'Yuck, are *you* the girl I've got to go to school with?' he asked.

I certainly wasn't going to snuffle my nose at *him*. I felt like bursting into tears – but I didn't. I pulled a face back at him.

'Yuck, are *you* the boy I've got to go to school with?' I said.

'Come on then. My mum says your name's *Beauty*. Is that right?'

'Yeah, so what?' I said, pretending I didn't care in the slightest. I felt horribly shaky and peculiar inside.

He ran full-tilt down the terrace and banged at the door of number two. Another boy came tumbling out, smaller, with curly hair.

'Hi, Toby!' he yelled excitedly.

'Hi, Ben,' Toby said, and they did this silly high-five routine.

Ben totally ignored me. I didn't know if this was better or worse. Either way, I hated the thought of going backwards and forwards to school with these two boys. But then a girl came out of number nine, much older, about fourteen, a big bouncy girl with spiky black hair and a lot of black eye make-up. I blinked at her, biting my lip. She smiled at me.

'Hi, I'm Angie. You're Beauty from Lily Cottage? Mum said you'd be coming on the bus with us. I hope for your sake you're not in Ben or Toby's class! They both drive me absolutely nuts. It will be so great to have a girl to go to school with. I'm in Year Nine at Seahaven High. It's right next to the primary. Hey, I *love* your boots! Where did you get them from?'

'They were a present,' I said shyly.

I wondered if Angie was somehow winding me up, ready to start teasing me any minute – but she chatted away happily all the way to the bus stop. There were some girls from the High School already on the bus and they called to Angie to join them, but she just waved and said she was sitting with me.

'It's OK, you don't *have* to sit with me,' I mumbled.

'I want to! I can't stick those girls, they just want to natter on about their boyfriends all the time. They're so boring. You don't have a boyfriend, do you, Beauty?'

She *was* teasing a little now, but in a sweet way.

'No, I haven't got a boyfriend!' I said.

'Well, we could maybe fix you up with Toby? Or even Ben, if you like younger men?'

'No thanks!' I hesitated. 'I like *older* men, actually. There's this guy Sam . . . but he doesn't even know I exist.'

'Oh well. I expect you'll be in Mr Pettit's class with Toby, and Mr Pettit is *definitely* an older man, but I don't somehow see him as fanciable. His glasses are all smeary and he wears knitted ties and those terrible trousers with an elasticated waist.'

I pulled a face. 'Is he strict?' I asked anxiously.

'No, he's OK. He can be quite sweet, actually. He tells the funniest stories if he's in a good mood. Tell you what, I'll come in the school with you and we'll find him and I'll introduce you. Toby's supposed to take care of you but he's hopeless.'

Angie was *so* lovely to me. She got off a stop early at Seahaven Primary and came into school with me. It was such a relief. Toby and Ben hared off in different directions without a backward glance. Angie took me to the school secretary and then led me up two steep flights of stairs, along a corridor, through some swing doors and round several corners.

It was all so much bigger than I was used to. There were kids charging around everywhere. I wanted to take Angie's hand like a baby.

'I don't think I'll ever find my way on my own,' I said shakily.

'Yes, you will, it'll be easy-peasy,' said Angie. 'Ah, here's Mr Pettit's class. Oh, look at all those sunflower paintings. *I* did one of them!'

She led me into the classroom, which was half full of chattering children. A man with smeary glasses, a red knitted tie and terrible trousers was sitting on his desk reading some papers, his big thick-soled comfy shoes propped on a small chair. He looked up as we came in.

'Hello, Angie!' he said, smiling. 'My goodness, you're so grown up now!'

'Hi, Mr Pettit. This is Beauty. She's come to live in our road in Rabbit Cove. She's meant to be in your class, isn't she?'

'She is indeed. Hello, Beauty.'

I ducked my head shyly.

'I'll be off then, Beauty. When school finishes this afternoon just go to the bus stop. Wait for me if I'm not there, OK?' said Angie. She put her head close to mine and whispered, 'Good luck!'

I smiled at her gratefully, wishing she was my age so that she could be in Mr Pettit's class with me.

'Now, where can we sit you, Beauty?' said Mr Pettit. He took off his glasses, wiped them in-effectually on his tie, and popped them back on his nose. 'We're all a bit crammed together, but there *is* a spare chair – this one!' He took his foot off it and dusted it down with his cardigan sleeve. 'Now, whose table shall you join? There's a space at the boys' table at the back with Toby and all his mates—'

'No fear, Mr Pettit! We don't want *girls*,' Toby protested.

Mr Pettit laughed at him. 'You are so *predictable*, Toby. I'd never dream of inflicting your company on Beauty.'

'Beauty!' said Toby, sniggering.

Two of his friends started chortling too.

'I think maybe you could park your chair next to Princess, Beauty,' said Mr Pettit.

Princess! Mr Pettit was pointing towards a big smiley girl with elaborate little plaits in rows all over her head. She was wearing a bright pink T-shirt with *Princess* in sparkly silver lettering – the same T-shirt I'd given Rhona for her birthday!

I manoeuvred my chair towards her table. Princess squashed into a corner to make room for me. I sat down next to her, breathing in a beautiful rosy smell.

'Are you wearing perfume?' I whispered. 'It's lovely!'

'It's my mum's Red Roses cologne. She'd kill me if she knew I was wearing it,' Princess giggled. She sniffed her own wrists appreciatively. 'Mmm, I don't half pong!'

'Is your name *really* Princess?'

'Yeah. See, it's on my T-shirt too!'

'I gave that exact same T-shirt to a friend at my old school!' I said.

'So was she called Princess too?'

'No, no, she was called Rhona.'

'That's cool. I like being the *only* Princess. Well, Jordan's little girl is called Princess too, but I tell everyone she copied me.' Princess chuckled. 'And you're Beauty. That's an unusual name too. I don't think I've heard of *any* other Beauty so your name's even more unusual than mine. Hey, maybe we can start an unusual name club, you and me? Would you like that?'

'Oh yes!' I said.

We got it all sorted out at lunch time. Princess and I were UNCles – founder members of the Unusual Name Club. We discussed letting other children join too. There was an Anastasia in our class, and also a Britney-Lee but we decided these weren't quite unusual enough. There was a boy called Ezra which definitely qualified as unusual, but we decided we didn't really want boys in our club.

I designed a special logo and Princess put it carefully in her folder. She had a special badge-making kit at home and said she'd bring two UNCle badges to school the next day.

Then we shared our packed lunches. Princess had chicken in hers, and a special little pot of rice and peas. I just had cheese sandwiches and an apple – but Mum had made a special batch of cookies on Sunday. She'd found a little rabbit cookie cutter in amongst a whole load of kitchen junk at the Sunday car-boot fair at the Rabbit Cove community centre. She'd made her first bunny batch of cookies last night, and given them white icing fur. I had two in my lunch bag so I gave one to Princess.

'Oh wow, bunny cookies!' she said. 'They are so *cute*! They taste great too. I'm so glad you're my friend, Beauty.'

Eighteen

No one called me Ugly at Seahaven Primary, not even Toby. At first they called me the New Girl, which was a perfectly acceptable description. But after a little while they called me the Cookie Girl!

I started off just sharing cookies with my best friend and fellow UNCle, Princess, but soon I started taking a little bag of cookies each day and handing them round to anyone who seemed left out or lonely. Then the whole school got involved in raising money for some poor children in Africa. We were told to bring in cakes and biscuits to sell to each other at lunch time.

'*Right!*' said Mum, rolling up her sleeves.

She started making an enormous batch of bunny cookies, all different flavours, every one lovingly iced with raisins for eyes and a dab of glacé cherry for a mouth. Nearly everyone brought cakes and biscuits – but mine were the most popular! I sold them for ten pence per cookie, and they sold out in five minutes flat!

We had a summer fair for school funds at the end of June and Mr Pettit actually wrote to Mum begging her to run her own cookie stall. She made us both little lacy white aprons out of a net curtain. She got me to paint a sign for the stall.

'What shall I put?'

'I don't know. Dilly's Cookies?'

'That sounds too much like those cookies you can buy, Millie's Cookies. People will think you're copying. How about Bunny Cookies? Then I can draw little white rabbits scampering round and round at the edges of the sign.'

'OK, then, Bunny Cookies it is,' said Mum.

She made cookies all afternoon, all evening and half the night. I made cookies too, mixing and rolling and cutting alongside Mum. Mike helped too, finding endless tins to store them. He came with us on Saturday to help Mum set up the stall.

Princess was helping *her* mum on the tombola stall. Her sisters and brother were there too: Julep, Precious and little baby Marley.

'We're going to have to enrol your entire family in our UNCles club,' I said. 'What's your mum called, Princess?'

'She's called Petal so she's in too! What about your mum?'

'Everyone calls her Dilly. That's kind of un- usual, isn't it?'

Princess was looking at Mike, who was arranging hundreds of cookies on plates. He absent-mindedly nibbled the ears off one of the bunnies and Mum pretended to smack his hand.

'What about your dad? I thought you said your mum and dad had split up?' said Princess.

'He's not my *dad*,' I said.

'Well, I did think he was a bit old,' said Princess. 'Is he your grandad?'

'No, no, he's just Mike. He's lovely. We live with him,' I said.

Princess nodded, eyebrows raised. 'So he and your mum are, like, a couple?'

'No!'

Princess stared at Mum and Mike. They were still fooling around, pairing up the rabbits on the plates so that they were giving each other Eskimo kisses.

'They *look* like a couple,' she said.

'Well they're not,' I said, but I started to wonder about it. *Dad* had thought Mum had a thing going with Mike – but then Dad was so crazy he thought every other guy in the world was after Mum.

He was still leaving angry messages on her phone, demanding to know what was going on. He kept asking when we were coming back. He actually said it was lonely at home without us, which made Mum cry. But Auntie Avril rang to see how we were getting on and she told us she'd called round at Dad's and she said he seemed quite chirpy.

'We had a glass of wine or two and a nice little

chat. It was almost like old times,' said Auntie Avril. 'You don't mind, do you, Dilly?'

'I don't mind a bit, Avril,' said Mum. 'Why should I?'

'Well, dear, he is still your husband.'

'Yes, but I'm not with him now, am I? You do what you want, Avril. Go for it, girl!'

Maybe Mum and Dad would get a divorce now and then Mum would be free to marry Mike if she wanted. *I* wanted it more than anything. I knew Mike would be the most magical stepdad in the whole world.

Mum's cookie stall made a positive fortune for the whole school. Mike made his special fish pie for supper and we opened a bottle of champagne to celebrate. Mum let *me* have half a glass. It was lovely, though the bubbles went right up my nose and tickled. Mum had much more than half a glass and went to bed quite giggly.

'You are funny when you're drunk, Mum,' I said, giving her a hug.

'I'm *not* drunk! I've only had two glasses of champagne, silly,' said Mum. 'Well, maybe it was three. Anyway, I'm just *happy*, OK?'

'Are you *really* happy, Mum?'

'Yes. Well, sometimes I still wonder if I'm crazy, if we've done the right thing. I worry about what's right for you.'

'I think we've done exactly the right thing.'

'Well, we've certainly been so lucky, coming here, finding Mike—'

'Yes, Mike. I *do* like Mike, Mum.'

'Yes, so do I. He's been so kind, and he's such fun to be with. And he never ever seems to get cross,' said Mum.

'He likes you too, ever so. So what would you do if – if he wanted to – to be your boyfriend?'

'Goodness! Well, Mike's lovely, I know, and I'm very fond of him, but . . .'

'I know he's quite old, Mum, but that doesn't really matter, does it?'

'No, no. I mean, I fell for your dad, didn't I?'

'And Mike isn't terribly good looking, though I *like* the way he looks.'

'I like the way he looks too.'

'So, do you think you'll get together, Mum?'

'I don't think so, Beauty,' Mum said gently.

'It's not because he hasn't got much money, is it?' I whispered.

'Oh, Beauty!' Mum sounded shocked. 'As if that matters! I *like* it that Mike isn't rich and doesn't give a hoot about money. He's become a very special friend. If you must know, he did sort of hint that he'd love to be *more* than just good friends, but he was very understanding when I explained why I wanted things to stay just the way they are.'

'But *why*, Mum?' I asked, exasperated.

'Because I want to be on my own for a bit. No man in my life. Independent. I got together with your dad when I was fresh out of school. I've never learned how to stand on my own two feet. I want to prove I can cope. It's still a bit scary but it's exciting making decisions for myself. I always thought I was absolutely thick but now I seem to be doing OK. Do you understand, darling?'

'Well. Sort of,' I said. 'But I hope you might change your mind later on!'

'I know one thing,' said Mum. 'I'm not *really* on my own. I've got you, babes. I couldn't manage without you. We're a team, you and me, Beauty.'

Mum and I were a real team when it came to cookie baking. Suddenly our bunny cookies were absolutely in demand. We spent Saturdays and Sundays up to our elbows in cookie dough in an attempt to please all our customers. Mum had been supplying cookies for all the guest houses on Primrose Terrace for weeks, but now the big White Hotel wanted their own batch to offer to guests for afternoon tea, and Peggy's Parlour wanted a big jar of assorted iced cookies every single day. We'd had enquiries from several Seahaven hotels and teashops – and we were asked to provide a *hundred* bags of bunny cookies for the big Seahaven Carnival in July.

I designed a special bunny label to stick on each bag: a white rabbit on a bright green background. Mum and I set up a big cookie stall at the carnival, and dressed up in our white lacy aprons. The local television news came and filmed us. I didn't even know they were doing it. I was just busy selling cookies and then this guy jumped in front of me and told me to eat a bunny cookie and go 'yum yum' so I did – and then I saw the camera pointing in my direction! I just about died – but it was all over before I could object. My heart started thudding like crazy in case I looked stupid when Mum and Mike and I switched on the local news that evening, but to my great relief I was only on for two seconds! They said I made the cookies all by myself, which made me fuss, but Mum just laughed.

The next morning Mike came charging into the kitchen, eyes popping.

'There's a phone call for our little television star. It's *Watchbox*, that kids' programme on Saturday mornings. They want to have you on their show,' he said.

'What? Oh, Mike, you are a tease,' I said, shaking my head at him.

'Stop kidding, Mike, you're very bad,' said Mum.

'I-am-NOT-kidding! Come to the phone, Beauty.

Dilly, they need to talk to you too. I *promise* I'm not joking.'

I went to the phone, Mum following me.

'Hello? It's Beauty speaking,' I said uncertainly, still not quite believing Mike.

'Hello, Beauty. My name's Jules Latimer. I'm a researcher on *Watchbox*. Do you know our show? I've been watching various news items and I saw your little spot on the piece about the Seahaven Carnival. So you make all these wonderful cookies?'

'Well, my mum makes most of them. I just help out when we're really busy,' I said.

'And did you design the bunny logo?'

'The logo? Oh, the picture on the bags. Yes, I did that.'

'Well, we'd love to have you on our programme. You could maybe show our presenters Simon and Miranda how you make the cookies? Would you like to do that?'

Would I like to go on *television*? Oh goodness, it might be so scary. I'd have thousands and thousands of children watching me, Ugly Beauty. They'd all laugh and snigger at their television sets, saying horrible things about me . . .

'No thank you very much,' I said.

'What?' said Mum beside me. 'Don't be daft, Beauty! Of *course* you want to go on *Watchbox*!'

She snatched the phone away from me. 'Hello, I'm Dilys Cookson, Beauty's mum. I think she's a little bit overwhelmed. I'm sure she'd *love* to go on *Watchbox* – it's her second favourite television show.'

I heard the researcher laughing and asking something.

'Oh, her *favourite* has to be *Rabbit Hutch*. She's absolutely nuts on Sam and Lily,' said Mum.

'Shut *up*, Mum! They'll think I'm a terrible baby!' I hissed.

Mum wouldn't shut up.

'That's why she painted that lovely white rabbit for our bunny cookies. It's because she loves Lily,' she said.

She listened to the researcher for a while and then laughed. 'Yes, yes! OK, what day do you record the programme? Tomorrow!'

'*No*, Mum, I'm not going to,' I said, struggling to get the phone off her – but she held it out of my reach.

'Can you give me the full address? That's London, right? I'm afraid I don't know London very well. Will I be able to park at the studio or should we get the train? You'll send a special *car* for us? What, all the way to Rabbit Cove? Oh wonderful. It's Lily Cottage, nineteen Primrose Terrace. At nine o'clock? We'll be ready and waiting.'

Mum rang off and then gave me a huge hug. I stayed stony still, not responding.

'*You* can be ready and waiting. *I'm* not going,' I said.

'Oh, Beauty, don't be so silly!'

'I don't want to *look* silly on television.'

'But you *won't*. You were fine on the local news, completely natural.'

'Yes, because I didn't know what they were doing. But I'm *not* going on *Watchbox*. I'd *hate* it.'

'You'll *love* it, especially when you know what they've got lined up for you. I'd give anything to tell you but they want it to be a total surprise,' said Mum.

'I know what they want me to do: show Simon and Miranda how to make cookies. Simon is this big fat jolly guy who shouts all the time and Miranda is little and very bouncy and beautiful. I couldn't possibly make cookies with *them*. I'm not going on *Watchbox*, Mum, no matter what you say.'

'But—'

'Look, you're getting just like *Dad*,' I said, starting to shout. 'He was always always always making me do stuff I didn't want to do. *Please* don't you start, Mum. I'm sorry, but I'm not the sort of pretty show-off girl who'd be great on television. I'd be awful. You don't understand me one little bit, do you? You're a totally useless mum.'

Mum stared at me. Her eyes filled with tears and she rushed upstairs. I glared after her.

I was still glaring when Mike found me, kicking the skirting board in his living room.

'Are you looking for those rats again?' he said. 'Steady on, you'll scuff the paintwork – and it won't exactly enhance your new baseball boots either.'

'I'm sorry,' I said, feeling bad.

'That's OK, kiddo. Fancy saying sorry to your mum too? I think you were shouting at her – and when I listened on the stairs just now it sounded as if she might be crying,' said Mike.

'Well, it's not my fault,' I said. 'Just because I don't want to go on *Watchbox*.'

'What *is* this programme anyway? I've heard of it but I don't think I've ever watched it.'

'Oh, they have these two presenters on every day, and all these kids come on and do stuff, dance and sing and play around. All the girls at my old school were desperate to be on *Watchbox*, Skye especially.'

'Is she the one who was particularly mean to you? There, don't you want to be on the wretched programme, just to be one up on her?'

'Yes, but I'd make such a *total* fool of myself. Everyone would laugh.'

'What makes you think that?'

'I just can't *do* stuff in front of people. They'd

say my silly name and every child watching would give a double take and go, "*Beauty* – as if!"'

'Like they did at Seahaven Primary?' said Mike, with a little edge to his voice. 'You were so certain they were all going to laugh at you and tease you and make your life a misery, remember? And did that happen?'

He waited. I fidgeted. He cupped his ear, wanting a response.

'All right, they're all lovely at my new school,' I said. 'Well, except for Toby and Ben. And actually they gave me some of their perfectly disgusting home-made toffee that sticks your teeth together the other day, hoping I'd give them bunny cookies in exchange.'

'So you were *wrong* about Seahaven school and its pupils?' Mike persisted.

'Yes, OK, I've admitted that.'

'So don't you think you might just be wrong about this television show? You could go on it and actually be a little superstar.'

'No I wouldn't!'

'Yes, you *would*. But even if you come over all shy and can't say a word, does it really matter? At least you'll have had a go! And you'll have given your mum's cookies an enormous plug too. Do you know how much it costs to have an advert on television, Beauty? Thousands and thousands and thousands of pounds. Yet you can advertise Bunny Cookies for nothing on the most popular programme on kids television. Don't you see what this could mean for you and Dilly? She could expand properly, take on some staff – there are heaps of mums in Rabbit Cove who'd love to do a bit of baking part-time. It's her chance to turn Bunny Cookies into a quality product sold nationwide, Bunny Cookies in every up-market food emporium – Fortnum and Mason, Harrods, Selfridges . . .'

I stared at Mike open-mouthed. 'Do you really think that could happen?' I asked.

'Well, I'm maybe going a bit over the top to prove my point. I'm not sure Dilly would want to develop the business to such an extent. But she's taking it very seriously, Beauty. She's getting some con-fidence in herself at last. You should feel so proud of her.'

'I am,' I said.

'So you know how much this means to her. Though *you* mean much more to her than her pre-cious cookies. In a way she's doing all this for you – and yet what did I hear you shouting at her just now?'

'I said she was a useless mum,' I said, my voice going all wobbly.

'And do you really think that?'

'No, of course I don't. I just said it because I was

cross and wanted to hurt her. Because I truly still *don't* want to go on *Watchbox* – but I will if you really make me.'

'I'm not going to make you do anything, sweetheart,' said Mike, putting his arm round me. 'But I'm hoping like anything you'll say you will! I'll be so proud of you, Beauty.'

I gave him a big hug.

'You're very clever, you know. You don't shout and yell, you don't even really tell me off. You just say stuff that makes me do exactly what you want. You must have been a great dad, Mike.'

'I think I was rather a rubbish dad, actually. Not much cop as a husband either. I just wanted to do my own thing and expected everyone else to fit in. I try not to think about the past too much. I'm not very proud of the way I behaved. Maybe I've learned my lesson now. That's the only thing I've really learned about life. You don't have to go on making the same old mistakes over and over again. You can't change other people but you *can* change yourself. There! Wise old Mike has done enough mumbling in his beard. Scoot upstairs and make it up with your mum, poppet.'

I ran up to our room. Mum was lying on our bed, sobbing into her pillow.

'Oh, Mum, don't! I'm sorry,' I said, lying down beside her.

'I'm sorry too, Beauty. I just got so excited I forgot you'd find it a terrible ordeal. It's OK, you don't have to go on the silly old programme.'

'But I will,' I said. 'I'll do it, Mum – for us. To advertise Bunny Cookies. I'll probably be absolute rubbish on the telly and you'll die of embarrassment, but I'll give it a go, OK?'

'Oh, you darling!' said Mum. 'You're the best daughter in the whole world.'

'And you're the best mum,' I said.

I was glad I'd changed my mind and made Mum happy and Mike proud – but in the middle of the night, wide awake, I wished wished wished I didn't have to. I kept imagining what it would be like. I'd be in a studio with a lot of cool, confident, talented, beautiful girls like Skye. They'd all dance and sing and I'd make a muck-up of my cookies and they'd all goggle at me and chortle – and children from John o'Groats to Land's End would goggle and chortle too.

I didn't get to sleep until about five o'clock. Mum bounced out of bed very early. I huddled under the duvet while she got ready. She seemed to be making a big performance of it, swishing clothes along the rail, opening drawers, snapping her suitcase . . .

She woke me up with a cup of tea at eight o'clock.

'Rise and shine, my little television star,' she said, giving me a kiss.

I sat up in bed, looking Mum up and down. She looked lovely, wearing her cream dress, her hair newly washed and fluffy round her shoulders. I took a sip of tea and made my voice gruff.

'Your neck looks a bit bare, Dilly. Why don't you wear your diamond collar?' I said.

'Oh *don't!*' said Mum, and we both laughed shakily.

'Do you think I should tell your dad you're going to be on the telly?' said Mum.

'No, because I know I'll muck it all up,' I said. 'I wish *you* were doing it. You look fabulous, Mum, really.'

'Do you really think so, babes?' Mum glanced at her suitcase. 'I've got another outfit in case they all look dead casual. I don't want to let you down, darling. Now, I've ironed your grey dress and your white pinafore and polished your grey boots. We don't want them to get all creased in the car so we'll pop them on a hanger and you can wear your comfy jeans and stuff for the journey, OK?'

I nodded, touched that she'd gone to so much trouble. I still wasn't sure I'd actually be able to stand there in front of the cameras. My tummy flipped over at the thought and I could barely swallow my tea.

Mike insisted on doing breakfast by himself. He made Mum and me sit down as if we were ordinary guests on holiday at Lily Cottage. All the other guests made a great fuss of me and when the big black car drew up outside they all crowded on the doorstep and patted me and kissed me and wished me luck.

Mike gave me a big hug and whispered in my ear, 'Good luck, kiddo.'

He gave Mum a hug too and whispered in *her* ear. She blushed and giggled. I wondered if they *might* just get together, in spite of what Mum said.

Then Mum and I got in the back of the car. The chauffeur was a nice fat man called Harry who hung my dress and pinafore on a special little hook inside the car and stowed Mum's suitcase in the boot.

'Are you comfy now, ladies? You just sit back and relax,' he said.

I felt a horrible pang as we drove out of Rabbit Cove. I knew it was silly but I was scared I'd some-how made it all up, and once we were back on the main road to London it would vanish into the sea, a never-never land we'd never be able to reach again.

I knelt up on the seat and peered back.

'It's OK, babe. We'll be back this evening,'

said Mum softly. 'Rabbit Cove's our home now. We're going to live there all summer – and winter too.'

'And the *next* summer and winter, for ever?' I said.

'Yes, yes, if that's what we both want,' said Mum.

I turned round and cuddled up to her.

'You bet it is,' I said.

Harry let us choose CDs to play in his car and we sang along for a while, but then my head started nodding. When I woke up again we were in London.

'Oh help!' I said, suddenly horribly scared. 'Oh, Harry, are we nearly there?'

'Five minutes away.'

'I don't want to go now!' I said.

'It'll be fine, Beauty,' said Mum, holding my hand – but *her* hand was cold and clammy too.

'You'll *love* being on *Watchbox*, young lady,' said Harry. 'That Simon is a right laugh – and as for Miranda – *phwoar*!'

We drove into the studios. I couldn't help feeling a *little* bit thrilled when Harry told the security man at the gate: 'Here's Miss Beauty Cookson and her mum for *Watchbox*.' We were let through straight away. Harry parked the car, handed over my grey outfit and the suitcase, and promised he'd be waiting to take us all the way home after the programme.

'Wish us luck, Harry,' said Mum.

'Oh, yes. I wish you *lots* of luck – but you won't need it. You'll be brilliant.'

'Well, if Beauty makes a batch of bunny cookies we'll make sure we'll bring you some,' said Mum.

We were met by Jules, the researcher. She was much younger than I'd imagined, with a ponytail and a very short skirt. I thought just at first she might be one of the child performers on the show. She took Mum and me to our very own dressing room. It even had our names on the door!

'Now, we'll probably have a little rehearsal and you'll meet Simon and Miranda and all the other kids in the show,' she said. 'You're going to start the show, Beauty, making cookies. You'll be showing Simon and Miranda what to do. Then while the cookies are baking – we have our own little oven, no expense spared on *Watch-box*! – all our other guests will do their turns. We've got a singer, a conjuror, and two different dancers, and then we'll finish with you, Beauty, taking the cookies out of the oven. We were wondering if you'd maybe draw a little rabbit for us, seeing as you designed the Bunny Cookies logo.'

'Oh yes, that would be great,' said Mum. 'Look,

I've brought lots of Beauty's drawings. She's even done some oil paintings.'

She unfastened her suitcase. She didn't have spare clothes in there at all. She had all my Sam and Lily drawings and paintings.

'Oh, Mum!' I said, terribly embarrassed. 'They don't want to see all that silly old stuff.'

'Oh yes we do!' said Jules, seizing an armful. 'Do you mind if I take them away to show the producer? They'll fit in brilliantly with the special finale.'

'What special finale?' I asked.

'Oh, we've just thought of a good way of rounding off the programme,' said Jules. She winked at Mum and Mum winked back.

'What's all the winking about?' I asked Mum, when we were left on our own in the dressing room.

'What winking?' said Mum. 'I just had something in my eye, that's all.'

I didn't have time to quiz her further, because we were called to go into the studio for a run-through rehearsal. It was a great room full of cameras with cables snaking all over the floor. There were two big red squashy sofas in our corner, a mini-kitchen in another, and a round stage with a spotlight.

There were four other children standing around with their mums. They all looked comfortingly anxious too, apart from a beautiful girl with long fair hair in a very short skirt and a sparkly top. She was wearing very high heels.

'She is *so* like Skye,' I whispered to Mum.

'Maybe she'll trip in her heels and fall over and show her knickers,' Mum whispered back.

The fair girl looked positively ordinary compared to Miranda. She was simply dressed in jeans and a little T-shirt and sneakers but she looked stunning, her long ultra-curly black hair flying everywhere, her honey-coloured skin shining, her dark eyes huge and luminous. She smiled at everyone, asking our names, chatting away. Simon was very friendly too, bounding about pulling funny faces and tweaking the nose of the very little boy who was the conjuror.

I smiled shyly at Miranda and Simon but I felt paralysed with fear. I didn't know what I was going to do. I knew how to make cookies – but what was I supposed to *say* when I was mixing and baking? I asked Jules in panic.

'It's OK, Miranda and Simon will ask you stuff and you just say whatever you want. We're not going to go through it word by word just now. We find it makes things much fresher when we start recording,' said Jules.

I had to stand in the kitchen and pretend to make cookies, while Miranda and Simon bobbed about. I felt so shy I barely said a word. Then a tall red-haired girl called Megan did an acrobatic dance, a tiny kid called Tina sang a song in a surprisingly deep strong voice, the little boy Darren did his conjuring tricks, and then the blonde girl in the short skirt and high heels, Nancy-Jo, sang and danced. She was depressingly good at it too.

'Then we'll come back to you, Beauty, and we'll look at the cookies and you'll draw the bunny and then . . . well, we'll just chat for a couple of minutes and that's the end of the programme,' said Jules. 'OK, let's take you back to your dressing room. I'll come and fetch you for Make-up in a tick, Beauty.'

'Should Beauty change into her best dress now?' Mum asked.

'Well, we think Beauty looks great for the programme just the way she is,' said Jules.

'Oh yes, wear your jeans. I'm wearing mine,' said Miranda.

'And we all love your red boots,' said Simon.

'*Sooo* much more sensible than some of the others,' Jules muttered in my ear, raising an eyebrow at Nancy-Jo.

So I didn't change after all. I think Mum was a bit disappointed and worried people would think I looked a scruff in my jeans.

'Let's hope your dad *doesn't* get wind of this and watch. He'd go bananas,' said Mum. 'I wonder what they're going to do to you in Make-up? I hope they don't plaster it on you.'

The make-up lady was lovely. She just put a little foundation on me so I wouldn't look all shiny, and the palest pink lipstick, and then she combed my hair and said my pageboy style really suited me.

'There, you look fabulous, pet, even though I say it myself,' she said.

I stared at myself in the mirror. I didn't look fabulous – but I looked kind of OK. I gave myself a soppy little grin and the girl in the mirror smiled back at me encouragingly.

Then Jules came to collect me and we went back into the studio ready for the start of the show.

They stood me in the kitchen with all the ingredients in front of me. I suddenly felt so sick and so scared I wondered if I was going to throw up right there and then in my mixing bowl.

'Are you OK, sweetheart?' said Simon, suddenly gentle.

'I'm scared!'

'I know, I know. Don't worry, Miranda and I get scared too before the start of the show. But it'll be fine once the cameras start rolling.'

'But what about all those thousands of people who'll be watching us?' I whispered.

'Forget about them. It's just you and me and

Miranda and the other kids having fun, OK?'

'OK,' I said, swallowing.

'That's the girl. Now listen, I want at least *four* of these famous cookies, OK? I'm a growing lad,' he said, patting his big tummy.

Then they started the countdown to the programme and Simon whizzed over to the red sofa beside Miranda. I heard the *Watchbox* signature tune and Simon and Miranda started singing it too.

'Hi, everyone!' said Miranda, smiling at the camera.

'Welcome to *Watchbox*,' said Simon. 'We've got a *g-r-e-a-a-a-t* show for you today. You just wait and see! First of all, we're going to do some baking. Are you any good at cooking, Miranda?'

'No, I'm total rubbish, but I know a girl who's a *great* cook – and that's Beauty Cookson,' said Miranda.

They both walked over to me. That was my cue to start mixing the flour and the sugar and the butter. I started so determinedly that some of the flour flew up all over my T-shirt. I froze.

'Whoops, it's snowing!' said Simon, flicking a tiny bit of flour too.

'Hey hey, stop messing about, you two,' said Miranda. 'OK, Beauty, tell us how to make your special bunny cookies. I hear they've become ever

314

so popular where you live, in Rabbit Cove. That's a lovely name!'

'It's a lovely place. It's the seaside and it's so special,' I said, suddenly not shy at all. 'My mum's great at making all sorts of cookies and I'm her number-one helper. Now we specialize in making these bunny cookies with this special cutter.'

Simon held it up, making the bunny run up my arm and across my shoulders. It tickled and I couldn't help laughing.

'They've become really popular and we sell heaps,' I said, still mixing.

'And you've designed the special bunny logo on the packaging?' said Miranda, holding up one of our bags of cookies. 'You like rabbits, do you, Beauty?'

'Yes, I love them,' I said, slowly adding my eggs and milk to the cookie mixture.

'Can I have a stir, Beauty?' said Simon. 'Have you got a favourite rabbit, then?'

'Well . . .' I said, hesitating.

'Come on, tell us,' said Miranda, her head close to mine.

'I like Lily. She's Sam's rabbit on the *Rabbit Hutch* show,' I said. 'I know I'm an awful baby to watch it, but—'

'*I* watch Sam and Lily. I love Lily too,' said Simon.

'I love Sam!' said Miranda. 'Well, we've got a little

315

surprise for you at the end of the show, Beauty. But now while you're rolling out your cookie dough and popping the cookies in the oven let's meet some of our other guests. Megan is going to do a special acrobatic dance for us.'

'And, boy, is she bendy!' said Simon.

The cameras switched to Megan, who did a handstand and then arched over so her feet touched the floor. By the time she'd finished her display I'd rolled out the dough, cut out forty-eight bunny cookies, and put them in the oven.

Simon looked over at me, did a thumbs-up, and rubbed his tummy. I peered into the darkness at the back of the studio and there was Mum, waving wildly and blowing kisses at me. Tiny Tina came on and sang and then did a short duet with Miranda. Darren did his conjuring tricks and Simon joked around with him.

'You haven't got a top hat with you, have you, Darren? Then you could make a white rabbit appear for Beauty,' he said. 'How are those cook-ies getting on, Beauty? They're starting to smell good.'

'Another couple of minutes, that's all,' I said, peeping in the oven.

Simon helped Darren through a complicated card trick and a funny routine with a 'magic' box. Then it was Nancy-Jo's turn.

I took my cookies out of the oven, Jules helping as the cameras weren't on us. We put them out on cooling trays.

'They look wonderful, Beauty. Well done!' she whispered.

Nancy-Jo threw back her head and went for a high note, thrusting out her arms and tapping her high heels. She wobbled precariously. Jules shook her head and I had to bite my cheeks to stop myself giggling.

Miranda and Simon had a chat with Nancy-Jo and then she tottered off while I was gently shoved towards the red sofas, a plate of bunny cookies in either hand.

'Oh wow, Beauty, they look fantastic!' said Miranda. 'May I have one?'

'Of course,' I said. 'They're for everyone. Though Simon has to have lots because he says he's a growing boy.'

They both laughed as if it was my joke.

'Now, you're not just a good cook, you're also brilliant at drawing, Beauty. Will you draw a bunny for us?' said Simon, his mouth full of cookies. 'Mm, these are delicious.'

I started drawing on the pad he gave me – while to my embarrassment Miranda held up lots of my Sam and Lily pictures to the camera.

'I love the oil paintings, Beauty,' she said.

'My special artist friend Mike showed me how to use oils,' I said proudly.

'There, that's a lovely rabbit,' said Simon, peering at my page. 'Now, I've borrowed this magic wand from our friend Darren. If you tap your drawing it *might* just turn into a real rabbit, Beauty.'

I stared at Simon.

'Go on, give it a try,' he said.

I tapped my drawing, feeling a bit daft. I sensed someone coming up behind me. Then suddenly there in my lap was a huge, soft, oh-so-familiar white rabbit with floppy ears.

'*Lily!*' I said.

'Hey there, Beauty,' said Sam, coming to sit beside me.

It was the *real* Sam, his shiny hair flopping over his forehead, his eyes bright, his face one big smile. I still wondered if I was dreaming – but Lily felt so warm and heavy cuddled up on my lap I knew I had to be wide awake.

'We're so pleased you like our show, Beauty. Lily's particularly thrilled that she inspired your special cookies. They are *so* good,' said Sam, biting one in half. 'And I love all your artwork!'

'I drew them all for you,' I whispered. 'I never dared send any because I was scared you'd think me a silly baby.'

'Maybe you'd like to give Sam and Lily one of your paintings now?' said Miranda.

'Oh yes! What about the oil painting of you and Lily? You're meant to be on holiday in Rabbit Cove,' I said, shyly handing it to Sam.

'We'll have to go there some day. It looks just our sort of place,' said Sam. 'We'll hang your picture in pride of place in the Rabbit Hutch, won't we, Lily?'

Lily snuffled sleepily, taking up an awful lot of my lap.

'Lily's almost as fat as me,' said Simon, leaning over to stroke her.

'Yes, she's always been a big girl but she's even bigger now,' said Sam. 'I think she's got a sweetheart at rabbit school, because our Lily's going to have baby bunnies soon.'

'Oh, how wonderful!' I said, stroking her too. 'Congratulations, Lily.'

I had a little nibble of a cookie myself, just to check they were OK.

'Tell you what, Beauty. You've given us a very special present so maybe we can give you one in return. Lily won't be able to keep all her babies. Would *you* like one of the baby rabbits?'

I choked on my cookie. *'Really?'* I spluttered.

'Yes, really,' said Sam.

'Aah!' said Simon. 'Isn't that sweet?'

'Time to go now, folks,' said Miranda, waving.

Simon and Miranda and Sam and Megan and Lucy and Darren and Nancy-Jo all waved. I couldn't wave because Lily was fidgeting and I had to hang onto her, so I gave a great grin to the camera.

'You were so great, Beauty,' said Miranda.

'You're a little natural,' said Simon. 'A total little beauty!'

'Well done, babes!' Mum shouted.

But I hardly heard them. I stroked Lily and looked at Sam – and he smiled specially for me.

☆ CHECK OUT ☆ JACQUELINE WILSON'S OFFICIAL WEBSITE!

You'll find lots of fun stuff including games and amazing competitions. You can even customise your own page and start an online diary!

You'll find out all about Jacqueline in her monthly diary and tour blogs, as well as seeing her replies to fan mail. You can also chat to other fans on the message boards.

Join in today at
www.jacquelinewilson.co.uk

And to view the exciting book trailers including *Lily Alone*, *Sapphire Battersea* and *The Worst Thing About My Sister*, visit Jacqueline's official YouTube channel at
www.youtube.com/jacquelinewilson.tv

Jacqueline Wilson

The Story of Tracy Beaker

Illustrated by Nick Sharratt

*Feisty, funny Tracy lives in a Children's Home –
but she'd love a real home one day, with a real family . . .*

Jacqueline Wilson

MY SISTER JODIE

Illustrated by Nick Sharratt

*Pearl adores her wild sister. But will life
at their new school tear them apart?*

Jacqueline Wilson

Lily Alone

Sometimes Lily wishes she really was home ALONE

Illustrated by Nick Sharratt

Sometimes Lily wishes she really was home alone . . .

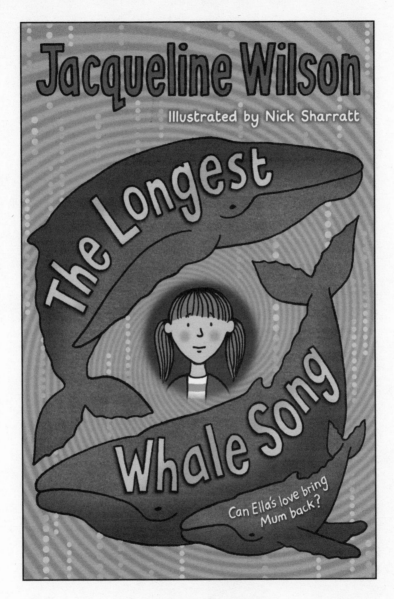

Jacqueline Wilson

Illustrated by Nick Sharratt

The Longest

Whale Song

Can Ella's love bring
Mum back?

*Can Ella's love bring
Mum back?*

The incredible stories of Hetty Feather, the Victorian foundling determined to find her real family and start a better life!

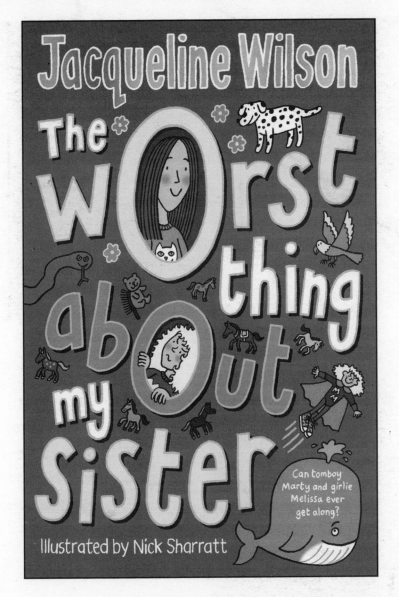

Jacqueline Wilson

The Worst thing about my Sister

Illustrated by Nick Sharratt

Can tomboy Marty and girlie Melissa ever get along?

*Can tomboy Marty and girlie Melissa
ever get along?*

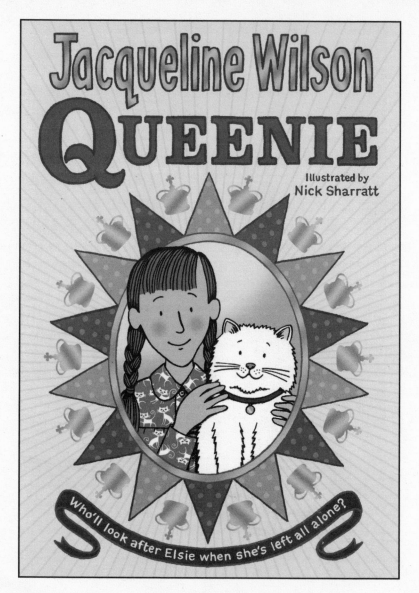

COMING SOON!

YOLO

wrote on
25/12/13
christmas
Day